Full Fathom Five

A Caleb Hayes Thriller

James L. Nelson

This is a work of fiction. Names, characters, places and incidents either are the product of the author's imagination or are used fictitiously. Any resemblance to actual events, locales, organizations, or persons, living or dead, is entirely coincidental and beyond the intent of either the author or the publisher.

Fore Topsail Press
64 Ash Point Road
Harpswell, Maine, 04079

Lobsterboat diagram by Michelle L Sirois Jean

ISBN: 0692794883
ISBN-13: 978-0692794883

For Elizabeth and Patrick Lockard.
This new adventure story is dedicated to you, as you begin to create the adventure story of your own lives, and to spread the branches of the Nelson and Lockard family trees.

Historical Fiction by James L. Nelson

The Norsemen Saga: Novels of Viking Age Ireland

Fin Gall
Dubh-Linn
The Lord of Vík-ló
Glendalough Fair
Night Wolf

The Brethren of the Coast Trilogy: Piracy in Colonial America

The Guardship
The Blackbirder
The Pirate Round

The Revolution at Sea Saga: Naval Action of the American Revolution

By Force of Arms
The Maddest Idea
The Continental Risque
Lords of the Ocean
All the Brave Fellows

The Samuel Bowater Books: Tales of the Confederate Navy

Glory in the Name
Thieves of Mercy

The Only Life that Mattered
The French Prize

Nonfiction:

Reign of Iron
Benedict Arnold's Navy
George Washington's Secret Navy
George Washington's Great Gamble
With Fire and Sword

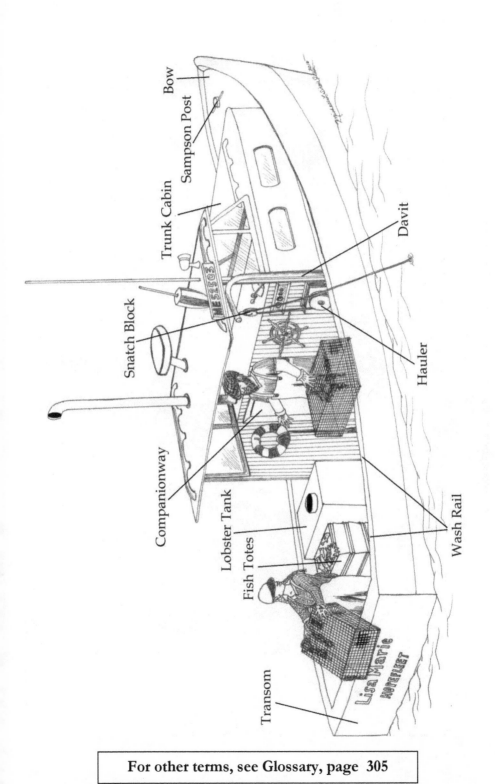

Bow

Sampson Post

Trunk Cabin

Snatch Block

Companionway

Lobster Tank

Fish Totes

Transom

Davit

Hauler

Wash Rail

Lisa Marie
HOPEFLEET

ME5503

For other terms, see Glossary, page 305

Chapter One

Caleb Hayes always thought there was something eerie, even unworldly, about the way a lobster trap rises up out of the depths of the sea.

First there is only a rope coming up from that unseen place, a cable from the ocean floor, the great seafarers' graveyard. And then a shape materializes out of the murky green, and then it resolves itself into a trap that seems to fly up through those last fathoms before it breaks the surface.

As a teenager, working as a sternman on his Uncle Dick's boat, and later when he had a boat of his own, he used to think about that as he watched the traps rising silent from the bottom of Casco Bay. Now, fifteen years later, having returned to lobster catching after a long detour through various careers, most notably the bizarre, often toxic, often violent world of personal security for the reining elite of Hollywood, he was thinking it again.

And, because of the strange way the traps came up from below, Caleb always thought he would not be too surprised if someday a dead body came up as well. But he was wrong. Because when the body did appear, he was very surprised indeed.

He was hauling a string of traps on the edge of a deep hole southeast of Whaleboat Island when it happened. His boat was called the *Lisa Marie*, a thirty-five-foot Henry Barnes lobsterboat, oak plank on oak frame, built some time in the 1950s. She was one of the few wooden boats still working and Caleb liked her. The heavier hull had an easy motion in a seaway, and he appreciated her traditional, organic quality, so lacking in fiberglass. Other than that, she was an utter pain in the ass, as wooden boats were wont to be.

Fifty feet off her starboard side, one of Caleb's buoys, painted in red and white vertical stripes, bobbed in the short chop. Caleb spun the wheel and aimed the boat's flared bow at the bright-colored marker. He eased the throttle back and nudged the wheel again, then reached over and grabbed up the gaff that lay on the wash rail beside him.

He straightened and dropped the transmission into neutral and let the momentum carry the boat the rest of the distance. At six foot two Caleb fit perfectly under the cabin's roof, as long as his hat was not standing too proud on his head.

The *Lisa Marie* swooped up alongside the buoy and Caleb leaned over the side and snatched the marker with practiced ease. He pulled it inboard until he could get his gloved hand on the rope. He tossed the buoy onto the deck of the boat and looped the rope through the hauler's snatch block and then around the round, grooved wheel of the hauler itself.

There was no thought needed for this operation; it was so ingrained in his muscle memory that his hands and arms worked of their own accord, letting Caleb's mind ponder thoughts profound or otherwise. The hauler whirled, spraying water over the deck, and the line ran through the snatch block and Caleb absently picked off the bits of seaweed clinging to it as it whirred past. He looked down over the side. The line, like old weathered bone, was visible for twenty feet or so before it disappeared into the pea-green depths.

He was staring down into the water when the dead guy began to materialize, five fathoms down. Caleb's eyes saw something resolving out of the watery haze and his mind said *trap* and at the same time he knew it was not a trap. The look of a trap coming up from the bottom was as fixed in his mind as anything in life, and he knew this was not it.

"Ahh! Shit!" he shouted, loud, as he realized what he was looking at. He leapt back from the rail and his hand lashed out and turned the brass handle that controlled the hauler and the hauler came to an abrupt stop.

For a long moment Caleb just stood there, the only motion the slow rocking of the *Lisa Marie* in the small, early morning swells. Caleb stared outboard, over the water, toward the long, low, tree-covered length of Whaleboat Island and the shoreline of Casco Bay a few miles beyond. It was a flawless July morning: clear blue skies, save for the odd puff of cumulous, a gentle breeze from the southwest. The kind of morning that drove Maine's multi-billion-dollar tourist industry, but Caleb saw none of it.

Okay...there's a dead guy on my trap... he thought.

He let his breathing settle back to normal. It was not as if he had never seen a dead body before. He had seen plenty in the course of his security career in Southern California. It was just the shock of the thing that threw him off.

And then his mind conjured up an image of the last dead body he had seen, just over a year earlier. It was an image that had come to mind every day since then, an image he had fled three thousand miles to escape. But it had followed him, and it followed him still.

Caleb shook his head, trying to clear his mind, because he had another body to deal with now. He frowned and stepped forward and leaned over the rail. The corpse had made it to about ten feet below the surface before Caleb managed to turn the hauler off. He could see him quite well through the clear salt water. His face and hands were so white they seemed to glow. Khaki cargo shorts, a shirt with buttons. Not a lobsterman, but then if any local lobsterman or boater had gone missing Caleb was sure he would have heard about it.

"You haven't been down there so long, have you?" Caleb asked the dead guy. From what he could see the body did not look too bad. All limbs seemed to still be in place. The *Lisa Marie* rocked in the swell and the dead guy's arm waved as if beckoning to be brought up, or for Caleb to come on down. Caleb sighed and stepped away from the rail. He pulled off his gloves and ran his fingers through his thick beard. He reached up and snatched the mic from the VHF radio.

His thumb was just pressing the transmit button when he thought better of it. There were half a dozen lobster boats and even more yachts buzzing around that part of the bay. If he called the Coasties on the radio they would all hear it, and soon it would be like a multicar crash on the highway with all the rubberneckers coming around. Caleb was not in the mood for that, and he doubted he ever would be.

He put the radio mic back and picked his cell phone up off the dashboard in the cabin. He considered calling 9-1-1 but decided this was not really an emergency, so he found the number of the Coast Guard Station and punched it in.

A woman answered. She sounded young and her accent was decidedly not Maine—she was "from away," as the locals would say. "United States Coast Guard Group Portland, how may I help you?" she asked. Professional, with just a touch of chipper.

3

"Hi, yeah, my name is Caleb Hayes," Caleb began, wishing now he had thought of what he would say before dialing. "I'm hauling traps here about half a mile southeast of Whaleboat Island and I seem to have brought up a dead body on my buoy line."

There was a pause at the Coast Guard's end. "A human body, sir?" the woman asked.

"Seems to be," Caleb said.

"Please hold, sir," the woman said and then the line went quiet.

Oh, God, friggin' Coasties, they're putting me on hold! Caleb thought, but even before the thought was complete another voice came on the line.

"Search and rescue, Boatswain's Mate Cummings, how may I help you?" Another woman, this one considerably less chipper than the first.

Caleb repeated what he had said to the first Coastie, but it sounded more coherent with the second telling.

"Understood, human body on your buoy line," Boatswain's Mate Cummings said, apparently unfazed by this news. "Could you give me a more precise location, sir?"

"I'm about two hundred feet south of the green and red WS buoy off Whaleboat Island."

"Roger that. Do you need me to dispatch emergency medical personnel, sir?"

"I don't think so," Caleb said. "I'm okay, and the guy on my line isn't complaining. Just send someone to pick him up, would you?"

"Roger that," the woman said. Caleb heard the clicking of computer keys coming over the phone. "I'm dispatching a boat now, estimate time of arrival at twenty minutes."

"Roger that," Caleb said. It seemed the proper Coastie response.

"Please remain where you are, and don't disturb the body, sir," Boatswain's Mate Cummings said.

Disturb him? Caleb thought. The fellow seemed beyond disturbing. But Caleb said only, "Roger that."

He answered a few more of Boatswain's Mate Cummings's questions and then they disconnected. Caleb sighed and sat down on the wash rail, facing the port side, back to the snatch block and buoy line and the unwelcome catch that hung from it. He looked southwest at the smattering of islands that crowded Casco Bay, low-lying and bristling with spruce for the most part, as familiar as the streets in the neighborhood in which one grew up, which was pretty much what they were to him.

Caleb Hayes, thirty-six years old, native of Hopefleet, Maine, come back now like a salmon returning to the place of its birth. He had not come to spawn (though he was not adverse to the idea), but to rewind his life, spin it back to what it had been before he had tried making a new one on the West Coast, the wild roller coaster of the past decade and a half, before that had all turned to a great steaming pile of crap.

That turnaround had so far been a limited success.

Caleb stared off toward the west, past Stockman Island to the larger mass of Great Chebeague behind it and the tall stacks of the power plant on Cousin's Island. He was trying to focus on which string he would haul next, and if he should shift the one by Stockman closer inshore, but the dead guy on his buoy line seemed to call to him.

"Don't do it," he said out loud. "Don't do it." But even as he spoke those words, he knew he could not resist.

Caleb Hayes had a nearly insatiable curiosity. He could not leave anything unexplored. Since his earliest days, poking with a stick at whatever had washed up on the beach, he had to examine anything, odd or mundane, that crossed his path. It had led to a surprising breadth of knowledge, and it had led to considerable trouble.

He sighed again, stood, snatched his binoculars off the dashboard. He looked to the southwest, down Luckse Sound toward Portland. There were a dozen lobster boats plying back and forth, a few sailboats motoring in the light morning air. No sign of the Coast Guard forty-seven-foot motor lifeboat that Boatswain's Mate Cummings had dispatched.

Caleb set the binos down and stepped over to the starboard rail and looked down through the water. The dead guy was still there, looking back at him. Caleb reached over and twisted the hauler control just a bit and the buoy line came reeling in slowly and the dead guy rose the last ten feet.

The corpse broke the surface with a gush of water and Caleb stopped the hauler again when the dead guy was about level with the wash rail. The buoy line was wrapped around him in a haphazard sort of way, leaving him to hang at an odd angle. He reminded Caleb of Ahab tangled up in the lines that trailed from Moby Dick. It seemed the floating corpse had fetched up on Caleb's buoy line and become twisted in the rope, a random happenstance. Or maybe not.

Caleb leaned closer, studying the place where the line wrapped around the man's right thigh and realized it was not wrapped. It was tied. A slip knot, tied in the middle of the line, the loop slipped over the man's leg to a high point on his thigh.

"Hmm," Caleb said as he looked at the knot. It was certainly possible that the line had tied itself that way by accident. Caleb had seen ropes tie themselves into knots, sometimes quite impressive knots. But it was unusual. Very unusual.

He stepped back and ran his eyes over the corpse hanging at waist height. One foot was bare, but the other was clad in a topsider. Shorts, belt with nautical signal flags embroidered on it, light blue button-down shirt. L.L. Bean, Caleb guessed. The guy looked like a professional something or other, dressed for outdoor recreation.

Finally Caleb looked at the guy's face. It was white like some cave-dwelling creature, with a tinge of blue, and there were some bits taken out. Most of one ear was gone. But his having been caught in the line had kept him off the bottom, clear of the crabs and the lobsters, and that had likely done much to preserve him.

Caleb tried to guess how long this guy had been in the water. He had last hauled those traps three days earlier, and he was pretty sure the dead guy had not been there then. He was sure he would have noticed.

"A day? Two days?" Caleb speculated out loud. Probably not two days. He looked too good for that.

A wallet bulged in the back pocket of the guy's pants, calling to Caleb, who once again tried and failed to resist the temptation. With a twinge of guilt he looked over his shoulder, southwest toward Portland. No Coast Guard motor lifeboat. He reached out and eased the wallet from the man's pocket, not the easiest task with the wet cloth clinging to the leather.

Caleb stepped back from the rail and flipped the wallet open. About one hundred dollars in cash, twenties and fives. Sandwiched in the middle was the usual array of clear plastic sleeves. The first of those held a picture of a woman, pretty, in her thirties, perhaps, with her arms around two kids, a boy and a girl, somewhere in the eight- to ten-year-old range. They were on a beach, smiling.

"Ah, crap..." Caleb muttered. That would be the guy's family.

They were out there, somewhere, and they were probably already worrying because they had not heard from Dad in a few days.

He flipped through the other sleeves. A couple of credit cards, Anthem Blue Cross health insurance card. In a pocket in the back of the wallet he found a small stack of business cards, which he carefully extracted. "Richard Forrester" it read, and below it, "Senior Site Manager."

"Whatever the hell that is," Caleb said. He looked at the logo on the card. Atlantic Gas and Oil. Caleb made a noncommittal sound. The name meant nothing to him.

He carefully tucked the cards back where he had found them and pulled another stack from another sleeve of the wallet. They appeared to be cards the late Mr. Richard Forrester, Senior Site Manager, had collected. There was one from the manager of a hotel in Brunswick and another from a local restaurant. One card, simple and elegant, read "Susan Collins," and below that, "United States Senator." In the upper right-hand corner was a seal depicting an eagle that looked flattened, like it had been splattered on a windshield, and around the border the words "United States Senate."

"You keep impressive company," Caleb said. "Kept," he corrected himself.

He flipped through the rest of the cards. Mostly businesses in the New England area. A cream-colored card near the bottom of the stack bearing the logo of the Town of Hopefleet, a lobster boat floating above an enormous red lobster, caught his eye. He looked at the name.

"Howard Cox, Selectman, Town of Hopefleet," Caleb read. "Huh…" The name was familiar, but in truth in the ten months since his return from Los Angeles he had not paid much attention to local politics. It was a source of guilt—he felt like he should have a handle on what was happening in his hometown—but he did not feel guilty enough to actually do anything about it.

He carefully worked the stack of cards back into the wet leather of the wallet and with some difficulty returned the wallet to the late Richard Forrester's pocket. Curiosity sated, he grabbed hold of the hauler control and lowered the body back down into the water. He let about ten feet of line pay out, then stopped the hauler again. He picked up the binoculars and turned toward Portland. He could make out the dull gray of the Coast Guard's motor lifeboat just passing

Peak's Island and entering Luckse Sound. The boat was up on a plane, moving fast, a white, foaming bow wave spreading far out on either side.

"About time," Caleb muttered.

Chapter Two

The Coast Guardsmen were quick and thorough. The coxswain of the motor lifeboat looked to Caleb as if he was barely out of high school, but he oversaw the retrieval of the body with a calm, efficient and professional demeanor.

There were three Coasties in the boarding party, including the cox. Caleb used the hauler to hoist the late Richard Forrester up again, and with rubber gloves on their hands, the Coast Guardsmen and one woman pulled him inboard and laid him down on a body bag stretched out on *Lisa Marie*'s deck. They knelt beside him and began to disentangle him from Caleb's buoy line.

"Look at this," one of the crewmen said, getting to the end of the rope. "The line tied itself around the guy's thigh."

The others looked where he was pointing and made noises to express their surprise, but made no mention of it beyond that. Anyone who had been to sea for any length of time had seen such odd things before.

"You know this guy?" the coxswain asked Caleb as the others zipped up the body bag.

"No," Caleb said. "We just met this morning."

The coxswain nodded, jotted down a note on a small, spiral bound pad. Caleb had already described his discovering the dead man. If asked, he was ready to say he had not touched the body, based on the fact that he had only touched the wallet. But happily the coxswain did not ask, saving Caleb from his morally dubious obfuscation.

"All right," the coxswain said. "I've got all your contact info. I would guess the cops will want to talk to you, particularly if they decide this was something more than an accident."

As they were speaking, the Coast Guardsman who had remained

on the lifeboat passed a body board over the rail. It was the sort used to move people with back injuries, and the other two set it on the *Lisa Marie*'s deck, hefted the body bag onto it, and fastened the straps around the late Richard Forrester. They lifted the body and, with the help of the third man, passed it back aboard the motor lifeboat.

The coxswain looked around Caleb's boat as if trying to decide whether or not to do a safety inspection for good measure. Instead, he shook Caleb's hand and stepped up on the wash rail and then onto his own command.

The Coasties cast off and headed back toward Portland, and Caleb turned his attention to the buoy line still wrapped around the hauler. He hit the control handle again and watched the rest of the rope snake up from below. He half expected to see another body come up with it, but none did, only the first trap on the trawl, emerging from the green depths and breaking the surface with a gush of water.

Caleb swung the trap onto the wash rail. There were five lobsters in it, three of which looked to be keepers. There was little chance that any of them had been feasting on the late Richard Forrester, and even if they had, it would not really make any difference. That was the reasonable conclusion. But reason was not really playing much part in Caleb's thinking at the moment.

He opened the top of the trap and tossed all the lobsters, along with the sundry Jonah crabs, back into the sea. One by one Caleb hauled up the next seven traps on the trawl and hefted them onto the rail. He discarded the lobsters in those as well, baited the traps, and set them on a stack on the stern, leaving the last in the string on the rail beside him. He motored the *Lisa Maria* around in a wide arc, and when he was once again where he wanted the trawl set, he tossed the buoy overboard and shoved the trap into the sea.

One by one the others were pulled from the stern as the ground line came taught and jerked the traps off the back of the boat. This operation would have been much easier with the assistance of a sternman, but Caleb had no desire to share his hours on the water with another guy. He had a lot to think about, a lot to work through, and he did not care to fill his blessed solitude with banal conversation.

For the next six hours, Caleb hauled, emptied, baited and set traps, and then he turned the bow of the *Lisa Marie* for Kettle Cove, hidden beyond pine-covered Oak Point a few miles away. He pushed the throttle forward, felt the boat's bow rise out of the water as the hull began to plane. On the east shore of Kettle Cove was Hopefleet Lobster Co-op, an organization of local lobstermen who banded together to collectively buy bait and gear and sell their catches. Caleb, like his Uncle Dick, was a member.

He passed red nun buoy number two and eased the throttle back. The *Lisa Marie* came down off her plane and seemed to nestle into the water as her speed dropped by eight knots. There were four boats ahead of him, all making for the same place, and he knew there would be more once the harbor came into view. Working alone, and not being in any particular hurry, Caleb was often the last to reach the co-op's dock. And of course, the time spent with Richard Forrester that morning had only made it worse.

He rounded Oak Point and Kettle Cove opened up before him and he eased the throttle back further still. Kettle Cove was not large, a narrow indent in the coast maybe two hundred yards wide at its widest, and about a quarter mile long. A shallow granite ledge formed the shoreline, with a gravel beach tucked into the far end of the cove. From the water's edge the shore rose gently to stands of tall spruce and a few clearings where gray-shingled houses looked out to sea. Two dozen lobsterboats had their moorings in that small patch of water.

On the east side of the cove sat a series of floating docks with a small shack, open on one side, where the lobstermen who belonged to the Hopefleet co-op tied up to off-load their day's catch. A ramp led from the floating docks to a more substantial wharf on which sat a single-wide mobile home converted into the co-op office and the larger, white-painted storehouse in which bait and sundry other supplies were stored. Kettle Cove would not have been out of place on a postcard or a promotional brochure from the Maine Tourism Association, but it was home to Caleb, so familiar that the beauty of the place hardly even registered.

For twenty minutes Caleb let the *Lisa Marie* drift as the boats ahead of him finished up and motored back to their moorings. Then he put his boat in gear and made a slow approach to the dock. Jimmy Moody, a young guy, twenty, maybe, who worked off-loading and weighing the lobsters, grabbed up the *Lisa Marie*'s bow and stern lines and made them off.

"Caleb, how's it going?" he asked as he handed Caleb a plastic crate into which the day's catch would go. Caleb lifted the lid off the *Lisa Marie*'s lobster tank. At the bottom of the tank was a crawling, waving pile of mottled green, brown and orange lobsters.

"Good. All's good," Caleb said, pulling the lobsters dripping and protesting from the tank and dropping them into the crate. When the crate was filled he handed it to Jimmy to be weighed, and Jimmy handed him a second, which Caleb started filling. Apparently word of his finding Richard Forrester's body had not yet filtered down to the docks. But it would. Caleb's rendezvous with the Coast Guard motor lifeboat could not have gone unnoticed.

"Pretty good day," Caleb added. "I think the lobsters are coming in shore."

Jimmy jotted down the weight of the first crate on a receipt pad, then lifted a section of the floating dock and dropped the crate into the water below, where it joined a few dozen of its fellows, all stuffed with lobster. He took the second crate, weighed it, and dropped it into the water as well.

"Hey, Jimmy, I'll need two bushels of bait, too," Caleb said, but Jimmy was staring off toward the wharf, transfixed and oblivious.

"Dude, check this out," Jimmy said.

Caleb looked in the direction Jimmy was staring. A girl was coming down the ramp to the floating docks. Faded blue jeans, tight but not overly tight, a gray sweatshirt, long blond hair flying gently like a flag in the five knots of breeze. Even from one hundred feet away she looked good. But Caleb was not one to leer, so he turned back to Jimmy, who was still staring unabashedly at the approaching girl. "Bait?" he prompted.

"Dude, no way," Jimmy said. "She's gotta be twenty, at least." It took him a second to register that Caleb was not talking about the girl, and only then did he pull his eyes away. "Oh, yeah, dude, sorry," he muttered.

Caleb emptied the last of his crustaceans into a third crate and handed it over to Jimmy, aware that they were both making an effort not to look at the woman who was making her way down the floating docks, even as she approached Jimmy's hut.

"Excuse me," she said as she came to a stop near *Lisa Marie*'s bow. "Is one of you Caleb Hayes?"

"Yeah," Jimmy said, and Caleb was sure he heard both

disappointment and resignation in the man's voice. "He is."

"Hi, Caleb?" the girl said, pulling the windblown hair from her face, a bit of a smile on her lips. She stepped up, offered him a hand. Caleb slipped the cloth work glove off and shook, suddenly aware of the fishy smell that permeated his clothes and his person.

"I'm Katie Brennan," she continued. "Your uncle, Dick Hayes, said I should talk to you."

"He did?" Caleb said, stepping on the boat's rail and then onto the dock. "About what?" Katie was around five seven, he guessed, though even at that height she only came up to his shoulders. She had a comfortably fit look, like she was in good shape without really trying too hard.

"Here, Caleb," Jimmy interrupted, the words bitten off short and resentful, as if Caleb had purposely ruined his otherwise perfect chance to impress this girl. He handed Caleb the carbon copy of the receipt and retreated back into his hut, like a moray eel squirming back under its rock.

"Here's the thing," Katie said. "I've been looking for work as a sternman this summer."

Caleb nodded. She said "sternman" and not "sternwoman." A good sign. Women who really knew lobstering did not call themselves "sternwomen."

"Most of the guys I talked to had already hired someone on. And some of these younger guys..." Katie added, and by way of example she gave a sidelong glance at Jimmy, sulking in his shack.

"Yeah," Caleb said.

"So anyway," Katie said, "I ran into your uncle and he said you don't have a sternman and you're not a creep so I should come talk to you."

Caleb nodded as he considered this. Uncle Dick was his father's only brother. The two men had both grown up in Hopefleet, but their courses had gone off in different directions. Caleb's father had spent his career as an English professor at nearby Bowdoin College. He had retired five years earlier. He and Caleb's mom now lived most of the year in Florida, a thing Caleb's father had always sworn he would never do, right up until the moment that retirement had made it feasible.

Uncle Dick, like many local boys, had become a lobsterman, hauling traps from a skiff in high school and buying his first real boat soon after graduation. He was smart and hardworking and had made a good living from the sea, enough to send Caleb's three cousins to college. He was a mainstay in the Hopefleet fishing community. That was why Caleb had been welcomed back and allowed to start catching lobsters in those waters again.

"There's another thing," Katie said, and she said it sheepishly, as if she was about to reveal she had a criminal record or was a registered sex offender. "I'm in grad school, most of the year. I'm studying…marine biology and fisheries management."

"Ah!" Caleb said. "So that's your nefarious secret. You're going to join the Dark Side, work for the state's fisheries management. Is this part of your course work, learning to spy on innocent lobstermen?"

"That's right," Katie said. "I'm trying to spy on innocent lobstermen. But I haven't been able to find any."

"I'll bet not," Caleb agreed. He considered his uncle's motives in sending Katie his way. Dick was likely growing concerned about his nephew's self-imposed isolation, the hermit life he had taken to as he tried to sort out all that had gone down in Los Angeles over the past year, and the fourteen years before that. Dick no doubt thought that having a sternman might help draw him out, a sternman who was not some kid right out of high school whose idea of conversation was to talk about how insensibly drunk he had become the night before.

He was about to tell Katie that he would be happy to hire her on when Jimmy, who had emerged from the hut, interrupted again. "Dude, more company," he said, nodding toward the wharf.

Caleb looked over. Katie did as well. There were two men, wearing sports coats and ties, their hair cut short, their appearance neat.

"Cops," Caleb said.

"How do you know?" Katie asked.

"They look like cops," Caleb said.

"Are they looking for you?" Katie asked, a touch of concern in her voice.

"Not sure. Jimmy, any reason the cops would be looking for you?"

"No, dude," Jimmy said. "Those charges were all dropped, like, a month ago."

"Then I guess they're looking for me," Caleb said.

The three of them waited as the two men in the sports coats came down the floating docks. They stopped five feet short of Caleb and Katie. "Excuse me, are you Caleb Hayes?" the first asked.

"Yeah, that's me," Caleb said, then thought, *For a guy who gets ignored most of the time I seem to be getting a lot of attention today.*

The man reached into his back pocket and drew out a wallet with a badge and police ID. "I'm Detective Mike Berry of the Cumberland County Sheriff's Department. Can I ask you a few questions?"

"Sure, no problem," Caleb said. He glanced at Katie and almost laughed at her expression, which seemed to be an odd mix of intense curiosity and a strong fight-or-flight instinct. "I have an idea what this is about."

"No doubt," Detective Berry said. "You found the body of an adult male individual entangled in one of your lobster trap ropes this morning?"

"That's right," Caleb said. He wondered why cops had to say things like "adult male individual" rather than just, "guy."

"Dude, no way!" said Jimmy, who wasn't even pretending to not listen.

"Did you know the individual?" Detective Berry asked. Caleb knew with certainty that Berry had talked with the Coast Guard and already knew the answers he had given. Now he was looking for consistency.

"No, I don't believe I ever met him," Caleb said. "I didn't get a great look at him, of course. Frankly, I wasn't real motivated to look."

"I understand," Berry said. "Any idea how he happened to get tangled in your line?"

Caleb shrugged. "All sorts of weird things happen on the water, Detective. Isn't that right, Jimmy?"

"Weird shit, dude," Jimmy offered.

"Guy might have drowned. He was floating around. The swells and the currents and tides will do all sorts of things. Traps get tangled up all the time."

Berry nodded. He pulled a small notebook from his back pocket, briefly revealing the butt of the service weapon in a holster clipped to his belt.

Glock 19, Caleb thought as Berry jotted down a few notes. *Decent gun.*

There were a few more questions. Caleb answered them and Detective Berry seemed satisfied enough with the answers. Caleb recalled Mark Twain's words: *If you always tell the truth you don't have to remember what you said.* They were words he lived by. Mostly.

Caleb took Berry's business card and Berry wrote down Caleb's address and phone number. The detectives left and Katie turned to Caleb. She looked like she might explode if she didn't speak. That was the Irish in her, he guessed.

"You had a dead guy tangled in your buoy line?" she asked.

"Yeah, out by Whaleboat Island."

"Was it...I don't know..." Katie was looking for the right question to ask.

"Dude, was he messed up?" Jimmy prompted.

"He was dead," Caleb said. "I guess that's pretty messed up. But he wasn't all half eaten or anything. I don't think he was down there that long. Couldn't have been more than three days because I fished that trawl three days ago."

"Wow," Katie said. "Does that sort of thing happen a lot?"

"Tell you what," Caleb said. "Why don't you start working for me tomorrow and find out for yourself?"

Chapter Three

Howard Cox, one of three selectmen for the town of Hopefleet, Maine, sat in a small meeting room in the Hopefleet Town Office. It was a nice room, and a nice town office, built just a few years before on land that enjoyed a view straight down Hopefleet Sound to the Atlantic Ocean. It was one of the finest views in Hopefleet, and that was saying a lot.

Selectman Cox was trying not to appear bored. Or impatient. Or condescending. Despite his feeling all of those things at that moment.

Across the table from him, notebook laid out on the faux wood surface, was Alex Henderson, owner, editor, publisher, writer, janitor for the monthly *Hopefleet Buoy*, the town's only newspaper. Alex still looked more like a commercial fisherman, which he had been, than he did a newspaperman. Even if he had looked like Clark Kent, Selectman Cox was not much inclined to think of Henderson as a member of the press. Cox was accustomed to being interviewed by the *Washington Post* or the *New York Times* in his former K Street office, by men with journalism degrees from Stanford and not lobstering licenses from the State of Maine.

But they both had a part to play, Cox and Henderson, and Cox settled in to play his.

"So, Selectman," Henderson said, looking up from his pad and giving Cox the same genuine smile with which he seemed to greet the world. "I know you've been in Hopefleet a few years now, but you've only been on the board since the last election...which was..."

"Six months ago," Cox supplied.

"Six months, right. Damn, it goes faster and faster every year, doesn't it? So, if it's not too tedious, I'd like to get some background stuff for any readers who might not be as familiar with you."

Like you? Cox thought, but rather than say it he nodded and

said, "Of course."

"You are from Connecticut originally?" Henderson prompted.

"Yes, Darien, not far from New York City. My father was in finance. But we had a summer place in Hopefleet. Bought by my grandfather, actually, around the turn of the century. The nineteenth century, that is. We spent most summers here when I was growing up. Hopefleet's always seemed like my real home. When I retired it was only natural that I would retire here. To the home my grandfather built."

"Of course," Henderson said, writing as fast as his big hands could write. "And right after you moved here you had the Hopefleet Fire and Rescue burn the house down as a training exercise?"

"Yes, well…" Cox said. He hadn't seen that question coming and he cursed himself for letting some rube get in a potential jab. "The house wasn't winterized, you see, and it was too small for the grandchildren and all. I figured it would be a big help to the fire department to get the training burn in. It was something of a service to the community all around."

Henderson scribbled. He did not respond. Cox wondered if the question had been a deliberate gotcha or if the writer/fisherman had stumbled on it innocently. He was not sure what Henderson's angle was here.

"And you spent most of your career in Washington?"

"That's right," Cox said. "I was sort of a facilitator. I got people talking to each other, which is a feat in itself in that town, I can tell you."

He didn't even have to think about how to spin that answer. He had worked it out years before. "Lobbyist" became "facilitator." His efforts to keep the government from interfering with the profits of whatever organization paid his firm's fees became getting people to talk to each other. The hicks in Maine always bought that job description, even if the greenest DC lawyer or Hill staffer would have seen right through it.

"Do you miss it?" Henderson asked. "Washington, doing that work?"

"Oh, no, not really," Cox said. "I sure don't miss DC and all the nonsense that goes on there, all the acrimony. That's why I retired. All these years I've still spent summers in Hopefleet, you know, and I couldn't wait to get here full time.

"What I do miss, or did miss, was the helping part. Trying to do my bit to make people's lives better. I think government can do that, if it knows its proper roll. That's why I stood for selectman, so I could keep helping. And I'm delighted the folks in Hopefleet took a chance on me."

"Sure," Henderson said, his eyes on his pad as he wrote. "Now..." he began, but he was interrupted by a buzzing sound, like a bee caught behind a window. Howard Cox's cell phone, taking an incoming call.

"Excuse me," Cox said. He picked up the phone, looked at the number. No name, an anonymous caller. He didn't recognize the number, but he recognized the area code: 212, New York City. That meant it was a call he probably did not want to miss.

"I'm sorry," Cox said to Henderson, "I have to take this. Just be a moment." He stood and walked quickly out of the room, down the hall and out the door on the side of the town office building. It was a gorgeous day, the sky blue, the humidity tolerable, the temperature just right, but Howard Cox did not care at all about any of that. He poked the answer button on his still-buzzing phone.

"Yes?" he said, not trying to disguise his irritation.

There was a pause on the line, like a beat for emphasis, and then a voice he did not recognize said, "Dick Forrester is dead."

Cox felt his lips press together, his eyebrows knit. That one, simple sentence was fraught with implications and danger, and Cox took a beat of his own to consider his approach.

"Do I know a Dick Forrester?" he snapped, more to buy a few more seconds to think. The caller clearly knew he did.

"Yes, you do," the caller said.

"Who is this?" Cox demanded. His equilibrium was coming back.

"I'm the guy calling to tell you about Forrester," the man said. "What happened to Dick, it's too bad. And it means some of the arrangements are going to have to change. You understand?"

"No, I don't understand," Cox said, which was true on some levels, untrue on others. "I don't know who you are, I don't know what arrangements you're talking about, and I sure as hell have no intention of talking to you over the damned phone!" He pressed the little red circle on the screen and the call was ended. He looked up at the pine-covered hill that loomed to the east of the town hall and drew a deep breath.

Dick Forrester dead? Shit... He wondered what had happened. Had the man been killed by accident, hit a deer driving the back roads, got hold of some bad seafood? No, of course not. There was an implied threat in the caller's voice. Not so subtle a threat.

Then Howard recalled that Alex Henderson was still waiting inside. He took another deep, cleansing breath and stepped out of the warm afternoon sun into the air conditioning of the town office.

"Sorry about that," Cox said, taking his seat once again. "My mother-in-law is in the hospital, and I'm afraid it's not looking too good. My wife's with her."

"Oh, I'm sorry," Henderson said. "Would you like to reschedule?"

"No, this is fine," Cox said. "They're down in DC. I'll probably fly down tomorrow. Now, where were we?"

"Right," Henderson said, glancing down at his notebook. "Well, there's one subject that you knew we had to get to, so we might as well get to it. You know what that is."

"LNG," Cox said.

"LNG," Henderson agreed.

LNG. Liquid natural gas. That arcane substance was the hottest and most divisive subject in Hopefleet, and had been for the past six months. In earlier, Cold War days, the United States Navy maintained a deep-water port in Hopefleet where ships would bring in aviation fuel to be stored in great fuel tanks and piped to the naval air station in Brunswick, ten miles away. The dock and the land, known locally as "the fuel farm," had since been abandoned by the navy and turned over to the town.

The fuel tanks had long ago been removed. Of the infrastructure, only a few old brick buildings and the massive concrete dock remained. The rest of the property consisted of one hundred acres of beautiful open meadowland, rolling down to the island-dotted waters of Middle Bay. It was a stunning piece of real estate.

The question then was, what to do with it? No one was really sure. Turn it into a public park of some sort? Lease it to a private commercial venture? Those discussions were just getting started when International Gas and Power arrived.

IGP was one of those corporations that had its fingers in any number of energy interests worldwide: oil from Russia, coal from West Virginia, wind power in Kansas. And now natural gas in New England. Which was where Hopefleet came in.

For transport, natural gas was cooled to the point where it became liquid, and in that state it could be moved by tanker ships and stored just like any other liquid. More or less. The chief problem was that LNG was incredibly volatile, and while there had not been any major disasters with the stuff in many years, still the potential existed.

International Gas and Power knew this, and they were willing to make the risk worth Hopefleet's while. They would lease the fuel farm for eight million dollars per year, enough to all but eliminate the town's need to levy a property tax. They would build and equip a new fire station, since the old one was both inadequate and within the blast zone of any potential catastrophic failure. They would bring good-paying jobs.

What seemed like an offer dropped from heaven had so far torn the roughly five thousand residents of Hopefleet apart. The working class folks, the carpenters and mechanics and truck drivers and nurses, were delighted at the thought of having no property tax, and at seeing good-paying jobs come to town so their kids would not have to move elsewhere to find work.

But Hopefleet also had a large and growing population of well-off retirees who had discovered in the town a quaint and largely unspoiled fishing community where real estate was not yet so wildly expensive. They didn't care about property taxes, they just wanted Hopefleet to remain as they had found it, and they were strongly opposed to any industrial development.

In the middle of all this were the lobstermen. They were not at all opposed to having their property taxes eliminated, but they had other concerns. The huge tankers that carried the LNG would be sailing right through some of the prime spots for setting traps. Worse, because the ships' cargoes were so volatile, the Coast Guard would set and enforce a five-hundred-yard perimeter around each vessel as it went in and out, effectively shutting down the lobster fishing in wide swaths of Hopefleet waters whenever the ships arrived.

This put the lobstermen in league with the wealthy retirees, strange bedfellows indeed.

The mood in the town had become as volatile as the LNG itself. And the decision to accept or reject the offer presented by International Gas and Power fell to Howard Cox and his two fellow selectmen.

"Of course," Cox continued. "I expected a good part of this discussion would revolve around LNG. How could it not?"

"It's an explosive topic, for sure," Henderson said, "if you'll pardon my choice of words. Your two fellow selectmen are in favor of the project. You oppose it. Could you talk about that?"

"Certainly I can. In fact I would like very much to do so," Cox said. He had long ago perfected the ability to sound as if he were speaking off the cuff while reciting arguments he had labored over and rehearsed until he could deliver them like a Broadway actor in a show's fourth season.

"Here's the thing," Cox continued, speaking slow enough for Henderson to keep up with his note writing. "A lot of the folks, they think guys like me are against the LNG thing because we don't want to see Hopefleet spoiled by industry. You know what? They're right. But it's not for my sake I want to keep this town the way it is. I don't want to see this beautiful place, where I've been coming all my life, ruined for our kids and grandkids."

Henderson looked up from his pad. "A lot of folks would say the natural beauty of Hopefleet doesn't do them much good if they can't afford to live here. If their kids can't get jobs here," he said.

Cox nodded. He wasn't sure where Henderson's sympathies lay.

"Look, there are plenty of economic opportunities here, based on the natural beauty you're talking about. It's our most important asset," Cox continued. "If we ruin that, and then the LNG terminal closes up because the Saudis have ramped up oil production and LNG is no longer viable, then we've lost everything."

Cox felt he was on a roll now, so he continued, though Henderson had opened his mouth to ask another question. "Here's the thing," Cox went on. "If I trusted International Gas and Power to do what they said, to have as little impact as they say, to bring all the jobs they say they will, then I might be in favor of this. But I've dealt with these sorts of people my whole career. They'll say whatever they think the locals want to hear, and then when they get their nose under the tent they do whatever damage they want, and by then it's too late. If they violate the contract and we try to do something about it, do you think Hopefleet can go up against the lawyers they'll throw at us? The town would be bankrupted by the legal fees alone."

Henderson was nodding now, and Cox had a notion he had reached the guy, that the nearly unassailable logic of his argument had struck home. The subtext, of course, was that Cox, as someone who had moved in international circles, knew better than the provincials what could happen if they tangled with IGP. Hopefleet, indeed all of Maine, needed the worldly experience of Howard Cox.

"So you'll be voting against the LNG terminal?" Henderson asked. "Even though the other two selectpersons are in favor of it?"

The other two selectpersons are a couple of ignorant dolts whom evolution seems to have bypassed, Cox thought, but he said, "As of now, yes. If I can be persuaded that I should vote otherwise, then I'll change my vote. I like to keep an open mind about these things. But as of now, I don't see what might alter my opinion."

He paused while Henderson scribbled. "Okay, Selectman, just a couple more questions, if you don't mind," he said, and then lobbed a few queries about shore access issues and brown tail moth issues and pesticide run-off issues, all the tedious nonsense through which a selectman had to wade.

*Two more years of this crap…*Cox thought. He had an end in sight, a path marked out, but until then he had to tolerate this small-town nonsense and make it seem as if he cared.

There was a knock on the doorframe that thankfully cut Henderson off short. The two men looked up. Eleanor, who manned the front desk of the town office, was there, and behind her, two men with ties and short hair and the unmistakable look of cops.

"Mr. Cox, these gentlemen were looking for you," Eleanor said.

"Come in, come in," Cox said, waving them into the room. Eleanor stepped aside. The two men came in. The one in front pulled out a wallet with badge and ID.

"I'm Detective Mike Berry of the Cumberland County Sheriff's Department. Can I ask you a few questions, sir?" the man said.

"Of course, of course," Cox said. He turned to Alex Henderson. "You'll excuse me, I hope. I seem to be a popular guy today."

"Of course, Selectmen, and thank you," Henderson said, standing and scooping up his notebook and pen. He nodded a friendly greeting to the detectives, and headed out of the door.

"Please, have a seat." Cox gestured toward the chair Henderson had just vacated. "I have to say, I'm intrigued," he added quickly, before Henderson had left the room. "I can't imagine what it is you want with me." That was not the first lie he had told that day, and he doubted it would be the last.

Chapter Four

It was just past 5:00 a.m., the first gray vestiges of dawn showing in the east, when Caleb Hayes steered his Ford F-150 into the dirt parking lot by Hopefleet Lobster co-op and moored it in line with the other Fords and Dodge Rams and GMCs and the occasional Toyota Tundra.

There were many things about lobstering that Caleb liked, but this was not one of them. He had never been a morning person, and ten months of rising before dawn had not changed that. This had not been an issue during his time in Los Angeles, since no one with whom he worked there was up at 5:00 a.m. More often they were going to bed at that hour.

But the lobstermen started early. In part this was because the seas were flatter, the wind less likely to be blowing in those early morning hours. But it was also a matter of pride. Lobster catchers were not lay-a-beds. They were up and they were hard at work by the time the office-dwellers were just staggering toward the coffee pot.

Caleb climbed down out of his truck and took a deep breath. The air was cool and smelled of balsam pine and salt water and fish. There might have been birds singing, but they could not be heard over the low growl of half a dozen diesel engines out on Kettle Cove, the lobster fleet waking up.

He looked around the parking lot. He had told Katie to meet him there at that hour and he hoped she would arrive on time. He considered it something of a test—if he had to wait more than ten minutes for her, her first day as his sternman would be her last.

The irritation was just starting to form when he saw a car's interior light come on at the far end of the parking lot, revealing Katie Brennan inside. The car was a PT Cruiser, looking well past its prime and like it had not received all the care it might have liked. Even if he had not seen Katie inside, Caleb would have known that was her ride. No lobsterman or male sternman would have arrived at Hopefleet Lobster in a PT Cruiser.

Caleb heard the car door slam and the light went off and Katie came around the back and walked toward him. She was just visible in the dawn's early light, wearing jeans and the same sweatshirt she had been wearing on the dock the day before. Over her arm was a pair of orange rubberized bib overalls. Oilskins, the lobstermen called them, a term that was a throwback to an earlier era. The brand was Grundens, as close to a uniform as anything in the lobstering fleet. But it was not Katie's Grundens that greedily drew Caleb's eyes. It was the tall, white, cardboard-clad cups of coffee in her hands, the Starbuck's logo just visible in the gloom.

"Good morning," she said as she handed one of the cups to Caleb, and Caleb, so grateful for the hot liquid, did not even think to be annoyed by her chipper tone.

"Thank you," Caleb said as he took the cup and lifted it to his lips. "And bless you." It had been a bad night. Caleb had done a bit too much self-anesthetizing with a bottle of vodka and he had not managed to pull himself out of bed with enough time or energy to brew a pot of coffee. "You haven't even stepped on the boat and I'm ready to give you a raise," he added.

"Really?" Katie asked.

"No," Caleb said.

"What are you paying me, by the way?" Katie asked. "I guess I should have asked that yesterday. The cops kind of threw me off my game."

"Me too," Caleb said. "I'll pay you fifteen percent of every day's catch after the costs of fuel and bait are subtracted. That's standard pay for a sternman."

"Fair enough," Katie said.

"It is," Caleb agreed, "as long as we catch lots of lobsters. But the fishing's been pretty good and the boat price is decent."

They walked down the hill from the parking lot and out along the floating docks where the two had met the day before. This was rush hour, lobsterman style, and there were men and a few women, ranging in age from sixteen to their sixties, moving along the dock, casting off skiffs, motoring their boats alongside. It was loud, boisterous, but there was a sense of community, of shared effort, despite the notorious independence of the Maine lobsterman.

They reached Caleb's skiff, a battered, flat-bottomed wooden boat with worn green paint on the freeboard and dirty, worn gray paint on the inside. There were sundry bits of rope, a hand-operated bilge pump and a few empty coffee cups strewn around the bottom. Caleb stepped on board. He turned to help Katie and was gratified to see that she stepped aboard without hesitation and with considerably more grace than he had done.

Caleb set his coffee down, set the choke on the outboard, then tugged the starter cord a few times. The engine caught and chugged and settled into a smooth idle. Caleb always made certain his outboard was in top running order. There was almost nothing he hated more at any time of the day than fighting to start an outboard engine. At 5:00 in the morning it was intolerable.

He gave Katie a nod and she untied the painter and sat. Caleb backed the skiff away from the dock, swung her bow around, then shifted the motor into forward and steered for the *Lisa Marie* as he sipped his coffee. It was not a long boat ride, two minutes across Kettle Cove, and the familiar shape of his Henry Barnes-built hove into view.

"Who's Lisa Marie?" Katie called aft as Caleb eased the throttle and brought the skiff along the port side.

"Don't know," Caleb said. "That was the name of the boat when I bought her. It's bad luck to change a boat's name."

"Really?" Katie said. She reached up and grabbed the *Lisa Marie*'s wash rail and climbed up on board, the painter in her hand. "So you're stuck with the name, even if you want to change it?"

"As I understand it, you can change the name once you've run the boat aground. Probably won't be long before that happens," Caleb said. "Or I could just admit I'm too lazy to pick a new name and repaint the transom." He stood, set his coffee on the boat's rail and climbed aboard. "Tie the painter to the mooring line up on the Sampson post, would you?" he said next.

"Sure," Katie said, walking forward and pulling the skiff along.

"You can tie a knot, right?" Caleb asked.

"If you can't tie a knot, tie a lot. That's what I say," Katie said. Caleb smiled. He would find some excuse to go forward and check her knot tying before they got underway.

He put the key in *Lisa Marie*'s ignition and turned it and the big diesel engine made a few chugging noises and then caught. For all the problems that a wooden boat presented, *Lisa Marie* was in good shape. Caleb had put a significant amount of money into her hull and drive train because he had the luxury of having a significant amount of money to spend. That investment showed in the reliability of the engine and the relatively minor amount of water that leaked into the bilge.

"Okay, go ahead and cast her off!" Caleb called forward and Katie nodded and tossed the mooring line off the Sampson post. Caleb put the boat into reverse and backed away from the mooring and the skiff and thought, *Damn it!* He had forgotten to check the knot that Katie had tied in the painter.

Well, if the skiff's still here when we get back, that'll tell me something, he thought.

They motored over to the floating dock and hefted aboard four fish totes: battered and stained gray plastic crates about three feet long by two wide and ten inches deep, filled with the bait they would use to lure the lobsters into the hundreds of traps on Caleb's trawls. They cast off and Caleb whirled the *Lisa Marie* around and they motored out of Kettle Cove, giving friendly waves to their fellow lobster fisherman standing behind the wheels of their own boats, all motoring out for the fishing grounds of Casco Bay.

The sun was up by the time they cleared the cove and the water and the islands and the mainland were lovely in the low-angled light. The sky was a perfect blue once again and the morning was already warm, an ideal day for hauling traps. Or for going to the beach or going sailing or pretty much anything that could be done out of doors. Caleb stretched, took a deep breath, arched his back.

"Nice morning," Katie observed.

"Finest kind," Caleb said. "At least, that's what the tourists expect us to say."

"Gotta keep the tourists happy," Katie said.

"Ayuh," Caleb agreed.

They motored out beyond Kettle Cove with the islands of Casco Bay spread out before them: Jewel, Stave, Great Chebeague, Cousins. They could see the promontory of Cape Elizabeth more than ten miles away to the southwest.

Caleb throttled back and the *Lisa Marie* settled down into the water, making no more than five knots now. "Time to get to work," he said, taking one last look beyond the bow before stepping away from the wheel. The hydraulics would keep the helm centered, and it would be fifteen minutes at least before they were in danger of hitting anything.

"Better suit up," he said to Katie, taking his own Grundens oilskins down from a hook in the open cabin. He stepped into them and Katie did the same with hers and Caleb could see Katie's were not new; they had seen some use. Another good sign. Caleb handed her a pair of cloth work gloves, which Katie took with a thanks.

Katie pulled a baseball cap from her back pocket, put it on her head, and pulled her ponytail through the opening in the back. The cap bore the logo of the University of Southern Maine Huskies. Caleb smiled.

"What's so funny?" Katie asked.

"Your hat. I always wondered how the gals on the USM teams liked being referred to as 'Husky women' in the sports pages."

Katie smiled as well. "Not our favorite," she said.

"So," Caleb said, moving on to a more relevant topic. "Do you know much about lobstering?"

"I've been out on boats a few times," Katie said. "But I don't really know that much."

"Ever get bait bags ready?"

"No."

"You're in for a treat. Here, let me show you." The fish totes were stacked three high and Caleb lifted the lid off the top one. Inside was a nasty stew of silvery fish about ten inches in length and long dead, along with a mixture of water and blood, all covered with salt like the dirty snow of late spring.

"These are a fish we call menhaden, or pogies," Caleb said.

"*Brevoortia tyrannus*," Katie said. "Omnivorous filter feeders. They tend to cluster in large, slow-moving schools."

"Yeah," Caleb said. "That's what I was going to say next."

From a box mounted on the side of the lobster tank Caleb pulled out a few mesh bags about a foot long, six inches wide. "These are bait bags," Caleb said. "First thing is to fill about a dozen of these, like this." He opened the bag and stuffed it full of the stiff pogies, then pulled the drawstring closed.

"Now you take one of these bait irons," he said, holding up a twelve-inch-long stainless steel rod with a wooden handle on one end and the other end flattened with a hole through it like an oversized needle. "Go ahead and open that other tote," he added.

Katie leaned over and opened the fourth tote. Like the first, it was filled with fish and brine and blood and salt, but these fish were larger, with a reddish hue.

"These are redfish," Caleb said. "Do you know the scientific name of these?"

"No, I don't," Katie said. Whether she really didn't, or was just trying to not come off as a know-it-all, Caleb could not tell, but he didn't pursue the question.

They hefted the tote filled with redfish and dumped some in beside the pogies. Caleb grabbed one of the redfish and bent it in two, the bones making an audible cracking sound as they broke, then he thrust the pointed end of the bait iron through the folded fish. He looked over at Katie to see how she would react to this unpleasant task, but her expression was one of interest and focus, nothing more.

"Now take the bait iron and run it though the bait bag," Caleb continued, pushing the sharp end through the mesh bag filled with pogies, "and that's it. There should be a dozen bait irons here. Go ahead and load them all up and we'll be ready to haul the first trawl."

"Got it," Katie said and took up another bait iron. Caleb left her to it and returned to the wheel, pushing the throttle forward and swinging the boat off to the south, toward the trawls he had set down by Eagle Island Ledge.

Ten minutes later Caleb came up on the first of his red and white buoys, grabbed it with his gaff, and pulled it aboard. He set the buoy on the wash rail, put the line through the hauler block and around the hauler and began winching the rope on board.

"Is there going to be a dead guy on the trap?" Katie asked.

"Don't know," Caleb said. "Come look."

Kate leaned over the side, watched the line rising up from the depths. Suddenly something larger materialized through the green haze of water. Caleb made a loud gasping noise and Katie sucked in her breath and jumped back. And Caleb laughed.

"Don't laugh, you jerk," Katie said.

"Sorry," Caleb said, though he wasn't.

With a gush of water the trap broke the surface and they swung it onto the rail, happy to see three good-sized, flapping lobsters within. Caleb walked Kate through the steps of opening the trap and tossing back the various less desirable creatures. He showed her how to use the state-issued measuring gauge to determine if the lobsters were "keepers," within the size limits, not too small or too big.

One of the lobsters was of legal size but was V-notched; a wedge-shaped notch had been cut in her tail fin by some previous lobsterman to indicate she was an egg-laying female, an activity the lobstermen wished to encourage.

"That notch will keep her alive until the next molt, at least," Caleb said as he tossed the lobster back. The other two were within specs and Caleb showed Katie how to use the bander, a scissor-like device that stretched the short, thick rubber bands so they could be slipped over the lobsters' claws. They dropped the lobsters through the short pipe on the top of the lobster tank, took the old bait bag out of the trap, shook the contents into the sea to the squawking delight of a small flock of eager gulls, and replaced it with one of the bait bags Katie had prepared.

"Okay, that's done," Caleb said. "Only a hundred and ninety-nine more to do today." He pushed the trap down the rail to make room for the next one.

They worked well together and Katie quickly got the hang of the work, though, as Caleb assured her, it wasn't rocket surgery. Through a flawless morning they hauled traps, banded lobsters, baited traps and set them again. They worked their way around Eagle Island Ledge and then north toward the trawls tucked in between Jewel and Cliff Islands.

It was about 10:00 when Caleb killed the *Lisa Marie*'s engine and announced it was time for lunch. Katie had failed to bring a lunch since Caleb had failed to mention the need for one. But happily Caleb had at least remembered that he had failed to mention it, so he'd brought extra food for her.

"You're not a vegetarian, are you?" he asked, handing her an overstuffed roast beef sandwich.

"Good Lord, no," Katie said, taking the food gratefully. They sat on the *Lisa Marie*'s wash rail as the boat moved up and down, side to side in the easy swell and the sun blazed down on them and their ears were filled with the cry of the gulls and the lap of the water and the distant buzzing of lobster boats racing from buoy to buoy.

Katie took a big bite, chewed and swallowed. She took a long look around. "I can see why you love this," she said.

"Not hard to love it," Caleb agreed. "Are you a Mainer by birth?" He realized he knew nothing about her, really. They had worked together all of four hours and that time had been taken up with talk of lobsters and bait and trawls. Their conversation had not even extended to cabbages and kings.

"No, far from it," Katie said. "I'm from Sibley, Iowa, if you can believe it."

"I can believe it," Caleb said. "Someone has to be."

"My folks are farmers. Organic farmers. Actually, they're pretty chill. That's how I grew up...on a farm."

Caleb nodded. "That's why the bait bags didn't gross you out."

Katie gave a dismissive wave of the hand. "Bait bags? I've been butchering chickens since I was ten."

"Okay. A Midwest farmer's daughter," Caleb said.

"Right," Katie said. "And one who doesn't much appreciate jokes about the same."

"Got it," Caleb said. "So how'd you get out here?"

"After high school I was pretty eager to get out of Sibley, Iowa. Maybe desperate's the word. So I applied for schools in Washington and Oregon and Maine. I'd only been to the ocean a few times and it seemed very romantic to me and I wanted to be near it."

She took a bite and swallowed, then took a long draught of the Snapple Caleb handed her. "I got accepted to USM," she continued, "and it sounded cool, Portland seemed cool, so I came here. I thought I'd major in agriculture, maybe go back and work on the folks' farm, or start a farm of my own. But then I got here, got a chance to really experience the sea.... That was it. I never wanted to be away from the ocean again. Spent the past six years getting out on the water as much as I could."

"I can understand that," Caleb said. "But fisheries management? Not fishing or anything like that?"

"I guess my mind works in a more scientific way. That's what I like," Katie said. "But I sure as hell don't want to be stuck in some lab. I thought working at the juncture of science and fishing, you know? That might be the way to go. I mean, honestly, scientists and fishermen look at each other like they're friggin' enemies. That really has to stop. We've got to get on the same page. I'm hoping I can be part of that."

Caleb nodded. His first impulse was to make some comment about Katie's naiveté, the impossibility of what she was proposing. But he didn't. Because jaded as he was, he knew she was right.

Over the soft lapping of the water on the hull they could hear a vessel coming closer, the sound of the engine building in pitch and volume, and together they swiveled and looked off to the east.

Green boat, gray topsides, an odd, boxy-looking trunk cabin, the boat was up on a plane and coming fast, a long plume of black smoke streaming from its upright exhaust pipe and trailing off astern. Caleb recognized the boat, kind of a ratty affair, but could not place the owner.

"Know this guy?" Katie asked.

"Not sure," Caleb said.

The boat slowed as it swept in toward *Lisa Marie*'s stern. It came down off the bow wave it rode and settled into the water as the skipper jammed the throttle into reverse, stopping with a flourish ten feet from *Lisa Marie*'s transom, the wake making Caleb's boat roll side to side. Caleb could read the boat's name at the bow. *Bait & Bitch*.

"Hey, Caleb!" the driver of the boat called, stepping out from behind the wheel. Big guy, stained orange oilskins, a filthy cap pulled over a round head. Mike Morin, Caleb remembered. Fished out of Marsh Cove.

"Hey, Mike, what's up?" Caleb called.

"Came looking for her," Mike called, pointing a meaty finger at Katie. "We still on for tonight?"

"Sure," Katie said, not sounding so sure.

"Cool," Mike said, face brightening. "I'll pick you up around seven. Hope you don't smell like fish, still!" He smiled and his weasely little sternman, whose name Caleb could not recall, laughed out loud. Then Morin stepped back into the cabin, shoved the throttle forward, spun the wheel and the green boat accelerated fast into a wide arcing turn.

"Impressive wake," Caleb said as the *Lisa Marie* bucked in the turbulence cast off by Morin's boat. "You're boyfriend?"

"No," Katie said quickly. "He just asked me out. A lot of times, actually. At a certain point it's easier to say yes and get it over with. You know him?"

"A little," Caleb said. "Hard worker." *And a friggin' yahoo, from what I can see,* he thought, but he kept it to himself.

"So," Katie said in a tone that heralded a change of subject, "I told you my life story. What about yours? Your uncle said something about you being out in California for a while, and just coming back here last year?"

"Yeah, a few years after high school I moved to Los Angeles."

"Were you fishing out there?" Katie asked. "They fish for sardines, right? And tuna?"

"No. I was a bodyguard. If you can believe it."

"I can believe it," Katie said. "Someone has to be. You work for a security company?"

"No," Caleb said. He took a big bite of his sandwich, took a long time to chew and swallow. The conversation was starting to move toward a subject he did not care to revisit. But neither did he want to be rude.

"No," he said again. "I started out as a bodyguard for Trevor Middleton. Do you know who he is?"

"Trevor Middleton, the actor?"

"Yeah, that one."

"Do I know who he is? Duh! He's like the biggest star in Hollywood. You'd have to live on Mars to not know who he is."

"Or in Sibley, Iowa."

"Believe it or not we have television and all sorts of highfalutin stuff there," Katie assured him. "So how did that happen?"

"Long story. But basically I went out to LA to be an actor. Majored in drama at UCLA. I got a bit part in the first movie that Trevor starred in. *Surf Line* it was called. Friggin' awful. But Trevor was kind of a rising star at the time, and he was getting some hassling e-mails and stuff, so the producer asked if I'd just sort of act as his bodyguard. I think they figured since I was a big guy I could do it. And they knew I was from Maine, and they knew Maine was not really civilized so they figured I was used to beating people up. It just went from there."

"Huh," Katie said. "So what made you give all that up?"

"Just got sick of it," Caleb said, his tone polite but not inviting further inquiry. "I'd lobstered around here with Uncle Dick when I was in high school and a few years after, saving money for college. I always loved it. When it was time for a change I knew this was where I wanted to be."

Katie drained the last of her Snapple and handed the bottle back to Caleb. "And the lobstermen here, they were okay with you fishing this area because you're a local?"

"Yeah, pretty much. But more because of Uncle Dick. He's a real pillar in the local fishing community. If he says it's cool for me to fish here, that's all the others need to hear." He stood, stretched, rolled the empty wrappers into a wad and put them back in his cooler.

"Okay, lunch break's over," he said.

Katie stood and she also wadded up her wrappers. "Thanks again for the sandwich," she said.

"My pleasure," Caleb said. "Next trawl's over beyond that red and green buoy, there." He pointed off to the north. He was eager to get back to fishing and away from the subject of his former life in LA. He had drained nearly a pint of vodka the night before trying to forget about it, and had barely succeeded. He had no desire to bring it all up again while sober.

Chapter Five

Twenty-six years in Washington DC, in the trenches of K Street, and Howard Cox, former attorney-at-law, former chief lobbyist, was no rube. The clients his firm serviced were not always the kindest or most civic minded. Far from it. Many were as vicious as they came, both American and offshore.

Howard and his partners didn't seek that sort out, of course. It was just that the most vicious were often the ones who were willing to pay the most and had the need and the ability to do so. The Sierra Club or the Red Cross might be of greater benefit to society in general, but they could not dole out cash the way the extraction industries or the tobacco producers could.

Cox had played in those leagues and he knew the rules. Sometimes you flaunted your connections, and sometimes you kept them an absolute secret. And now was the time for secrecy.

No calls from home, no calls from his cell phone. You never knew who might be listening. He understood that the trend now was to buy some cheap disposable cell, use it once and destroy it. But he was sixty-seven and old school and he liked to do things the way he had always done them, including his clandestine communications.

He climbed into his car, a Lexus LX, which he thought sufficiently luxurious without being ostentatious, and drove the ten miles along the single winding road that led from Hopefleet to Brunswick. With a population of twenty thousand, Brunswick was near enough to a city for Cox to find what he needed. He wound his way through streets laid out two hundred years earlier and pulled into the parking lot of the Hannaford's supermarket.

He climbed out of the Lexus, moving from the cool of the air conditioning to the heat of the summer day, hot by Maine standards, at least. Mild by those of Virginia. He paused and looked around but saw nothing out of place. Mothers dragging reluctant children in and out of the store, employees with bright safety vests pushing great trains of shopping carts. Young men carrying twelve-packs of Budweiser and Shipyard beer. All was as he would expect it to be.

He crossed the parking lot, the heat radiating off the blacktop, to the sheltered area just outside the supermarket doors. There, looking like the anachronism that it was, was one of the few pay phones to be found within the city limits. Cox wondered if anyone besides himself ever used it. He wondered if he should request that it be buried with him when he died; two relics from another generation.

He picked up the receiver and was relieved to hear a dial tone. He fed quarters into the slot. He was not entirely certain what this phone call would yield; it was as much an exploration as anything. He was probing now, looking to see who knew what. He had to know if his plans had come to an end when Dick Forrester had taken that last, deep breath and sucked in a lungful of seawater, or if all he had been working for was still moving ahead.

He punched in a number. He waited. Two rings and a woman answered, her voice professional but friendly.

"Atlantic Gas and Oil, a division of ConWest Industries, how might I direct your call?"

Cox paused. He had rehearsed this, but now his confidence was wavering. But not for long; a heartbeat, no more.

"Yes, hello," he said. "My name is Charles Benton. I'd been working with Richard Forrester in your site management department. I hadn't heard from him in a few days, and now I hear he's had some terrible accident."

"One moment, please," the woman said as if she had to check something, as if she had to find out for herself what the hell he was talking about. She was back on the line inside ten seconds.

"Yes," she said, "I'm afraid Mr. Forrester is not available right now."

I'll say, Cox thought. He had an image of Forrester laid out on a morgue table. They would have to do an autopsy, he was certain.

"Yes, that's what I hear," Cox said. "But this is the thing; he and I were involved in some pretty important business, and despite this tragedy I can't let it drop. But I never knew who Dick's supervisor was. Could you find out and connect me to him?"

"Certainly, Mr. Benton, let me see what I can do," the woman said, crisp and professional. She had recalled his name, likely written it down. Which was why Cox had not given his real name. He knew how these things worked.

"Mr. Benton?" The woman was on the line again. "I'm going to connect you to Mr. William Davis who's head of our site management division. He should be able to assist you."

"Thank you," Cox said and listened as the phone went through a series of clicks and pauses, transferring the call up the corporate ladder. Cox took advantage of the silence to feed more quarters into the phone.

Head of our site management division, Cox mused. *What a crock of shit...* These corporations, he knew, were masters of creating such innocuous-sounding division titles. God alone knew what actually went on in the Site Management Division. They were probably the ones who kept track of where the bodies were buried.

Another woman answered the line, announcing Mr. Davis's office. Cox braced himself for another round of blowing smoke, but to his surprise she took his name and sent his call on through.

"Hello, Mr. Benton, this is Bill Davis," a male voice answered on the second ring. Professional, not nearly so friendly as the women had been, with an edge of impatience. "What can I do for you?"

"Yes, I've been working with Dick Forrester," Cox began and Davis cut him off.

"Dick, yes, tragic, tragic accident. We'll be putting a new field rep in his place and..." Davis set in with his well-rehearsed spiel, but Cox cut him off.

"Are you recording this call, or is there some idiot means of having it traced?" he asked.

There was a pause as Davis adjusted to this sudden shift. "No," he said.

"Good," Cox said. "My name's not Benton. It's Howard Cox. I'm calling from Hopefleet, Maine."

There was another pause, longer this time. This was the crucial moment, the moment of truth, as they say. This was when Cox would learn if the deal he had been working with Forrester went any higher up the corporate chain. Learn how real it was. The pause was encouraging.

"You're calling from your home phone?" Davis asked at last.

That question told Cox volumes. If Davis's first concern was that the call might be traced, then he knew the subject was hot, very hot. And that meant that Davis knew, and had no doubt authorized, what Forrester had been doing.

"I'm calling from a pay phone. This isn't my first rodeo, okay? I've been dealing with corporate putzes like you for twenty years," Cox said. "What I need to know is, does Forrester's death change anything?"

There was another pause. Then Davis said, "No, it doesn't change anything on our end. And I hope it doesn't change anything on yours."

"No. It changes nothing. Those assholes think they can scare me, but they can't. They want to play hardball? They don't know what hardball looks like."

"Good," Davis said. "What about the police? Have they talked to you?"

"They talked. Forrester had my card in his wallet. But he had a lot of cards in his wallet. He had Susan Collins's card in his wallet, and I'm guessing they don't suspect she's involved either. I don't see any problem there."

"Okay, good," Davis said. "We stay the course, then. And I'll find someone to take Forrester's place."

"You do that," Cox said. "Someone with a little more testicular fortitude. Our friends are stepping up their game; they're getting desperate. Forrester caught the business end of that desperation."

Another pause. "Forrester drowned in a kayaking accident," Davis said. Cox almost laughed out loud.

"Sure he did," Cox said. "Or maybe it was mermaids."

"You need protection?" Davis asked. "You need someone out there watching your back?"

"No," Cox said. The last thing he wanted was some babysitter from Atlantic Gas and Oil. He didn't need that crap and he didn't need the questions it would raise. "I'm all right," he continued. "They're not going to do anything to me. Forrester can be written off as an accident. No one knew he was in town anyway. But they can't afford to do anything to me. After Forrester, if I turn up dead even the cops are going to know something stinks. It'll point right to International Gas and Power, and that's the last thing they need."

"Okay," Davis said. "Keep in touch." He hung up, no doubt eager to end the conversation before it got any further into the muck.

Cox replaced the handset and stood there for a minute, looking out over the parking lot, the pickup trucks and the minivans and the cars all whirling around in their complicated parking lot quadrille. International Gas and Power had certainly raised the bar more than a few notches, taking out Forrester that way, putting him on the rope of that dumb sap's lobster trap. What was his name? *Caleb Hayes, that was it.* The cops had told him that, asked him if he knew the guy.

No, never heard of him, Cox had answered, truthfully. He wondered idly if this Hayes was tied up in any of this. He'd done a little asking around, found out Hayes was a local boy, had gone off to California, worked as a bodyguard or something like that. Nephew to Dick Hayes, a prominent lobsterman, vocal critic of the LNG terminal. If that was the case, this Caleb should be on Cox's side, because Cox was the only thing preventing construction from beginning in a month.

Just some dumb bastard, hit the dead body jackpot, Cox thought, his final evaluation of Caleb Hayes. He turned to go back to his car and the blessed AC when behind him the pay phone rang.

Cox froze and he felt a cool wave of dread pass over him. *What the hell?* he thought. But he knew it could be anything. A wrong number, someone calling for someone else. He looked around, but there was no one waiting for the phone. The ringing continued.

Davis calling back? Cox thought. That could be, but he would have to be one stupid bastard to get that on the company's phone records. The phone rang again. Cox snatched up the receiver, held it to his ear.

"Hello, Mr. Cox," the voice said. Not Davis. It was the man who had called before, during his interview with Henderson. Despite all his bravado Cox felt his stomach twist. He resisted the urge to look around. Whoever this was, he was far too professional to let himself be seen if he did not want to be. The call to the pay phone proved that.

"Who the hell is this?" Cox demanded.

"I told you before," the voice said, "I'm the guy who's telling you about Richard Forrester. And what we do now that he's dead."

"I told you before," Cox said, "I don't know who Richard Forrester is. Or at least I didn't until the cops told me."

There was a pause, unnerving as it was intended to be. "That's not what Forrester told me," the voice said. "But then, he was under duress at the time. Extreme duress."

Cox swallowed hard, pressed his lips together. "I don't know what the hell you want," he started in, "but I suggest—"

"You know what I want," the voice said. "I want one word from you. One syllable. 'Aye.' That's all you need to say when it's time to vote on the contract with IGP."

"Or what?" Cox demanded. "You come after me? Rough me up? I know you can't kill me because if I'm dead I can't vote your way. And don't think my people can't connect you to International Gas and Power. That's not going to do much for your cause."

"Oh no," the voice said. "I won't come after you. No one from IGP will come after you. Someone else will. And when he does, you'll know it, and it won't be pleasant."

There was a pause and Cox could hear nothing but his own breathing. Then the man on the phone was speaking again. "Or you can save yourself all this trouble and do what would be best for everyone. Then you don't get hurt and nothing you discussed with AGO sees the light of day."

"I don't know what you're talking about," Cox said, his voice growing louder as genuine anger blotted out his fear. "And you know what? You don't either. You might think you know something, you son of a bitch, but you have no proof. None. You start spreading unsubstantiated rumors and you know who takes the fall? Not me. You. You and International Gas and Power or whatever bastards you work for. So back off, or I take you down, not the other way around."

He slammed the receiver down hard and stood there for a moment, letting his breath return to normal, letting his swirling thoughts settle. *Son of a bitch*, he thought, the words directed at no one in particular. The whole world.

It had been set up so perfectly and now it was falling apart.

No, not 'had been', Cox thought. *Is. Is set up so perfectly.* This was a hiccup, a temporary problem. He had done plenty of deals like this, and there was always some screw-up, some problem that arose. He had done deals where people had died as a result; this was not something new.

He had told Davis that the people who killed Forrester would not dare touch him, and that was true. Forrester could be written off as an accident. It seemed the police were doing just that. They might wonder why he was there in Hopefleet, but for lack of any evidence suggesting otherwise, they would have to call it an accidental drowning. But if something happened to him? That would raise some questions.

There isn't one damn thing they can do to me, Cox thought, and he mostly believed it. He crossed the parking lot, walking quickly back to his car, resisting the urge to look around for the caller. He still had two errands to do. He had to stop at that place on Pleasant Street that did home security systems. After that he would run down to L. L. Bean and buy a handgun.

I've been meaning to do this for some time, he told himself. *Might as well do it now.* That decision, of course, had nothing to do with the events of the past few days.

Chapter Six

For a week, a ridge of high pressure sat over the Gulf of Maine and brought with it the kind of weather for which Maine's tourist industry would sacrifice their firstborn children. The skies were blue and dotted with humped cumulous clouds, gray on the undersides, heaping white above like scoops of the most luxurious whipped cream. The weather was in the mid-seventies, the winds light from the southwest.

By the fifth time Caleb assured Katie that she could not count on that sort of weather lasting for long, she told him to shut up, that she was not fresh off the boat from Iowa, that she understood how weather works. But they were able to enjoy it while it lasted, the finest sort of days to be out on the water, pulling trawls and baiting traps.

A couple of days of that and Katie had the routine down well enough that Caleb had no need to instruct her in the basics, and instead began to teach her some of the more advanced lessons: how to set the traps with the tide and haul against it, what the bottom of the bay looked like in various places, where the deep holes where the lobsters like to live were located, and where they didn't.

"Over there." Caleb pointed to a placid stretch of sea around the west side of Whaleboat. "There's some ugly ledge there. Good place to lose traps."

Katie shook her head. "Dude, it's like you can see right through the water, like you can just see the bottom like dry land."

"Thanks," Caleb said. "But I don't really know the bottom that well. These older guys, like my Uncle Dick, to them it really is like there's no water all. They know every inch of the bottom of Casco Bay. Those guys are amazing."

He turned the helm over to her and told her to find their next

43

trawl up between Whaleboat and Little Whaleboat and she took the challenge with pleasure, spinning the little brass and wood wheel and pushing the throttle forward to get the *Lisa Marie* up on a plane.

Caleb sat on the rail, enjoying the warm breeze in his face, the occasional spray coming up from under bow and showering him with cool salt water. Enjoying Katie's company. As much as he had been embracing the solitude of his time on the water, the space to think, to work through things, he had to admit he liked having her on board.

Maybe I was giving myself too much time to think, he mused. *Maybe that's not so healthy. Maybe Uncle Dick understood that.*

He looked over at Katie, one hand on the wheel, eyes scanning the water through the windshield, looking for the red and white striped buoy that would mark Caleb's trawl. Her blond hair, thrust through the back of her Huskies cap, was whipping in the wind that snuck around the side of the open cabin. She was noticeably more tan than she had been even a few days before, despite the copious sunblock she smeared on herself and insisted that Caleb smear on himself as well. She looked good in her orange Grundens and faded tee shirt and rubber boots, and looking good in that garb was no mean feat.

Katie spun the wheel and the *Lisa Marie* heeled with the turn and Caleb braced himself so he would not go tumbling over the side. She eased back the throttle and snatched up the gaff and, coming up alongside the buoy, snagged it with the hook.

"Excellent," Caleb said. "Tomorrow I'm staying home and watching my soaps. You do all the lobstering."

Katie wrapped the buoy line around the hauler and hit the brass control lever. A moment later the first trap broke the surface and she swung it onto the wash rail. Half a dozen decent-sized lobsters were flailing and snapping inside. The fishing had been good; they'd been averaging more than two pounds per trap, a couple hundred pounds of lobster coming up every day.

They emptied the trap and baited it, and Katie slid it down the wash rail to the stern as Caleb hauled the next one aboard. She was singing to herself as she moved. The tune was familiar, like something from far away, the words vaguely remembered.

And then Caleb remembered. He turned to her. "What the hell?" he asked, more surprised that anything.

"What?" Katie asked, her face all faux innocence, her smile more like a suppressed grin.

"Where the hell did you hear that?" Caleb asked.

"You know that song? It's from that hit movie *Surf Line*. Trevor Middleton starred in it. Great supporting cast."

"Where the hell did you find that?" Caleb asked.

"They have this new thing called the internet," Katie said, picking up a loaded bait iron and handing it to Caleb. "You can find all sorts of things."

Caleb pushed the trap down the rail, shook his head as he hoisted the next one aboard. "Damn," he said. He felt a mix of emotions: amusement, sheepishness. He felt honored that Katie had gone to the trouble of searching out his one big screen effort, and embarrassed that she had watched it.

"It was good!" Katie said, and she sounded genuine in her praise. "Really. And you were great. Really funny. Why didn't you keep up with the acting?"

Caleb sighed. "It's a long, sordid, messy tale."

"Oh, look, I'm sorry. It's really none of my business," Katie said, realizing, apparently, that her prying might not be welcome. And in truth, had it been anyone else, it would not have been. But Caleb liked her and was starting to trust her and was starting to think that maybe talking would help, rather than bottling it up and letting it fester and then drinking to forget, which had been his approach up to that point.

As Katie would say, *Well, duh...*

"No, it's okay," Caleb said. "It's not really that long or sordid. I'll admit I was the finest thespian in all of Mt. Ararat High School in Topsham, Maine. Which, as it turns out, is not so impressive when you get out to Los Angeles. Anyway, I went to UCLA and got a degree in theater and did a few little things, some ads, a couple of bit TV roles. *Surf Line* was my first real part, per se."

Caleb secured the bait bag and its contents of redfish and pogies in the kitchen section for the trap, shut the door on the top of the trap, and slid it down the rail.

"Yeah, I was pretty excited getting that part," he continued. "Trevor had done a few things, too, but there was this sense that he was really coming up, that he would break out soon, be a big star. Some nut-job started sending him threats, little stupid stuff really. Not so serious that the cheap-ass producer wanted to spring for real security. So I was there and I was a big guy and they asked me to sort of fill in. So I walked around behind Trevor when we were off set and tried to look scary and it seemed to work."

"Huh," Katie said. She grabbed up the trap that Caleb had baited and set it on the boat's transom. "I suppose it helps, being a big dude like you."

"Yes and no," Caleb said, hoisting the next trap aboard. "Being big can be intimidating to some guys. But at the same time there are a lot of guys who are eager to kick some big guy's ass, just to show they can. It's kind of like a red cape to a bull. In that case, if you don't know how to really fight, then you can get stomped."

"So what happened with you?"

"I got stomped a few times. And then I got some formal training and learned some things about real defense."

"But you kept working as…Trevor's bodyguard? You didn't go back to acting? You really were good, you know."

"Thanks, I appreciate that," Caleb said, and he did. He was wandering into territory he had not talked about in some time, and he was tentative. It was like pulling off a Band-Aid. He knew he should do it quick, but instead he was pulling it free bit by bit.

"The thing is, I wanted to be an actor. But wanting it isn't enough. To really make it you need that fire-in-the-belly, throw your grandmother under the bus level of desire. Trevor had that. I didn't. As he started getting more famous he wanted me to keep on as his bodyguard because he liked me and trusted me. We were friends, really. The money was good. There was a certain degree of excitement. So I just started doing that. You want to set this trawl?"

"Sure," Katie said. She stepped into the shelter of the cabin, took the wheel and pushed the transmission forward. She spun the wheel and the *Lisa Marie* turned in a wide circle, leaving a curving white wake astern. She lined the boat up until it was running to the southwest, the orientation that lobstermen in Casco Bay set their trawls.

She glanced around to see she was not dumping this trawl on top of another lobsterman's, then tossed the buoy overboard and shoved the first trap in after it. The ground line to which the eight traps were attached began to whip out over the side, twisting in the bottom of the boat like a living thing, and then one trap after another was jerked from the transom and disappeared into the green-blue water.

Caleb did not say a thing. He didn't have to.

"Next trawl to the west of here?" she asked.

"Ayuh," Caleb said so he would sound like a Mainer. Or a tourist's idea of a Mainer.

"So, you worked as Trevor Middleton's bodyguard," Katie said, speaking at a near shout to be heard over the engine and the wind rushing by.

She had the boat opened up nearly all the way, the bow climbing up on a plane. She was an aggressive driver, Caleb could see that. He considered telling her to back off, not out of fear for the speed she was making but concern over the amount of diesel she was eating up. But Katie seemed to be enjoying herself and Caleb didn't have the heart to make her slow down.

"Yeah, at first that was what I was doing. Then I met this girl, who's now my ex-wife. She was the ambitious one. I had all these contacts with Hollywood A-listers, you see, because of Trevor. Susanna...that's my ex...Susanna convinced me to partner with her in a security firm. Cater to all these celebs. Trevor was happy to help build a client list. So pretty soon we had this company. C&S Security, we called it."

"You worked with some big stars?"

"Very big stars. Names you probably even heard of in Sibley, Iowa."

"Like who?"

"Ahh...confidentiality, you know."

"Okay, sorry," Katie said and flashed him her smile. "So what happened? Why'd you give that up?"

That was a question that was inevitable, of course, the natural progression of the conversation. Any number of images roiled up in Caleb's mind: that last night with Trevor, the girl that he, Caleb, had invited to party for Trevor's benefit, the beach house packed with celebs and hangers-on. All stuff Caleb did not care to remember. Things that even the lovely Katie Brennan would not motivate him to speak about.

"Oh, you know," Caleb said, sounding as nonchalant as he was able. "It sucked, really. Down deep. So unbearably fake, all of it. It was exciting for a while, but then it all sort of fell apart. Susanna and I broke up, I sold my interest in the company to her and bailed out.

Came back here. And I'm a hell of a lot happier, I can tell you."

Katie took her attention from the water ahead and looked him in the eye and her expression suggested that she did not believe him, not entirely. About the reasons he packed it in, about his being happy, he was not sure what, but she was not buying everything he was selling.

"So that's it, the life and times of Caleb Hayes," he said by way of concluding the conversation.

"Wow," Katie said, looking ahead again, eyes scanning for the buoy at the end of the next trawl. "You got my life story all beat to hell."

They were a few more hours hauling traps, and the tank was near capacity when they finally turned the bow toward Kettle Cove. They were tired, the sort of tired that comes from hard work on the water, and filmed with sweat and dried salt water and sunblock. They loved it all.

Katie hosed the boat down and scrubbed it with the deck brush, a sternman's lot, while Caleb took the boat into the cove and up to the dock. Jimmy seemed to have forgiven him for absconding with Katie and he greeted them in a friendly way, handing the plastic crates over the *Lisa Marie*'s wash rail.

They had finished off-loading, and Jimmy was just scribbling the total for the catch on his receipt pad when the stranger came down the ramp and onto the floating docks. He was wearing deck shoes and khaki shorts with cargo pockets, a clean, new polo shirt with some sort of logo on the breast and a round, wide-brimmed hat, like yachtsmen wore. He had a short beard, neatly trimmed, and round glasses. In either hand he carried a hard plastic case, the kind the secret service guys carried when they accompanied the president somewhere.

"Hey, check out this guy," Katie said in a low voice. "Isn't that Hooper from *Jaws*?"

"I hope not," Caleb said. "We have enough crap to contend with around here without man-eating sharks."

The man approached with some hesitation, clearly unsure of where he was going, or not finding what he had expected to find, so Caleb was not at all surprised when he stopped by *Lisa Marie*'s bow and said, "Excuse me, are you Tom Merryman?"

"I'm not, I'm afraid," Caleb said.

"Oh," the man said, clearly not pleased. "I was supposed to meet him here...." The man looked back toward the wharf, the big white building with the shredding American flag flying from the pole, the words Hopefleet Lobster Co-op painted in a somewhat professional manner on the side. "Yeah," he said, turning back. "Hopefleet Lobster Co-op. His boat's the *Island Lady*."

"Yeah, that's right," Caleb said. The *Island Lady* was a former lobsterboat that Tom Merryman used to run people around to the islands and down to Portland. Tom had discovered some time earlier that there was nearly as much money and considerably less work in running a water-borne taxi service than in fishing for lobsters.

"*Island Lady* is hauled out at the boatyard down the road, I'm afraid," Caleb went on. "Nearly sunk at the mooring. Stuffing box, I think."

"Damn," the man said. "I made these arrangements two weeks ago. I don't know why he didn't call me and tell me."

"I don't know," Caleb offered, though he had never thought that customer service was Tom Merryman's strong suit. "What do you need?"

"He was going to run me up by the old naval fuel depot. I need to take some water and bottom samples a ways off shore."

The day was fine and the catch was good and Caleb was feeling in a generous mood, so he said, "I can give you a lift, if you like. Nice day for a boat ride."

The man's face brightened. "Really? I would sure appreciate it. I'm happy to pay you what I was going to pay Merryman."

"Not a problem. Happy to help in the name of science. Katie, you want to come, or no?"

"Sure," Katie said. "I'm game. Like you said, nice day for a boat ride."

Caleb reached up for the man's cases, which he handed over. Then he stepped aboard, dropping to the deck with an easy motion. Caleb extended a hand.

"Caleb Hayes," he said. "This is my sternman, Katie Brennan."

"Please to meet you. And thanks again. I'm Billy Caine."

"Billy," Caleb said. He and Katie took a moment to strip off their rubber Grundens, which was always a great relief on a hot, sunny day. In the absence of the rubberized material the cool breeze enveloped them and felt wonderful. Then Katie cast off the bow and stern lines and Caleb put the boat in gear and swung the bow around and they headed back toward Casco Bay.

"So why are you taking water samples?" Caleb asked over the roar of the engine. Billy was standing to his left, under the cabin roof, studying the water ahead. Katie was sitting on the wash rail to his right and a little aft, clearly enjoying the wind generated by their forward momentum, the spray kicked up by the bow.

"It's all part of this LNG thing," Billy said. "Before they start stirring up the bottom with any new construction they have to be sure they're not releasing any nasty crap hiding in the mud."

"You work for the LNG company?" Caleb asked.

"No, I work for a private environmental firm." He pointed to the logo on his polo shirt. Caleb looked closer. It showed what he guessed was a stylized mountain and a lake, and in a circle around those images the words "New England Environmental Testing and Analytics."

"The state hired us to do the testing," Billy explained.

"Huh," Caleb said. He slowed the boat as he made his way through a tricky channel between two smaller islands, then swung around northeast. Ahead, Middle Bay opened up, a little more than a mile wide at its widest and seven miles long, one of the many long, narrow indents in the Coast of Maine.

"Here," Billy said, holding out a business card. Caleb took it and glanced down. The left-hand corner showed the same logo that was on Billy's shirt, and across the front of the card was "William Caine" and below that "Environmental Science: Field Division" and phone numbers and e-mail below that.

Caleb pushed the throttle forward and the *Lisa Marie* surged ahead. Whaleboat Island was passing down the port side and Hopefleet Neck was to starboard, with its thick growth of spruce and the shoreline dotted with those grander, more expensive homes that could not be seen from the roads.

About a mile north along the neck, the tree line yielded to acres of open ground, grassy meadowland that rolled uphill from the water's edge, and standing out from the shore, a massive concrete pier built to accommodate large tankers bearing holds full of aviation fuel.

"When I told you I was doing water samples at the fuel depot I thought you'd throw me off the dock," Billy Caine said. "Anyone doing anything that has to do with LNG doesn't seem to get a very warm reception around here. At least not among the lobstermen."

"Well, I let *her* on board," Caleb said, nodding toward Katie, "and she's going to work for the fisheries department, so I guess I'm not too discriminating."

"You're lucky to get anyone to risk their life out on the water with you," Katie pointed out.

"Anyway," Caleb said, "I don't really know what's going on with the whole LNG brouhaha and I don't much care."

"Really?" Billy said. "You're the first one I've met in Hopefleet who feels that way."

"I guess I don't pay a lot of attention to that stuff. But it seems like a lot of fuss about nothing," Caleb said and that made Billy laugh out loud.

"Nothing? Are you serious?" he asked. "You must spend a lot of time at sea."

"What's the big deal?" Caleb said. "You build an LNG terminal. Or you don't."

"Look, Caleb," Billy said, and he was still smiling. "Do you know what IGP offered the town of Hopefleet?"

"What's IGP?"

"IGP. International Gas and Power. The company that's proposing to build this thing. They offered eight million dollars a year to lease this land. Now, if a company like that will shell out eight mil a year just for a lease, how much do you think it's worth to them? 'Cause they ain't looking to just break even, I can tell you."

"I imagine not," Caleb said. "So what's the holdup?"

"Right now it's one guy. Howard Cox."

"He's a selectman, right?" Caleb said. That much Caleb knew, and he knew it only because he had seen the man's business card in the wallet of the dead Richard Forrester.

"Yeah, that's right," Billy said. "He's the one selectmen who's against the project, but it only takes one to put a stop to the whole thing." He looked forward, through the windshield. "If you could get in just to the south of the pier, that would be great," he added. "Tide's high, you should be able to get in pretty close."

Caleb eased off the throttle and brought the *Lisa Marie* down to a crawl and continued toward the pier, one eye on the depth sounder. "So you must be right in the middle of all this crap," he said to Billy.

"Hell no," Billy said. "I'm just here to do my samples and then get the hell out of Dodge. I don't want to be around when the shit really hits the fan." He turned to Caleb and smiled. "You, however, as a local guy and a lobsterman, are going to have a hard time keeping clear when the bad stuff really starts to fly."

Chapter Seven

The corporate headquarters of International Gas and Power occupied a twenty-story building on Forty-Ninth Street in Manhattan. The offices on the higher floors enjoyed a view of Central Park below, the clusters of trees, the ponds and paths, a glimpse of the Met in the distance.

The office of Daniel Finch, Executive Vice President of Resource Development, was one of those. Floor-to-ceiling plate glass windows made up the eastern wall, stretching forty feet side to side and affording him a view that was breathtaking and intriguing. But he had been in that office for two years now, was used to it, and it held no thrill for him. He was ready for a new office, on a higher floor.

Worse, the luxury surrounding him—the view, the leather furniture, the massive ship-like desk made out of polished mahogany with ebony accents, the original art from some of the hottest new working artists in Manhattan—could not stem the enormous and growing frustration that Finch was feeling.

In his hand, hermetically sealed in its clear plastic container, was the cheapest of prepaid cell phones, one of six he had bought that morning. He had bought them at a Wal-Mart on the outskirts of White Plains where he had his home. He had never been in a Wal-Mart before, had not looked forward to the experience, and had not been disappointed.

If anthropologists ever needed proof that homo sapiens *interbred with Neanderthals*, he'd thought, looking around the massive, florescent-lit store, *they need only come check this place out.*

He had gone there with the intention of buying only one prepaid phone, thinking that buying more than one might raise the suspicions of the sales staff. He would need more than that, of course, but he intended to buy them one at a time. After wandering around the aisles for some minutes, however, he understood that he could not stand to ever set foot in a Wal-Mart again, so he'd purchased all six that were hanging from the metal rod in the electronics section. In the end, no one seemed to care or even notice.

Now, standing in his office, he clawed at the edge of the plastic that encased one of the phones and realized he could not even open it. No matter where he pulled or pried, the packaging would not yield. This was all getting so complicated, the danger to him personally was mounting, and he could not even open the damned phone.

"Son...of...a...bitch," he muttered. He thought about calling his secretary and having her do it, but he didn't, for the same reason he had gone himself to Wal-Mart, the same reason he had bought the disposable phones in the first place. Anonymity. And so here he was, surrounded by some of the most sophisticated electronic communications and computing hardware and software available, and not only was he forced to use the crudest of devices, he couldn't even get it out of the packaging.

He jerked open the top drawer of his desk, snatched up a pair of scissors, and attacked the plastic like a shark in a feeding frenzy. Five minutes later the phone was in hand and the packaging lying in shards on the off-white Berber carpet.

Finch went through the process of activating the phone as outlined on the instructions, which happily had been spared from his frenzied hacking at the package. He looked at the note on his desk, a single telephone number. Who was at the other end of that number, he did not know.

He glanced up at the computer screen on his desk. It displayed, as it usually did, a website that monitored stock in real time. There were only two lines on the graph. One was IGP. The other was Atlantic Gas and Oil.

IGP's trend line was not bad, a steady uphill slant, slow growth over the past six months. But AGO's trend line was something else, a steady rise like IGP's and then a sharp upward spike, representing the moment they had announced their new deal for Canadian tar sands. Finch felt his stomach turn at the sight of it. He was not happy, the board was not happy, the stockholders were not happy. Bad things would happen soon if those trend lines did not reverse, if IGP was not able to pick up the sweet toehold of an LNG terminal in this shitty little town in Maine. The reverberations of failure, Finch knew, would certainly be felt in his suite.

He punched the buttons on the phone and listened to it ring. Four times, and then it was answered. There was a pause. Then the voice. "Yeah?"

"It's Finch."

"What are you calling on?"

"Pre-paid phone."

"Okay," the voice said.

Finch pressed his lips together and looked out the plate glass window. He let his anger subside. Fighting with the troglodytes at Wal-Mart, fighting with the idiot phones, he had nearly forgotten why he had to call this man, and how furious he was. But now, hearing the voice, he remembered.

"They found the body," Finch said. "They found it tangled up in some fucking lobsterman's trap. It was in the newspapers, for God's sake."

"I know," the voice said.

"How could you be so damned sloppy?" Finch said, speaking low. He was seething now. "How could you screw up that badly?"

"I didn't screw up," the voice said. Calm, unhurried. Patient. "I made sure the body was tangled up in that rope."

At that Finch paused, taken aback. He had been boiling since the early morning hours when he had first seen the article in the online version of the *Portland Press Herald*. "Lobsterman Gets Unwelcome Surprise." They had the man's name. Richard Forrester. They had his employer, Atlantic Gas and Oil.

"You put the body on the rope?" Finch said, this surprising revelation not doing much to cool his fury. "Why would you do that?"

"A guy just disappears, it doesn't send much of a message, does it?" the voice said, still patient, a touch pedantic. "A guy who's found dead, under dubious circumstances, that's a different matter. We want people to know the potential consequences here."

Finch was quiet again, looking for the flaws in this thinking. "A dead body is evidence of a crime. It will get the cops involved."

"It depends on how the body gets dead. Did the paper say anything about the police suspecting foul play?"

"No," Finch admitted.

"No," the voice said. "It was a kayaking accident. The cops might have their suspicions, but there's nothing that points definitively to...what actually happened to our friend."

"So you just tied him to some lobsterman's trap? You had to be so ostentatious with this?" Finch demanded.

"Not some lobsterman's trap. A specific lobsterman's trap. A guy I can use, if I have to. Just more insurance."

"I don't see..." Finch began, but this time the voice cut him off, and there was a note of irritation there.

"Look, this isn't the fucking amateur hour, okay? I'm not out here making this stuff up as I go along. We have one specific result we are looking for, and I am here to see that we get that result, and I am doing it in the most efficacious manner."

Finch pressed his lips together. The voice was only that to him. He did not know the man, did not know his background, his credentials, his experience. For lack of anything else to call him, at least in his own mind, Finch thought of him as the Enforcer. It was silly, he knew. Histrionic. But that was the name that came to mind and it fit the role the man played.

What the Enforcer's actual job description might be, Finch had no idea. He knew only that he was in some way employed by IGP. He knew that he was the one who was going to make things right, by whatever means were necessary. He was going to make sure the Town of Hopefleet saw the light and welcomed IGP and their new liquid natural gas terminal. He was going to make sure all the selectmen voted the right way.

There was a reason that Finch knew nothing more. Deniability. Levels of remove from the boardroom and the executive suites and whatever was going down in that crappy little fishing town in Maine. Daniel Finch was not a man who liked to cede control over any aspect of his life, but he could see that this was one place where he would have no choice.

And he realized he was glad of it.

"All right," Finch said. "I'm not going to tell you how to do your job. You know what has to happen, and I'll assume you know how to make it happen. Keep me posted." He disconnected the phone before the voice had a chance to make a reply, one last tiny gesture of dominance.

That done, Finch walked over toward the plate glass windows

where the wool carpet yielded to marble tile. He put the phone down on the hard surface and brought a heel of his Tanino Crisci shoe down on the device, grinding it into its component parts. He was a bit more thorough than was absolutely necessary, but he wanted the phone gone, and he wanted to vent some of his anger and fear on the hated thing.

He worried that this was getting out of hand. He had been in the world of big-money energy production for many years, and he had been involved in more than his share of unethical, even illegal dealings. Price manipulation, rationing production to jack up profits, industrial espionage and sabotage, he had been complicit in all of it. But this was something else.

Natural gas was hot. The profit potential was huge. Atlantic Gas and Oil had their tar sands and if they got an LNG terminal in Maine, and IGP did not, they would leave IGP in the dust. This Hopefleet thing had to happen. No matter what it took.

Daniel Finch swore and drove his heel harder into the cheap plastic phone.

Chapter Eight

They spent about an hour just off the old fuel depot, Billy Caine dropping weighted sample collectors on lines off the side of the *Lisa Marie*, Caleb and Katie watching with interest, chatting about this and that, enjoying the fine afternoon.

"Steamers and cold beer," Katie said.

"Huh?" Caleb said.

"Steamers and cold beer. If we had those right now, this would be about as perfect as it could get."

Caleb nodded. He had to agree. The sun was bright, but the heat was moderated by the sea breeze filling in from the southwest. The seas were calm, rocking the *Lisa Marie* like a cradle. Puffy white clouds marching off toward the horizon, bright points of color on the blue water where the lobstermen's buoys marked their trawls. Perfect. Lacking only steamed clams and beer.

"Sorry about this, but would you mind bringing us in a bit closer and a little to the south?" Billy asked as he pulled a dripping sample up over the rail.

"Not a problem," Caleb said. "Katie, bring us in a bit closer and a little to the south."

Katie rose from her reclined position on the stern. "A woman's work is never done," she grumbled as she kicked the boat's engine to life, pushed the gearshift forward and eased the *Lisa Marie* ahead.

"Good," Billy called over the rumble of the engine. Katie gave her a shot of reverse to bring the boat to a stop, then turned the ignition key to off. Quiet settled over them once again.

For another twenty minutes or so Billy pulled samples from the bottom in his fussy, meticulous way. He made careful note of the GPS coordinates, wrote on the jars with a Sharpie, then settled the jars in cut-outs in the foam inside his hard-shell brief cases.

Katie pulled her cell phone from her canvas bag and clicked off a few pictures. "If I show my advisor these pictures I might be able to convince him I was doing scientific work over the summer, and not just slopping around with dead fish," she explained.

Finally Billy closed the lid on the second case and snapped the latches closed. "Okay," he said. "I think I'm done."

Caleb rose with a slight groan. "All right, let's head back." He stepped under the cabin roof, fired up the engine once again, swung the *Lisa Marie* away from the shore. "So, what do you think of this? You in favor of the terminal being built?" he asked Billy. He spoke loud over the dull roar of the engine, though Billy was standing nearly at his side.

Billy Caine shrugged. "I get paid either way. But look, there are communities all up and down the coast that'd love to get this terminal in their town. If Hopefleet doesn't go for it, some other community will. If I lived here I guess I'd be for it. Snag the money before some other town does."

Caleb nodded. He could appreciate that argument, though he still had not put enough thought into it to have an opinion one way or another.

"So, you heading back to where you came from after this?" Caleb asked.

"No, I have some more work here," Billy said. "Soil samples from the fuel farm, a few other things. I'll be honest, this is more like a vacation than work for me. I'm going to drag this out as long as I can!"

They ran southwest with Hopefleet Neck off the port side and then swung around the point and into Kettle Cove. Most of the boats that fished out of the cove were back at their mooring, the day's work done. Caleb brought the *Lisa Marie* up against the dock. Jimmy was gone and only a few people could be seen on the wharf from which the floating docks extended.

"Here you are, safe and sound," Caleb said and Billy lifted his cases of samples.

"You're sure I can't pay you?" Billy said. "It's the company's money, and it was going to go to Tom Merryman."

"Naw, I'm good. Let's call it my contribution to science," Caleb said.

Billy smiled. "Okay, thanks. Katie, good to meet you. Maybe

we'll see you around."

"Sounds good," Caleb said. Billy stepped onto the dock and Caleb eased the boat off and motored slowly back to the mooring where the battered green skiff was tied. Kate went forward with the gaff, grabbed the mooring pendant as Caleb eased the bow up to it, and then she slipped the loop of rope over the Sampson post and the *Lisa Marie* was home.

The two of them gathered up lunch boxes and various other bits of gear and climbed down into the skiff, quiet and companionable. Caleb started the outboard and Katie let go the painter and they motored back toward the dock where the dinghies were tied like cows ready for milking.

Caleb switched off the outboard and let the skiff glide up to the dock, and in the quiet he heard Katie say, "Ah, shit."

"What's up?" Caleb asked. He could not recall her having used a four-letter word before.

"Oh, nothing," Katie sighed, her tone suggesting it was certainly not nothing. She stood, hopped nimbly onto the dock, painter in hand, and Caleb followed.

"No, seriously, what is it?" Caleb asked. Katie's mood had clearly made a massive, hundred and eighty-degree shift.

"That," Katie said, nodding toward the shore. Partway up the steep road that led to the parking lot Caleb could see the looming bulk of Mike Morin, apparently watching them. He was more than one hundred yards away from where they stood, but the shape of the man was large and distinct.

"What, your boyfriend?" Caleb asked, but Katie gave him a look that made it clear the joke was not appreciated.

"Sorry," Caleb said. "Things didn't go well, I take it?"

"Things sucked, majorly," Katie said. "So, he picked me up at my apartment. In his truck, which is fine, but a guy who was at all considerate would have cleaned it at least, you know? Would have tossed out the empty beer cans and removed the *Sports Illustrated* swimsuit calendar.

"Then he takes me to this dive bar he and his yahoo buddies hang out at and we're there for hours while he drinks beer and plays pool and acts like a total douche. Then, I swear, he thinks he's going to get lucky after that, and he gets pissed when I just want him to take me home. I mean, I didn't exactly expect cordon bleu and the opera, but that was a whole different level of douchiness."

"Huh. Sorry to hear that," Caleb said and he meant it. "So what do you think he wants?"

"Don't know. But I can guess. He's been calling me and texting me nonstop since then, but I've been ignoring him."

"You want me to go talk to him? I can be persuasive," Caleb offered.

"No, I'll talk to him. I'm sure you being here with me just pisses him off further."

Caleb handed Katie her lunch box and her canvas bag with her sweatshirt and sunblock and whatever other girly stuff she insisted on bringing, and they headed toward shore, the floating dock moving gently under foot, the aluminum ramp amplifying their footsteps. They reached the wide wharf with its worn, sun-bleached timbers and headed across to where it met the blacktop and the steep drive leading to the parking lot above. Mike stood waiting, hands on hips, as they approached.

"All right, here goes," Katie said, the words coming out more like a sigh.

"You're sure you don't want me to come?" Caleb said. "I have a lot of experience standing behind people and looking scary."

"No, I'll go alone. I have a lot of experience dealing with jerky guys. Not sure why that is, but that's how it seems to have worked out." She headed off toward where Morin stood waiting, fifty feet away, as if he thought it was her duty to come to him. Caleb watched her go, watched Mike's body language as she approached him. He straightened, chest thrust out a bit, head cocked slightly back. Caleb shook his head.

"This is not going to go well," he said to himself. And he understood these things, understood them very well.

Since coming back to Hopefleet, Caleb Hayes was often asked by the folks who knew him about his former business, bodyguard in the glamorous world of Hollywood. It was a reasonable thing for people to ask about. It was intriguing, exotic. And Caleb tended to downplay it all. *It was no big deal*, he would say. *I'd just stand there and try to look intimidating, and if some fan got too grabby I'd step in and make sure my principal was safe. Just a glorified goon, really.*

And that was true. To a degree. In the same way that the top of the iceberg sticking up from the water was truly an iceberg, but only a small part of the whole thing.

C&S Security was a multi-million-dollar company, *the* boutique, go-to security firm for all aspects of personal protection and more, much more, catering to the Hollywood elite. Caleb and Susanna had not built the company to those heights by offering their clients just a stable of hired meatheads with Glocks. Caleb did not discuss all the services that C&S offered. Even back in the day, the firm's literature did not mention all the services that they offered.

Caleb had told Katie the truth when he said he had had his ass kicked on a few occasions, until he figured out that he had to either learn his trade or quit it. But by then Trevor Middleton was making some serious bank and he was eager for Caleb to stay on as his bodyguard and so was willing to shell out the money Caleb needed for training. Personal combat, weapons training, defensive driving, Caleb learned it all and mastered it all because he liked it.

Once Susanna and her heated ambitions came into the picture, it all got stepped up a notch, and then another. Caleb's skill sets branched out, and C&S took on other employees with similar talents, and still others who could expand the firm's offerings. They learned to keep individuals safe in crowds and how to keep groups of people safe in crowds and how to analyze potential threats and how to neutralize them.

Caleb had personally been in more scraps and ugly scenes than he could recall, and he had never suffered more than a superficial bullet wound or slash from a knife, and he had never had a principal who had so much as been touched. Reading a situation and seeing how it would play out was instinct for him now. He was a predator, and his prey was anyone who might do harm to someone he intended to protect.

And that was why he stood motionless as he watched Katie Brennan approaching the surly, angry Mike Morin. That was why he appeared bored and disinterested when in fact he was keyed up tight and ready to move. That was why he felt pretty sure this whole situation was about to fall apart fast.

Katie stopped a few feet away from Morin, her hands on her hips. She was directly between Caleb and Mike, but Mike was a bit uphill from her and quite a bit bigger and Katie did not block Caleb's view of him in any meaningful way. He could see Morin's red and scowling face, his filthy cap tilted back on his head. He could see

Mike's hand come up as he pointed an accusatory finger at Katie.

They were speaking, Mike low and angry, Katie conciliatory, trying to diffuse the situation. Caleb could hear the sounds of their voices but not the words. He didn't have to hear the words. The tone told him all he needed to hear.

Their voices rose in volume. Caleb heard the change in Katie's voice as she gave up on conciliatory and shifted to angry. He heard her parting words. "Look, just leave me the fuck alone!"

She turned her back on Mike, took a step toward Caleb. Mike's meaty hand shot out, grabbed her arm, jerked her back and turned her around so she was facing him once again. Caleb heard something like, "You don't walk away from me!" but he was already moving by that point.

"Whoa, whoa, whoa!" he shouted to distract Morin, to give himself the few seconds he needed to close with him. Morin looked up, but he maintained his grip on Katie's arm as Katie twisted and tried to break free.

"Hold up there, Mike," Caleb said, his voice lower and calmer now. Almost casual. He slowed his step as he saw he would reach the two of them before things became any uglier.

"This is none of your business. Got nothing to do with you," Morin said. He let go of Katie's arm as Caleb came to a stop five feet away. Katie stepped clear, off to the side, and the two big men faced one another.

"Dude," Caleb said, still trying to keep his tone light, still hoping to end things peacefully, but feeling pretty certain that would not happen. "I gotta have my sternman. Let's just forget this, okay? Time to move on."

Mike Morin took a step in Caleb's direction. This was the downside of the approach Caleb was taking—idiots like Morin would confuse diplomacy with weakness and it only encouraged them.

"Why don't *you* forget it and mind your own friggin' business, Caleb? Shouldn't you be hanging out with your pussy California buddies?"

"Seriously, man, back off," Caleb said. "Katie's not interested. Just get out of here, leave her alone, and we'll forget this whole thing."

Morin's eyebrows were bunched together, his hands balled in fists. Caleb could see the muscles in his arms and shoulders tense. He might as well have been wearing a sandwich board that said *I'm going to throw a punch.*

Caleb's hands were up, palms facing Morin, a gesture that seemed to be calling for calm. And it was that, to some degree. Caleb still hoped for a nonviolent resolution, though such a thing was looking more and more unlikely.

But Caleb's hands, held as they were, served another purpose as well. They created an avenue for the punch Mike would throw, a clear path right between Caleb's upraised hands and right at his face. They would direct Mike's fist right where Caleb wanted it directed.

"Back off?" Morin said. "Here, back this!"

Back this? That makes no sense, Caleb thought as Mike's right fist came around in a wide arc. Caleb had guessed the punch would be slow, and it was, though not as slow as he had imagined, and with a lot of power behind it. Mike Morin was a big guy, and a powerful guy, and he no doubt used that to his advantage in most situations.

But not this one. As his fist passed through Caleb's hands, Caleb smacked Mike's forearm with the palm of his left hand, sending the punch wide. In the same instant Caleb stepped in and drove his right fist in low, a sharp punch to Mike's ribs, which doubled him over.

In the instant that Mike Morin had moved, Caleb had made an unconscious decision as to how much hurt to inflict. His options ran from mild pain to serious agony to permanent damage to near instant death, any of which he could have brought about and there was nothing Mike Morin could do to stop him.

Caleb opted for something easy, medium-rare. Mike Morin folded over Caleb's fist and Caleb brought his knee up into Mike's gut, knocking the wind from him with an audible expulsion of air, and Caleb pushed down on his neck, dropping him to the blacktop.

The fight had lasted less than two seconds. Mike Morin, Caleb knew, had no idea of what had happened. One instant he was throwing a punch that he imagined would lay Caleb out cold, and the next he was on the ground in a world of pain, gasping for air. Caleb knew this was Mike's experience because he himself had been on the receiving end of such punishment many times during his training over the painful months and years during which he had learned to dole out such treatment.

Caleb stood over Mike as Mike writhed and gasped on the ground. He waited patiently until he heard Mike pull in a decent lungful of air, until he knew there was a chance that Mike would hear what he had to say. He leaned over and spoke softly into Mike's ear, his tone calm and reasonable as if concluding some amicable negotiation.

"Mike, listen, Katie just isn't into you, okay?" He waited for some reaction but got none. "Mike, nod if you hear me and understand what I'm saying."

Mike lay on his side, motionless in a fetal position, but he managed to nod his head.

"Good, okay," Caleb said. "So I want you to leave her alone, okay? Don't call, don't text, don't stalk her. Okay? So we don't have to do this again. Because next time I promise I won't go easy on you. Nod if you understand."

There was a pause this time, and then Mike Morin nodded again.

"Good," Caleb said. "Really, this is good, all around. Take it easy, okay?"

He straightened. Katie was ten feet away and her expression was hard to read. Horror, relief, surprise, guilt. It was all there, it seemed to Caleb.

"I think we're done here," Caleb said. He nodded to the cars in the parking lot up the short hill. "You ready to head out?"

Katie nodded. Neither she nor Caleb took another look at Mike Morin, still lying on his side, as they walked up the road to their vehicles, the long work day finished at last.

Chapter Nine

Local Lobsterman Makes Grisly Catch

Hopefleet – Caleb Hayes, a lobsterman who fishes out of Kettle Cove, had an unpleasant surprise when he found the body of a deceased kayaker tangled in the buoy line while hauling traps near Whaleboat Island last Monday morning.

"I was all alone. Third trawl of the morning, I think," Hayes told the Hopefleet Buoy shortly after the incident. "He came right up, leg tangled in the buoy line. I nearly had a heart attack right there."

Hayes immediately called the Coast Guard who sent a motor lifeboat from the Coast Guard Station in South Portland to retrieve the body. "This did not have to happen," said Coast Guard Boatswain's Mate Danny Larson who commanded the motor lifeboat dispatched to Hayes's assistance. "We see maybe five or six of these a year. A lot that are associated with kayakers. This was a calm day, good visibility, but the deceased was not wearing a life jacket, which is never a good practice. Even the best kayakers can overturn their boat. If he'd been wearing a PFD he probably would have been all right."

So far this year there have been twenty-two recreational boating deaths in the Coast Guard's Northeast region, eleven of them attributed to canoe or kayak accidents. The region stretches from New Jersey to Maine, and the numbers include inland and coastal accidents.

Cumberland County Sheriff's Department detectives identified the deceased as one Richard Forrester, 42, of Greenwich, Connecticut. Forrester was employed by Atlantic Gas and Oil, a division of ConWest Industries. AGO is the chief competitor of

International Gas and Power, the energy company currently in negotiation with the town of Hopefleet for construction of a liquid natural gas terminal on the site of the old naval fuel depot. Officials at AGO say that Forrester was not in Hopefleet in any official capacity and was in fact on vacation at the time of the accident.

An avid sea kayaker, Forrester rented the boat he was paddling from Middle Bay Canoe and Kayak in Brunswick, but it is not clear where he first put in or how long he had been underway before meeting with his accident. Forrester's kayak was discovered by recreational boaters several miles from where his body was recovered later that same day.

An autopsy revealed that the cause of death was drowning and no foul play is suspected. "It looks like a tragic accident," said Detective Mike Berry of the Cumberland County Sheriff's Department. "The victim apparently fell out of the kayak and was unable to get back in. The water wasn't that cold, if he'd been wearing his life jacket he probably would have made it."

Forrester is survived by his wife, Jane, and their two children, William, 9, and Abigail, 11. Funeral services will be held Saturday at the St. Paul Episcopal Church in Greenwich, Connecticut.

Daniel Finch, Executive Vice President of Resource Development for International Gas and Power finished reading the words on the screen. He let his face drop into his hands and sat there for a long moment, his thoughts swirling. The morning sun was well above the rampart of buildings surrounding Central Park, driving the deep shadows out. It streamed in through the plate glass windows of his office, making elongated rectangles of light on the off-white carpet.

Daniel Finch did not look up.

For a week he had been monitoring the papers—Portland, Maine, Hopefleet, Greenwich, Connecticut. The *Portland Press Herald* and the *Greenwich Times* had run articles, of course. And after that, nothing. More importantly, neither of those papers had made the connection between Richard Forrester and Atlantic Gas and Oil and International Gas and Power. Until now.

The Hopefleet Buoy...Finch thought, torturing himself with the absurdity of it. He had thought the whole thing had blown over, but now this ridiculous little make-believe newspaper had brought the whole thing up again, including Forrester's connection to LNG.

He lifted his head, leaned back, stared at the computer screen that showed the online version of the *Buoy*, which he checked whenever it came out, which was once a month.

*This is bad...*he thought, though in truth he did not know if he was overreacting, which, he had to admit, he did do on occasion. He turned from the screen, looked out the window at the buildings on the far side of the park. He had to make a phone call, he knew it, but he did not want to. Any of the hundreds of men and women below him in the hierarchy of IGP would act the eager sycophant in his presence. Not one of them would intimidate him in the least. Save for the one man with whom he had to speak.

He looked at the computer screen again and the shot of anger that accompanied the sight of the article boosted his resolve. He pulled open his desk drawer and extracted the second of the disposable phones he had purchased at Wal-Mart. After having negotiated the extraction and activation of the first, Finch had the good sense to get the others ready for immediate use. The last thing he needed, at a time when he had a phone call to make, was the maddening frustration of just trying to get the damned thing out of the plastic.

Finch flipped the phone open and punched in the number that was scrawled on the pad on his desk. He waited as the call connected, the phone rang on the other end. The ringing stopped and there was a moment of quiet.

"Yeah?" said the voice, slightly garbled by the cheapness of the phone and the lousy cell service in the backwater from where the man was answering. The man that Finch thought of as the Enforcer.

"There was another article," Finch said, forcing a low menace into his voice. "In the idiot local paper."

"Old news," the Enforcer said. "It's already been in the Portland paper. And the paper in Greenwich, Connecticut."

"Yes, but this time the connection was made between Forrester and IGP," Finch said.

"Yeah, and what did it say?" the Enforcer asked. "Never mind, I'll tell you. It said Forrester was on vacation, that he was not in Hopefleet in any official capacity."

"And people believe that? The cops believe it?"

"Why not? Forrester's superiors at Atlantic Gas and Oil said it was the case. And they're not going to say anything different. They're as up to their armpits in the shit as we are. They don't want the cops poking into this."

Finch paused, frowned, stared at his computer screen. This man had a way of deflecting any argument or criticism and it was maddening. Finch let his thoughts organize themselves before he went off on another tack.

"Okay, the cops think it was an accident. Does Cox think it was an accident? Or did he get the hint?"

"The cops have no real reason to think Forrester was purposely eliminated," the Enforcer said, with that patient, pedagogic tone that drove Finch nuts. "But Cox does. He's a crooked, nasty piece of work, but he's not stupid. He got the hint."

"Okay, so he'll cooperate? We have his vote?"

There was a pause on the line, the first hint of failure, no matter how minor, he had ever had from the Enforcer. It delighted Finch and terrified him all at once.

"Cox is not being as cooperative as I would wish," the Enforcer said at last. "He has a lot of experience with this sort of thing, so he's not going to be pushed around easily."

"Damn it!" Finch said, his anger driven by fear. "We have two weeks until the selectmen vote and if Cox isn't with us we're screwed."

"I know," the voice on the line said. "I haven't even begun to put pressure on him."

"You can't…" Finch said and stopped. The phone he was using was untraceable and he knew the man he was talking to would not be so sloppy as to allow any access to their conversation, but still he could not bring himself to say the words that came to mind.

"You can't handle this the way you handled Forrester," Finch said instead. "If something happens to Cox, if he isn't there to vote, then the other selectmen will just table the whole thing and we have to start over again. This only works if Cox is alive and votes our way."

"I understand," the voice said. "Cox will be…encouraged…to do what we want."

"Yes, but whatever you do, it can't get back to us," Finch said. "IGP can't be implicated in any way."

There was silence on the line, a clear and effective rebuke. The Enforcer did not need to be reminded of so elemental a consideration and he was letting Finch know it. Finch shifted nervously in his chair.

"Don't worry," the voice said. "Someone else will be delivering the message. Not me. Not anyone associated with IGP."

"Good," Finch said. "Take care of it." He disconnected the call. Then he stood, walked over to the stretch of tile in front of the floor-to-ceiling windows and crushed the phone under foot with particular vehemence.

Chapter Ten

The Hopefleet Tavern was a cheesy affair, in Caleb's mind. The building that housed it, built between the wars, had been home to any number of establishments over the years —a general store, an antique shop, a United States Post Office. But for the past three decades it had been the Hopefleet Tavern, the only genuine local drinking establishment in town. And in all those years, Caleb doubted it had ever had anything like a thorough cleaning.

It was not well lit, probably a good thing. What light there was came from a few hanging fixtures, old-time wooden ship's wheels with lightbulbs mounted on the underside. The walls were made up of tired pine paneling, varnished and festooned with weathered wooden lobster traps and wooden buoys, relics of an earlier time in the lobster fishery.

There were two large wooden plaques mounted as well, and on them the fading shells of massive lobsters, twenty-five pounders at least, that had been hauled up years before, at a time when it was still legal to catch such monsters. The mounted shells of giant lobsters were so ubiquitous in restaurants on the coast of Maine that Caleb often wondered if they were required under some sort of state regulation.

A long, dark, wooden bar ran nearly the length of the main tavern room, separated by a ten-foot-wide space from a series of booths that ran along the opposite wall. There were neon signs for various brands of beer, faded posters from past events in town, signed, framed photos of the various B and C list celebrities who had passed that way. It was all so tacky that Caleb chose to believe the tavern had been decorated with a healthy dose of irony, that it was really someone's humorous take on what a Maine coast dive should look like. Still, he loved the place and would not trade it for all the fern bars and boutique microbreweries in Portland or Los Angeles.

So it was to the Hopefleet Tavern that Caleb took Katie Brennan to celebrate their having worked together for eight days. It was a Saturday night. The catch had been good, as it had been for the past week, and Katie was quick to ascribe that good luck to her own presence aboard the *Lisa Marie*. And while Caleb knew that the other boats, *sans* Katie Brennan, were also landing good catches, he did not argue the point.

They came directly from the boat, still smelling of sweat and bait and lobsters and, in Katie's case, coconut-scented sunblock. This was not a problem; half the clientele were lobstermen and they all smelled that way, save for the sunblock. They found stools at the bar.

"Caleb!"

May Cousins, owner of the Hopefleet Tavern, was behind the bar. She was in her sixties now, stout and gray-haired, her face weathered and lined from years of working the water. "Lobsterman to the stars! What can I get you?"

"Two Shipyards, *por favor*," Caleb said.

"You got it," May said, pulling two frosted glasses from a place below the taps. Caleb turned and looked around the room. Maybe twenty people there, mostly men, but not all. A couple of obvious tourists taking in the local flavor, looking like they were not so sure it was to their taste. Caleb haunted the Tavern often enough to know that Mike Morin rarely went there, and he was not there now. He had not, in fact, contacted Katie in any way since his and Caleb's discussion a few days before.

May set the beers down on the bar. Condensation beaded up on the glass and ran in streams down the sides in a way that made Caleb desperately eager to take that first long, refreshing draught. He lifted one beer up and Katie lifted the other. Caleb touched his glass to hers. "*L'chaim*," he said.

"*L'chaim*," Katie said. She took a swig and Caleb took a gulp. "Spanish, Yiddish, you are one multicultural son of a bitch, aren't you?"

"Yeah," Caleb said. "It all comes with being a man of the world." Caleb fished in his pocket, pulled out his wallet and his cell phone. He set the cell phone on the bar, pulled a twenty from his wallet and laid it down on the dark wood. He left phone and wallet on the bar, not wishing to stuff them back in his pockets.

"So, I've been meaning to ask you…" Katie began.

"Yeah?"

"What you did to Mike Morin? At the wharf? Was that, like, karate or something?"

Caleb smiled, took another long swig of beer. The first glass, in particular, always went down so quick and smooth. The second, third and fourth ones were nearly as good. *I'm drinking too much these days*, he thought.

"Naw, nothing so fancy as karate or one of those ancient disciplines. It's a technique called *krav maga*. It was developed by the Israelis, so you know it's kick-ass. Doesn't involve any kind of philosophy or personal enlightenment, it's just designed to take down an adversary as quick and efficiently as possible."

"Sure seemed to work," Katie said. "You'll have to teach me some things."

"I can do that. Might help with all these jerky guys you seem to attract. Maybe if you didn't smell like bait all the time…"

The door opened and the late afternoon sun spilled in and lit up the interior of the Hopefleet Tavern. Caleb turned his head. Billy Caine was there, looking around the room as the door swung closed behind him. His eyes fell on Caleb and Katie and he smiled.

"There you are!" he said, still smiling behind his round glasses as he walked toward them. He held up a copy of the *Hopefleet Buoy* like it was a rare artifact he had just discovered. "I didn't know you were the guy!"

"I am the guy," Caleb said. "What guy?"

"The guy who found Dick Forrester's body," Billy said, holding up the paper as proof.

"That's old news," Caleb said. "The Portland paper had it almost a week ago."

"Yeah, but I never read that paper. Like I told you, this is practically a vacation for me."

"'Dick' Forrester?" Katie asked. "You knew him?"

"Sure," Billy said. "Not well, but I knew him. We traveled in the same circles, you might say. It's actually kind of a small community, the people who are involved with this sort of thing. LNG. Tar sands. Extraction industries."

"Huh," Caleb said. He drained the last of his beer. "Can I get you a drink?" he asked. There was something about Billy's nebbish enthusiasm that he liked.

"Shipyard would be great, thanks," Billy said.

Caleb looked at Katie. "You ready for another?"

"Not even close," she said, holding up her half-filled glass.

"Lightweight," Caleb said. He turned, caught May's eye, pointed to his empty glass and held up two fingers, like the silent communication of a catcher and a pitcher. May nodded.

"So," Caleb said, turning back to Billy. "The cops and the papers all say that this Forrester guy worked for the rival of this company that wants to build the LNG terminal."

"International Gas and Power," Billy supplied. "They're the ones who are in negotiations. Dick worked for Atlantic Gas and Oil."

"Right," Caleb said. Or at least he assumed Billy was right. He could never keep it straight in his head. "So, they all said it was just a coincidence he was here in Hopefleet. On vacation. By himself, apparently, wife and kids left at home. You think that's true?"

"Hell of a coincidence," Katie chimed in. She had taken a step closer, Caleb noticed, drawn in by the promise of intrigue.

"Like Katie said," Billy replied, "hell of a coincidence."

"So?" Caleb asked. Billy shrugged.

"I don't know," Billy said. He glanced side to side, took a step closer. "He might have been here snooping around. That would make sense. But...you know Howard Cox, the selectman?"

"The guy who says he'll vote against this LNG thing?" Caleb said. "Shut the whole thing down?"

"Yeah," Billy said. "Well, I can tell you, he's a nasty piece of work. He comes across as this sort of gruff-old-guy-with-a-heart-of-gold type thing. But he was a K Street lobbyist for years. Repped some pretty bad actors. Had Saddam Hussein as a client before that all went south. A corporate attorney before that. Guy like that, who knows what he's capable of?"

May set two more beers down on the bar. Caleb handed one to Billy, picked up the second and took another long drink.

Katie leaned in, speaking in a low, conspiratorial tone that was almost comic in its dramatic effect. "You think Cox killed this Forrester guy?"

Billy held up his hands in a *who knows?* gesture. "No, I'm definitely not saying that," he protested. "I'm just saying, I did a little digging into all this, out of professional curiosity, and I found out he's a guy who plays rough."

"This was no boating accident!" Katie said in her best Hooper-from-*Jaws* voice.

"You really have a thing for Hooper, don't you?" Caleb said. "You keep mentioning him."

Katie smiled, shrugged. "Smart, salty guys with beards," she said.

"Well, I got two out of three," Caleb said. He took another deep swallow, half the glass drained already. "Okay," he said to Billy. "Cox plays rough. And smart, because the cops and the coroner didn't find anything that suggests it wasn't just a boating accident, Mr. Hooper notwithstanding. Why would he kill Forrester? Forrester must have wanted to stop these IGP goons as much as Cox does."

"Sure," Billy said. "Honestly, I don't think this Cox guy had anything to do with Dick's death. And, like you said, the cops say it was an accident, and I have no reason to think otherwise. Or to think that Dick wasn't here on vacation. Occam's Razor, you know, the simplest explanation. Unless there's more going on than any of us understand."

"We can only hope," Katie said, draining her beer. "We could use a little excitement around here."

"What?" Caleb protested. "Catching lobsters isn't exciting enough for you?"

"Here," Billy said, stepping toward the bar. "Next round's on me." He pulled his wallet and cell phone from his pocket, set them on the bar, and raised a hand to signal May who was chatting up a couple of carpenters at the far end of the long counter. A minute later May put three fresh beers down. Billy flipped his wallet open, handed her a twenty, said he didn't need change.

"So," Caleb said to Billy. "What did you think of the mud you pulled up from the fuel farm? Clean?" He was coming to like the enthusiastic, slightly fussy scientist.

"Don't know," Billy said. "I'm just doing samples. I have to get it back to the lab for the actual testing. But my guess is it will be okay. In fact, my guess is that IGP already had someone out to secretly test it. I don't think they'd have gotten this deep into it if they didn't already know the tests would be okay."

"Really?" Katie asked. "They're doing this clandestine stuff, secret tests and things?"

"Sure," Billy said. "This is the big league. Literally billions of dollars at stake. They don't screw around."

The conversation drifted from there to lobstering. Billy seemed to have a curious mind, an interest in learning about any subject that came up, and he asked insightful questions about the state of the fishery, the health of the lobster population, techniques used in catching the crustaceans. They drained another round of beers.

"Okay, that's it for me," Billy said, putting another empty down on the bar. "I can't drink like you fishermen."

"I'm working on it," Katie said, "but I have a ways to go before I can keep up with Caleb."

"Not a life goal you should be aiming for," Caleb said.

Billy leaned in, grabbed his cell phone and wallet off the bar. "So, I'm here another few days. I hope I see you around." He paused, looked Katie in the eye and then Caleb. "And seriously, watch yourselves. Probably nothing going on, but like I said, this is the big leagues and you don't know what any of these bastards are capable of." He gave a quick smile, turned, and pushed his way toward the front door.

"Comforting," Katie said.

"Well, we pose a threat to no one but the population of *homerus americanus*, so unless they organize and rise up, we should be safe."

Caleb grabbed up his wallet and phone, Katie grabbed her bag and they made their way to the door. They stepped out of the hot and humid tavern, the fetid climate of many bodies pressed into a small space, food cooking, beer spilling, and into the cool and fresh night air. They both breathed deep. There was a hint of salt, and a trace of a campfire burning somewhere off in the distance. A lovely night. Perfect.

"It's Sunday tomorrow, a day off," Caleb said.

"Yeah, I don't know what I'll do with myself," Katie said. "Maybe have some friends over for a big lobster dinner."

"Really?" Caleb asked.

"No," Katie said. "I'll be happy to go a day without seeing a lobster."

They said their goodbyes, Caleb heading to his truck, Katie to her battered PT Cruiser. Caleb pulled the cab door open, stepped up and sat in the familiar seat. He could feel a slight swimming in his head, four beers slammed down on an empty stomach and a long day's work. He did a quick mental inventory of the booze that was in his refrigerator and freezer at home and nodded to himself. Still plenty there.

He picked up the cell phone he had just dropped in the cup holder between the seats and swiped at the screen in the unlikely event he had received a text or voicemail. The wallpaper flashed to life, the smiling faces of two children he had never seen in his life, and instantly they were half covered by the icons of half a dozen apps.

"What the hell?" Caleb muttered. And then he recalled Billy Caine setting his phone down on the bar, reaching over and snatching it up later. Caleb looked down at the wallet, still in the cup holder. It was his. Billy had grabbed the right wallet, wrong phone.

"Crap," Caleb said. He looked out the windshield at the cars in the parking lot. Most were dark and stationary, a few coming in and out, swinging headlight beams like lances held by knights of old. His brain was muddled and he was not sure what to do when it dawned on him he could use Billy's phone to call his and Billy would no doubt answer.

He lifted the phone, scrutinized it and realized it was identical to his: same model, same operating system, even the rubber Otter case was the same. Easy mistake for Billy to make. He pressed the phone icon and the dial pad sprung up bright. Caleb was reaching a meaty finger for the screen when someone knocked on the window by his head and made him jump.

He turned to his left. In the glow of the floodlight over the tavern's front door he could see Billy smiling at him and holding up a cell phone identical to the one in his hand. Caleb turned the key in the ignition, pressed the button on the power window.

"I was a mile down the road before I thought to pull over and check for texts, and lo and behold, wrong phone!" Billy said.

"Yeah, I was wondering why I suddenly had strange children on my wallpaper," Caleb said, handing the phone through the window and taking his from Billy.

"Yeah, they're strange, but I love them," Billy said. He nodded, Caleb nodded, and Billy turned and headed back to his car.

Caleb watched him go, but his mind was elsewhere. He could feel the warm buzz in his head fading into a headache. But he was only five minutes from his home. He had time to get there before the numbness was gone completely. He would be alone there, sure, a thing he both craved and feared. But there was beer and rum enough to ease him through the night.

Chapter Eleven

The Penalty Box was a sports bar the way Hooters was a family restaurant; the descriptions may have reflected the owners' vision for the place, but they had nothing to do with why people actually went there.

In the case of the Penalty Box, housed in a free-standing building that had started life as a Pizza Hut and then served a brief stint as the Chow Maine Chinese Restaurant, the chief attractions were a half dozen pool tables, a decent selection of video games, an even more decent selection of cheap beers on tap and frequent promotional events that made the beer cheaper still. Added benefit: there was little expectation of proper or even civilized behavior on the part of the men and women (though mostly men) who frequented the place.

Several flat-screen TVs playing sundry sporting events, and framed posters of chiefly New England teams were the Penalty Box's only nod to being a sports bar. In truth the decidedly un-athletic patrons came there night after night looking for a good, affordable, raucous drunk.

The bar was on the Bath Road in Brunswick, Maine, about ten minutes' drive from the Hopefleet town line, which was another thing in its favor. Hopefleet was a small town. Tales of bad behavior spread quickly. By the third or fourth time the sheriff's deputies had to respond to a disturbance by the same individual it could affect his ability to do business there. Better to keep that sort of thing in Brunswick, deal with the Brunswick cops. Better not to shit in the nest.

All of those factors were part of Mike Morin's decision to make the Penalty Box his third home, along with the single-wide trailer he had set on blocks in a cleared patch of wood he bought years before, and his lobsterboat, which he had named the *Bait & Bitch*. Most of his life, he had just recently come to understand, was spent at one of those three places, or driving from one to the other. But in his mind that was only an observation, not a cause for concern.

He had hoped to add the little one-bedroom apartment Katie Brennon rented near Bowdoin College to the list of places he frequented. He had never been inside, of course, had only seen it from the street, watching from the cab of his truck, sometimes for hours on end. He imagined it was cute in a girly sort of way: books crammed on shelves, a futon mattress and frame, which he feared would not be strong enough for the activity he envisioned taking place on it, posters with strange pictures and words in foreign languages.

He had never seen the inside and now it looked as if he never would. Weeks of pursuit and he'd finally had his chance, but she had turned out to be too stuck up to enjoy the simple charms of the Penalty Box and the good company of his buddies there.

"Well, she can bite my ass," he muttered to himself. He was leaning on the bar, letting those thoughts swirl around, watching a few of his friends shoot pool. He would have played the winner under normal circumstances, but he had begged off, said he was sick of pool. Which was not true. In truth he was still having trouble bending over after the blow Caleb Hayes had delivered to his ribs, something like five days earlier. Some kind of karate shit or something.

Mike still was not sure what had happened. One minute he was throwing a punch that should have been lights out for Hayes, the next minute he was on the ground with Hayes whispering something about Katie not being into him.

Whatever had happened, Mike Morin did not care to have it happen again. He had stopped calling Katie, stopped texting, even stopped parking outside her apartment. Luckily, none of his buddies had asked about her, so he didn't have to lie. It was almost as if they'd expected it would not work out.

Mike picked up the beer that had just been set on the bar beside him and took a deep drink. Number five or six for the night, he couldn't recall, but it was pretty much doing the trick. The pain in his side was hardly noticeable as long as he didn't move much. The anger and the self-loathing were dulled, as if he were looking at those emotions through frosted glass. He took another drink.

The front door opened and a smallish man, lean, wearing a leather coat like a motorcycle jacket and sunglasses came walking in. He was clean-shaven, his hair trimmed close. Mike had never seen him there before, but that meant nothing, as people often drifted in and out.

The sunglasses were stupid. If the Penalty Box was any more poorly lit the people there would have to feel their way around. Only the pool tables received adequate lighting. Had Mike been feeling more belligerent he might have made some snarky comment, but the blow to his ribs had knocked much of the belligerence out of him.

The new guy stepped up to the bar next to Mike, nodding his thanks as Mike stood aside for him. The guy raised a hand, and the bartender came over. "Budweiser," the guy said. He had a voice like a growl, like a dog you should be wary of.

The man in leather got his beer and stood, elbows on the bar. Mike continued to watch his buddies play, their shooting skills falling off in direct proportion to the amount of beer they poured down their throats, which was quite a bit. He and the man were looking in opposite directions. They did not speak.

A minute or so passed and then Mike saw movement in the corner of his eye. The guy was looking up at him, checking him out, but before Mike could turn his head, the guy looked away.

This guy some kind of fag? Mike wondered. If the guy came on to him, he wasn't sure how he would react.

From the corner of his eye he saw the guy looking up again, and this time Mike turned and looked right into the lenses of his dark glasses.

"You got a problem?" Mike asked. The guy shook his head but did not respond. And he did not look away. For half a minute the two of them stood like that.

"What the fuck are you—" Mike began, but the guy in the sunglasses cut him off.

"I've seen you before," he said, his growl of a voice matter of fact.

"Yeah?" Mike said, trying and failing to match the low menace.

"Yeah." The man with the sunglasses was quiet again and still he did not look away. Mike suddenly felt a desperate need for alcohol and he took a long pull of his beer. He was about to speak, but once again the man beat him to it.

"Down on the dock. In Hopefleet. I saw that guy, what's his name, sucker-punch you."

"Caleb Hayes."

"Was that it? Yeah, I was there. Guy comes up, starts giving you shit, and then before you can even defend yourself he hits you, right like that. Real chickenshit move, I thought."

"Yeah, it was," Mike agreed. He didn't remember it exactly like this guy remembered it, but he liked this guy's version better, and he was too drunk to argue about the details.

"Yeah," the guy said. "Caleb Hayes. There's a real asshole."

"You know him?" Mike asked.

"Yeah. Some. Mostly I know guys who know him. Guys who don't like him."

"Yeah," Mike said, "a lot of guys don't like him. Me included."

"I'll bet. After what he did to you. And in front of that hot chick, too."

"Yeah," Mike agreed. "He's a real asshole." He drank again, turned his attention back to his buddies. He watched one of them put the cue ball in, swear loud and emphatically, and make a move to break the cue over his knee. Then he thought better of it and threw the cue on the floor. Some behavior was out of bounds, even for the Penalty Box.

"Be nice to teach that asshole a lesson, wouldn't it?" the guy with the sunglasses said, so low Mike could hardly hear, and it took a few seconds for the words to process.

"Yeah," Mike said, drinking again. And he meant it. In his mind he had played out various scenarios, all of which involved beating Caleb Hayes bloody while Katie stood watching and screaming in horror. He got a warm feeling when he thought of those things, a glow of satisfaction. And then, like a bucket of cold seawater in the face, came the memory of finding himself crumpled in pain on the blacktop, not even knowing how he got there.

"Yeah, be nice," Mike Morin said, draining the last of his beer. "But Hayes, he knows karate or some shit."

He turned to the man in sunglasses and was surprised and pleased to see him holding out a sweating cold bottle of beer like an offering, and Mike realized he must have silently ordered a second round. Mike took it, raised it in salute, too drunk and grateful and slow-witted to wonder why the stranger had done him this kindness.

The stranger gave a short snort of laughter, a derisive sound. "Karate," he said. He took a long drink from his own beer. "Karate's okay when you're sucker punching a guy in a parking lot. Up against three or four guys with baseball bats? Naw. It ain't like the movies, like friggin' Spiderman or something, where all those guys get taken out. You get three, four guys, and the karate guy's dead meat."

Mike Morin nodded as he drank. That made sense. He'd always thought four guys with bats could take out one guy no matter how good a fighter the one guy was. But that still didn't solve the problem.

"Yeah, I bet you're right," he said to the guy in sunglasses. "If I could get three or four guys, I'd do it."

The guy with the sunglasses turned around, leaned back with elbows on the bar the way Mike Morin was standing. He pointed with his chin toward Mike's buddies, now racking the balls for a new game. "Those are your buds, aren't they? They're some big dudes. Tough-looking dudes."

Mike nodded, but there was an uncomfortable feeling creeping over him. He had thought about this very thing, recruiting his buddies to teach that son of a bitch Hayes a lesson. The bunch of them, they'd known each other since grade school and they were not strangers to fighting. They'd kicked some serious ass in their day. Now two of these guys were lobstermen and the other one worked for a guy who built stone walls. They were not pussies. They knew how to dole out some hurt.

But still Mike Morin was not so enthusiastic about this idea. He had never met anyone who could fight like Caleb Hayes, and he didn't know the further extent of his skills. What's more, he had not mentioned to his buddies that Caleb had kicked his ass, and if he was going to recruit them, he would have to tell them why.

"You're thinking your buddies might not be so into this?" the guy said.

Mike nodded.

"Here's the thing." The stranger turned his dark-shaded eyes toward Mike. "Like I said, I know people who hate this bastard Caleb Hayes. And they'll pay money to see he gets taught a lesson. You'd like to make him pay for what he did to you, right? So let me pay you money, and you make him pay with pain. Get it?"

Mike Morin squinted at the guy with the sunglasses. He understood that money was being offered here, and that would do a lot to convince his buddies. In fact, if this was a job for hire, he wouldn't have to tell his buddies at all about what had gone down between him and Hayes. But still, there was something odd about the whole thing.

"You sure you didn't know I was here?" Mike Morin asked. "You just happen to see me when you come in?"

"That's it," the guy said. "Just a big, happy coincidence."

Mike Morin nodded, but he was still not sure he believed the guy. "So, what kind of money are we talking about?" he asked.

"Tell you what," the guy with the sunglasses said. "I'll give you a thousand dollars, cash. You divide it up with your buddies any way you want. That work for you?"

Mike squinted, not certain he had heard right. *A thousand dollars? And I can split it up however I want?*

He was too drunk even for simple arithmetic, but he knew if he offered each of his buddies a hundred dollars they'd be happy as shit, and that would still leave him… it would be a lot, whatever it was. To do the one thing on earth he most wanted to do: beat Caleb Hayes bloody.

"Awright," Mike Morin said. "Let's do it. Let's friggin' do it."

The guy with the sunglasses nodded. "Good. Good decision. But not tonight."

Mike frowned. He had just started working himself up into a fever, and he had insight enough to know he would not be so enthusiastic when he was sober. "Why not?" he asked.

"Because you need to convince your buddies. And I need to get the money. And you need to not be so drunk. Got it?"

Mike nodded. He was not happy, he wanted to strike while he was still fired up, but he understood what the guy was saying.

"Okay, then," Morin said. "What's the plan?"

"The plan is," the guy with the sunglasses said, taking a long pull of his beer, "you listen to what I'm about to tell you, and you do exactly what I say."

Chapter Twelve

Sunday was a day of rest, but not by Caleb's choice. It was regulation; the State of Maine prohibited lobstering on Sundays during the summer months. That decree, and limits on the number of traps a lobsterman could fish, and sundry other rules, generally infuriated the lobstermen but also assured that the tasty crustaceans continued to populate the dark, deep waters of the Gulf of Maine.

The regulations also left Caleb Hayes at loose ends on Sundays. He liked to work, to keep his body and his mind focused on the task. Lobstering was a physical game but it was a mental one as well, keeping note of where the trawls were set, which were catching lobsters and which weren't, trying to guess, based on what came up in the traps, what was happening on the unseen bottom of Casco Bay. These things kept him from having to think too much about other, less uplifting things.

And then Sunday came. He had no pressing reason to rise early, and he often slept until 7:00 a.m. before climbing with a groan from his king-sized bed. A year or so before, during the climactic days as head of C&S Security, the wild rollercoaster ride of Hollywood and Palm Springs and London and Paris and Monte Carlo and Dubai, the idea that 7:00 a.m. was a late hour for rising would have seemed ridiculous.

Whether he was going to bed drunk or sober, dead tired from a long night of stressful work or a long night of industrial-level partying depended on the role he filled.

If he was there in a professional capacity, heading up the security detail, overseeing the dozen or more men brought on for that particular job, he would be absolutely sober. All of them: the site security, the personal bodyguards, the rent-a-cops, the real, off-duty cops making some extra cash, they all answered to him and he was responsible for making certain they were where they should be and doing what they should be doing.

And it went beyond mere traffic regulation. The homes and suites and shooting locations that C&S Security protected were populated by the top of the A-List celebrities, the A+ list, the people everyone wanted to be near, even just to catch a glimpse. Autograph seekers and fans and gawkers crowded the approaches. And so did stalkers and sundry other sickos. And so did the paparazzi, who could make serious bank with one good compromising photo. It was Caleb's job to put up the impenetrable wall between those people and the principals he was hired to protect.

And there were still more considerations. It was incumbent on him to know who was sleeping with whom, and who should or should not know about it, and to do his best to see that situation did not change. He had to know which of his celebrity clients were not ready to have their publicists leak word of their affairs or their sexual orientations, and to make certain there was no chance that word got out anyway. There were plenty of times when Caleb had escorted some major bankable star from a Beverly Hills eatery such as Spagos or CUT or Urasawa to some filthy loading dock, in through a delivery entrance and up a service elevator to a suite that cost five figures a night.

All that had grown from the seed of Caleb Hayes and Trevor Middleton both being cast in that silly surfing movie, and from the parsimonious producer who hadn't wanted to pay for real security. And from the driving ambition of the lovely, stiletto-sharp and powerfully persuasive Susanna Simpson, his ex-wife.

Now, as he did most Sunday mornings, Caleb sat on the edge of his bed and let the fog of the previous night's alcohol-induced numbness dissipate. His mind wandered back to a party he had worked at St. Bart's three years back and he smiled. He had been on duty so he had been sober and had been checking the inner perimeter of the venue, the party around the massive pool in some record producer's estate.

A fight had broken out between one of the producer's top recording artists—a woman—and a rising starlet whose sense of self far eclipsed her actual fame and bankability. It had ended in the water, and it had drawn in a dozen others, top celebrities, drunk and thrashing in the pool and beating on one another. It occurred to Caleb that he could pull his phone from his pocket, shoot a video of the affair, and sell it to network television for enough money that he would never need to work again.

But he didn't. Instead he ordered his men to make certain that no one else was shooting video of the fight while he himself waded into the pool and began pulling the combatants apart. He had a job to do and he felt a moral obligation to do it properly. What's more, C&S Security was by then so profitable that money was no longer much of a temptation.

And then his mind wandered, inevitably, to another party. The last party. Trevor Middleton's Malibu home, the girl from Kansas, beautiful, the music pounding against the walls.

Jenny Carter.

Swarms of people moving like schools of fish in the dim light.

Trevor Middleton, panic in his eyes.

Caleb shook his head, trying to physically drive the memories away. He stood and wandered out into the kitchen and fumbled with the coffeemaker. The house had a modern, open floor plan, and as the water began to spit and gurgle and drip through the grounds, Caleb leaned on the marble counter and looked out through the plate glass windows that lined the living room. The yard in the back sloped away gently to the wide, blue-green stretch of Hopefleet Sound, half a mile wide at that point, the far shore a bristly carpet of evergreen.

Eager as Caleb had been to exit Los Angeles and his marriage and the life he had built there, he was not so eager that he was willing to let his ex-wife take it all. He had insisted that she buy out his part of C&S Security for exactly what it was worth, and that was considerable. In Los Angeles he could have set himself up nicely. By Maine standards he was rolling in it. He had bought the *Lisa Marie* with cash. He had taken out a mortgage on the house, with a thirty percent down payment, though he could likely have paid cash for that as well.

The house was not huge, three bedrooms on two floors, 2,000 square feet perhaps, but it was all he needed. It was new-built, everything modern, all the appliances top-end but not ostentatiously so, the best quality windows and lots of them, so that the house was flooded with light. It was gray shingled on the outside, mostly white on the inside, done in the vernacular of the seaside cottage but with none of the tired, cobweb quality of those houses that had been standing for generations. It was more than Caleb needed, but not much more, and it made him happy.

When the coffee was done Caleb poured a mug and stepped out through the French doors and onto the patio that extended like a dock from the back of the house. He leaned on the railing and breathed deep. The air smelled of balsam and salt water and rockweed. There was nothing to hear but the calls of the cardinals and nuthatches and chickadees darting through the brush.

Caleb straightened. "All right. Fine. It's paradise," he said to no one.

Twenty minutes later he was in his truck, which he had also bought with cash courtesy of his C&S buyout, and heading down to the dock at Hopefleet Lobster Co-op. Hopefleet, like so many of Maine's coastal towns, was situated on a narrow peninsula running northeast to southwest with a single road cutting along its spine and all the secondary roads like tributaries running into it. Caleb drove down his own road, called Ash Point, and turned southwest on the twisting, two-lane road that was Route 54, Hopefleet's main artery.

On the seat beside him sat a new bilge pump, destined to replace the aging and unreliable one currently in the *Lisa Marie*'s bilges. There may have been no lobstering that day, but there was most certainly work to do. He had a wooden boat. There was always work to do.

For the next hour he tinkered and cursed and sweated in the sweltering, cramped cabin under the *Lisa Marie*'s foredeck. In truth it was more a storage area than a cabin, with a portable toilet, what the sailors called a "head", and a couple of bunks half filled with spare buoys and coils of rope and boxes of sundry parts. Sweat ran down Caleb's face and arms as he labored to get the new bilge pump in place, twisting wires and screwing in mounting bolts and tightening hose clamps. At last he reconnected the battery and was greeted by the welcome sound of the float switch kicking the new pump on and the water from the bilge spewing over the side.

He set all things to rights again then drove home, showered, had a beer, then climbed back into his truck. This time he was bound to his parents' home for Sunday barbecue, a near weekly tradition, easier than changing out a bilge pump in a sweltering, dark cabin, but in some ways more dreaded.

In the end it was not so bad, the Adirondack chairs and cold beers, his father fussing with the barbecue, his mother fussing with everything else. His parents' house, like his, was on the water, but theirs looked out over the open Atlantic. It was a spectacular view, though having thousands of miles of unbroken ocean as a front yard would have made for brutal winter conditions if his parents had spent winters there. Which they did not.

His Uncle Dick was there as well, a welcome addition for Caleb, a buffer between himself and his concerned parents.

"Caleb!" his father, Bob Hayes, said as he saw Caleb coming around the side of the house. He rose from his chair and Caleb's mother did as well. Uncle Dick raised a beer in greeting but did no more than that.

"Dad," Caleb said, giving his father a quick hug. His father was a big man, like Dick and Caleb himself. The size was a Hayes family trait.

Caleb's father was still in good shape, if growing a little soft around the middle. He had the hands and the face of a man who had spent his life mostly in intellectual pursuits. He was collecting wrinkles around the eyes and mouth and on his forehead, but his skin still had a smooth and pliable quality and ran to a pinkish color.

Uncle Dick was nearly the polar opposite, a man who had spent most of his life on the water, his face bearing the brunt of fifty years of sun and wind and rain and snow and spray, his hands battered by handling miles of rope, thousands of traps, from mechanics and woodworking and boatbuilding and house carpentry. Robert Hayes and his older brother, Richard. Hopefleet natives, two men who had taken so very different paths, who still loved and respected one another as much as Caleb had ever seen two men do.

"You get that new bilge pump in?" Dick asked.

"Yup," Caleb said, pulling a cold beer out of the ice in the cooler.

"Good thing," Dick said. "She was like to sink at the mooring."

"Nonsense," Caleb said, then added, "It better be nonsense after what I paid Buddy Johnson to put her to rights."

"Everything okay?" Caleb's mother, Dorothy Hayes, asked.

"Oh, sure. Just a broken bilge pump on my boat. Everything's fine," Caleb said.

Dorothy nodded. Her question, Caleb knew, was ostensibly

about the boat, but in truth it ran much deeper than that. It was this very reason that he dreaded spending these afternoons with his parents, love and respect them though he did, and he genuinely did. They worried, as parents were wont to do. And they knew everything was not fine.

They had stopped prying, at least, but it was still there, just below the surface: his parents' worries, their certain knowledge that there was more wrong with their son than he was letting on. And that worry was always just visible.

Dinner proceeded as it generally did, an amiable time, pleasant conversation. They could talk politics because they all pretty much agreed with one another, and Bob and Dorothy knew enough about lobstering that they could talk about that, too. The steaks were perfection in meat, as ever, Dorothy's macaroni salad a blissful mix of noodles from a box and vegetables and spices from the raised bed garden sheltered by the house from the ocean winds. The beer was cold and plentiful and Caleb refrained from drinking so many that his mother would start suggesting he sleep in the guest room, a mistake he had made only once.

The sun was behind the tall pines to the west and throwing long shadows and orange light along the distant shoreline when Caleb and Uncle Dick took their leave. Once again, as Caleb climbed into his truck, he took mental inventory of the amount and variety of liquor waiting at home, and once again deemed it sufficient to get him through the night. He would not need that much, of course. The next day was Monday and that would see him back at the docks, loading trays of bait in the first light of the early summer dawn.

With Katie. And that thought gave him a shot of pleasant anticipation that surprised him.

Ten minutes later he pulled into the dirt drive by his house and climbed out of the truck. The motion sensitive light above his front door snapped on, but like any good Mainer Caleb eschewed the front door and went in the side door by the garage. He stepped into the mudroom, closed the door without locking it. People in Hopefleet did not lock doors, generally. He moved without thinking to the bar on the side of the living room, poured rum into a glass and pineapple juice over that and took a deep drink. Then another.

Caleb wandered over to the couch, a massive white affair that faced the high windows looking out over the water, as well as a flat screen TV mounted on the wall above an array of electronics. He picked up the remote and flicked the TV on. It was tuned to the History Channel, which was showing a documentary about pirates.

He watched for an hour more, enjoyed the show, and refreshed his drink a few times, happy to let his mind wander off into a world of rum and piracy in the Caribbean. Then his eyes flicked over to the downstairs bedroom that he had converted to an office for the few times when he actually had office type work to do, and the good feeling faded away.

It was there in the desk. He knew it. The file he had compiled over the past year. Newspaper clippings, mostly. Some police reports. Photos. Scribbled on the outside of the manila folder was a series of numbers, meaningless to anyone but Caleb. Somewhere out there were people whose lives would be changed completely if they knew those numbers. He had only to mail them anonymously. He had only to work up the moral courage.

How long has it been? Twelve months? What would be left after twelve months? Caleb felt the old questions rising up, coming up fast, like the body of Dick Forrester, a horror from the depths, and he could not stop them from rising.

He stood, looked at the desk. He took a step toward it and stopped. He wanted to open the file and look at it, though it was no more than self-flagellation. It would do no good.

You coward, you useless coward, he thought. He took another step toward the desk and once again he stopped. Someone on the television was going on about the pirates Ann Bonney and Mary Read. Caleb changed course, headed toward the bar.

He was unscrewing the cap from the rum bottle when he heard the pounding on the door. Not knocking. Pounding. He stopped and set the bottle down. In the old days, the old life, he had surveillance cameras everywhere. He would have been alerted to any approach, would know who was at the door long before they were close enough to knock.

But those were the old days. The ones he had hoped to leave in his wake.

"So who's this?" he asked out loud. He did not know, though he had his guesses. And whoever it was, he could tell by the impact on his door, the shudder it sent through the house, that it would not be pleasant.

Chapter Thirteen

The pounding stopped and Caleb heard a voice, muffled and loud, coming through the heavy wood door.

"Hayes! You bastard! Hayes!"

Caleb set the rum bottle down, nodded to himself. The voice, he was pretty sure, belonged to Mike Morin. It had the same bovine sound he associated with Morin and he could think of no one else who would come pounding on the door like that. He sighed and crossed the living room to the foyer and the front entrance.

He won't be alone, Caleb thought. As it was, Caleb was surprised that Mike had come back for more, but he knew he would not come back alone. Either he would have some of his yahoo buddies with him or he'd be armed. Or both.

He was ten feet from the door when the pounding started again. "Yeah, yeah, I'm coming, stop hitting the damn door!" Caleb yelled. Morin wasn't pounding with his fist, he could tell. He must be using whatever troglodyte weapon he had brought with him and it was no doubt doing considerable damage to the paint.

Caleb twisted the brass doorknob and threw the door open. As he imagined, Mike Morin was standing there, a baseball bat in hand, and the look of surprise on his face suggested he had not really expected Caleb to answer.

"Mike, what can I do for you?" Caleb asked, pleasantly enough. The motion sensitive light had gone on and now it revealed a sheen on Mike's eyes that suggested he had indulged in a little liquid courage before this encounter.

Fair enough, Caleb thought. Mike Morin used booze to bolster his physical courage, while he himself used it to dull thoughts of his own moral cowardice.

Caleb's training and experience were kicking in now as he evaluated the threat. His eyes moved past Morin to the two guys standing behind him. Like Morin they were holding baseball bats, and like Morin they did not look entirely sober, or entirely confident in their ability to carry out the task at hand.

Morin was taking the lead. It was his party, so Caleb would take him down first. But the guy behind Morin looked like the meanest of them, the most sure of himself, the most ready to kick ass. Caleb knew he'd have to put Mike down fast and take care of that one. Number three might be a problem too, but once he saw Mike and number two go down a lot of the fight would go out of him.

Where should we do this? Caleb thought next. He had an advantage, standing in the doorway, because it meant they could only come at him one at a time; they could not surround him. But he was afraid that one of them might slip past. On the table just to the right of the door was a ship-in-bottle he'd bought from an antique dealer. It was late nineteenth century, clearly done by a sailor, probably a model of the very ship he was aboard at the time. Made to be traded for a few rounds of drinks or a roll in the hay with some seaport hooker. It was one of Caleb's most prized possessions and he did not want to risk its getting smashed.

Okay, outside then.

All of this evaluation took no more than a few seconds, enough time for Morin to recover enough from his surprise to speak. "We're gonna kick your ass, Hayes, and you know why?"

"'Cause I asked you politely to leave Katie alone?" Caleb offered.

"No," Morin spit. "The hell with that little slut. You can have that whore, for all I care."

Caleb nodded. He had not planned on doing too much damage to Mike Morin, just a bit more than last time, enough to reinforce the lesson. That plan changed even as those ugly words left Morin's mouth.

Then Morin was talking again. "We're gonna kick your ass because Mr. Cox, he's sick of your shit, you hear? He knows what you've been doing and he wants it to stop."

Mike Morin's words were so much of a surprise that Caleb felt his whole train of thought, which had been moving in a straight line toward the coming fight, go entirely off the rails. He frowned and his eyebrows came together in confusion.

Cox? he thought. *Why do I keep hearing this guy's name?* A week ago he had never heard of the man, not until he had seen his business card, soggy and stuck to the rest, in Richard Forrester's wallet. Since then his name seemed to keep cropping up. And now this.

"What, exactly, is Mr. Cox's problem?" Caleb asked. He could see his questions were throwing Mike and the other guys off. They had expected to launch right into an ass kicking, not stand there yapping like missionaries from the Jehovah's Witnesses.

"Like you don't know, you son of a bitch," Mike Morin said and Caleb could see those were the last words he intended to speak. He took a step forward and raised his bat. Caleb took a step back, and even as he did, a part of his brain once again recalculated the hurt he would do the man. There were questions he needed answered and that meant when this was over Mike had to still be in a condition to speak.

Mike was over the threshold now, bat over his shoulder, and Caleb cocked his leg for a front kick. It wasn't something he would normally do fighting multiple assailants—too much chance someone would grab his foot and toss him—but it was only Mike now and his hands were full of the bat and Caleb knew he would not drop his weapon for anything.

Caleb grunted as he brought his knee up to his chest. He could feel the muscles and sinews protest, could feel the lousy range of motion he now had. A move that would have been fluid and effortless a year ago was considerably harder now, with his training, workouts and stretching ignored.

But the action had started, the adrenaline was pumping. Most conscious thought was erased from Caleb's mind, but he was still processing, still evaluating, moving by instinct. A front kick to Mike Morin. He could deliver it with the ball of his foot right in the gut or solar plexus and that would double him up, but that was not what he wanted. He wanted him out of the house, away from his precious ship-in-a-bottle. He wanted him to go crashing into the guy behind him.

Caleb's foot drove forward, leading with the heel, all the power of his quads behind it. Even eight months earlier he could have kicked Mike square in the chest, but now he couldn't get his foot up that high, so he got him in the stomach instead.

But that did the trick. Mike stepped into the kick as Caleb

delivered it and the impact was significant. Caleb felt his whole body jar with the blow. He saw Mike's eyes go wide and his arms fly up and his mouth come open as he was driven back into the big goon behind him, the two of them stumbling back through the door and just managing to avoid tumbling in a heap onto the red brick path.

Muscle memory kept Caleb on his feet. He came back from the kick, legs spread, ready to move. He could see the thrashing, confused men outside his door and he charged, but as he did he took the extra second he needed to grab the doorknob and slam the door behind him as he advanced. He did not need these idiots with baseball bats rampaging through his house.

There was a price for that, however. The extra second or two had allowed Mike and the two behind him to disentangle themselves, and by the time Caleb stepped clear of the door jamb, Mike was coming at him again, fury on his face, in his eyes, bat over his shoulder like he was going to swing for the bleachers.

Caleb did not back away. Just the opposite. He moved forward, driven by instinct and hours and hours of training at krav maga, training that taught him that defense and offense happened at the same time, that a fight should be violent, decisive and quick.

With his right hand, palm out, held up by his face, and the left held down over his ribs, Caleb stepped into Mike Morin's swing. The bat came around with tremendous force, but by then Caleb was well inside the deadly arc, nearly pressed against Mike's chest. Mike's arms slammed ineffectively against Caleb's shoulder as Caleb cupped his right hand behind Mike's neck and pulled him down, hard and fast, right into the knee that was coming up.

The impact drew an ugly grunting noise from Mike's throat, but Caleb did not drop him yet. The second yahoo was on them, swinging his bat as Mike had done, a powerful roundhouse blow. Caleb shifted his hand from Mike's neck to a place under his chin and through brute force alone stood the big man up again, pushing him upright just as the second guy's bat completed its swing.

He had been aiming for Caleb's head, but Mike Morin made an excellent defense against the strike. The second guy had the wherewithal to adjust his swing as he saw Mike coming up, and the bat hit Mike on the upper arm with force enough that it would have cracked his skull if it had connected there. Mike groaned again and Caleb let him fall. The second man was already bringing the bat back, but Caleb managed to grab the end of the weapon and jerk it toward him, bringing the man with it.

He grabbed the man's forearm, kept the other hand on the bat, and brought his knee up on the man's hand as if he were snapping a branch, breaking the man's grip. Caleb now had the bat in his right hand and was bringing it back over his shoulder before the second yahoo even knew he had lost it.

The man looked up, his eyes reflecting the light over the door, bright with booze and sudden terror. He held his hands up as Caleb swung, turned his head away, and so did not see Caleb change the angle of the swing and catch him in the side of his torso. The man gasped, dropped his hands, and Caleb was certain he had broken more than a few ribs. But he recalled the vehemence with which this bastard had swung at his head. Power enough to kill. This one would have to go down and stay down.

But not yet. Number three was charging up, and, having learned nothing in the five seconds of combat that had already gone down, he had his bat cocked back over his shoulder like the others.

Once again, Caleb used the wounded man in front of him as a shield. He pressed the bat down on the man's neck, grabbed his right arm and pulled it back, and slammed his knee up once, twice, to soften the guy up. He could smell the beer and sweat and bait rising off the guy's shirt.

Lobsterman...I knew I'd seen him around, Caleb thought as he twisted the man to keep him between himself and number three. Number three drew up short, swung the bat with less enthusiasm than number two had. Caleb leaned back and let the tip swish by, so close he could feel the breeze from its passing.

He gave number two another knee to the gut. He could sense that his grip on the man's arm was the only thing holding him up. He let him drop just as number three completed his follow-through and started to draw back for another swing.

In the light of the doorway lamp Caleb saw number three glance over to his right, heard a rustle behind, and he realized that these dumb bastards were not quite as dumb as he had thought. There was a fourth one, and he had been hiding behind the tall, pointed cedar bush by the door. He had apparently been waiting his chance to get into the fight and now, with the casualty rate at fifty percent, he decided it was time.

Number three was back in business, winding up again. Caleb dropped the bat he was holding; it would be easier to take number three's weapon than fight him with one hand occupied. Once again he leapt at his attacker, coming inside the arc of the swing. He felt the man's arms hit his shoulders and he wrapped his left arm around the man's right and drove his right elbow into the man's chin.

Number three's head snapped back and Caleb grabbed his outstretched arm and pivoted him around, putting number three between himself and the new, unseen attacker.

Number four was almost as big as the first three, which was plenty big, but he was thinner and Caleb could see right off he was more nimble. And unlike the others, he seemed to have figured out a few things in the now eight seconds of fighting he had witnessed. Lesson one: don't rush in heedlessly.

Five feet from Caleb, number four stopped, bat held high. He shifted left and right and Caleb pivoted with him, holding number three, who was still staggering from the elbow to the head, between them.

Caleb could hear himself gasping for breath. *Pathetic*, he thought. A year before he would hardly have broken a sweat with this sort of encounter.

Left and right they moved, number four like a snake waiting for a chance to strike. He looked angry, but he did not look afraid, which was too bad because Caleb hoped he might talk his way out of messing anyone else up.

"You don't have to be a hero," Caleb said, shifting number three as he spoke, keeping up this weird three-man dance. "Just drop your bat and run. Chalk this up to a bad night. Someone's gonna have to drive these morons home."

It was a good argument, reasonable, but Caleb could see it would not work. Number four growled, "Fuck you," and he charged, done with the dance. He grabbed a fistful of number three's shirt to pull him clear, but Caleb let the man go, snatching the bat from his hand as he did. Number four cursed again and stumbled, but he was able to push number three aside and take a one-handed swing with the bat at Caleb's head.

Caleb raised his own bat vertically and the two wooden shafts hit with a resounding crack. It was like sword fighting in some pirate movie and Caleb had just an instant to enjoy it before he brought his foot up between number four's legs in a very unpiratical move. The impact with the man's crotch was not as bad as it would have been if Caleb had been wearing shoes or boots, but it was solid enough to double the man over.

Hands on his crotch, howling with pain, number four folded at the waist. Caleb drew his bat back over his head as the adrenaline pulsed. He almost started the swing at the man's skull, realized that, best case, he'd be doling out a massive and permanent brain injury, and even furious as he was, pumped up as he was, he was not ready for that.

He stepped forward, put his hand on the back of the man's head and brought his knee up in two rapid blows to his chest and stomach, then stepped aside as his erstwhile attacker collapsed in a meaty heap on the ground. Caleb stood there, gulping air, letting the adrenaline drain away. He ran his eyes over the four men on the ground. Two were making small, desultory movements; the other two were motionless. The occasional low groan told Caleb they were still alive.

His eyes came to a stop on Mike Morin, the figure slumped closest to the front door. To Caleb, the fight and the run-up to the fight had been business; his focus had been on what he had to do to be the last man standing. He had not been angry. His mind had been too preoccupied with other concerns for him to be angry. Anger was for amateurs.

But that was over now. The four men were down and Caleb could feel the fury boiling up in him. And he knew that it was not all about the senseless violence they had tried to visit on him, violence ordered, for some reason, by this Cox guy whom Caleb had never met. It was also the file he had nearly opened, the girl, the personal torment he had been suffering this past year or more. He felt like a volcano. He could sense the earth shifting under him.

Three steps and he was at Mike Morin's side. He put the heel of his foot on Morin's shoulder and rolled him onto his back. Mike gave a low groan. There was a thin line of blood running from the corner of his mouth.

Caleb crouched down on his heels, got close to Mike's face. His first impulse was to punch him, a series of quick jabs that would mess him up in a big way, but he made himself resist. Instead he said in a low voice, "Who's Mister Cox and what does he think I've done to him?"

Mike turned his head and seemed to be struggling to focus. He opened his mouth and at first nothing came out. And then he said in a low voice, "Go to hell..."

Really? Caleb thought. He picked up Mike's hand and held it in such a way that he could bend the thumb back and exert excruciating pain. But before he had to apply more than a minor amount of pressure, Mike Morin seemed to rethink his reticence.

"Okay, okay!" he gasped. "Mr. Cox, he paid me. Me and these guys. Five hundred dollars. To come mess you up."

"Why?"

"I don't know. He just said he was sick of your shit."

Caleb frowned and tried to make sense of this, but the comedown from the fight and the rum and beer in his bloodstream were not helping. *What shit?* he wondered. Could this have something to do with his bringing up Forrester's body? What other possible connection did he have to this Cox guy?

"This Cox," Caleb said, "is this Howard Cox, the selectman?"

"I don't friggin' know," Morin said, a touch of defiance in his voice. Caleb gave his thumb a press, not enough to inflict real pain but enough to give Morin a sense for how much pain could be inflicted if he so chose.

"Really, I don't friggin' know!" Mike said, squirming, all defiance now gone from his voice.

"What did he look like?"

"He was...I dunno. Not big. Clean-shaven. He was wearing sunglasses the whole time."

"Was he old?"

"Not really. Thirties, maybe."

Caleb frowned. Cox, as he understood it, was an old man, retirement age. "And this Cox found you and hired you to do this?"

"Yeah, he ran into me at the Penalty Box," Morin began and then paused.

"Just ran into you?" Caleb asked. "Like, by coincidence?"

"Yeah, I think so," Morin sputtered. "That's how he made it sound."

Caleb dropped Mike's hand, stood and looked out into the dark. He had not learned much, just that some guy named Cox, who was apparently not Howard Cox, had hired these yahoos to rough him up. Howard Cox's son, maybe? It was all so absurd he had to guess it was some grand mistake. But he could tell he would not be getting any useful information from Morin, because Morin had none to give.

In frustration Caleb kicked Mike Morin in the gut, hard enough to drive the air from him, not hard enough to do any real damage. He stood thinking as Mike writhed and thrashed and tried to suck in air. When Morin's breathing had finally returned to something near normal, Caleb squatted at his side once again.

"Mike, you hear me?" he said and Mike nodded his head. "You're not going to ever try anything like this again, right?"

Mike shook his head emphatically.

"Good. And here's the thing. If anything happens to me...my truck gets messed up, someone screws with my boat or my traps...I'm going to just assume it's you and I'm going to beat your ass in a way it's never been beat. Got it?"

Once again Mike nodded emphatically. Caleb looked over at the other three. They were starting to move a bit. He looked past his own truck, parked in the gravel driveway. There was a down-on-its-luck Dodge Ram with an extended cab parked behind it. These dumb bastards hadn't even thought to park where their truck couldn't be seen.

"Okay, I want you to get these other idiots in the truck and drive away and never let me see you again. Got it?"

More nodding. Caleb patted Mike on the shoulder, stood and went back into his house. He had a lot to consider. What was happening here was not senseless. There was a reason for it. He just didn't know what it was. But he would have to find out, because someone who would go to the trouble of paying four guys to beat him up was not going to stop just because they had failed at their job. He would have to look into it. Put some serious thought into it.

But first he had to sleep, because suddenly he felt very, very weary.

Three hundred feet away, tucked into the tree line of the woods that ringed Caleb Hayes's lawn, the man whom Daniel Finch thought of as the Enforcer stood watching the action by Hayes's front door. In his hand he held a pair of powerful night vision goggles which he realized he would not need as soon as he saw the motion sensitive light go on above Hayes's door.

He had met with Mike Morin and the other three idiots an hour before, in a parking lot on the far side of Hopefleet. He had given Morin the money and watched as the man had nearly started drooling at the sight of it. He had told them what to do, when to do it, what to say. He had told them he wanted Caleb Hayes beaten but not to the point of hospitalization or death. He had to know who had ordered this, even if Morin and the others could not tell him why.

The morons had listened and nodded and the Enforcer had felt there was a reasonable hope that they would remember and do as they were told. He handed Mike a baseball bat. "Here. It's a good weight. Good grip. Take it."

Mike took it and hefted it and nodded approval. The Enforcer turned to the others. "You guys have weapons?" he asked. They shook their heads, looked embarrassed.

Dumb bastards, the Enforcer thought. He went back to his car, pulled out three more bats. His final instructions: "Wait an hour or so, then go beat the crap out of him."

He left them there and made his way to Hayes's property well ahead of them. He parked his car in a place it would not be seen, a precaution he guessed that the four half-drunk goons would not think to take, and he was right. From his spot in the trees, he watched them drive up, park, exit the truck with the subtlety of a cattle drive. He adjusted the fit of the earpiece in his ear. The UHF micro bug implanted in the bat he had given Morin was in range now and he could hear their muttered conversation as they approached the front door, the plan to have one of them hide in the shrubs.

Good, good, the Enforcer thought. Maybe there was some hope.

He stood motionless, watching and listening, and just managed to pull the earpiece out of his ear before the idiot Morin began pounding on the door with his bat.

If he broke that bug I'll rip his lungs out, the watching man thought. He put the earpiece back and to his relief it was still broadcasting as Caleb Hayes pulled the door open.

The conversation took no more than a few seconds, but the watching man nodded his approval as he listened to what Morin said to Hayes.

Good, he thought. He wondered how Hayes might react. He was surprised to see Hayes stepping back as if he was going to fight those guys in his house. Then he saw Mike Morin come flying back, driven by the force of Hayes's front kick, and then it all played out pretty much as he had expected it would.

The subsequent action was too fast and too distant for the watching man to see the subtleties of what went down. The fight lasted maybe ten seconds, if that, and then the four meatheads were lying on the ground in immobile heaps.

"Damn..." the watching man said to himself.

He was not entirely surprised. He had done considerable research into Caleb Hayes, as he had into a number of the people of Hopefleet, anyone who didn't fit into the regular mold. He knew about the security company, the years of training in everything from wiretapping to krav maga, Hayes's inability to let anything go. The fact that some secret had driven him from Los Angeles, prompted him to chuck that whole life. What that secret was the man did not know, but he was still looking. If he found out it would likely mean serious leverage.

Caleb Hayes was standing straight, hands on hips, leaning slightly back, a classic posture of catching one's breath.

"You're getting soft," the watching man said. Hauling lobster traps would keep a man's arms strong, and his back as well if he managed to avoid blowing it out, but it would not do much for aerobic fitness.

At last Caleb had caught his breath and stepped back to where Mike Morin was lying on the ground. The watching man pushed his earpiece in tighter, hoped the bat had not fallen too far from where Mike lay for the bug to pick up. He was rewarded with muffled but audible voices.

He listened closely to the conversation, nodding to himself as he did. It played out just as he had hoped. Morin, defiant at first, a pointless exercise since he didn't know anything that would be of value to Hayes, though Hayes didn't know that. A little pressure exerted and soon Morin was singing like a goldfinch, telling Caleb Hayes exactly what the watching man wanted Caleb Hayes to hear.

At last the conversation was done. Caleb Hayes retreated into his house and Mike Morin began the labored process of getting to his feet. The watching man took a few cautious steps back into the woods. He was happy, perfectly happy, with the way this had played out. He didn't care if Hayes had been hurt or not, as long as he was not too hurt to act. In the end it seemed Hayes had not been hurt in the least; only the four yahoos had been, and they had received some real punishment. But the watching man cared even less about that.

The important thing was that Caleb Hayes got the word that Cox was gunning for him, and now he had. And next, Hayes would act on it. He wouldn't call the cops or anything like that. He would act on his own, and he would act decisively. Thoughtfully. The way the watching man wanted him to. Of this, the watching man was sure. Caleb Hayes was the perfect tool for what he had in mind. And like any good tool, he was working just as expected.

Chapter Fourteen

The idyllic weather they had enjoyed for the past week and a half could not last, and it didn't. On the morning after his brief and violent encounter with Mike Morin and his posse, Caleb stepped out of his house and into a morning of thick clouds overhead and the smell of pending rain in the air. Three of the four baseball bats were still lying on the ground; only the one that Mike Morin had wielded was gone. Caleb thought briefly about donating them to some local little league as he fished his truck keys from his pocket.

The rain held off as he drove to the wharf and parked and climbed out of the cab to the welcome sight of Katie Brennan with her usual two cups of Starbuck's joe. They took the skiff out to the *Lisa Marie*, cast off, picked up half a dozen trays of bait, motored out of the harbor. The talk was casual and intermittent. No real need to discuss the work at hand. They had the routine pretty well down.

They were halfway to the trawls set east of Great Chebeague Island when the rain set in. They were under the cabin roof, Caleb steering, Katie seated on the tall chair beside him, both of them drinking their lukewarm coffee and enjoying the early morning boat ride.

"Here we go," Caleb said, nodding toward the rain splattering on the windshield and ruffling the surface of the sea ahead.

"Here we go," Katie agreed. She took the orange coat that matched her oilskins down from the hook and slipped it on. It might have been raining, but it was still warm, so she left it unbuttoned and left the University of Maine ball cap on her head in lieu of more waterproof headgear.

Caleb throttled back as the first of his buoys came into sight. "Time to make the donuts," he said, their now standard line regarding the morning's first trawl. He grabbed up the gaff and hooked the buoy and tossed the buoy line over the snatch block and around the hauler. He took down his own oilskin coat and pushed his arms through the sleeves.

Hand on the short brass shaft that controlled the hauler, Caleb drew the line in, water spraying off the snatch block, and he picked bits of seaweed off the rope as it spun inboard. Katie stood ready, and as the first trap broke the surface she grabbed it and swung it onto the rail and pushed it aft to make room for the next. Through the green wire mesh of the trap they could see a thrashing, snapping pile of brown and orange and green lobsters.

"Nice," Katie observed.

"Nice, indeed," Caleb said. "That trap alone should pay for about twenty seconds of your high-falutin' graduate program."

Katie smiled. "Maybe," she said. She flipped the top of the trap open and began extracting lobsters, tossing the shorts and the v-notches back, placing the keepers in a tray for banding, using the gauge she kept tied by a cord around her waist to measure the ones that were not obviously legal or not.

The next trap broke the surface and Caleb grabbed it and set it on the rail, stepping out from under the roof of the cabin. He was not wearing a hat and the rain fell cool and refreshing on his head and ran down his face. In colder weather it would be damned unpleasant, but on the warm summer morning the rain felt good, and if it kept up it would make for a fairly pleasant day of fishing.

But his mind was elsewhere: on the fight the night before, the words Mike had spoken, voluntarily and otherwise. There were questions he had to ask Katie, but he was not sure how to go about it, not sure how she would react.

"Something on your mind?" Katie asked, and her words took Caleb by surprise.

"What?"

"Something on your mind?" She looked up at him, lobster in one hand, measuring gauge in the other. Her cheeks were ruddy in the rain, her blond hair plastered against her oilskin jacket. "Normally I would have endured half a dozen stupid jokes by now and a thorough interrogation as to what I'd been up to over the weekend. But so far, nothing."

Caleb smiled. "Not *stupid* jokes," he protested. "Do you think

I'm nosey?"

Katie measured the lobster, tossed it in the keeper tray. "No, not nosey. Not in an obnoxious way. Curious, maybe."

"Well, sure," Caleb said, pulling a short from his trap and tossing it flailing back into the sea. "I have to live life vicariously, since I have no life of my own."

"You *could* have a life, you know," Katie said. "There's no reason I can see why you have to be like Gollum, just crawling out of your cave to haul traps."

"Yeah, I suppose I could," Caleb said. This, he realized, was a perfect opportunity to ask the question he wanted to ask, since he also wanted very much to change the subject. "Hey, do you know this guy Howard Cox?"

Katie tossed a Jonah crab into the sea and picked up a bait iron from the bait tray. "He's the selectman, right? The one Billy Caine was talking about? I know who he is, but I don't know him."

"Yeah, that's him. So, do you know if there's any connection between him and Mike Morin? Do they know each other? Related, maybe?"

That question caught Katie by surprise and she paused, bait iron in hand, and looked at Caleb. "Mike Morin? God, I don't know. I don't know Mike Morin very well. You probably know him better than me. Most of our conversation involved him grunting at me. But as far as I know they're not related. And I can't believe they travel in the same circles."

"He never said anything to you about Howard Cox?"

"No," Katie said.

"Huh," Caleb said. "Okay." He spit rainwater, grabbed a lobster out of the trap, measured it, checked for a v-notch, tossed it into the keeper tray.

"Oh, no," Katie said. "Oh no, you don't."

"What?" Caleb asked.

"You're not going to ask me a question like that and then not tell me why you're asking. Uh uh."

He looked up at her. She was holding the empty bait iron in her right hand and while he knew, or imagined, she would never try to impale him with it, it did seem as if was preparing to do just that. He knew he would have to tell her, at least most of it. But he had understood all along that such was the price of asking her about Cox and Morin.

"Well, it's the weirdest thing," Caleb said. He baited his now-empty trap and slid it down the rail as Katie hefted her trap and set it on the transom. "Mike and three of his goombah buddies came by my house last night. I thought they were going to give me a hard time about what happened in the parking lot last week, but instead Mike says Mr. Cox sent him. Said Mr. Cox was sick of my shit and he wants it to stop."

"What shit?" Katie asked.

"That's what I'm wondering. I have no idea."

"Huh," Katie said. She grabbed the next trap as it broke the surface and began the routine of emptying it. This one did not hold quite the bounty that the first one had. "So their showing up at your place had nothing to do with me?" she asked, and Caleb was sure he heard just a touch of irritation in her voice.

"Apparently not," Caleb said. "Apparently it was about this Cox guy. Who I've never met, and have nothing to do with. Though I seem to hear his name a lot, all of a sudden."

"Weird," Katie said. "So these guys showed up to threaten you? Did they try to hurt you at all?"

"No, it was no big deal. A lot of big talk, that was about it. But the whole thing is kind of mystifying."

Katie pulled the near-empty bait bag from the trap, dumped the contents overboard, took up a new bait iron and bag. "So what are you going to do? Are you going to go to the cops? You should go to the cops. Maybe that guy...what was his name...Detective Berry? The guy who questioned you about the dead guy you brought up on the trap."

"Maybe," Caleb answered in a noncommittal way. He waited, wondering if Katie would speculate on some connection between the dead guy and Howard Cox, but she didn't. Which was not too great of a surprise. The LNG thing was pretty tenuous. There were a lot of people in Hopefleet now who had some interest in LNG. Caleb did not see how there could be a connection between Forrester and Cox.

And at the same time he did not see how there could not be.

And he did not see how he could leave this alone, how he could avoid digging deep into Howard Cox to find out why the old man seemed to have this inexplicable interest in him. His former career had left Caleb Hayes with many tools that he could use to achieve that goal, and now he had to decide which he would deploy.

The weather remained variable for the next few days as he and Katie kept to their established routine, hauling traps on a three-night set, baiting, banding, selling the catch. They were landing enough lobsters that Katie was making well above minimum wage with her fifteen percent minus bait and fuel. Caleb was happy about that. He would have felt very bad indeed giving her crap wages after all the hard work she did.

It was Thursday morning when they were fishing trawls by Whaleboat Island. The job was much nicer under the thick overcast than it was in the direct sun, and Caleb had to endure only minor grumbling from his sternman about her fading tan. They broke for lunch at the usual time, shutting the engine down and letting the *Lisa Marie* drift as they ate.

"So," Katie announced after swallowing a meaty bite. "I've been making some inquiries into one Howard Cox, Hopefleet selectman,"

"You what?" Caleb asked, feeling a momentary stab of alarm. "You haven't talked to him or anything, have you?"

"No, no," Katie said, reassurance in her tone. "Dude, I'm like Sherlock friggin' Holmes. Just asking some discreet questions, seeing what I can find online and such. Turns out he's a retired lobbyist, a pretty high-powered guy in Washington, apparently. Summered in Hopefleet, now retired here. On the board of selectmen, as you know. Pretty much what Billy told us that night at the Hopefleet Tavern. As far as I can tell there's no line of connection between him and Mike Morin."

"Huh," Caleb said. "Interesting." Actually she had not told him anything he had not already discovered by using the same resources she had used, and some others from his previous life that she would not have access to or indeed any knowledge of.

His conclusion was the same as hers: what Billy had told them was pretty much accurate. Caleb had unearthed a few things Billy had not mentioned, work Cox had been involved in that was kept as far from the light of day as it could be, and for good reason. It was not pretty. The amiable, gruff Howard Cox was indeed one nasty piece of work.

"So, what's next?" Katie asked. "Go to the police?" Caleb could see she was intrigued by this whole thing.

"No, I don't think it's time to talk to the cops. I don't know what I'd say to them. And I'd just as soon they not go poking around."

"Wow, very mysterious," Katie said. She took a handful of potato chips from a bag and munched them down. "So what, then? You can't just let this go."

"No," Caleb agreed. "No. I'll look into it some more."

"How? I don't know what more you can find. Are you going to go talk to Cox?"

"I don't want to talk to Cox until I have some idea what I'm talking about."

"So how do you find that out?" Katie asked, exasperation creeping in around the edges.

"I'll look into it," Caleb said, hoping his tone would end the discussion without offending his sternman. Which he knew it would not. She continued to munch her chips as she regarded him.

"You're going to spy on him, aren't you?" she said at last. "Are you going to break into his house, bug him or something? Isn't that what you used to do?"

"I told you, I was a bodyguard," Caleb said, "and I had a company that provided personal security. We weren't the friggin' NSA."

"Uh huh," Katie said. She sat more upright, leaned closer to Caleb, as if there were someone on the boat who might be eavesdropping. "So, when do we break into his house?" she asked.

Chapter Fifteen

Two days later they broke into the house of Hopefleet Selectman Howard Cox.

Honestly, Caleb thought, *this stuff is getting too friggin' easy…*

They were kneeling in the bracken, right at the line of trees surrounding the Cox home. He and Katie Brennan, whom he had only with great reluctance agreed to take with him. She had cajoled him, nearly begged him; her desire to be part of this was near insatiable. He had finally given in on the condition that she remain hidden and serve as a lookout of sorts. She would not come into the home. This was a felony, breaking and entering, and he would not have her be a part of that.

He had done plenty of this sort of thing in the old days. It was much harder to pull off in LA and the environs of Southern California. Strange cars parked in affluent neighborhoods for very long drew suspicion, and that would soon bring the police, or at least a patrol from a private security firm. There were close-circuit cameras and motion detectors and very few places to secret oneself.

But this was a brave new world. Most of the Hopefleet peninsula had been stripped of trees by the late ninetieth century, but now it was all but covered in second-growth forest. Building lots were carved out of the woods, trees cut back only as far as they had to be to provide for the desired stretch of lawn. That meant nearly every home in town was ringed by forest, ideal for observing and not being observed. Most people could not even see their neighbors' homes, which cut down dramatically on prying eyes. People tended to park their vehicles wherever the hell they wanted and no one much cared and so the vehicles attracted little notice.

This was part of the reason that Caleb Hayes loved Maine. There was a libertarian quality to it. Not the sort of libertarian quality he associated with the west, Montana and Idaho and such, where libertarianism seemed to mean building a compound to hold off federal troops. No, in Maine people were concerned with their neighbors' well-being, and that generally meant not getting into their business.

"So what, we just wait until he leaves?" Katie asked in a whisper. "How long will that be? Can I watch Netflix on my phone?"

"Friggin' millennials," Caleb said. "No attention span. Shouldn't be too long. He usually leaves in the evening for a few hours." It was dark, the last vestiges of daylight showing over the trees to the west.

"How do you know that?" Katie asked. "Have you been spying on him for a while?"

"No need," Caleb said. He held his cell phone low so the light of the screen would be hidden by the brush and pressed the button on the side. The screen lit up with a series of bar graphs and buttons that linked to other screens. "I put a GPS tracker on his car. Gives me real time and past location data. I know everywhere he's been for the past week. When and where."

Katie leaned over and peered at the screen. "Wow," she said softly. "I thought you said you were just a bodyguard, that you just stood behind people and looked scary."

"Well, sometimes it was more than that. These folks I worked for, they were often very curious as to what the other folks in town were doing. Rivals for parts in movies, producers, directors. People liked to keep informed. We kept them informed."

"And that was legal?" Katie asked.

"No," Caleb said.

"So this"—she nodded at his cell phone—"is part of your big-time spy operation? Equipment from your old company?"

Caleb smiled and shook his head. This was another reason this was all so easy: the availability of modern surveillance equipment.

"Naw," Caleb said, "I just bought this stuff. You know, when I first started doing this kind of thing, none of this stuff existed, except maybe for the government agencies. When we could finally get our hands on tech like this it was unbelievably expensive. I think we spent around twenty grand in late '90s, dollars for something that couldn't do a fraction of what this can do. Now? You just order it over the internet."

"Wow," Katie said again. "Modern living."

They waited for a while more, eyes on Howard Cox's house two hundred feet away across a well-manicured lawn.

"Aren't you afraid he has an alarm or something?" Katie asked after a while.

"He definitely has an alarm. Just had it put in."

"How do you know that?"

"The sawdust from the installation is still on his front stoop," Caleb said.

"So how do you get past that?" Katie asked. "Do you have some kind of high-tech James Bond thing for that?"

"Not really," Caleb said. "I'll just watch Cox punch the numbers in." He swiped at his cell phone's screen and the image changed to a greenish night-vision picture of an alarm keypad.

"What's that?" Katie asked.

Caleb nodded toward Cox's house. "It's an image of his keypad. I put a camera on the porch. Tiny thing. I got it on the internet."

"So when he punches in the numbers we just write them down?" Katie asked.

"Right," Caleb said. He pulled a thin, cylindrical object from his pocket and handed it to her.

"Wow, what's this?" she asked.

"It's a pen," Caleb said. "Get ready to write down the numbers I tell you."

"Oh," Katie said. "Okay." She bent her elbow and poised the pen over her forearm.

"Not on your arm," Caleb said.

"Why not?"

"Because if this goes south and you get picked up by the cops it's not going to help your case to have Cox's alarm code written on your arm."

"Oh, right," Katie said. "Boy, you think of everything."

"It's why I make the big bucks," Caleb said.

They waited another fifteen minutes and then Caleb saw the light in what he guessed was Cox's living room go out and the porch light turn on. He lifted his cell phone close and peered at the image of the alarm's keypad. Since the alarm was new he guessed Cox would not be so quick at punching in the numbers, but he would be quick enough, and Caleb knew he would only get one shot at this.

Across the open ground he heard the sound of the front door opening and an instant later the image on the phone went dark then light again as Cox stepped in front of the camera. A cautious man like Howard Cox would use his body to shield the keypad from anyone watching from beyond the house, so Caleb had positioned the camera to focus on the keypad from the other direction.

Sure enough, Cox stepped around so no one watching from the lawn or woods would see what he was doing, but Caleb's camera had an unobstructed view.

"Ready…" Caleb whispered. Katie had found a slip of paper and was ready to write. Caleb stared at the image of the keypad as Cox's boney finger pushed the buttons. "One…zero…one…two…four…four…"

10, 12, 44, that's your birthday, Cox, you dumb bastard, Caleb thought. He knew that from the research he had done into Cox's history.

"Okay, got it," Katie said, breathing the words. They watched as Cox got into his car and fired up the engine. The headlights went on and Caleb and Katie ducked low as Cox swung the car around and the lights swept the tree line like searchlights in an old prison movie. They were silent as Cox's car moved down the gravel drive and then the red tail lights disappeared from view.

"Do you go now?" Katie asked, her voice just a little louder.

"Not yet," Caleb said. He changed his screen to the GPS tracking app, punched a button. A map of Hopefleet and Brunswick, a tiny red dot moving northeast. "We have to make sure he'll be gone for a while and he's not just running out to pick up a pizza."

Katie nodded and the two of them stared at the small screen, watching the red dot moving away, steadily away, and soon it was clear Cox was heading for Brunswick or some point beyond that. Worst-case scenario, if he turned around now, Caleb would still have fifteen or twenty minutes inside. The house would be empty until then. Cox's wife was still in DC and there was no one else living there. Caleb had made sure of that.

"Okay, time to make the donuts," Caleb said.

He handed Katie a small earpiece with a microphone an inch or so long. She put it in her ear and he put another in his. They had played with the devices earlier in the day and were familiar with their operation.

"You hear me?" Caleb asked, speaking in the softest of whispers.

"10-4," Katie said, her voice coming in through the earpiece. "I read you five by five." She liked that kind of talk, Caleb knew.

"Roger that, you're five by five as well," Caleb said. "Okay, I'm going in. Keep an eye on the house and the driveway and most of all on that GPS tracker. If Cox changes direction in any way that suggests he might be heading back, you let me know."

"10-4," Katie said. She leaned over and gave him a quick kiss on the cheek. "Good luck," she said.

"Thanks," Caleb said, standing, but the kiss, unexpected as it was, had thrown his concentration off a bit. He found his mind sorting through a number of questions and considerations, conscious and otherwise. He physically shook his head to clear his mind, forcing himself to focus only on the matter at hand.

He stepped carefully through the bracken, moving as noiselessly as he was able, which was not very noiselessly at all, but no louder than the wind in the trees or a porcupine trudging through the undergrowth. He paused at the edge of the lawn and looked around. Nothing moving. He stepped from the woods and moved across the open ground.

Caleb had decided against wearing anything so cloak and dagger as black pants or a black turtleneck, but he had put on jeans that were new enough to still be dark blue and a long-sleeve navy blue tee shirt. Not blatantly cat burglar wear, but close enough to help him blend into the dark, and now he was glad he had dressed that way. He felt exposed and vulnerable as he crossed the lawn.

I haven't actually broken the law yet, he reminded himself, *at least nothing worse than trespassing.* That would remain true for the next thirty seconds or so.

He crossed the drive and grimaced at the grinding sound the gravel made under his rubber-soled shoes. Two steps and he was up on the porch and facing the keypad. He retrieved a pair of thin leather gloves from his back pocket and pulled them over his hands.

Some alarm systems, he knew, had apps that would alert the owner if the alarm was disabled, but he was counting on an old guy like Howard to be too uncomfortable with such technology to use it. The fact that he had used his birthday as a password made Caleb even more certain he was right.

10, 12, 44. Caleb punched the numbers into the keypad. He

waited as a series of lights blinked across the top of the unit. He felt the perspiration standing out on his forehead. And then a tiny red light blinked on and the word "Disarmed" appeared on the screen.

Caleb let out a breath. He turned, reached up and pulled down the small camera he had trained on the keypad a few days before. He put the camera in a fanny pack he wore around his waist, a pack for which Katie had already given him a healthy ration of grief and mockery.

The lock on the front door was a decent brand, the sort that a conscientious but profit-minded contractor would install. Good but definitely not top-end, a brand Caleb knew well, and so in less than a minute's work with his steel picks he heard the satisfying click of the lock disengaging. He twisted the doorknob, stepped inside, and shut the door behind him.

"All good?" he heard Katie's voice whispering like his conscience in his ear.

"All good. I'm in, alarm's off. I'm going to look around."

He hoped Katie was not the sort who, in the excitement of the moment, was going to keep blathering over the com system, but to his relief she said only, "10-4," and then fell silent.

The inside of Cox's house was nearly black, save for the little bits of light creeping in from the porch around the curtains and shutters. Caleb reached into his fanny pack and pulled out a pair of night vision goggles and pulled them over his head, then switched them on. Suddenly it was all visible, as visible as day, if the colors of day had all been replaced by greens and blacks.

He stood motionless, save for his head, which scanned side to side. A nice place, art on the walls, good quality furniture that didn't seem to have seen much use. Various lights on the components of an entertainment center flared bright in his lenses. To his right was a coffee table bearing several stacks of big, illustrated books. *The Architecture of Frank Lloyd Wright. Hidden Treasures of the Louvre.* Caleb wondered if they had ever been opened.

As he moved his eyes around the room he listened to the sounds of the house at night. He knew Cox lived by himself, and he would not have set the alarm if there were anyone else inside, but caution was never wasted. Caleb heard the soft hum of the refrigerator running in a kitchen off to the left. He closed his eyes, focused on what his ears were taking in. Aside from the refrigerator there was nothing.

He opened his eyes again, moved quietly across the room. There was nothing in particular he was looking for. He didn't know enough about Howard Cox or why Howard Cox had any interest in him to even guess at what he might find. He just hoped that, like pornography, he would know it when he saw it.

A big arched entry led to the kitchen at the back of the house. Caleb could see stainless steel appliances, marble countertops. He moved on toward an open door on the far wall. He looked in. It seemed to be an office, and that, Caleb guessed, would be the happiest hunting ground.

"Hey, you there?" he whispered into his earpiece. He had told Katie the transmissions on the com system were not necessarily secure and that they should not use names. He had nixed her suggestion they come up with code names instead.

"Yeah," he heard Katie's voice come back.

"Any movement?"

"Target seems to be stopped, somewhere in Topsham," Katie came back.

Target seems to be stopped... Caleb thought. *Oh, brother...*

"10-4. Keep monitoring."

He stepped into the office and looked around. One four-drawer oak file cabinet, a big desk with sundry papers scattered across the top, a cordless phone. In the middle of the desk, a keyboard, a mouse on a pad, a flat screen monitor.

Files or computer? Caleb thought. If he had to abort early, would he rather have what he could find on the computer, or in the file cabinet?

Computer, he decided. He looked over at the windows. The canvas curtains—L.L. Bean, he was certain—were pulled down all the way, which was good. He did not want the light from the computer screen to be visible from outside.

He sat in the desk chair and removed his night vision goggles and gave the mouse a jiggle. The screen burst to life, brilliant in the dark room, and it made Caleb uneasy, though he knew that little or no light would show around the shades. There was a welcome screen, a generic icon with Howard's name under it.

Will you have set a password? Caleb thought. *And if so, will it be your birthday?* He clicked on the icon and the desktop flashed onto the screen. No password needed. The background image was a blue field and on it a photo of a much younger Howard Cox posing with Ronald Reagan. Both men in tuxes.

He's either too dumb to password protect this or too smart to put anything he doesn't want seen on this computer, Caleb thought. He suspected, in all honesty, it was the latter.

He pulled a small, battery-powered external hard drive from his pack, found a USB port on the computer and inserted the business end of the hard drive's cable. There would be time later to sort through what he found; right now he just had to take it all, and so with a few clicks and drags he began the process of copying the contents of Cox's hard drive onto his own.

With that process in motion he stood and opened the top drawer of the file cabinet and began to thumb through the file folder tabs. There was light enough from the computer screen to read the neatly typed labels and he did not see anything that looked particularly interesting. *Taxes, 2010, Taxes 2011, Taxes, 2012, Mortgage Information...* He closed the drawer, opened the next. Nothing of any greater interest than the first.

There has to be something... Caleb thought. Howard Cox was deep into some business he should not be, Caleb was certain, something bad enough that he was seeing threats where they did not exist, sending goons to rough up enemies who were not really his enemies at all. The evidence was somewhere. But it might not be here, in this house.

In fact, if Cox was smart, which he apparently was, it would not be.

"You there?" he asked, soft, into his microphone.

"Yeah," Katie's voice came back. "Target's in Topsham, it seems, still not moving."

"Roger. Looks like I have time to look around some more. Keep monitoring."

"Roger," Katie's voice came back. Caleb looked at the screen. The download was done. He pulled the external hard drive's cable from the computer, put the slim black box back into his pack. He stepped out of the office and put his night vision goggles back on. There were stairs on the far end of the room.

Upstairs, maybe? Caleb thought. *Worth a look. Cox is still in Topsham. I have time.* He knew that that was true. He did have time.

But thinking those words did not ease his tension in the least. Because he knew from experience that this sort of thing could go south, very fast.

Chapter Sixteen

By Saturday evening Howard Cox still had heard nothing and he was sick of waiting. In the old days he would be given constant updates on every project he had in the works. Even if there was nothing to report he would get updates telling him that, so he knew that nothing was being ignored. It was like the stupid music playing while you're on hold—annoying and pointless as it is, at least you know you have not been cut off.

He was not so sure anymore. And he was not the kind of guy to wait by his phone. So he stuck his gun in his coat pocket, left his house, set his new alarm, got in his car and he drove.

He drove northeast, through the town of Brunswick and across the bridge to Topsham, turning into the parking lot that headed a bike path by the Androscoggin River. It was a little after ten o'clock, full dark, and Cox parked in a place where there were no street lamps illuminating the area.

Years of this sort of thing had taught him caution. In the old days, in his office on K Street, the phones and the rooms were regularly swept for bugs, and they had encrypted communications for the really sensitive stuff. But those days were gone, and Cox knew better than to make a call from his home phone or his cell phone, or even from his house. Who knew what sort of listening devices might be hidden there? He could have had the place swept, but if someone was listening he did not want to let on that he knew. A wiretap or bug could be a good way to spread disinformation.

Cox swung the door open and, with a groan brought on by age and the stiffness in his legs, he climbed out of the seat and stood. He was the only one in the parking lot, one of a half dozen such open spaces he chose at random when he had to make a sensitive call. He pulled a pre-paid cell phone out of his pocket and scowled at it.

"Stupid piece of crap," he muttered.

It had always been his habit to use pay phones, rare as they were becoming. But he had grown lazy and fallen into the habit of always using the one by Hannaford. When the stalker had actually called him on that phone it had unnerved him more than he cared to admit, and he knew from that point on he was done with pay phones.

He bought the pre-paid cell phone at Wal-Mart and quickly realized he had no idea how to activate it. He went back and made the kid at the counter do it for him. The problem was that he needed half a dozen of them, at least, and he couldn't make the same kid activate them all without raising eyebrows. So he had gone to every Wal-Mart and Target and Best Buy and every other damned place that sold pre-paid phones and bought one at each store and had whatever pimply faced kid who worked there activate it for him. So now he was set. For a while.

He peered at the face of the phone and punched in the numbers he knew by heart. The man at the other end would not recognize the incoming number, but he would pick up anyway because the line Cox was calling on was the highest degree of private and if someone called it, it meant that the call should be answered.

It was, on the second ring. "Yeah?" the voice said.

"Ryan? It's me, Howard."

"Hey, Howard," the voice said. Ryan Miller, the young hotshot Howard had discovered and groomed to take over the K Street firm when he, Howard Cox, moved on to better things. Cox thought he heard impatience there and it annoyed him. "What's up?"

"What's up? That's why I'm calling you," Cox snapped. "You tell me what's up. You look into this Caleb Hayes bastard? You know who he is yet?"

"We know a lot about him," Miller said. "Failed actor, started as a bodyguard for the actor Trevor Middleton. He and his wife started C&S Security. They specialized in personal security for the A-list crowd, but my people tell me they were involved in a lot more than that. Domestic surveillance, maybe a little muscle work, that sort of thing. All unofficial. He left it all pretty suddenly last year. It's not clear why."

Howard Cox gritted his teeth as he listened. *I know all that, you damned idiot!* he thought. He had been doing some digging of his own, simple, superficial stuff he could do with his now-limited resources.

He had begun digging a week earlier, ten minutes after he got the text message from Hayes. One simple line. *I know what you're up to.*

Cox had stared for some time at that text lighting up his phone like some ill omen. *Caleb Hayes…* he thought. He knew that name, but he did not know why.

And then he had remembered. Caleb Hayes. He was the lobsterman who had brought up Dick Forrester's body. It had seemed an unimportant part of the story at first, this Hayes guy just the winner of some grisly lottery.

But then Hayes sent the text, indicating as clear as if he had carved it in granite that it was not a coincidence at all. How could it be? The message, the implied threat, was unmistakable. And Cox knew perfectly well who would want to send him a message like that.

"I don't care about what the hell Caleb Hayes was doing in Los Angeles," Cox hissed into the phone. "I want to know what his connection is to International Gas and Power."

"Ah, well, that's the thing," Ryan Miller said. "We weren't able to find any connection at all. No big bank deposits, no records of Hayes having any kind of dealing with IGP."

"Bull," Cox snapped. "It has to be there. Who did you talk to?"

"Listen, Howard," Miller said, "we're…is this line secure?"

"Yes, it's secure," Cox snapped. "You think I'm some senile idiot?"

"No, Howard, I don't. Look, we're not without resources, you know that. We have people inside IGP. They've been looking around. Caleb Hayes has no connection with them."

Cox said nothing, just stared off into the dark. Miller was wrong and whomever they had inside IGP was wrong, he was sure of it. Hayes was the guy IGP was sending to lean on him, to get him to change his vote. It was the only explanation. If they found no connection between Caleb Hayes and IGP, it didn't mean it wasn't there, it just meant that Hayes had done an extraordinary job of covering his tracks.

And that meant he was more dangerous than any of the other dumb bastards that IGP had sent so far. If Cox could connect Hayes to IGP, he could expose that connection and the whole thing would blow up in IGP's face. If he couldn't, then he had nothing to use against them.

Not only had Cox found out what he could about Hayes online, but he had actually tracked the man down, watching him from a distance. He had seen him bring his boat up to the dock at Hopefleet lobster, him and his pretty young sternwoman. He was a big bastard, Caleb Hayes, big chest and arms, powerful-looking. With his scruffy light brown beard he looked like central casting's version of a Viking warrior.

But he did not look or act different from any number of lobstermen in the area. He was a local boy, come home. Cox might have concluded that he was wrong about Hayes being an operative for International Gas and Power. Except for Hayes's past work. And Dick Forrester dead on Hayes's trap. And the text.

It unnerved Howard Cox in a way he had not been unnerved before. It actually frightened him, and he would not have thought that was even possible.

"Howard?" Miller's voice came distorted through the cheap phone. "Did I lose you?"

"No, I'm here," Cox said.

"So, like I said," Miller continued, "I don't see any connection here. But if you do, I won't argue. I'm thinking maybe we should send someone to help, look into things. Maybe give you a little backup."

Howard nodded. William Davis at Atlantic Gas and Oil had offered to send protection, but Cox had turned them down. He didn't care to leave any trace of a connection between him and AGO, and he did not trust any meathead that those idiots might send. But someone from his old firm was another matter, and he knew they would be genuinely capable.

"Who you got in mind?" Cox asked.

"You remember Travis, did some work for us overseas?"

"Travis? Yeah, I remember. About six feet tall, black guy, slight South African accent?"

"Yeah, him. He's good," Ryan Miller said.

"Sure, he's good. And he'd blend right in here on the coast of Maine. Wouldn't stand out at all. You putz. Who else do you have?"

Miller was quiet for a second. "Well, there's Marco Scott. I think he's around."

Marco Scott. Despite the vaguely ethnic first name he looked as white as anyone in the lily-white State of Maine. Average height, quiet. Very smart. Brutal and deadly.

"Yeah, he might do," Howard said. "Let me think about it." Before Miller could reply, Cox felt his cell phone, his real cell phone, his smart phone, buzzing in his pants pocket.

"Hang on," he said to Miller. He pulled the smart phone free, swiped the face. Some sort of message coming in through some app he hardly ever used and barely understood. He poked the icon with his finger and the screen opened to show an image, difficult at first to make out. Howard held the phone closer.

It was his office. The image was from some night-vision camera, all green and black, but Cox could see it was his office. And he could see there was someone sitting at his computer. And that person was Caleb Hayes.

"Oh, son of a bitch..." he said as he felt the panic sweeping over him. Through the speaker of the prepaid phone he could hear Ryan Miller, his voice sounding small and distant.

"Howard? Are you all right?"

Chapter Seventeen

The man whom Daniel Finch, Executive Vice President of Resource Development for International Gas and Power, called "the Enforcer" was sitting in the semi-dark of his hotel suite doing the one thing he least wished to do, speaking to Daniel Finch.

"It's one week until the selectmen vote. One week," Finch was saying, his voice not entirely clear, coming through whatever crappy disposable phone he was calling on. "I'm not seeing any indication that Cox is changing his mind on this."

What do you think you'll see? the man thought. *A billboard? Facebook post?* The statement made him wonder if maybe Finch had someone else in Hopefleet working some other angle. That would be just like these corporate idiots, falling all over each other, the left hand not knowing that the right hand is stuck up their butt. So he figured he had better ask.

"What indication do you expect to see?" the man asked.

"I don't know..." Finch stammered. "Something in the paper, some word he's changing his mind?"

That's what I figured. You're panicking, you weak piece of crap, the man thought.

"Listen, I'm rocking Howard Cox's world, okay?" he said to Finch. "He's running scared, and once he's scared enough he'll be plenty open to suggestion."

"But this can't be tied to us, right?" Finch asked. Again.

"It can't be because it isn't. Has no connection to us. Cox just thinks it does. That's what's scaring the crap out of him. He's been around too long to be frightened by any situation he understands. But give him a threat he doesn't understand, an angle he can't figure out, and that scares him. And that's where we're at."

"Okay, so what are you doing now?" Finch asked.

Wasting my time talking with you, the man thought, but instead he answered, "Do you really want to know?"

There was silence on the line for a second, then Finch said, "No, I guess not."

"Get back to me in a few days," the man said and disconnected the line, happy to be free of Daniel Finch, VP, a man in over his head. He set the phone down and turned back to the small array of electronics splayed out on the table in front of him. He smiled, nearly laughed out loud, a thing he rarely did.

*This is so damned easy...*he thought.

When he had first started dipping his toes into these kinds of black ops, years before, the surveillance and other high tech gear had been limited, crude, expensive and very hard to find. Now, anyone with a credit card and internet access could get their hands on the sort of thing only government agents formerly enjoyed.

He pulled his tablet closer, looked down at the screen. The grainy, greenish image showed Caleb Hayes moving cautiously through Howard Cox's home. He had gloves and night vision goggles on. He looked elongated and distorted in the fisheye lens of the surveillance camera.

You've done this sort of thing before, haven't you? the man thought. After the way Hayes had gone through the four bat-wielding goons, and now this, he was gaining a grudging respect for the man. Training a surveillance camera on the alarm keypad had been simple, elegant and effective. He himself had gone to quite a bit more trouble to defeat the alarm, and it embarrassed him a bit that Hayes had found so much easier a solution.

But you didn't think to sweep Cox's house for UHF, did you? If Hayes had done a sweep he would have known that the place was wired like the Iranian embassy.

Sloppy, sloppy...

He watched Hayes step through the living room, scanning the space with his enhanced vision. He saw him move toward the office and then disappear through the door. The man punched a few virtual buttons on the screen and the screen changed to a view of Howard Cox's office as Caleb Hayes stepped into the frame.

Files or computer? the man thought, taking a guess at what Hayes might be thinking at that very moment. He watched Hayes pull Cox's chair up to the desk and sit.

Computer. Good choice. But a pointless choice as well, the man knew. He had been through every inch of Cox's house and he knew there was nothing there. Not that it mattered much to him. He knew what Cox knew. Dick Forrester had been pretty vocal there at the end. And he knew Cox was not so stupid as to risk anything incriminating falling into the wrong hands. In truth, there probably was nothing incriminating. Cox was probably smart enough not to commit anything like that to paper or electronic file.

He watched as Hayes pulled out a hard drive and plugged it into Cox's computer and he nodded to himself. So far Hayes was doing everything he expected he would, everything he himself would do.

The man thought of himself as the Clockmaker. It was how the thinkers of the Enlightenment envisioned God. Someone who created, who set things in motion, and let them play out as they would. He knew better than to try and make people do what he wished them to do. People were too unpredictable, their reactions too variable. He could not make them do what he wanted; he could only set them on the path. The trick was in knowing what paths each of them was most likely to follow.

Caleb Hayes would not go to the police and he would not leave this alone, nor would he confront Cox until he knew what was going on. That much the man had guessed from what he had been able to dig up on Hayes, and so far he had been right.

Howard Cox would not be swayed by any situation over which he had control. He was the manipulator, not the manipulated. But present him with a threat he did not understand, turn up the heat, let him see this was a very real threat indeed, and the man guessed he would start to crumble, would be willing to do as he was told just to make it stop.

Time to turn up the heat, the man thought. He pulled another tablet over until it sat beside the first. The GPS tracker told him that Howard Cox was somewhere in Topsham, Maine, a dozen miles from his home. The man had put the tracker on Cox's car a few weeks before. He imagined Hayes had also put a tracker on the vehicle.

Damn car's going to blow a tire from the weight of all the surveillance gear on it, the man mused. He guessed that Cox had driven to some place where he could make a call on a disposable phone. Cox knew enough to never talk about anything of interest on his landline or in his house. Both Cox's house and car were bugged, but the devices had yielded nothing.

But that didn't matter much either. He had a pretty good idea of who Cox was talking to and what he was saying. He leaned toward the tablet and tapped a few icons, dragged an image across. Somewhere out there, moving at the speed of electrons, a live stream of Caleb Hayes seated at Cox's desk was winging its way toward Cox's phone. In a matter of seconds Howard Cox would be presented with the image of the man he now feared most in the world sitting in his home, screwing with his computer.

The man shifted his eyes to the tracking device. Cox's car was moving, and moving fast. Message received. The man smiled to himself. *This is too damned easy...*

There was one more thing left to do. This was gravy, really. The important part was accomplished, but if he could pull this off it would make things even better. *We'll see if it's amateur hour at Chez Cox*, he thought as he punched numbers into a cell phone.

Katie Brennan had squatted on her calves for as long as she could, which was longer than most people could, but eventually she shifted forward on her knees. The brush was about at eye level, but she could still see the house on the far side of the lawn. The antique-looking lamp over Howard Cox's door made a bright pool of light around the entrance, but the rest of the property was lost in the dark.

In her earpiece she could hear the soft rustling of Caleb moving cautiously through the house. Her eyes moved from window to window, but she could not see any sign of him as he stepped from one room to another.

Good... she thought. This was all going very well, and the idea of pulling it off and getting clean away gave her a bit of a thrill.

Caleb, she well knew, had not wanted to bring her along. That was not because he didn't trust her. She was all but certain of that. It was because he did not want to put her at any risk.

She had argued that she was already at risk. He had told her what he planned to do, which meant she was already an accessory. She wasn't sure that was true, and she could see Caleb didn't really buy it, but in the end he relented—after she had assured him that she would do nothing more than keep watch, and if any danger appeared she would bugger out as fast and as stealthily as she could.

So far she'd enjoyed every minute of it: trying out the com systems and the night vision goggles, parking some distance from Cox's house on a dark, half-abandoned road in the woods, making their way through the trees to a spot where they could observe the house. The GPS tracker and the hidden camera and all the other spy gear that Caleb had produced only added to her sense of playing some elaborate game. It made her even more curious than she had been previously about all the things in Caleb Hayes's past, the things he would not tell her.

She thought about making contact again, checking on Caleb's status, but she had sense enough to know that the less communication the better, so she swept the area visually, strained to hear anything out of the ordinary. She remembered with a flush of guilt that she had not checked the GPS tracker for four or five minutes. She reached out for the phone nestled on the pine needles when she felt her own phone buzz in the back pocket of her jeans.

What the hell? she thought. Her first impulse was to ignore it, but everything seemed quiet at the Cox house and this could be important. Could be Caleb, if something had gone wrong with his earpiece.

She pulled the phone from her pocket, swiped the screen to life. A text message, sent by someone she did not recognize. No picture, just the phone's generic icon. She touched the screen and the message appeared, the only one in a brand new thread.

Hey, Katy, Aunt Jean's in the hospital. Maine Med. Car accident.

What the hell? Katie thought again. She squinted at the message as if that would help clarify it. Her thumbs flew over the virtual keyboard.

Who is this? Who's Aunt Jean?

She sent the message off into the ether and waited. Ten seconds and the phone buzzed again. *This is Tony.*

Tony who?

Tony your cousin Tony.

I don't have a cousin Tony.

Isn't this Katy LaPaglia?

No.

There was another long pause as Tony on the other end seemed to be absorbing this information. The phone vibrated in her hands once again.

How long have you had this number?

About a year.

Oh. I must have an old one. Do you know Katy LaPaglia?

No.

So how did you get her number?

Katie looked at the phone. *Dumb bastard, the phone company gave it to me,* she thought and was about to type just that, perhaps leaving out the dumb bastard part, when she remembered, and a wave of panic swept over her. She dropped her phone, snatched up Caleb's, and swiped the screen on. The GPS tracker showed the same map it had been showing since Caleb had activated it. Her eyes moved to the top of the screen, where she had last seen the red dot that represented Howard Cox's car, but it was not there.

"Oh, shit, oh, shit…" she muttered. She ran her eyes down the screen. There it was. On Route 54. Heading back toward them. Moving fast.

"Oh, shit…" A rush of emotions came over her: anger, humiliation, fear. Like being swept by wind and rain and spray all at once.

"Caleb…" she said, and as she did she wondered why he had not reacted to the expletive she had spoken into the microphone. "Caleb, are you there?" Silence. "Caleb!"

She looked back at the tracker. Cox's car was coming fast, it was a couple of miles away, no more, and had to be doing fifty or sixty on the narrow road that ran down Hopefleet Neck. She felt panic in her gut. She stood, staring at Cox's house, pressing the earpiece into her ear.

"Caleb! Damn it! Caleb!" She spoke in a harsh whisper, as loud as she dared, as if that would make it more likely Caleb would hear her. Nothing. The com was dead.

"Shit!" She looked back at the GPS tracker. Cox was much closer, half a mile from the turn-off onto the smaller road which led to his driveway. She looked back at the house. No sign of Caleb, no sound from the earpiece.

Katie had this vague sense that she should be analyzing options, seeing different scenarios playing out in her mind. She should be cool, she should not panic. But all of that was swept away by the single screaming thought that she had to warn Caleb, that she had to get him the hell out of the house, and now.

From a standing position she broke into a full run, like a sprinter, crashing through the bracken, heedless of the noise she was making. She raced across the lawn, pushing as fast as she could, which was fast, since she generally ran three miles a day after the day's lobstering was done. As she crossed the open ground she felt herself tensing, waiting for the sweep of headlights to come up the driveway and catch her in their beams.

But no headlights came. She leapt over the front steps and onto the porch and wondered if Caleb had locked the door behind him, and if she dared pound on it if he had. Hand on the knob and twisting, and to her relief the door swung open and she raced through, remembering to shut it behind her.

She stopped and stood absolutely still in the dark room. From the porch light filtering in around the shades and shutters she could make out vague shapes: a couch, a chair, an entranceway into the kitchen. No Caleb. Somehow she had thought he would just be standing there. Now she realized she would have to find him.

"Caleb? Caleb?" she said in a harsh whisper, but there was no response. "Caleb?" she said a little louder and she felt herself tense at the sound of her own voice.

Just yell for him! she told herself. No reason not to. But she had been so focused on silence she could not bring herself to do it. She ran off to her left, looked through an open door. The glow of a computer screen revealed an empty office. She ran off in the other direction, looked through the wide entrance to the kitchen. Nothing.

"Katie?" She heard Caleb's voice behind her and she nearly jumped out of her skin. She spun around but she could not see him in the dark room.

"I'm on the stairs, just stand still," he said and she heard the soft sound of his rubber soles on the stair treads.

He has the goggles, she realized. He could see her as if the lights were on.

"What's going on?" Caleb asked. Katie had expected him to be angry with her for abandoning her post, for coming into the house when she had promised she wouldn't. She expected to hear in his words the fear she was feeling. But Caleb's voice was calm, as if he were making small talk.

"The com is down, I couldn't reach you," she said, the words tumbling out. "Cox is on his way back!" She pulled the phone from her pocket, swiped the screen, handed it to Caleb.

"Shit," Caleb said, the first indication that he found the situation at all concerning. "Okay, we have to get out of here. If we have time." They both turned and looked toward the windows that faced the driveway, expecting to see them lit by oncoming headlights, but they remained black. Katie felt Caleb's hand on her upper arm as he guided her around the furniture back toward the front door.

"Shouldn't we go out the back?" Katie asked.

"We have to reset the alarm," Caleb said. He opened the door a crack and peeked out. Katie leaned down and looked past him. Nothing but darkness beyond the light of the porch.

"Okay, wait here," Caleb said. "Lock the door, and when I tell you, step out and shut it behind you."

Katie nodded. Caleb gave one last look around, then stepped through the door onto the porch. He was fully illuminated by the porch light and looked terribly vulnerable and exposed.

With her left hand on the edge of the door, Katie felt with her right hand for the knob. She twisted the button that engaged the lock.

She looked up at Caleb, waiting for the signal. Caleb was facing the keypad, in the very act of raising his finger to tap in the numbers, when the tense silence was ripped apart by gunfire, two quick shots, close, like thunder right overhead.

The muzzle flashes were brilliant in the dark beyond the porch and Katie saw the wood by the keypad shatter into two ragged holes. Caleb staggered back and Katie opened her mouth to scream, but before she could, Caleb pushed her back through the door, back into the darkness of Howard Cox's home.

Chapter Eighteen

For twenty minutes Howard Cox alternated between driving as fast as he was able down Route 54 and keeping his speed at just above the speed limit. He was frantic to get back to his home, the image of Caleb Hayes seated at his computer playing over and over like some kind of GIF in his head. At the same time, if he got pulled over for speeding there would be no chance of catching the bastard, and the irony would be too much for him to bear.

He had no idea how the video had appeared on his phone; he did not understand the technology. He did, however, know perfectly well who had sent it. It had to be that son of a bitch who had been calling him, the one who was clever enough to have called the pay phone. The one who had been pressuring him to change his vote. The one who had sent this Caleb Hayes bastard to threaten him.

He could feel the pressure mounting, like he was sinking down miles under the water, and the weight of it was crushing him.

The familiar bend before the turn-off to Pinewood Lane, his own road, appeared in the headlights and Cox braked and spun the wheel and heard the tires squeal as he made the turn. And only then did he wonder what exactly he meant to do when and if he caught Hayes in his home.

He knew Hayes would not find anything incriminating there because he knew better than to keep anything of that nature in so insecure a place. Should he call the cops? Hopefleet didn't even have a police force; the dispatcher would have to send one of the Cumberland County sheriffs. And even if Hayes was arrested, he would be asked why he had broken into Cox's house and that might lead to all sorts of speculation Cox did not particularly want aired.

And then he remembered the gun.

It was a Smith & Wesson SD9 VE nine millimeter. He had purchased it the same day he got the call on the pay phone from that mysterious bastard, the same day he had ordered the alarm installed, for all the good that had done him. He hadn't owned a gun in years and so he tended to forget about it. But it was with him now. He had put it in his coat pocket, then jammed it down between the car's seats where he could grab it fast. Loaded, ready to go.

His Lexus bounced as the front end hit frost heaves left over from the past spring and his mind ran though the options, and he liked what he was coming up with. Caleb Hayes had broken into his house. Catch him in the act, pop him with the nine millimeter and he wouldn't be telling the cops a damned thing, and the message to IGP would be clear: don't screw with Howard Cox.

And he, Cox, would take no blame. Not for killing an intruder. It would actually bolster his reputation in certain demographics, help him politically. He could look for NRA money, if nothing else.

The mailbox, brilliant white-painted metal, seemed to bob at the far end of his headlight beam, and Cox pressed the brake until he was going slow enough that he dared turn the headlights off. He slowed even more as the darkness enveloped him, but then his eyes began to adjust to the light of the bit of moon showing, enough that he could see the pale road ahead.

He drove for another twenty feet, then pulled over to the side of the narrow road. He would have to approach cautiously, quietly, if he hoped to catch Hayes in the act. Once he'd dropped the bastard he'd go back for his car, bring it into the driveway so it would not look to the police as if he had been stalking the man. He hoped Hayes had a gun on him—that would help—but the fact that he had broken into the house was justification enough for whacking him.

Cox reached up and switched off the dome light so it wouldn't go on when he opened the door. He pulled the gun from between the seats and chambered a round, then pushed the door open and stepped out.

The night was quiet. Rural Maine quiet. Cox moved down the driveway, stepping carefully, keeping to the shadows at the edge of the woods that lined the way. His own footfalls made almost no noise at all, and he strained his ears as he walked down the narrow dirt road. Nothing, beyond the normal sounds of the night.

Twenty more feet and he heard the soft thud of feet on wood, the sound of his own door being opened then closed.

"Damn!" he whispered to himself. He had to catch Hayes inside. If he was outside, running away, it would be harder to justify deadly force. Maybe he could claim Hayes was attacking him. That could work. But it would certainly be easier if he plugged him inside the house.

He picked up his pace, and as the tree line opened up to the yard and the house beyond, Cox stopped and surveyed the scene. He could see no one moving. If the sound he had heard was Hayes leaving, he was gone by now. Cox lowered the Smith & Wesson to his side and moved out across the lawn, sure he would not be seen with the light from the porch obscuring anything in the darkness beyond.

His eyes searched the windows of the house as he approached. It was just as he had left it, no lights on, nothing out of the ordinary that he could see. The closer he came, the more certain he was that he had missed his chance, that Hayes had buggered off half a minute earlier. He started walking faster still.

And then to his surprise the door cracked open and Caleb Hayes, massive and dressed in dark clothes, stepped out on the porch.

"Crap!" Cox said to himself. Hayes's appearance on the porch took him completely by surprise, so certain had he been that the man was gone. He broke into a jog, closing the distance to the porch fast, and brought the gun up to a firing position. Hayes was going for the alarm keypad, probably going to re-arm it. It crossed Cox's mind that it would not be ideal to gun him down on the porch, but he did not have time to really examine the ramifications of that decision. He stopped, aimed, squeezed off a double tap. The sound of the shots was staggering, the muzzle flash looked like a flamethrower.

The bullets punched two ugly, jagged holes in the wall just to Hayes's right, and Hayes seemed to stagger back from the point of impact, but Cox could see he had not hit the man.

"Damn it!" he shouted out loud, and in the wake of the gunshots his own voice came soft and muffled, like he had cotton in his ears. He should not have missed from that distance, he was a better marksman than that, but he had just reflexively raised the gun and pulled the trigger, had not paused even a second to collect himself and take decent aim.

He saw Hayes stumble back and Cox kept the gun raised, expecting Hayes to leap from the porch and bolt for the woods. He could still drop him, then think of some story to tell the cops. Hayes would be dead and thus in no condition to contradict the tale.

But Hayes did not bolt for the woods. He turned the other way and pushed into Cox's house, slamming the door behind him.

"Oh, you son of a bitch!" Cox shouted. His mind raced through the possibilities. Either Hayes would race for the back door or he would lie in wait and kill Cox as Cox came through the door. Which one?

He did not think it would be the second option. Most people had a genuine aversion to killing, even bastards like Hayes, and would not do it unless there was no other choice. Most likely Hayes would be running out the back door before he could come in the front. But maybe he could catch Hayes inside, in which case he would get a second chance to kill him in the act of breaking and entering.

Howard Cox had never killed anyone, though on several occasions he had given orders that he knew would result in someone's death. And he had no real aversion to personally killing someone when doing so was in his interest. He took a moment to collect himself, then headed for the door to his house, moving as fast and quiet as he could.

The gunshots, the gray cedar shingles blasted apart, startled Caleb more than he would have cared to admit. He stumbled back. Instinct told him not to run across the open ground but to go back into the house. Instinct, and the need to keep Katie from blundering into the line of fire.

He turned and rushed for the door, pushing Katie back inside and closing the door behind them. In the dim light he saw Katie start to race for the far side of the room, heading for the back door, and he lunged out and grabbed her arm and stopped her. The shock of the gunfire was starting to fade and Caleb's mind was working again. They could not go running around with an armed man after them. They had to turn him into an unarmed man.

Caleb pulled Katie back to him, then wheeled her around and positioned her against the wall just beyond the front door. He reached down and felt the door handle. Katie had locked the door as he had instructed, but now he unlocked it. Partway across the room, at a right angle to the couch, stood an armchair with a side table and reading lamp. Caleb crossed the room in three long steps, knocked the table and lamp over and upended the chair, as if someone had upset those things in a panicked rush through the dark room. He moved back quickly, standing beside the door where he would be hidden when it opened.

Then it was quiet again, an ugly, unnatural quiet. The crickets had stopped. Everything seemed to have stopped. He could hear Katie breathing beside him and then heard her suck in a breath and then let her breathing settle into a normal and silent rhythm.

What is that son of a bitch doing? Caleb wondered. Was he circling the house, hoping to catch them going out the back? Was he calling the cops? Caleb didn't think so. He didn't think Cox was the sort to want cops prying into his business. He would not want Caleb blathering about Cox's hiring Mike Morin and his goons to work him over. It would be much better for Cox to kill an intruder in his home, even if he would have to find a way to explain the bullet holes on the porch.

Then, from the other side of the door, the faintest of sounds, the slight groan of the porch as it took up the weight of someone stepping onto it. Then silence again. Cox was coming through the front door, but he wasn't stupid enough to come barging in. He was taking his time. He knew he had to make this count.

Nothing moved for what seemed a very long time, and then Caleb was aware of another step, and another. He seemed to feel the change in pressure as much as hear the sounds of the step. Then, to his right, and down by his waist, he heard the doorknob turn, and in one quick move the door swung open. Not far enough to hit Caleb where he stood, but close. And then again, nothing.

The light from the porch spilled into the room, partially illuminating it, and Caleb braced himself. Cox was no more than a foot or so away on the other side of the door. He could smell the man's cologne. Cox would have his gun raised and he would be looking over the barrel as he swept the room with his eyes. He would see the overturned chair and table and Caleb hoped he would reach the conclusion he wanted the man to reach.

And apparently, Cox did. There was another footfall, soft as a sheet of paper hitting the floor, and the barrel of the silver semi-automatic pistol appeared beyond the edge of the door. It hovered there, as if it were levitating.

And then Cox took another step and the rest of the gun was visible, lock, stock and barrel, and then Cox's wrist was there and Caleb made his move.

Caleb's right hand lashed out and clamped down on Cox's wrist, held it in a vise-like grip as he jerked the older man into the room. His left hand clamped down over the barrel. He twisted the gun sideways and back and wrenched it right out of Cox's hand, the surprise and Caleb's strength of arm combining to make the move all but effortless.

He heard Cox gasp and stammer, as if the words were crowding his mouth and he couldn't get them out. Caleb pulled him the rest of the way into the room. He was little more than a silhouette in the dark room with the porch light illuminating him from behind.

Until that moment it had been all business to Caleb, but now, suddenly, with Cox's wrist in hand, he felt the rage well up, as he had when he had seen Mike Morin lying on the path to his house. The anger seemed to explode inside him, surprising him, driving him. It was a foreign thing, like nothing he had experienced before. He could shatter Cox's arm with little effort, cripple the man, kill him if he wanted to, and in that blinding moment he wanted to very much.

Then he thought of Katie, standing in the dark behind him, thought of how she would react if he broke this old man, if he inflicted such pain for no more reason than his wanting to. And he knew then he would not do it.

All that flashed through Caleb's mind in a second, less than a second. He released Cox's wrist, bent low, and drove a shoulder into the man's midriff. He wrapped an arm around Cox's thin waist and stood, coming up with Cox draped over his shoulder.

Two steps and he was at the back of the couch and he unceremoniously tumbled Cox off his shoulder and onto the cushions on the other side, the back of the couch effectively screening Caleb and Katie from Cox's sight, at least until he managed to sit up.

Caleb wheeled around. He could just see Katie, still standing where he had put her, her eyes wide. He pointed toward the open door and she nodded and ran and Caleb ran after her, trying to mask her footfalls with his own. Cox had probably not seen her, had not even been aware that there was someone besides Caleb in the house, and he wanted to keep it that way.

They came off the porch at a full run and pounded across the lawn back toward where they had been watching in the woods. Caleb still had Cox's gun in his left hand and as he crashed into the tree line he flung it away into the bracken. They were ten feet into the trees when Caleb called in a strangled whisper, "Hold up!"

Katie stopped, turned, stepped back to where Caleb stood. Caleb tilted his head back, gasping for breath, and he could not help but notice, with a touch of irritation, that Katie was not even breathing hard. He turned back to the house to see what Cox was doing, which was the other reason he had wanted to stop. No lights had been turned on and Cox was still inside, as far as Caleb could see.

He's being cautious, Caleb thought. He was sure he had not hurt the man. Even someone older and less robust would not have been injured by that drop onto the couch. But Cox knew that Caleb had his gun, and he did not know what Caleb wanted, so he would not be stupid enough to come chasing after him.

They watched the house for another minute, but there was no activity at all. Caleb still did not think Cox would call the police, but it was possible. Time to go.

He turned to Katie, nodded toward the woods. He led the way back down the vestige of a path they had followed from Pinewood Lane. They broke out onto the road and jogged the half mile to where Caleb's truck was hidden. They climbed in and for a moment they just sat, breathing, looking out the window into the dark.

Caleb turned and looked at Katie and Katie looked back at him.

"Well...damn," Caleb said. He could think of nothing else to say.

Chapter Nineteen

Caleb started the engine and with some reluctance switched on the headlights. He was pretty sure they had made a clean escape, but after hours of maximum stealth it was hard to do something so visible as illuminate their getaway vehicle. He put the truck in reverse, backed out of the overgrown road on which he had parked.

They drove in silence, each processing the events of the evening. Caleb wondered what was going on in Katie's head, if she was frightened, angry, confused, exhilarated. When he thought the time was right, he would ask, in a roundabout way, work his way into a place where he could gauge her reaction. But not just then. It was still time for quiet, time for processing.

Katie had parked her PT Cruiser in the parking lot of the Grange Hall, a place where enough people parked that it would not attract notice, but Caleb understood that he could not simply drop her off and bid her goodnight. The evening had been too traumatic for that. There was too much to consider and work through for him to send her home as if they had just finished an uneventful day of lobstering.

Instead, he pulled into the parking lot and stopped by Katie's car. "Why don't you follow me back to my place?" he said, and Katie nodded.

She hopped out and a moment later Caleb was again driving down Route 54 with Katie's headlights bright in his rearview mirror. He had no reason to think that Cox had recognized him as the shadowy figure in his house, and no reason to believe his own house was any less safe than any other place. More safe, probably, with the hardware he had stored there. He turned onto Ash Point Road and then into the driveway of his home by the water. He turned off the ignition and let the quiet settle over him.

Caleb had been shot at before, but not often. Four times, maybe? Still, he had been in plenty of scrapes, many of which he had escaped only after suffering some injury, laceration or ugly bruises, broken ribs, a tooth knocked out once. He understood the gamut of emotions that welled up as the adrenaline drained away and the reality of what nearly happened asserted itself.

Katie pulled into the gravel drive and stopped next to his truck. She switched off her lights and engine. Caleb opened his door and hopped down to the ground as she was stepping out of her car. "Rough night," he said. "Can I buy you a drink?"

Katie smiled and Caleb was glad to see it. If she could still smile then she was not too traumatized by the whole thing. "God, yes," she said.

Caleb found his house key on his ring and put it in the lock and twisted it. Until the past few days he, like most people in Hopefleet, had never locked his door. But with some of the ugly things that had been brewing he thought it might be time to start, at least until he had all this straightened out.

He flipped on the lights and tossed his keys and the fanny pack in a boat-shaped bowl on a small table by the door and led Katie into the living room. He turned to ask her what she wanted to drink, found her staring up at the high ceiling, down at the wool Berber carpet, and over at the various framed pictures on the walls, some prints of paintings Caleb loved, some originals.

"Wow," she said. "This is your house?"

"Yeah," Caleb said, surprised to realize that she had never been there before. "Is it okay?"

"It's lovely. Beautifully done."

"You're surprised?"

"I don't know," she said. "Maybe I was expecting paintings of wolves or motorcycles on black velvet. A Hooters calendar. Pyramids of beer cans."

"Thanks a lot," Caleb said. He was not sure if she was kidding or not. He chose to believe she was.

"You decorated it yourself?" Katie asked.

"My mother helped, I'll admit," Caleb said. "She has wicked good taste. What are you drinking?"

"Vodka tonic?"

"You got it," Caleb said, crossing over to the bar and pulling out the requisite ingredients. Katie stepped up to the plate glass windows and the French doors that led out onto the deck, black now with the dark of night, and reflecting her image like a full- length mirror.

"What do these windows look at?" she asked.

Caleb poured tonic into their drinks, squeezed a quarter of a lime into each. "They look out over Hopefleet Sound. If there was light enough you could see my lawn's only about a hundred feet to the edge of the water."

"Really? Wow," Katie said. "You must have had one hell of a year lobstering to afford this."

Caleb smiled and handed her her drink and they touched glasses. "Hardly," he said. "I think I told you I sold out my half of my security company to my ex. We'd built a fairly profitable business. I made out pretty well."

In truth he had made out quite a bit better than pretty well, but that was something he kept to himself. He loved lobstering, he needed the release, and he didn't want Katie or anyone to think he did it as some sort of hobby.

"Here, let's step out on the deck," Caleb said, pushing the French door open. The night was lovely, the air warm and pungent with the salt water and the woods nearby. But more of a concern to Caleb was the fact that, standing in the living room in front of the windows, they made a perfect target for anyone in the woods with a rifle.

He didn't necessarily think an assassin would be lurking there, but caution was what had kept him and his clients alive so far, and by now it was ingrained in his DNA. But he didn't mention those concerns. He did not want to alarm Katie or make her think he was paranoid.

"Sounds good," Katie said. She stepped through the door and Caleb followed, steering her off to a corner where the light from the living room did not reach. They leaned on the rail and looked out into the dark, and as their eyes adjusted they could just make out the dark band of water beyond the sloping lawn, the tall pines standing like sentinels near the shore. Caleb's ears strained for any sounds out of the ordinary, but there was nothing beyond the brackish water tumbling along the shore and chirping of crickets and frogs.

Caleb took a long sip of his drink. *Just friggin' relax*, he said to himself. He realized he was holding his shoulders tense and he let the muscles ease away.

"So," Katie said. "Think Cox will call the cops? Will we be in jail by this time tomorrow?"

Caleb had been waiting for the question. It had to be asked, the night's events had to be dissected. A "post mortem" is what they called it in the old days, a review after an operation.

"No, I don't think so," Caleb said. "If he wanted to do that he would have called them once he realized we were in his house. Instead he tried to shoot me. I don't think he wants the cops poking around."

"What about the gunshots? You don't think the neighbors might have called the cops?"

"No," Caleb answered truthfully. "This is Hopefleet. A couple of gunshots at night are nothing to get too worried about."

"People in Hopefleet spend a lot of time shooting each other?" Katie asked.

"Not each other," Caleb said. "Just shooting."

Katie nodded, took another long pull of her drink.

"I think we'll be okay," Caleb said. "Cox didn't get a good look at me, and he never saw you at all. He might guess it was me, but he has no proof. We have to be alert, see how he reacts. But I don't think we're in much danger. Either from Cox or the police."

Katie nodded again. Took another drink. Her expression suggested that she believed him, which was good, because he had meant what he said. Even if he had been putting the best possible spin on it, it was still the truth as he saw it.

She leaned her elbows on the rail around the deck and looked out toward the water. "Beautiful," she said in a soft voice.

For just an instant Caleb thought she was talking about herself, because at that moment he found himself reflecting on just how beautiful she was. The indirect light from the living room was falling over her tanned face and her thick hair, blond but streaked with variegated shades by the sun, her tight-fitting shirt and jeans that accentuated her form.

"Beautiful night," Katie added.

"It is that," Caleb agreed.

Katie set her drink down on the rail, straightened and looked at him. Caleb straightened as well, looking down into her face, her eyes bright in the dim light. He had a feeling about what would happen next, a good feeling, a cautious feeling, because he knew he might well be wrong. Then Katie reached up and put her arms around his neck and he leaned down and he kissed her, soft and a bit tentative, then more boldly as she kissed him back.

He wrapped his arms around her back and drew her in and their kissing grew more vigorous. Caleb could feel the muscles in her shoulders, the strength in her core as he held her close. He knew what was happening here. He had experienced this before, this rush of passion in the wake of some traumatic event, the come-down from some adrenaline-pumping adventure. He knew what this was and he did not care.

Katie took her arms off his neck, drew back a bit and pulled the hair tie from her ponytail, letting her long hair cascade down her shoulders. She gave her head a slight shake. Caleb had rarely seen her with her hair untied and the effect was electric. He reached out for her once again, pulled her close, pressed his lips against hers.

For some time—Caleb had no sense for how long—they stood on the deck, lost in the dark and each other's arms. He ran his lips over her neck and she tilted her head to the side and he could hear her breathing grow just slightly more pronounced.

He could smell the scent of her soap and shampoo and sunblock, a bit of lavender and coconut. He could detect just a trace of pogie and redfish, a scent that even multiple showers could not eliminate completely. But Caleb did not mind at all. He had only good associations with that smell.

He ran his hands down her back and over the well-defined curve of her waist. He grabbed handfuls of her shirt and tugged the tail end free of her jeans and eased the dark cloth up her midriff. She released him again and held her arms up and he pulled the shirt up and over her head.

They explored one another for some time more, then Katie pulled Caleb's shirttail from his pants and he pulled the shirt over his head with a deft and practiced move and tossed it aside. They pressed close, the delicious feel of skin on skin making Katie gasp a bit as Caleb once again ran his lips along her neck. His hands traced lines over her back and his fingers found the clasp of her bra, but she pushed him away, just a bit, and whispered, "We should find some place more private than the deck. Before the mosquitos find us."

She was right. Mosquitoes were a prime hazard to outdoor lovemaking in Maine in the summer. "I think I know just the place," Caleb whispered.

He took her hand, led her back into the living room and over to the stairs leading to the bedroom in the loft above. He switched off the lights as he crossed the room and the house fell into darkness. With the lights off, Caleb knew they would be invisible to anyone watching from the darkness outside, and he felt his tension ease.

The master bedroom was large, nearly a quarter of the floor plan, with a king-sized bed and a skylight above which filled the room with the bluish light of the moon and stars. Caleb stopped at the edge of the bed and turned to Katie and put his arms around her again and kissed her again and she wrapped her arms around his neck and kissed him in return. Once again his fingers found the clasp of her bra and he unhooked it and relished the familiar feel of the tension coming off the elastic. He eased it away and ran his hands over her now-bare back.

They tumbled onto the bed and soon all of the night's events, and all of the miserable things that had led up to them, were no more, blotted out by the pleasure they took in one another, all of their trouble, all of their worry, happily, gladly, forgotten, for that time at least.

When they were finished they found themselves sprawled at an odd angle to the direction of the bed, so they realigned themselves, Caleb's head on the pillow, feet toward the foot of the bed, Katie's head on his chest. They lay like that for a long time, quiet, savoring the feel, like the aftermath of a fine and satisfying meal.

Caleb ran his hand over Katie's flawless skin. He had expected the usual lobsterman's tan lines, face and arms burned dark brown, the rest pasty white, but she seemed to be pretty evenly tanned all over. He found that intriguing and intended to ask her how she managed to achieve that look. At the same time he found himself embarrassed by his own starkly chocolate and vanilla flesh.

After a while, when Caleb was pretty sure Katie had fallen asleep, he tried to ease himself out from under her, but before he could she made a little guttural noise and adjusted her head and ran her hand over his chest. He stroked the hair on her head and ran his hands over the long strands splayed out over his stomach.

"So," Katie said at last, her voice a soft and sleepy murmur.

"Sternman with benefits? How does that work for you?"

Caleb smiled. "It's an unusual arrangement," he said, his voice soft like the night air. "In most cases I wouldn't be much interested, but right now I think it's working very well indeed."

"Hmm," Katie said. She pushed herself up on her elbows, looked him in the eyes, then bent her head down and kissed his chest. "Me too," she said.

They made love again, and soon after Katie was unequivocally asleep, mouth open, her breathing deep and regular. Her hair was spread out on the pillow, her face relaxed and expressionless, the shape of her body clearly defined under the light sheet she had pulled over herself. She was lovelier than anything Caleb had witnessed in a long, long time.

Slowly, carefully, Caleb eased himself out of bed and crossed to the closet on the far side of the room. The space was huge, designed for the sort of people who had extensive wardrobes and shoe collections. Caleb's pathetic smattering of clothes looked comically anemic. His wardrobe consisted mostly of jeans and chamois shirts and flannel shirts and cargo pants. He had one suit, custom made by Carroll & Company of Beverly Hills, left over from his former life and worth three months' catch when the fishing was good.

He reached up to the shelf and found a small key hidden far back. He took it down and crossed to the end of the closet. It was dark, only a touch of light filtering in from the skylight, but that was enough. He inserted the key into the lock of a gun safe he'd had built into the wall and swung the heavy metal door open. It was not the most secure arrangement, but he had considered it overkill when he had installed it. Now he wasn't so sure.

Caleb could see almost nothing, but his hands knew where to go. His fingers brushed over his Beretta 92FS and wrapped around the grip. Hundreds of hours on the range had made that weapon an extension of himself, as much a part of him as his hands and feet. He reached back into the gun safe and found a magazine, felt the satisfying weight of the ten rounds it held.

He slipped the magazine into the grip. Normally he would push it in quick and enjoy the bold click as the slim metal box seated itself with machined perfection. But he did not want to wake Katie, or worse yet alarm her if she recognized that sound, so he slid it in slowly and pressed it with his thumb until he heard the soft snap of it locking in place.

Caleb held the gun down by his side and stepped out of the closet and walked silently back to the bed. He set the gun down gently on the nightstand, between the digital alarm clock and the novel he was midway through, a series about Vikings in medieval Ireland, a great book. Then he climbed carefully back into bed. He shuffled close to Katie until he was spooning her. He wrapped his arm around her and she snuggled close and made a soft, sleepy sound. Caleb closed his eyes and a minute later he fell into a deep and profound sleep.

Chapter Twenty

Howard Cox remained on the couch long after the sounds of footfalls and Caleb Hayes crashing through the woods had faded away and the crickets had taken up their song again. Then he stood, a bit uncertain. He shut the front door, turned on the lights in the living room and crossed straight to the bar. He needed a drink. Scotch on the rocks. With a twist.

These sons of bitches are really turning up the heat, he thought. He knew perfectly well the amount of money that was on the table here. It came as no surprise that International Gas and Power would play this kind of hardball. What was surprising was that they were playing it better than he was.

Who the hell is Caleb Hayes? Cox thought. In the past, if someone like Hayes had been sent to shake him up, Cox would have had a dossier an inch thick on the man by now. He would know who he worked for, why he was playing the game he was playing, his weaknesses, pressure points. He would hit back at the people who sent him, call in favors, make it clear that he could hurt Hayes's people more than Hayes could hurt him.

But now he had nothing.

It could not be a coincidence that Hayes had owned and run a high-end security firm, but none of Cox's people could find any connection between that and IGP. Maddening. He couldn't threaten IGP with exposure if he had nothing to expose. He could try bluffing, but they would never fold that easily.

I want one word from you. One syllable. 'Aye.' That's all you need to say when it's time to vote on the contract with IGP. That's what the voice on the pay phone had said. Was that Caleb Hayes? The man on the phone had suggested he was not Hayes, that Hayes was the one who would be coming for him.

"Ah, damn them all to hell!" Cox said slamming his glass down hard on the bar. *Maybe I should just give the hell in*, he thought. *Just do what they want. I don't need Atlantic Gas. I can do what I need to do without them…*

It would make all this go away. One vote. He didn't really have any convictions one way or another about LNG, or about any other damned thing for that matter. One didn't become a wealthy and influential lobbyist by having values or convictions. Those things only got in the way.

"No, son of a bitch, no!" Cox said out loud. He might not care one way or another about LNG or Hopefleet or any of that, but he sure as hell cared about Howard Cox and he would not allow himself to be intimidated or manipulated. Give an inch in that direction and it was over.

His mentor, decades before, had told him a man was like a knot in a piece of rope. It couldn't be loosened as long as it stayed drawn so tight it was like a solid thing. Work at it enough, get just one part of it to give in the smallest way, and soon the whole thing comes apart.

"Fuck them," Cox said. He would not give, not in the slightest. He crossed the living room, turning on more lights as he did, and stepped into his office. He could see in his mind the image on his phone, Caleb Hayes sitting at this desk, and it only made him madder and more resolved. He sat down at the desk, pulled open the drawer and snatched up one of half dozen prepaid cell phones he had left. He powered it up, pressed the talk button. Cell phone coverage was not always all that strong in Hopefleet, but the dial tone sounded steady enough.

Cox looked at the small clock by the computer monitor. 11:38 p.m. *Too damned bad*, he thought. He punched numbers into the phone. It rang at the other end, over and over, but Cox was certain there would be no voicemail picking up.

On the eighth ring it was answered, the voice tired and agitated. "Yes?"

"Ryan? Cox here. Sorry I cut you off earlier. I had an incident."

"Oh, yeah?" Ryan Miller sounded more awake now, which was good. "You okay, Howard?"

"Yeah, I'm okay. But listen, these sons of bitches are really turning up the heat, and they're being smarter about it than I would have given them credit for. I need to stop screwing around, I need to hit back hard."

"Are we talking about Marco Scott?" Miller asked.

"Yeah, is he available?"

"I'm pretty sure he is," Miller said. "I talked to him a few days ago. You want me to send him up to Maine? He can be there tomorrow."

Cox had made this late-night call to Ryan Miller before he had really thought this through, but he was thinking now. He had tried every avenue he knew to discover who Caleb Hayes was and what game he was playing, but he could find nothing. If intrigue was not going to work, maybe a more physical approach was in order.

Marco Scott was a tough bastard, dangerous, but with the look of a guy who would hardly dare drive his Prius over the speed limit. He could do what Howard Cox needed him to do.

"Yeah, send Scott up here," Cox said. "You know what to tell him. I'll give him the details when we make contact. I've got this Hayes bastard trying to put a scare into me, so I need to show him what fear is all about."

"Okay," Miller said. "I'll get him up to you." Cox took the phone from his ear and was about to press the button to disconnect when he heard Miller say, "Oh, yeah, one other thing...." He put the phone to his ear again.

"What is it?" Cox asked.

"I forgot. I just got a call from a guy I know in Los Angeles. About that guy Caleb Hayes. He thinks he's found something."

As Caleb woke he became aware of a sound he could not identify, a soft swooshing sound, not too far off. He opened his eyes and rolled his head to starboard. The bathroom door was open and he could hear water running in the sink, but from that angle he could see only the sliding glass doors of the granite-tiled shower.

Then Katie stepped into the doorframe, a toothbrush working in her mouth, toothpaste foaming around her lips, making her look rabid. She smiled around the toothbrush, then disappeared back into the bathroom and Caleb heard her spitting into the sink, then rinsing and spitting again. She reappeared in the bathroom door.

"I used your toothbrush. I hope you don't mind," she said.

"I don't mind," Caleb said. "*Me toothbrush es tu toothbrush.*"

Kate was wearing one of the few dress shirts he had brought with him from Los Angeles. Like all his better clothes, it had been handmade by a tailor in Beverly Hills. Vanity was only part of the reason for the tailor-made clothes. It was hard enough to find clothing in his size on the coast of Maine, all but impossible on Rodeo Drive.

The shirt was white silk, multiple sizes too big for Katie. The tail hung down to mid-thigh and the sleeves had been rolled up to her elbows. At her current wage of fifteen percent of the catch minus fuel and bait it would have taken Katie a month and a half at least to afford that shirt, if she didn't spend a penny on anything else.

The sight of her in it, however, gave Caleb a reaction that was both instant and profound. He raised an arm and beckoned her closer. She crossed the room with that strong, feline walk he knew so well, more mountain lion than house cat. She stopped at the edge of the bed.

"Aren't we supposed to be out sending poor, innocent lobsters to their doom?" she asked.

"The governor called," Caleb replied. "He said the lobsters get a twenty-four-hour reprieve of sentence."

Katie climbed onto the bed and walked over to him on hands and knees, stopped when her arms were straddling his chest. "I expect you to make me breakfast, you know."

"I'll be happy to make you breakfast," Caleb said. He grabbed her under the arms, lifted her and tossed her aside, rolling over so that he was above her now. "I'll even help you work up an appetite."

An hour later Katie was seated at the polished granite counter of the island in Caleb's kitchen, a mug of coffee between her hands. She had shed Caleb's dress shirt and was wearing the quasi-burglar outfit she had worn the night before.

"Okay," Caleb said, "I'm taking orders."

"Excellent," Katie said. "Do you have eggs?"

"Yup. Fresh from the farm stand on 54."

"Sweet. I'll have two eggs over easy. Do you have any decent bread?"

"Sourdough. From Borealis." Borealis was one of the surprising number of top-quality boutique bakeries springing up in Maine.

"Not a Wonder Bread guy. Good. I'll have two slices of toast, with butter, and any bacon or sausage you might have."

"I'm impressed," Caleb said. "I had always pegged you as a fruit and yogurt for breakfast type."

"Midwest farmer's daughter, remember?" Katie said.

Caleb turned to his short order cooking tasks and Katie took her coffee and wandered out onto the deck, enjoying the view in the light of day. The tide was ebbing and the water was piling up around the various mooring balls anchored in the stream and holding the boats still on their moorings so their bows pointed unwaveringly upstream. She came back in just as Caleb was sliding the over-easy eggs onto the plate with the deft and expert use of his spatula. He arranged bacon and toast beside them.

"Beautiful," Katie said.

"Thanks," Caleb said. "You mean the eggs? The view? Me?"

"You, of course," Katie said, sliding onto the stool and taking up the knife and fork.

Caleb cracked two more eggs for himself and let them slide into the still-hot frying pan. "*Manga, manga,* don't wait for me," he said. He heard the click of Katie's knife and fork on the plate and his mind wandered back to their earlier tussle in bed. In the full morning light he had in fact detected tan lines, suggesting the past use of a not terribly modest bikini, but the lines had been faint and not terribly distinct.

"Tell me," he said, turning from the stove, "how is it you manage to avoid tan lines, like the rest of us get?"

Katie had piled a big heap of eggs on her toast and smiled at him as she did. "Wouldn't you like to know," she said.

Caleb nodded. He would like to know. But he could see he was not going to find out from her.

They finished breakfast, cleaned up, poured more coffee. "Okay," Caleb said, "one last little bit of tidying up to do." He left Katie in the kitchen, went through the side door into the garage. He never bothered to park his truck in there during the summer, and so now the space was crowded with a couple of kayaks, an old skiff his uncle had given him, a workbench overflowing with tools, piles of rope and buoys, at least two outboard engines he knew of and sundry lawn care equipment.

The back wall was lined with shelves and Caleb worked his way through the clutter until he reached the far corner. He had left his old life in California, but some of the accessories from that life, such as the tailored suit and the Beretta 92FS, he had retained. Why, he was not entirely sure. Something had told him he might need those things again, and it seemed that that instinct had been right.

He took down another of those artifacts from his old world, a black metal case the size of a lunchbox, and brought it back into the kitchen. He set it on the island's granite counter. He pressed the "on" button and was happy to see there was still life in the battery.

"Okay," Katie asked, looking around his shoulder, "what's that?"

Caleb didn't answer. He fished a small pad of paper and a pen out of a drawer in the kitchen, wrote, *OSCOR Green hand-held spectrum analyzer.*

"And that is…?" Katie asked.

Caleb wrote, *Sweeps for bugs. Listening devices.*

Katie nodded. Caleb waited as the spectrum analyzer booted up. When he had first moved into the house he had swept it to get a baseline of RF signals. He had had no rational reason to do so, but old habits, particularly those associated with safety, privacy and protection, died hard. And now he was happy they had never quite expired.

A series of colored spikes, like an EKG gone mad, appeared across the small screen and Caleb scrolled through the various frequencies. He picked the unit up, walked around the ground floor with it, eyes focused on the undulating lines. Nothing. The house was clean.

"Okay, good," he said, setting the unit down and turning back to Katie. "Looks like no one's listening in."

"Glad to hear it," she said. "And I'm glad you didn't tell me last night that someone might be."

Caleb shrugged. "I don't know why anyone would. But then, there seems to be a lot going on I don't understand. So let's see if last night's wild adventures were worth it."

Katie raised an eyebrow.

"I mean the adventures in Howard Cox's house," Caleb clarified. He retrieved the small external hard drive from the boat-shaped bowl where he had dumped the fanny pack the night before and sat at his desk in his small office. Katie took a chair from the dining room table and sat beside him. Caleb brought the computer to life, pushed the hard drive's wire into a USB port and brought up a list of the files stored there.

For a long moment the two of them looked at the titles that appeared on the screen. There were ten with the file name "Tax Info" and the year, going back a decade. There was one called "Pictures." Caleb opened it. It contained pictures. Not a lot of them. Howard Cox and people he took to be Cox's kids and grandkids. Caleb took out his phone and clicked off pictures of each as he scrolled through.

There was a file called "Videos" which contained nothing at all. None of the other files yielded anything of greater interest.

"Either Cox isn't into anything he shouldn't be, which I doubt," Caleb said, "or he's smart enough not to put it on this computer, which seems more likely to me."

Katie nodded. "Here, this looks more promising," she said, pointing to a file labeled "E-mail." Caleb clicked on it and two subfolders appeared, labeled "Received" and "Sent." He clicked on "Received" and a long list of e-mails appeared on the screen, saved in order of the date they had arrived. He began to randomly open messages. E-mails from his kids, e-mails from friends, invitations to Cox to visit people in other states, chatty e-mails from people who seemed like they must have been longtime friends. Still nothing of interest.

He closed it, clicked on "Sent." Another list, much like the first. Subject lines with a wide range of innocuous-sounding titles. Then Caleb's eye caught an e-mail that stood out from the others. The subject line read simply "Printing," which was more businesslike than its fellows, and there was an attachment which few of the other e-mails had. Caleb put the pointer on that e-mail and double clicked.

The e-mail was brief and there was nothing chatty about it. Caleb read:

> *Have to place this order now. Looks like we'll need more lead time on this than I thought. This will have to be dealt with before I announce. Could you people handle payment directly and discreetly? It will make things easier in the long run. The attached was sent to this e-mail by mistake. Please reply to the other e-mail address you have for me.*

Caleb frowned. Katie said, "What do you think that means?"

"Don't know," Caleb said. He glanced up at the heading, saw the name of the recipient and he felt a punch of excitement. "Holy shit," he said softly. "Look at who this was sent to."

There was a pause and then Katie said, "R. Forrester.... Okay, why is that name familiar?"

"Because he's the dead guy who was caught up in my buoy line," Caleb said. "The day I hired you. Remember? Billy, the soil sample guy, he told us about him."

"Right," Katie said. "Holy shit."

"Check out Forrester's e-mail address," Caleb said. "R.forrester@ago.com. Atlantic Gas and Oil. Cox was e-mailing him at his business e-mail. And telling him to reply to some other e-mail address he was apparently using. Like I thought. Whatever Cox was doing here, he wasn't using his home computer to do it."

"So what's the attachment about?" Katie asked.

Caleb put the pointer on the link, double clicked. A PDF opened up, a long one, twelve pages. The top of the page showed a company logo, Twin City Printers, a printing company in Lewiston, thirty miles away. Below that it read,

To: Howard Cox
From: Twin City Printers
Re: Order for campaign material.

Caleb scrolled down. The text that followed outlined an order Howard Cox had apparently placed with the printers: thousands of bumper stickers, yard signs, hand signs, posters, buttons. Initial design concepts were included below. Total bill, $73,541. Fifty percent down payment due immediately.

"Scroll down," Katie said. Caleb worked the wheel on the mouse and the page scrolled up and the next one took its place. It showed what appeared to be a mock-up of a bumper sticker, bold letters with an artistic wave separating them top to bottom: *Howard Cox, Governor. A Man We Can Trust.*

They were silent for a moment, then Katie said in a low voice, "Ho-lee crap. That son of a bitch is going to run for governor."

Caleb nodded. "And look who he's sending the bill to? Atlantic Gas and Oil. That makes his position on this whole LNG thing a little more understandable, doesn't it?"

"He's doing all this just so AGO will buy him some bumper stickers?" Katie asked.

"I'm sure it's more than that. This is just one e-mail that went to the wrong place. My guess? AGO is pumping some big bucks into Howard Cox, enough to make this worth it to him."

"We have to tell someone about this," Katie said. "Like Alex at the *Hopefleet Buoy*? He'd love this. And we have proof!"

"We have proof we gained through breaking and entering," Caleb reminded her. "Not sure we want to make that public."

"Right," Katie said, and she looked away as if another thought had come to her. Caleb waited, watched her profile as she considered what she wanted to say. She turned back to him.

"About that," she said. "I have a confession to make. I think...I really screwed up. You know, when I was supposed to be watching the GPS to see if Cox was coming back? I got a text. And I took it and I got distracted. That's why he caught us. God, I'm sorry, Caleb." He could hear her voice catch in her throat as she spoke.

"It happens," Caleb said. "Happens to people with more training than you. Who was the text from?"

"I don't know," she said. "That's how I got distracted. I guess it was someone looking for the person who had my cell number before me."

"Is the text still on your phone?" Caleb asked.

"Yeah," Katie said. She fished her phone out of her back pocket, brought up the thread of messages, and handed the phone to Caleb. Caleb took it and read.

Hey, Katy, Aunt Jean's in the hospital. Maine Med. Car accident.
Who is this? Who's Aunt Jean?
This is Tony.
Tony who?
Tony your cousin Tony.
I don't have a cousin Tony.
Isn't this Katy LaPaglia?

Caleb stared at the messages for a moment. He said nothing at first, then asked, "This came in just before Cox started heading back our way?"

"Yeah," Katie said. "He used my name, but spelled it differently, and that's what threw me off."

The messages went on. *How long have you had this number? About a year. Oh. I must have an old one. Do you know Katy LaPaglia?* As if someone was trying to distract her.

Caleb felt a sick, hollow feeling in his stomach, the ugly sensation that came along with a final, complete and terrible realization. He looked at Katie and shook his head.

"We're being played," he said. "We're being played by an expert. Big time. And I still have no idea why."

Chapter Twenty-One

For the next hour, through another pot of coffee, they probed and examined the question. They walked down by the water, stood on Caleb's small private dock, because it was a beautiful spot on a beautiful morning and because, spectrum analyzation notwithstanding, Caleb was not entirely convinced his house was not under some sort of surveillance.

They sorted out what they knew. Cox was running for governor, and Atlantic Gas and Oil was apparently underwriting the campaign. Cox was voting against the efforts of AGO's chief competitor, International Gas and Power. Cox did not want anyone to know that because it might look like a quid pro quo. And it might look like a quid pro quo because that was exactly what it was.

How Caleb Hayes tied into any of this neither of them could imagine, and all the ideas they batted back and forth did nothing to clarify that mystery.

The only business that Caleb knew well besides security was the entertainment business, and he knew how rough they could play, with billions of dollars on the line. The big boys in the extraction business, he was learning, played even rougher still.

"Whoever killed Forrester and put him on my buoy line wanted to get me tangled up in all this," Caleb said, "if you'll forgive the choice of words. Why, I can't imagine. But we don't have to play their game. If we ignore them, they'll go away."

"Maybe you're saying that for my benefit, but I know you don't really believe it," Katie said. "For instance, I noticed that a nine millimeter semi-automatic appeared on your nightstand, as if by magic."

"Not a 'pistol' but a 'nine millimeter semi-automatic,'" Caleb said. "You know your guns."

"Don't try to change the subject," Katie said. "That was a lucky guess. But yeah, I do know something about guns. I grew up on a farm, remember?"

"Yeah, but wasn't it some kind of peacenik organic farm?"

"It *was* an organic farm," Katie said. "But my dad still liked to kill things. Deer and pheasants and stuff. We had a .22 and a 30.06 and a twelve gauge. And a .357 revolver. I've never shot a semi-automatic."

"Huh," Caleb said. "You like shooting?"

"I do," Katie said.

An hour later Caleb's truck turned off Route 54 onto a dirt road that skirted the fields surrounding one of many nineteenth century farmhouses in Hopefleet. The house stood on a rise overlooking the fields, a classic, rambling structure consisting of a big house, a little house, backhouse and barn, the way they built them in that part of the world two centuries earlier.

"This guy's an old friend of the family," Caleb said, pointing toward the house as they bounced past. "He set up a shooting range on his back fields, lets anyone he likes shoot there. First time I ever shot a gun was here."

They drove up over a grassy hill and down through a gap in a stand of trees to another wide, overgrown meadow, invisible from the main road. Caleb stopped at a cleared place where a couple of crude wooden tables stood in front of a mowed stretch two hundred yards long. Posts at fifty-foot intervals had been driven into the ground starting thirty feet from the tables and stretching to the far end of the range.

They climbed out of the truck and Caleb took out the two guns he had brought along: the Beretta, zipped into a soft, fleece-lined bag, and an AR-15 type rifle, what was generally referred to as an assault rifle, in the hard case made specifically for that weapon.

They started with the Beretta. Caleb showed Katie how to extract the magazine, how to work the slide to be sure there were no rounds in the chamber, how to insert the magazine again and chamber a round. He tacked a target up at thirty feet. They donned eye and ear protection. Caleb went first, putting ten rounds through the target in a fairly compact circle in the middle of the paper. He fetched it, leaving a new target in its place.

"Nice shooting!" Katie said, looking at Caleb's shredded target.

"Thanks," Caleb said. "But actually I kind of suck. A really good shooter would have had a much tighter grouping. I probably should have had more time on the range, but really, shooting people was not a big part of the security picture. In fact we tried to avoid it. Usually I wasn't even armed on an assignment, or any of my guys, either. The personal combat stuff was a bigger part of it."

Katie went next, taking her time between shots, getting a feel for the recoil of the gun. She put six of the magazine's ten rounds through the target, and Caleb said that was very good for her first time with an unfamiliar gun, which it was.

They went through two more magazines each and then Caleb put the Beretta back in the lined bag and flipped open the hard case of the AR, a .308 with three twenty-round magazines.

"Holy cow, you could start a war with that!" Katie said as Caleb lifted the gun out of the foam lining in which it was nestled. "How often did you use that bodyguarding?"

"Never," Caleb admitted. "I bought it 'cause I wanted it, mostly. It's made by a company in Maine, Windham Weaponry. It's mostly folks who got downsized when Bushmaster left the state. This is their Model R20FFTM – 308."

"Uh huh," Katie said. "You know, none of that means anything to me."

"That's okay," Caleb said. "It's a fun gun to shoot. That's all you need to know." He set a target seventy-five yards away, an easy shot for an experienced shooter, and put five rounds through it. He showed Katie how to work the gun, how to aim the weapon, and let her fire off the next five rounds, none of which found the target.

"I guess I suck worse than you," she said.

"No, no. You just got to get used to it," Caleb said. They plugged away for another hour, burning through a few boxes of ammo, and by the end of that time Katie could put most of her rounds through the target, though not in any pattern that might be considered "grouping."

"That is bitchin'!" Katie said, handing the empty .308 back to Caleb. "And I thank you for the bullets, but I should get going. I better take advantage of this surprise day off to get some stuff done."

"If you must," Caleb said. They packed the guns away, picked up the last of the brass, then climbed into his truck. He turned it around, the big tires raising dust clouds that wheeled away in the breeze, and he drove her to where they had left her car in his driveway.

"Will I see you tonight?" he asked as she reached for the handle of her door.

"I don't think so," she said. "I need to get some sleep."

"Okay, understood," Caleb said, and he was suddenly afraid that their night together had been nothing more than the fall-out from their mutual adrenaline rush, that in the wake of that, Katie Brennon would revert to being just a sternman, their brief romance written off as an anomaly. Or, worse yet, a mistake to be regretted.

Then she leaned over and kissed him and it was not the sort of kiss that signaled a cooling of passion or interest, and Caleb felt the sweet rush of relief.

"Oh dark thirty, at the dock," he said as she leaned back. She smiled, a lovely smile.

"Oh dark thirty. Roger that."

She hopped down from the cab and approached her car and Caleb wondered if he should have insisted on starting it for her while she stood in the shelter of the truck. And then he wondered how he had managed to get that paranoid, and then he wondered if he was indeed being paranoid or just sensible. But her car started up and did not explode. She gave him a little wave as she backed up, turned and headed down the drive, leaving Caleb sitting in the cab of his truck watching her go.

With Katie gone, Caleb cleaned his guns, mowed the lawn, which he had been ignoring, fired up the string trimmer and went after the tall grass where the mower could not reach. He went inside and had a beer. There were two coffee mugs on the counter, left over from that morning, and the sight of them made him happy.

Then, yielding to his growing though justified paranoia, he fished out a few wireless, high-definition security cameras he had stashed in his garage and mounted them at various vantage points around his property. He set up motion detectors as well, which would send a message to his cell phone if anything broke the invisible beam. It was a risk—he might be driven crazy with birds or animals setting them off—but they were chest height for a man and so would miss most woodland creatures.

That done, he had another beer. He turned on the television, stared blankly at it, then turned it off. He got in his truck and drove to the Hopefleet Tavern and had another beer and then another. He spent the evening talking to lobstermen with whom he had a casual acquaintance. They talked about boat prices and engine maintenance and yard fees and shedders and deep holes where morons set their trawls right on top of trawls already set there, and of the epic tangles of gear they had known.

Caleb liked the talk. He liked not thinking about the many things he had been thinking about, things that he should be thinking about but did not want to.

Finally, around 10:00 p.m., an hour that was late for lobstermen, early for most normal human beings, the crowd broke up and Caleb made his way home. He had another beer. And then he slept.

She was there in the parking lot the next morning, arriving before him as usual, the two big cups of coffee in her hands as usual. He took one, thanked her, took a deep sip. He was feeling a little shaky.

"You're welcome," she said. "But I have to say, I missed breakfast at *Chez* Hayes this morning."

Caleb smiled to match her smile. "Plenty more where that came from," he assured her.

The next hour and a half was taken up with the business of lobstering—getting bait on board, filling bait bags, motoring out to where their trawls were set. It was not until the first trap of the day had been swung onto the wash rail that Katie asked, "Any more thoughts on what's going on? Or maybe I shouldn't ask. Have you swept the boat for bugs?"

"We're good with the engine running," Caleb said. "We should watch what we say when the engine is off." He looked over at her and she looked vaguely surprised and he realized she had been kidding when she asked that.

"Really?" she said.

"Really," Caleb said. "*Semper Vigilantus*, that's my motto. I even say it in Latin, so you know it's serious."

"'Always vigilant'," Katie translated Caleb's made-up Latin. "I'll remember."

"I've been trying to drill down to who we know has some connection to this," Caleb said, "the connection between me and Howard Cox. I've only come up with one person I know of for sure."

"Is it Howard Cox himself?" Katie asked.

"No, not him," Caleb said. "I've never had any contact with him, I don't know if he knows me from Adam. You're not going to like this much, but I was thinking of your not-so-secret admirer, Mike Morin."

Katie looked up quick from the trap she was baiting. "Mike Morin? How the hell do you figure that?"

"He came by my house, him and his yahoo buddies, to beat the crap out of me. He told me Howard Cox ordered it. That's what he was told to say. But whether Cox did that himself or not, someone paid Morin to put me on Cox's trail."

"You don't look like you got the crap beat out of you," Katie observed.

"Yeah, it didn't go the way ol' Mike had hoped it would. But that guy, the guy who got Morin going, he's the one we need to talk to. So that means I need to question Mike Morin some more."

Katie frowned. "I see your point. I don't like it, but I see it. So where do you find him to talk to him?"

"He usually sets his traps out around Hopefleet Sound, right? And around Minot Island?"

"You want to go talk to him now?" Katie asked, surprised. "I'm not so sure about that."

"It'll be fine," Caleb assured her. "No place for him to run, none of his buddies around except his sternman."

"He probably has a gun on his boat," Katie said.

"Yeah, but he'll probably have a gun any place I find him. You stay on the *Lisa Marie*, drive the boat while we talk. It'll be fine. Let's haul the two trawls we have here and then we'll go find the man."

They hauled, emptied, baited and reset the traps they had set in that part of Casco Bay, then Caleb took up his binoculars and scanned the horizon to the east. He didn't think he would get lucky enough to see Morin's boat among the dozen or so currently visible to him, and he was right.

"Okay, we have to go hunt him down," he said, lowering the binos, his eyes still set on the distant water.

"Hey, Caleb, you remember that *Semper Vigilantus* thing?" Katie said.

"Yeah?"

"Well, you might want to *vigilantus* this." He turned to see her pointing north. A half mile away he could see a boat coming at them. It looked to be a Boston Whaler or some similar thing, a seventeen-footer with a steering console, a nice boat. It was coming fast, riding its bow wave and heading pretty much in their direction.

"Could be some guy heading to Portland for lunch," Caleb said, though he didn't really think so. With all the water around them, the course that the boat was on made it pretty clear it was coming for them.

"So, what do we do?" Katie asked. Caleb could hear the tension in her voice, the effort to keep it at bay. "Head out of here?"

"Yeah, let's get underway," Caleb said. "But if this guy wants to catch us, he'll catch us. This old wooden tub's not going to outrun that thing."

Caleb stepped up into the cabin, put the engine in gear and pushed the throttle forward. The *Lisa Marie* began to gather speed, but by then the Whaler was no more than a hundred feet off. There was one person aboard that Caleb could see, a guy at the console who throttled back as he made a wide turn toward the lobsterboat. He was half standing and waving his arm to get their attention and Caleb had to admit there was nothing particularly threatening in the look of him. He eased the *Lisa Marie*'s throttle back.

"Get ready," Caleb said to Katie.

"For what?" she asked.

"Don't know," Caleb said. "Just be ready for it."

The Boston Whaler came sweeping around the *Lisa Marie*'s stern and the driver brought it neatly alongside, coming to a dead stop with a five-foot gap of water between the two boats.

"Oh, man," the driver said. "I thought I was going to miss you."

"Well, you nearly did," Caleb said. "But what can we do for you?" His left arm was outstretched, resting on the davit that held the snatch block, drawing the man's eye away from his right hand, which was holding the grip of the Beretta he was wearing in a holster in the small of his back, under his orange oilskins.

"We're renting a cabin on Whaleboat Island," the man said, nodding off toward the north. "I was hoping I could buy some lobsters from you. Save me a real pain in the neck if I don't have to take the boat over to Hopefleet."

Caleb considered the man. He was wearing cargo shorts and a faded button-down shirt, a Tilly hat, like a flat-brimmed canvas fedora, popular among recreational sailors. He had something of a disarming smile, though Caleb did not intend to be disarmed by it.

"I think we can do that," Caleb said. "We've got about twenty in the tank, don't we, Katie?"

"About that," Katie said. Caleb could see she was relieved by the stranger's apparently benign mission.

"I was looking for a dozen, if that's all right," the man said.

Caleb did a quick calculation in his head. "Say…six fifty per lobster?"

The man's expression brightened. "Works for me!" he said.

"Okay, why don't you come aboard?" Caleb said.

The man in the Whaler tossed a couple of white rubber fenders over the gunnel and, with a twist of the wheel and a nudge of the throttle, he brought the boat smoothly alongside. Katie snatched up his bow line and made it fast to a cleat. The man jumped easily aboard and made off the stern line, then pulled a plastic bucket and a drawstring bag from his boat.

"I brought my own bucket," he said.

Katie took the bucket, lifted the top off the lobster tank and began to fish out lobsters. The man walked over, peered down into the swirling water. He looked up, looked around the boat. "You know," he said, "I've been visiting Maine for twenty years and I realize I've never been on a lobsterboat."

"It's pretty exciting," Caleb said. "Romance of the sea and all that." He was standing against the console under the cabin roof. His hand was off the grip of his gun, but his stance and his coveralls were arranged in such a way that it would take him a second, no more, to have the weapon out.

Katie paused, a flailing lobster in her hand. "A dozen, right?" she said.

"Yeah," the man said.

"Eleven…twelve…" Katie counted. She set the bucket down and put the lid back on the tank.

"Excellent," the man said. "So that's six fifty per lobster, so I owe you…."

"Seventy-eight bucks," Katie said. The man made an expression like he was impressed.

"She's in college," Caleb said. "Very smart."

The man smiled and picked up his drawstring bag and loosened it. Caleb reached around and took the grip of his gun in his fingers and loosened the weapon in the holster. The man pulled out a wallet, flipped it open and counted out seventy-eight dollars. He handed the money to Katie, dropped the wallet back into the bag and extended his hand.

"I'm Walter Barnes, by the way. I'm from Hartford. Connecticut. Just up with the family and some friends."

"Katie Brennan, pleased to meet you," Katie said, shaking. Walter Barnes turned to Caleb, extended his hand. Caleb let go of the Beretta and shook as well. "Caleb Hayes."

"You guys usually fishing around here?" Walter asked. "I'm just asking because, if you don't mind, I'd love to hit you up for more lobsters tomorrow. I try to get as much as I can when I'm in Maine."

"We should be hauling a couple of trawls a little north of here tomorrow," Katie said before Caleb was able to give a more noncommittal answer. "Always happy to sell retail."

"Excellent! Thanks! And maybe I'll see you tomorrow." Walter Barnes put the bucket aboard the Whaler, tossed his drawstring bag onto the passenger seat and climbed aboard. Katie cast off the bow and stern lines, and with a wave, Barnes brought the boat away from the *Lisa Marie*'s side and throttled it up onto a plane, heading back toward Whaleboat Island with a long, straight wake stretching out behind.

"He was a nice guy," Katie said. She looked over at Caleb. "What?" she said, and Caleb realized he was not keeping his expression as neutral as he had hoped.

"Yeah, seems like a nice guy," Caleb said. "I guess I'm just getting paranoid. Now, let's go find our good buddy Mike Morin."

Chapter Twenty-Two

Daniel Finch's home in White Plains featured several acres of manicured lawn that rolled down to a shallow, water-lily filled pond, which itself covered half an acre. The pond was man-made, but it looked as if it had been there since the end of the last ice age, thanks to the infusion of many tens of thousands of dollars in landscaping.

The home also enjoyed excellent cell phone coverage over every square foot of space, and Daniel Finch took advantage of both those things, the space and the cell coverage, to get as far from the house, his wife, his kids, the nanny, the cook to make a call on yet another in a long succession of prepaid phones.

His last conversation with the Enforcer had been pretty damned unsatisfactory. Finch was not a man used to being intimidated, but that calm voice, with its understated tones of menace, did just that. He was used to people giving answers quickly and unequivocally, but the voice on the phone spoke only in enigmatic and truncated phrases. Finch was coming to hate this son of a bitch even as his need for the man's services increased by the hour.

Get back to me in a few days... That was what the Enforcer had said as he cut their last discussion short. And now it had been a few days and Finch wanted answers and he was feeling less and less comfortable making calls from his office. It had occurred to him before that his office might not be entirely bug-free, and he was not thinking in terms of cockroaches.

He had no way of knowing for certain. The only way for him to check for listening devices would be to call International Gas and Power's security division; his superiors would never allow an outside company to conduct an electronics sweep. But it was pointless to have the IGP boys check because they would have been the ones who had bugged the office in the first place, done so on orders from the offices a floor above Finch's. No one was to be trusted. So Finch took two of his cell phones home.

He punched in the number. The phone rang once, twice, and then it was answered and the voice said, "Yeah?"

"It's Finch. What's the latest?"

A pause, meant as an irritant, Finch was certain, and it worked. "He's running scared now," the voice said. "I'm pretty sure he thinks the lobsterman is working for IGP. But he can't prove it, because the guy isn't."

"That's it?" Finch asked. "The vote is less than a week away."

"I know," the voice said. "There's more. I'm pretty sure the lobsterman has discovered Cox's connection to AGO. He broke into Cox's house, spent some time snooping around."

"He's not going to expose him, is he? We want Cox to change his vote, we don't want him to go down."

Finch had been growing more doubtful of the Enforcer's ability to persuade Cox to change his vote, so he did some digging into what would happen if Cox simply didn't vote at all. If, for instance, he was exposed as corrupt or met with some fatal accident.

He could find nothing about that in the selectmen's bylaws, but other language he found suggested that the two remaining selectmen could not make this decision on their own. Best-case scenario, there would be considerable argument and in-fighting. Worst case, they would have to wait until another selectman was elected and hope he or she would side with IGP. Too much risk. They still needed Cox's vote.

"Anything the lobsterman has," the Enforcer said, "he got by breaking and entering, so no, he's not going to spread it around. But I can still use it to turn up the heat."

"So what makes you think Cox is on edge?" Finch asked. "That he might be persuaded to change his vote?"

"He brought in some muscle," the Enforcer said. "He's done trying to finesse this, now he's going to play rough. It's a last resort. When that doesn't work, he'll fold."

Finch frowned. The Enforcer always sounded so sure of everything, like he was describing the plot of a novel he himself was writing. At first Finch had taken great comfort in that, but now he was starting to wonder if the Enforcer wasn't just blowing smoke.

"All right," Finch said. "I'll call for an update in a few days." He pressed the off button and disconnected the call. He snapped the phone shut and stared out over the pond. There was a light breeze blowing and it was making the surface ripple. It looked like the ocean might look when viewed out the window of an airplane from a very high altitude.

I think you might be full of crap, he thought. He was talking to the Enforcer, imagining what he might say to him. But of course he would never actually say it. Not because he was afraid of the man, but because he knew better than to reveal his real thinking to anyone. Once he did that, he lost all leverage. Better to let the Enforcer think he still had his trust, and act otherwise.

It might be time to bring this up to another level of negotiations, he thought next. The Enforcer was down there in the dirt, placing bugs and tracking devices, spying on the players, breaking into their houses. That wasn't the schoolyard Daniel Finch played in. He played in corner offices and executive suites, he made things happen in air too rarified for the likes of the Enforcer to breathe.

And now, he knew, it was time to start making other arrangements. What the Enforcer was doing might work, and it might not, and Daniel Finch knew he had to have his ass covered in either event. He flipped the phone open again and began punching numbers.

Caleb Hayes pushed the *Lisa Marie*'s throttle forward and spun the wheel to starboard. Walter Barnes in his Boston Whaler had put half a mile between them by then, as he made his way back to Whaleboat Island.

The lobsterboat began to gather way, the bow lifting with the building speed, and the air began whipping in around the cabin sides. Katie took her usual spot on the wash rail, squinting into the wind, her long, blond ponytail whipping behind her, her UMaine Huskies hat pulled low.

They passed Hackett Point, the southernmost tip of Hopefleet, to port, and Ram Ledge, and the wide mouth of Hopefleet Sound opened up in front of them.

There were a dozen lobsterboats in sight, some moving fast like the *Lisa Marie*, making their best time to the next trawl, some motionless, save for their rocking in the light swells as the crews aboard hauled the traps up from the bottom. Some were motoring in wide arcs as they swung around on a northeast to southwest line to set their trawls again.

"See him anywhere?" Caleb called over the throb of the engine and the rush of the wind. Katie looked up and shook her head, but Caleb knew she had not really been looking and his question was as much a suggestion that she look harder than it was a real query. She took the hint, stood, and grabbed up Caleb's binoculars.

She stepped aft, clear of the cabin, and swept the water off the starboard side. She turned and swept the water to port. "There!" she shouted, pointing just forward of the port beam. Caleb followed her finger. He could see the boat a half mile away. The green freeboard looked black, but he could make out the gray topsides and the unusual, boxy trunk cabin.

Bait & Bitch, Caleb thought. *That's what she's called. Ol' Mike Morin's a class act.*

"Okay, let's see how close we can get before he sees us," Caleb shouted. "Engage the cloaking device!"

Katie looked at him, a weary expression on her face. She stepped forward, under the cabin roof, stood close to him and leaned against the console, staring out through the salt-stained windscreen.

Lisa Marie closed to a quarter mile and Caleb backed off the throttle. They could see Mike Morin and his sternman were emptying and baiting traps and there was no sign that they had noticed the *Lisa Marie* closing with them. But there was no chance that Caleb would get all the way alongside unnoticed.

He slowed further, reached up and took down the microphone of his VHF radio. He keyed the mic, said, "*Bait & Bitch, Bait & Bitch,* this is *West Wind, West Wind,* please switch and answer 69."

Even from that distance Caleb could see Morin look up in surprise to hear his boat being hailed. He stepped into his cabin, reached up and took down his radio's mic. Caleb heard his voice come crackling over the speaker. "This is *Bait & Bitch* switching and answering 69."

Caleb reached up again and pressed a preset button that switched his radio from Channel 16, the hailing and emergency frequency, to 69, one of the frequencies open for general marine communication. He heard Morin say, "This is *Bait & Bitch* on 69."

"Hey, Mike!" Caleb said brightly into the radio. "This is actually

Lisa Marie. I'm just off your starboard side, heading your way."

There was a pause as Mike digested this, no doubt trying to match the man to the boat name. And then he figured it out.

"Fuck you," he said.

"Whoa! Don't swear on the radio, man, it's against FCC regs," Caleb said. "Look, I just need to talk to you."

"Yeah? Bite me. You copy that?" Mike's voice responded.

"No, dude, really, I just need to talk. Okay? I'm gonna come along your port side."

Morin, Caleb knew, was in an awkward position, his trawl half on the boat, half in the water. He could just dump the whole thing and run, but then he would have to come back later and finish emptying and baiting the traps. And if he just tossed it all overboard it might well be a tangled mess by the time he returned.

But neither, apparently, did he care to have Caleb Hayes aboard his boat. The *Lisa Marie* continued to close with *Bait & Bitch*, but Morin made no reply.

Not sure what to do, are you? Caleb thought. He turned to Katie. "Okay, you take the helm, bring us around his port side."

"Is he going to let you on board?" Katie asked.

"I plan on going, whether he does or not," Caleb said. "My guess is he's going to try something stupid, like gunning his engine just as I'm jumping aboard, so be ready for that."

Katie nodded. "Okay," she said, "but let the record show I think this is a friggin' bad idea."

She took the helm and spun a few spokes to port then back again, angling the *Lisa Marie* to pass down *Bait & Bitch*'s transom and along her port side. Caleb could see Morin conferring with his sternman, the two of them looking up at the approaching boat.

Caleb smiled to himself, then stepped up onto the wash rail, and with one hand on the davit he stepped forward along the side deck to the point where he knew it would be easiest to jump aboard Mike's boat as Katie brought them alongside.

He stopped and leaned back with his calves against the side of his trunk cabin and waited as Katie spun the *Lisa Marie* around the stern of Mike's boat and turned to bring her up starboard side to port. Caleb had only seen *Bait & Bitch* the one time, and he had never seen inside her cabin or on her deck, but he could see now she looked much as he had guessed she would: trash shoved up on the console by the windshield, streaks of grime on the deck and sides of the cockpit, rags and buckets and brushes in piles in the corners of the cabin, various bits of gear repaired with duct tape and tossed here and there.

Morin and his sternman were on the far side of the boat, the starboard side, trying to look as if they were not planning any sort of mischief and failing badly.

I want to play poker with you guys, Caleb thought, as Katie spun the wheel again to bring the boats up against each other. She throttled back to neutral, letting the *Lisa Marie* come to a near stop. Caleb stepped to the *Lisa Marie*'s gunnel and lifted his leg as if he was going to jump from one boat to another. As he did, Morin spun around and drove *Bait & Bitch*'s throttle forward, making the boat lurch ahead. If Caleb had not been ready for it, and had jumped, he would have been in the water.

Instead, he stepped back again as Katie, who had also been ready, punched *Lisa Marie* ahead. Caleb stumbled a bit as his boat accelerated under him, turning as the speed increased. The bow pressed against *Bait & Bitch*'s side, pushing *Bait & Bitch* sideways. Caleb stepped easily across and hopped down to the wet and grime-streaked deck of Mike Morin's boat.

Morin had been looking forward, through the windshield, but he turned back when he felt *Lisa Marie* nudge his boat, and as Caleb stepped down onto the deck he could see the look of anger, and a touch of fear, on his face. There was less fear in the sternman's face. He was a small guy, wiry, but he looked tough, like he was accustomed to fighting and to kicking ass.

Now he came at Caleb with a fish billy in his hand, a short bat sports fisherman used to knock out big gamefish before they thrashed the fishing boat to bits. Caleb frowned and shook his head at the silliness of it all. He wondered if Morin used the billy to take down lobsters that were getting out of hand.

"Don't do this, man," Caleb called as the sternman came at him, ignoring Caleb's words, bringing the fish billy back over his head to get maximum power in his blow. He was expecting Caleb to back away, but Caleb did the opposite, stepping in just as the fish billy began its descent. He locked the sternman's arm, bent it back so the smaller man was doubled at the waist. Then Caleb reached over, plucked the fish billy from the man's hand and shoved him forward, sending him sprawling on the wet deck.

"Stay there," Caleb said, pointing at the confused and furious man with the fish billy that was now in his hand. He heard the all-too-familiar sound of a shotgun shell being racked into a chamber and looked up to see Mike Morin, eyes wide, pointing a twelve-gauge roughly in his direction.

Caleb held his hands up in a mock surrender, but he did not let the fish billy go. "Come on, man, I said I just wanted to talk," he said, his voice calm, nearly to the point of being patronizing but not quite.

"Oh, yeah?" Mike said, nodding toward his sternman, who, seeing Mike now had the upper hand, was climbing back on his feet. "So why'd you do that to him?"

"Dude," Caleb said, holding the fish billy up a little higher. "He tried to take my head off. And I didn't hurt him. Here." He tossed the fish billy back to the sternman, an easy lob, and the sternman caught it awkwardly.

"Look," Caleb continued, "I just need to ask you some stuff. The other night, at my house? Someone was screwing with you as much as they were screwing with me. Whoever sent you knew what was going to happen, and he sent you in to get your ass kicked. There's no shame, I have a lot of training in this crap."

They were silent for a moment, then Caleb took a long and meaningful look at Katie, fifteen feet away on the other boat. Mike had throttled way back before grabbing his gun and now Katie had the *Lisa Marie* right alongside, and she was watching from her position at the wheel. "Kill me and you'll have to kill her too. And you'll spend the rest of your life in jail. For nothing."

Mike's gaze shifted between her and Caleb and his sternman and he seemed to realize the pointlessness of holding the loaded weapon. He lifted it, clicked the safety on and set the gun on the dashboard under the windshield. "Okay," he said. "What do you want to say?"

Caleb took a step forward, his hands still held slightly up and open. "You told me the other night a guy met you in the Penalty Box and said he'd pay you and your buddies to kick my ass, right?"

"Yeah," Mike said.

"He's the guy who's screwing with us. He's the guy I have to find."

"He paid me, man, he didn't screw with me," Mike protested.

"He paid you, sure, but he knew you'd get your ass beat. And he knew if I wanted to I could call the cops and get you in some big-time shit," Caleb said. "Any of you or your buddies on probation?" It was a guess, but by the look on Morin's face, it was a good one.

"Anyway, I have to find that guy so I can figure out what's going on. Have you seen him again? Had any thoughts about who he is?"

Morin shook his head. "Last time I saw him was when he paid me. Haven't seen him in the Penalty Box or anywhere since then."

Caleb nodded. "Tell me again what he looked like?"

Morin shrugged. "Dude, I was pretty hammered the first time I talked with him, and it was wicked dark the second time. He wasn't a big dude, about the size of Tom..." Morin nodded toward his sternman who was standing against the port rail with arms folded and a seriously pissed off look on his face.

"But older, you know? Like, thirties, maybe?" Mike was clearly warming up to the subject. "Dark hair, not bald. He always wore sunglasses, which was weird 'cause it was always dark when I saw him, but I guessed he just thought it was cool."

Caleb nodded. "And he said his name was Cox? No first name?"

"Yeah," Mike said, and then he hesitated as if another thought came to him.

"What?" Caleb asked.

"Well, the guy I talked to, I assumed his name was Cox. He kept saying 'Mr. Cox' wants this, you know, 'Mr. Cox wants you to kick Hayes's ass.' That was when he met us, to pay us. Right before... He never said any names in the Penalty Box. But when he met us he said to make sure I told you Mr. Cox sent us. I just thought he was one of those guys that talk about themselves like that. But maybe he wasn't Mr. Cox."

Caleb nodded again, though in truth the situation was getting murkier with each word out of Morin's mouth. The guy who hired them may or may not have been named Cox, but either way he had sought Mike Morin out and paid him and made certain that Morin said specifically that it was Cox who sent him. Someone who knew that Morin would be motivated to beat the crap out of Caleb, but that could be a lot of people. According to his Uncle Dick, word of their earlier fight over Katie had spread far and wide.

Someone wants me to think Howard Cox has it in for me, Caleb thought. *Why the hell would anyone want that?* He thought about Richard Forrester, tangled in his buoy line, Cox's business card in his wallet.

Did someone do that on purpose? he wondered. *How would they know I'd look in his wallet? Or maybe it didn't matter if I did.*

He pulled his phone out of his back pocket and brought up the photo gallery. He scrolled to the pictures he had taken of the photos from Cox's computer. Family pictures it looked like. Some of them showed Cox posing with men about the age Morin described.

"Here, check this out," Caleb said, stepping over to Morin and angling the phone so he could see it. "Any of these guys the one who paid you to come after me?"

Mike leaned down and held up a hand to shade the screen. He shook his head. Caleb swiped to the next picture. Mike shook his head again. Caleb swiped. They went through all the pictures that Caleb had taken, but Mike was certain that none of those men were the one who had approached him in the bar.

"Well, crap," Caleb said. He'd risked getting his chest blown open with a twelve gauge for nothing, it seemed. Then another thought struck him, and he wondered that he had not thought of it before.

"Hang on," he said and turned and stepped over to the port side, where Katie had the *Lisa Marie* idling a few feet off. Mike's sternman, Tom, watched Caleb warily, like he might watch a dangerous animal, hoping it will just keep moving.

"Hey, Katie," Caleb called, speaking loud to be heard over the rumble of the two diesel engines, "remember that day we took that guy Billy out to get the samples by the fuel farm?"

"Yeah."

"You took a picture of him. You still have it on your phone?"

"Yeah," Katie said. She pulled her phone from her pocket, poked at the virtual buttons on the screen, swiped the pictures in her gallery and handed the phone over to Caleb. Caleb looked at the picture as he crossed back to Mike Morin. Billy Caine in his dark blue polo shirt with the company logo on the breast, round glasses, smiling through a close-cropped beard.

"Here, any chance this is the guy?" Caleb asked, holding the phone at an angle so Mike could see. Mike squinted and leaned close. For a moment he was silent, staring at the photo, and Caleb could feel his hope building.

Why didn't I friggin' see this before? he thought.

Then Mike Morin straightened and frowned. "Man, I don't

know," he said. "This guy looks more like the guy, for sure. A lot more. But the guy I talked to didn't have a beard, and like I said, he was wearing sunglasses, not those round ones. And…"

"What?" Caleb asked.

"Well, the guy I talked to, he seemed like a pretty mean son of a bitch, you know? Like he could handle himself. Kind of a scary dude, actually. This guy"—he pointed at the picture on the phone—"he looks like kind of a pussy."

"Yeah, that he does," Caleb agreed. *And looks can be pretty wicked deceiving*, he thought.

Caleb put the phone on standby and slipped it in his pocket. "Hey, thanks, Mike, I really appreciate this," he said. He could see the confusion, and suspicion, on Morin's face. "And look, let's forget about all this bullshit between us, okay? It's past. Done."

Mike Morin nodded slowly, looking for Caleb's angle, but not seeing it. "Okay…" he said.

"Good." Caleb stretched out his hand and held it out for a few seconds as Mike Morin debated taking it. Then Morin reached out and took it, squeezed it harder than necessary, and shook.

"Okay, cool," Morin said. Caleb let go of his hand. He turned, gave Sternman Tom a small wave, then stepped up onto the gunnel of *Bait & Bitch* and onto the wash rail of *Lisa Marie* and then down on the deck next to Katie at the wheel.

"'Kill me and you'll have to kill her too'?" Katie said. "Thanks a friggin' lot."

"Ah, he wasn't about to do it," Caleb said. "Didn't even have his finger on the trigger." He looked over at the *Bait & Bitch,* the space opening up between the two boats. "Okay, let's get out of here," he said.

Katie gave Mike a wave, spun the wheel, pushed the throttle forward. *Lisa Marie* turned and gained speed as she pulled away from Mike Morin's boat.

"Well," Katie asked, "did you find out what you needed to find out?"

Caleb looked out at the water beyond the bow and the long, low, tree-covered peninsula of Hopefleet Neck. "I have absolutely no idea," he said.

Chapter Twenty-Three

Howard Cox was first to the diner and he took a booth against the back wall. It was a dump of a place in a strip mall in Lisbon, but he had checked it out a few days before and he knew it would do and there was virtually no chance that anyone who would recognize him would make an appearance here.

The waitress came by and Cox ordered coffee, even though it was late in the afternoon, closer to dinner than lunch. The waitress asked if he would like to see a menu and he said no.

As if I'd eat in some E. coli spawning ground like this, Cox thought.

The coffee came and Cox sipped it and found it drinkable. He wondered when Marco Scott would make his appearance, which was different from wondering when Scott would get there. Cox was all but certain that Scott was there already, somewhere, watching. Probably from a car parked in the lot. Making sure the meeting was as clean as they both wished it to be.

Cox had drained a third of his coffee by the time he saw Marco come in through the glass door and walk toward him, past the other booths. He walked neither fast nor slow, his expression neither happy, angry, or much of anything at all. He was medium height, medium build. Unremarkable in just about every way. Cox alone in that place, in all of Maine, he guessed, knew how very remarkable indeed Marco Scott was.

"Afternoon, Mr. Cox," Scott said, sliding into the seat opposite Howard's.

"Afternoon. No problem finding the place?" Cox asked. Both men understood they had to make small talk until the waitress came and went.

The waitress appeared and Scott ordered a cup of coffee and a cheeseburger, fries, coleslaw. The waitress jotted the order down, brought the coffee and left them alone.

"Can I see the image?" Scott asked as they settled into business. Cox pulled his cell phone from his coat pocket and powered it up, and that was approaching the limits of his technological literacy.

"It's on that…app…or whatever the hell you call it," Cox said, pointing to one of the ridiculous little pictures that littered the screen. "I don't know if it's still there. I don't know how the hell any of this works."

Scott took the phone and made a few stabs and swipes. He held it up for Cox to see. There was the image that was frozen in his mind: a grainy, greenish Caleb Hayes sitting at his computer, in his study.

"Yeah, that's it," Cox said. Scott flipped the phone around, studied the picture, put the phone on standby. "That's Caleb Hayes, who I told you about," Cox said. "The one that's been harassing me. He's working for IGP, he has to be. Putting the pressure on. And it's going to get worse, I can tell you. The vote is three days away. I swear, if Atlantic Gas doesn't start stepping up their game I'm going to throw them all to the wolves, vote for the damned LNG."

Scott nodded. He was being paid by Ryan Miller and Cox's old K Street firm; he didn't have a dog in that fight and Cox knew he did not care how any of this played out. His job was simply to find out who was putting pressure on Cox and why, and then make it stop.

"Can you show me the text?" Scott asked. Once again Cox fumbled with his phone, cursing under his breath. He found the single line of text that Hayes had sent: *I know what you're up to.*

"He sent this," Scott asked. "You're certain?"

"I had the number checked," Cox said. "It came from his phone."

Scott nodded. "And then he broke into your house?"

"Yes," Cox said, failing to keep the exasperation from his voice. They had been over this already, talking on the phone as Scott drove up from DC. "And then he calls me, threatens me. He makes it pretty clear what he wants."

Scott stared at Howard long enough for Howard to grow uncomfortable, then he said, "You're sure it's Hayes who's calling you?"

"Yeah, I'm sure," Cox snapped, then collected himself and said,

"Okay, no, I'm not sure. But who else? And if it isn't this Hayes guy, it must be someone he works for."

"Maybe," Scott said.

Cox waited for a moment and when Scott did not continue he said, "Maybe? What do you mean, maybe?"

"There doesn't seem to be any connection between Hayes and IGP. Or any other corporation," Scott said. "Just the security business he had in Los Angeles. I'm a little hard pressed to think we wouldn't find anything if it was there. We have pretty impressive resources."

"No shit," Cox said. "And I'm paying a pretty impressive bill to have you tell me what I already know."

"There are two of them, at least," Scott said. "There's someone else working this, not just Hayes. I doubt that Hayes sent you a picture of himself breaking into your house."

"Really?" Cox said. "Because I think he did just that. Sent it so I would come racing home and he could apply some physical persuasion."

"But he didn't," Scott said. "He had the chance, according to you. But he dumped you on the couch."

"All right," Cox said. "You can't find anything on Hayes, you think there's another guy. I didn't call you up here to do a fucking Hercule Poirot number. I think if you ask Hayes directly, in a persuasive way, he'll tell you what the connection is. And who this alleged other guy is."

Again Scott said nothing for a long time, and then he nodded his head. "I'm arranging an opportunity to talk to this Caleb Hayes," he said. "In fact, I've already made contact with him. I think he and I will be able to come to an understanding."

Cox leaned back. *Already made contact with him?* Scott could not have been in Maine much more that twenty-four hours. *Man, this guy does not screw around.*

"Good," Cox said, and he meant it. The past few weeks had been a nightmare, but now, for the first time, he felt like that was coming to an end, that he was kicking his way out of the fitful sleep. He felt himself waking to the pleasant recollection of all that he had going on in the world beyond the nightmare: the money, the influence. The governorship.

"Good," Cox said again. "I know you're on top of it. Please keep me updated on what you find."

He pulled out his wallet and withdrew forty dollars and tossed it on the table. They stood and headed out of the restaurant single file, just as the waitress was pushing her way through the kitchen doors, Marco Scott's cheeseburger and fries balanced on her tray.

Katie Brennan stayed at the helm and drove *Lisa Marie* back the way they had come, west of Hackett Point. She intercepted the next string of traps slated for fishing that day near the number eight nun buoy off Great Chebeague Island. She eased the throttle back as the heavy boat slid up to the red and white buoy, grabbed up the gaff and hooked the buoy rope, flipping it over the snatch block and around the hauler with a now-expert ease.

"All right," Caleb said, "I'm staying home from now on. You don't need me anymore."

"Not true," Katie said. "What would I do with that second cup of coffee I bring every morning if you weren't there to drink it?"

By two in the afternoon they had hauled and reset their traps for the day. The catch was good, but not outrageously good, the live tank half full of the snapping, crawling, waving crustaceans, now adorned with bright yellow rubber bands on their claws. Caleb took the wheel and turned the *Lisa Marie* back toward the co-op in Kettle Cove. Kate stood beside him, under the roof of the cabin. "So, you really think that that guy, Billy, is part of this?"

Caleb glanced over at her and smiled. He knew she had been aching to ask him about his showing Billy's picture to Mike Morin and what he thought Billy's part in all this might be. She had been waiting all afternoon for what she judged to be the right moment.

"I don't know," Caleb said. "I really don't. But think about it; he's someone new in town, a guy I don't know, and he seems to know a hell of a lot about all this LNG stuff. And he knew Richard Forrester, apparently."

"Yeah," Katie agreed. "But he's in the business, you know? Like he said. Small community."

"Yeah," Caleb agreed. "And that makes sense. Which is why I never really gave him another thought. At least not until I realized how much someone was screwing with us."

Kettle Cove opened up beyond the bow, the gravel beach, the granite ledge yielding to pines like rows of green dragon teeth along the shore, the lobsterboats milling about, waiting for their turn to off-load their catches. Katie pushed herself off the console and headed aft to scrub down the deck and rails as Caleb throttled back to take up his position in the queue.

It took another hour before the catch was disposed of and they made their way wearily up the hill to the parking lot. They stopped at the point where their paths to their cars diverged.

"So," Katie said, "do you still have any of that great sourdough bread you had?"

"Yeah," Caleb said.

"Because I'd love some for breakfast tomorrow," Katie said.

"That can be arranged," Caleb said. "But you know, I don't open the door for anyone in the morning."

"So I'd have to already be in your house?" Katie said. "Like, if I slept over?"

"Exactly," Caleb said.

"Okay," Katie said, "that can be arranged."

They drove back to Caleb's house in two cars, not wishing to leave Katie's PT Cruiser in the co-op's parking lot. Caleb unlocked the door and disarmed the security system which had been there when he bought the house but had never been used until that week. It was not a bad unit; like much of the house it was high-end without being extravagant, and between that and his own sweeping for bugs and the security cameras and motion detectors he was confident that his home was safe. They might be under surveillance from the outside, but no one was going to get near the house undetected or see or hear anything of interest from there.

"Beer?" Caleb asked.

"You're a bad influence," Katie said. "I used to go for a three-mile run after work, not drink beer."

"Carb loading, it's good for a runner," Caleb said, handing her an open bottle of Shipyard Summer Ale. He poured his own into a glass and fished out his wallet. He thumbed through the business cards there until he came to the one Billy Caine had given him a few weeks earlier. He looked at it and then handed it to Katie, who was watching him with curiosity.

She studied it. "New England Environmental Testing and Analytics," she read out loud, "William Caine, Environmental Science: Field Division. Very impressive. But I don't trust a guy who's named William but calls himself Billy."

"Nor should you," Caleb said. He reached out for the card and Katie handed it back. "I thought I would check the man's references." He took the cordless phone from its base, laid Billy's card on the island countertop and dialed the number. One ring, two rings, then a woman's voice, friendly yet efficient and businesslike.

"New England Environmental Testing and Analytics," the woman said. "How may I direct you call?"

"Hi, I'm looking for William Caine," Caleb said. "He's with your field division."

"Yes, of course," the woman said, perky and helpful. "I'm afraid Mr. Caine is out on assignment right now. I don't expect him back this week. Do you have his cell phone number?"

"I do, but I was hoping to speak with someone in the office. Is there anyone else in?"

"Let me check," the woman said, her voice betraying nothing but an eagerness to help. "It looks like Nathaniel James is in the office today. Would you like me to transfer you?"

"No, actually, now that I think about it I should just call Billy on his cell," Caleb said. "But I had one other question. Could you tell me again the name of your parent company?"

"No parent company, sir," the woman said. "NEETA is an independently owned LLC."

"Oh, okay," Caleb said. "I guess I was remembering wrong. Thanks for your help."

"My pleasure, sir. Thank you for calling New England Environmental Testing and Analytics."

Caleb pushed the disconnect button and looked over at Katie, who was tilting the last of her beer into her mouth. "Sounded pretty legit, from what I could hear."

"Sounded that way, for sure," Caleb said. "But it only takes one gal with good phone skills to sound legit. I could have been talking to someone in a trailer park in Kansas."

"True," Katie said. "So why did you ask to speak to someone else and then change your mind?"

"I wanted to see if there was anyone else besides her. The fact that she was willing to transfer me told me there was."

"So the company's legit?"

"Maybe," Caleb said. "Or maybe it's a cover that's several layers deep."

"Boy, are you paranoid!" Katie said.

"*Semper Vigilantus.* It's why I'm still alive and all my parts are still attached and working," Caleb said. "When there's big money involved, the game can get rough. You've seen that firsthand." He picked up his cell phone and opened the texting app.

"Now what?" Katie asked.

"Contacting a buddy from the old days," Caleb said. "This guy has the means to dig down through phone numbers and find out what their real origins are. Very useful. You'd be surprised." He scrolled through the contact list, found the name he was looking for, brought it up. He poked at the screen, typing out the message, his big thumbs making the task even more difficult.

"God!" Katie said. "I can hardly stand watching you do that!"

"Then don't," Caleb said without looking up. "Get us two more beers instead."

He finished the text, read it over to make sure the autocorrect didn't do anything that would embarrass him. *Paul, how's it going? It's been a while. All well with you?* Happy with the words and the tone, he hit the "send" button.

Katie opened two more beers; Caleb pulled steaks and corn out of the refrigerator. "Let's fire up the barbecue, whadda you say?" he asked.

"I say, huzzah!" Katie said, holding up her beer in salute. Caleb's phone buzzed on the granite counter and he picked it up.

All is good here, the text read. *It's still paradise and all. If you're texting me out of the blue I assume you need a favor?*

Caleb smiled, went at the keypad with his thumbs. *You wound me. But yes. Could you tell me who owns this phone number?* He looked down at Billy's card and typed the number in.

The reply came almost immediately. *No problem. It might take me a day or so.*

Thanks, Caleb replied. *Sooner the better. I'll send live lobsters to show my appreciation.*

Thanks, but I wouldn't know what the hell to do with them.

Caleb chuckled and set the phone aside, done with that, ready to embrace the evening. Both he and Katie were still infused with the strong and peculiar odor that comes with lobstering, so to save water and protect the environment they showered together. Katie threw her clothes in the washing machine and donned one of Caleb's flannel shirts while Caleb pulled on worn cargo shorts and an old button-down shirt, untucked. They carried the steaks and corn out to the barbecue on the deck and they cooked and talked about any number of things, none of which were Howard Cox, LNG or lobstering.

After dinner they cleaned up the dishes and then snuggled on the couch and watched an episode of a show called *Vikings*. Katie reached up, ran her fingers through Caleb's beard. "Definitely into the Viking thing," she said.

It was nine thirty when they went to bed and an hour after that that they fell into a blissful sleep. Caleb woke at 4:30 the next morning, rested enough and in a good enough mood that he happily climbed out of bed, padded down to the kitchen, made a pot of coffee and was just sliding the crisp bacon onto a brown paper bag when Katie arrived.

They ate, drove together in Caleb's truck to the co-op, went through the familiar routine of getting the *Lisa Marie* underway and headed off for the trawls west of Whaleboat Island. The day was overcast and threatening rain, but the air still held the warmth of summer and it promised to be an ideal day on the water, the sort of day that made certain people embrace a career on the water and all the obvious downsides, such as weather not nearly so amiable, that it entailed.

They hauled their first trawl, tossed back the shorts and the V-notches and the eggers—females with their thousands of tiny black eggs stuck to the underside of their tails—back into the sea, along with the crabs and the occasional fish. They banded the rest and dropped them in the tank. They dumped out bait bags to the delight of the screaming gulls, and rebaited the traps.

Caleb took the wheel and drove the boat around in a wide arc. He tossed the buoy overboard and pushed the first trap after it. The buoy line paid out and one by one the green wire traps slid off the transom and back down to the watery depths. Katie stood by his side, watching the twists of rope spin out over the side, taking care that none of the loops were around her ankle.

"I think we should shift that first trawl further away from Birch Island Ledge," Katie said. "I think it would fish better." Then she pointed through the windshield and called, "Look who's back!"

Caleb, who had been watching the traps go over, turned and

looked forward. The Boston Whaler from Whaleboat Island was making for them, once again riding the wave generated by its own forward momentum.

"Guess he liked doing business with us," Caleb said. "What was his name?"

"Walter something," Katie said. She paused. "Walter Barnes."

"Right," Caleb said. "We got a dozen for him?"

"Should have," Katie said. Caleb throttled the *Lisa Marie* back to a stop as Walter Barnes came up alongside.

"Ahoy, there!" Barnes called, smiling and waving from the steering console. "Ahoy the *Lisa Marie*! Any chance you can sell me a dozen this morning?"

"Yeah, should be," Caleb said. "We've caught at least that, even though Katie thinks I have my traps in the wrong place."

"Permission to come aboard?" Walter asked.

"Sure," Caleb said, wondering why people always felt the impulse to talk like they were in a Horatio Hornblower novel whenever they were around boats. Katie took up his bow line, as she had the morning before, and Walter came aboard, his stern line in one hand, bucket and draw string bag in the other.

"A dozen again?" Katie asked.

"Yeah, that was perfect," Walter said. He handed her the bucket and looked around enthusiastically. "What do you guys use for bait?" he asked, his eyes on the bait table.

"Menhaden, mostly," Caleb said. "A lot of people call them pogies. Redfish, too." He was still standing back a ways, and though he did not have his hand on the grip of his Beretta, which was still holstered in the small of his back, he was once again ready to pull it fast if need be. *Semper Vigilantus.*

Katie fished the mottled crustaceans out of the lobster tank, counting out loud as she dropped each in the bucket. "There you go, a dozen, fresh as can be," she said, putting the top back on the tank.

"Lovely," Walter said. "Seventy-eight bucks, if I remember correctly."

"That's right," Katie said. Walter opened his drawstring bag and reached in. He grabbed something, his wallet, presumably, and as he pulled his hand out a cell phone toppled out of the bag and fell with an ugly sound on the deck.

"Oh, damn," Walter said. "I hope that didn't break."

"Here, let me get it," Katie said, bending over. Caleb's eyes flickered down to the cell phone lying on the slick deck of the boat. His eyes flickered back to Walter Barnes, who was pulling something else from the drawstring bag. Caleb was expecting a wallet, but it was not a wallet. It was a Taser.

Chapter Twenty-Four

"Son of a..." Caleb managed to say. His hand whipped around his back and his fingers wrapped around the grip of his Beretta and then he saw the green plastic protectors on the end of the Taser burst apart. He felt two sharp jabs, like darts hitting him, one in the chest, one in the stomach, and in the next instant he was engulfed in a wave of pain.

He roared with the agony of it, felt his muscles contract as the pulses of current, 5,500 volts, coursed through him. He felt his knees begin to buckle. He tried to fight it, tried to will himself to move, but his body would not respond, his muscles would not unlock, as the pulses of current like machine gun fire hit him and tore through his body.

Katie, still bent over to retrieve the phone, began to straighten, and Caleb could just make out the confused look on her face when Barnes kicked her hard across her neck slamming her into the live tank and dropping her to the deck. Caleb roared in anger and pain, or at least he thought he did, and he tried to step forward, but his knees gave out and he came down on them with a jarring impact that only made the agony worse.

Barnes was moving now, racing toward him. In Caleb's mind he could see exactly what he needed to do; he did not even have to think about it. He could snap Barnes's arm like a stick, except that he couldn't move. The pain was like a blanket, smothering him.

He felt himself falling forward and he struggled to stay on his knees. Barnes reached out, put a hand on the back of Caleb's neck, and shoved him down to the deck. Caleb fell with an impact that made him shudder, unable to move his arms to break his fall and only just able to twist his face out of the way. He felt his arms pulled back, felt the sharp bite of plastic handcuffs, like glorified zip ties, encircle his wrists. He thought he was bellowing in anger and pain, but he was not sure.

And then suddenly the pain was gone. His muscles ached, like after a prolonged workout, and he felt light-headed, but there was no pain. How long it had lasted he did not know. It felt like a very long time, but he knew from past training that it was probably about thirty seconds, just enough for a skilled operative to get the cuffs on him. He felt Barnes's hand reach under his oilskins and pull his pistol from its holster.

He craned his neck to look aft. Katie was pulling herself to her feet and she looked stunned by the blow Barnes had delivered. She looked over as Barnes finished with Caleb and stood, moving aft. Caleb saw her raise her hands in a feeble defense as he advanced on her, saw Barnes push the Beretta into the waistband of his shorts, in the small of his back.

"If you hurt her I'll fucking kill you!" Caleb shouted, and that time he knew he had yelled as loud and emphatically as he intended, but Barnes had no reaction. Which was hardly a surprise, since Caleb was in no position to do anything of the sort.

Barnes grabbed Katie's arm, twisted it, forcing her around and down to the deck. He whipped out another set of cuffs and tightened them on her wrists, smooth and deft. Caleb understood then that Barnes might look like any of a thousand innocuous office workers vacationing in Maine, but he was in reality something very different from that. Something very dangerous.

"What the hell do you want, you son of a bitch?" Caleb said, keeping the control in his voice, and the tone of menace, but Barnes did not react at all, did not reply or even look in Caleb's direction. He grabbed Katie under the arm, and as he stood, he lifted her with him, spun her around and pushed her forward. She stumbled as she walked, and Caleb could see that the effects of the blow and the sudden turn of events were still working on her.

They walked past where Caleb lay and Caleb turned his head to follow them. Barnes stopped under the cabin and half lifted Katie up into the tall chair that stood inboard of the wheel, in case the helmsman got tired of standing. He stepped away and unlatched the small door that led to the *Lisa Marie*'s cabin in the bow and swung it open. He stepped aft, stood in front of Caleb where he lay so that

Caleb could see him if he twisted his head. The Beretta was in
Barnes's hand, pointing at Caleb's forehead.

"Up. Get below," he said. He wasn't about to try lifting Caleb,
and he probably knew enough not to get that close. If he got within
the arc of Caleb's legs, Caleb could do him some real hurt, maybe
even kill him, even with his hands cuffed.

For a moment Caleb did not move, did not speak, just to see
how Barnes would react. But Barnes did not react, he just waited. He
was not hurried, he was not flustered. He was a professional, and he
had complete control of the situation, and Caleb knew that at that
juncture there was no point in resisting. With a grunt he pushed
himself up to his knees and awkwardly stood.

Barnes grabbed hold of the wires running from the barbs that
were still sunk into Caleb's flesh and jerked. Caleb gasped in pain and
surprise and the barbs made a soft metallic sound as they dropped to
the deck.

"Go," Barnes said and nodded his head in the direction of the
cabin. Caleb felt weak from the tasing, but his legs functioned
properly and he stumbled along. He met Katie's eyes and he could
see the fear in them. He wished he could think of something that
might reassure her, but he could not. Anything he said now would
just be bullshit, and she would know it.

He stepped down into the cabin, ducking awkwardly to get
through the companionway, a tight fit for him even when he was not
cuffed. He stepped down onto the deck. Barnes shut the door and
the cabin was plunged into the gloom of the meager sunlight of an
overcast day coming in through the small, round portholes.

Caleb stood still and listened, but the rumble of *Lisa Marie*'s
diesel was even louder below and he could not hear anything above
that. He pressed his face to the small porthole, but all he could see
was the side deck and the water and the islands beyond. He craned
his head around. The end of the davit and the snatch block came into
view, but other than that he could see nothing. He stepped back to
the cabin door and pressed his ear against it. Nothing.

Barnes was clearly a professional and he clearly had a purpose in
mind, and that gave Caleb an odd sort of comfort. He felt certain
that the man would not harm Katie while he had her up on deck,
would not use her for any sadistic pleasure. There would be no
purpose in doing so. As long as Katie didn't try to fight she would

remain unharmed. For now.

The engine note changed as Barnes shifted *Lisa Marie* into gear. The bow lifted and Caleb stumbled back as the boat gathered way. He regained his footing and stepped over to the porthole again. He could see the spray sailing past as the lobsterboat's speed increased. He could see Hackett's Point and the long stretch of Hopefleet Neck off to starboard and he knew they were heading roughly north, back toward land.

He looked down at the door to the engine compartment. He considered opening it, doing some damage to the engine, but it would be difficult in the handcuffs, if not impossible. And even if he could, what good would it serve? Barnes was not about to abandon whatever mission he was on just because the lobsterboat was disabled.

Caleb's eyes were adjusting to the dim light and he looked around the cabin, searching for something he might uses as a weapon. There was a fileting knife in a sheath mounted to the bulkhead, and a toolbox that contained any number of things that would be lethal in his hands. But his hands were cuffed, immobilized, and even if he could get a weapon in his grip there was nothing he could do with it.

He toyed with the idea of trying to get the knife in his hands and using it to cut the handcuffs away, but he dismissed the thought. It was mounted high so that it could be easily reached from the deck and would be nearly impossible to reach now, with his hands cuffed. He considered using his teeth, but the knife handle was too near the overhead for that to work. What's more, he had seen Barnes put the cuffs on Katie and he saw they were professional grade, not some cheap plastic crap. Someone with his hands free could cut them with the fileting knife, but Caleb could not do it himself.

Those options eliminated, Caleb was reduced to staring out the porthole and watching the distant shore pass and waiting to see what Barnes would do next. It was easily the worst torment he had ever suffered, with Katie cuffed on deck, so close and completely beyond his reach. He would have gladly exchanged it for another half dozen tasings.

He could see the opening of Kettle Cove move past, and a few lobsterboats he knew motoring around. He had a sudden hopeful thought that one of them would see the *Lisa Marie* and wonder what they were up to, particularly if the Whaler was being towed astern, which Caleb guessed it was. But that hope died as soon as it sprouted. If a lobsterman was not in obvious distress, or calling for help, the other watermen did not inquire into his or her business.

Where the hell are we going? Caleb wondered as he watched the shore of Hopefleet Neck pass down the starboard side. Barnes, he was fairly certain, had some specific spot in mind. This whole thing, from the innocent purchase of lobsters the day before to the calculated fumble of the cell phone, had been flawlessly planned, and Caleb had no doubt that the rest of the day's activities had been as well.

Ten minutes later he heard the *Lisa Marie*'s engines back down, felt the boat settle in the water. They were coming into a little cove about five miles from the tip of Hopefleet Neck, just an indent in the shore, generally deserted. Caleb backed away from the porthole and faced the door, ready for Barnes to open it and come below. Now the fun would start.

The boat turned slightly underfoot, then Caleb heard the growl of the engine backing down, bringing the *Lisa Marie* to a stop. The boat rocked on an even keel and then, just behind him, Caleb heard the anchor chain paying out as Barnes dropped the twenty-five-pound Danforth over the bow. A moment later the engine turned off and an odd, unaccustomed silence fell over the boat. Caleb knew that change well, when the engine was finally silenced. It usually meant the end of the work day, and it carried a very positive connotation, but now it seemed ominous indeed.

At last the cabin door swung open and Katie appeared, framed by the companionway, and Caleb blinked in the light despite the overcast sky. Kate stepped down awkwardly, her hands still cuffed behind her. Caleb could see she had been crying.

"Did he hurt you?" he asked in a low voice and she bit her lip and shook her head.

"We'll be all right, don't worry," he said next, and he was sorry to hear that his words sounded as hollow as they were.

Barnes followed her below. He had the Beretta in his waistband, the drawstring bag in hand. He looked around, then pointed to a pile of rope against the starboard side, indicating that Caleb should sit. Once again there seemed no point in resisting, so Caleb shuffled over and sat. Barnes pushed Katie forward and sat her on the edge of one of the berths in the bow.

Next Barnes pulled a small black box out of the bag and pressed a power button. Caleb recognized the device. It was essentially a smaller version of the spectrum analyzer he had used to sweep his own house for bugs. Barnes moved it around the interior of the cabin, his eyes on the screen. He stopped, pressed a few buttons, scrutinized the screen some more. He looked over at Caleb and shook his head as if he was disappointed.

But still he did not say anything. He put the sweeping device back in his bag and pulled out another black box, switched it on and set it down. It was a small, battery operated acoustic noise generator that would render any listening devices useless.

"All right," Barnes said and he sounded vaguely bored, as if this was some minor but necessary task he had to carry out. He turned to Caleb. "Howard Cox. What is your business with Howard Cox? Why are you breaking into his house?"

"Bite me," Caleb said.

Barnes sighed, as if he barely had the patience for such pointless defiance, which was probably the case. "Okay, you know the drill here, Hayes," he said. He reached into his bag, pulled out his Taser, and with slow and deliberate moves he removed the spent cartridge and put a new one in its place. He pointed the Taser at Katie, four feet away.

"I'm sure you remember how the Taser feels," Barnes said. "That's what she'll get first. Then I use that fileting knife over there." He nodded toward the knife on the bulkhead.

Caleb grit his teeth and he tried to think of some way out of this, something he could do. But he could think of nothing, beyond telling Barnes what he wanted to hear.

And then he realized he couldn't even do that, because he didn't know a damned thing.

"So let me ask you again, what is your interest in Howard Cox?" Barnes said.

Caleb met his eyes and held them. "I will be perfectly clear, and I will be perfectly honest. Three weeks ago I had no idea who Howard Cox was. And the next thing I know, four guys come to try and beat me up, and they tell me Howard Cox sent them. Because Cox was sick of my shit, they said. And what that shit might be, I have no idea."

Barnes held Caleb's gaze for a second, two seconds, then he turned fast and took a step toward Katie. He raised his hand, backhand, and hit her hard across the face, twisting her around with the force of the blow. Caleb heard her gasp and he was on his feet, launching himself at Barnes, but Barnes had his foot up and he kicked Caleb hard in the gut, sending him back the way he had come, the breath knocked clean out of him. Caleb collapsed on the pile of rope, gasping to catch air.

Finally his breath caught and he breathed deep and scowled up at Barnes. "Let's try again," Barnes said. "Two weeks ago you sent a text to Howard Cox. It came from your phone. One sentence. It implied you had some knowledge of what he was doing."

"What was he doing?" Caleb asked.

"You tell me," Barnes said.

"I can't tell you because I don't know one damned thing. And I certainly never sent a text. I didn't know Howard Cox from a turd on the sidewalk."

"And yet you broke into his house. What did you find?" Barnes asked.

"I broke into his house to find out what the hell he wanted with me."

"Did you find out?"

"No," Caleb said. Barnes leaned back and considered him, and Caleb guessed he was gauging the truth of his words. "I found out he plans to run for governor. That was the only thing of interest I found out, and it wasn't very interesting."

"We know about Jenny Carter," Barnes said. He said it quick and matter of fact, as if it was the next logical part of the conversation, and it took Caleb a moment to register what he had said. And when he did, the name struck like the bolt from the Taser. He felt the rage and the fear surge through him like the 5,500 volts he had just endured.

He remained silent for a moment. "Who?" he said.

Barnes chuckled. "Jenny Carter," he said again. "We know everything. And we can see to it that everyone else does, as well. Trevor Middleton. The cops. The tabloids."

Caleb stared at him, the filtered sun coming in from the companionway casting him in light and shadow. Caleb's mind was thrashing like a fish on a spear and he felt his arms straining against the handcuffs. He was desperate to be free now, to get his hands around Barnes's neck. He had thought of Jenny Carter every day since he had left Los Angeles, but he had not heard the name spoken in almost a year. It had been six months since he had last broken down and opened the file folder, read her name splashed all over the articles and police reports.

He stared back at Barnes, the two men holding one another's eyes, and even through the anger and pain from the wound reopened, Caleb realized two things.

The first was that Barnes didn't know a damned thing about Jenny Carter. He was bluffing. He had her name, and what was written in the papers, and no more.

The second was that Barnes didn't really care that much what Caleb did or did not know or was willing to confess, because either way he had no intention of letting him and Katie live beyond the next hour. The threats of harm to Katie, of exposing Caleb's past, he was just doing that to squeeze whatever he could out of Caleb before he gave him the double tap to the head.

"Okay, okay," Caleb said with a tone the indicated defeat. "Yes, there's more to it. You know I was the one who pulled Richard Forrester's body up, right? On my buoy line?"

Barnes nodded.

"Well, I went through his pockets before the Coast Guard showed up. He had some papers…they were wet but I could still unfold them and read them. They were documents about how he was working with Cox to kill this LNG thing. A lot of crap about the payout Atlantic Gas and Oil was giving Cox for his vote, promises to underwrite his campaign for governor. Pretty damning stuff. I mean, stuff that could put Cox and Forrester and God knows who else in jail."

"Okay," Barnes said, interested but skeptical.

"Okay," Caleb agreed. He focused on Barnes's eyes, knew better than to let his gaze drop to the Taser in Barnes's hand or wander around the cabin looking for weapons. But as he spoke he took note of Barnes's stance, how alert he seemed, if his attention was divided. He was looking for a chance, whatever it might be.

"So," Caleb said, "papers like that, they're worth a friggin' fortune, you know? Forrester's dead, and Cox might even think I killed him. So of course I kept them, and got hold of Cox. Cox must have told you all this, right? That's who you're working for, right? Howard Cox?"

Barnes made no response, gave no reaction. "Where are the papers now?" he asked.

"Not here," Caleb said. "And not in my house, I'm not that friggin' stupid. I mailed them to my post office box. And there they sit. And no one can get them but me. Or, if something happens to me, this other guy who has the key. A guy I know, I told him to open the box if I get whacked. Not her," he added, nodding toward Katie. "A guy who'll bring it all to the cops."

Barnes was silent for a long moment, his eyes fixed on Caleb's. Finally he spoke. "I think you're full of crap," he said and without shifting his gaze he lifted the Taser and pointed it at Katie once more. Caleb heard Katie gasp, heard the sound of her trying to shuffle out of the way.

"Don't do it, you son of a bitch!" Caleb said. "I told you the truth!"

And then the *Lisa Marie* shifted, just the slightest motion, but out of time with the regular rocking caused by the small swells coming in from the southwest. Barnes seemed to freeze; it was almost as if Caleb could see his muscles tighten, could see his focus shift to the companionway and up on deck. And then came the slightest of squeaking sounds, a noise that would have gone unheard if their senses had not all been keyed up as high as they could be.

But they did hear it, and they all knew what it meant. Someone had just stepped on board.

Chapter Twenty-Five

It was quiet again. The slap of the waves against the *Lisa Marie*'s wooden hull, the slight shifting of gear as the boat rolled in the swell, the squeak of the snatch block hanging from the davit, all seemed unnaturally loud. Then, through the companionway, Caleb heard the tiny creak of the deck as someone eased their weight down off the wash rail.

Caleb knew exactly the spot where the newcomer had stepped. It always made that sound when someone stepped there. Whoever was on deck was moving with as much care as he could, but there was no preventing that board from making that noise.

Barnes heard it as well. He took a step away from the companionway, further toward the center of the cabin, closer to Caleb, standing against the bulkhead so he could not be seen from the deck. His eyes remained fixed on Caleb, but it was clear his concentration was on topside.

Then a voice called out and Caleb, his every sense concentrated, jumped in surprise.

"Marco Scott?" the voice called. "Up on deck, now. I'm not going to screw around here."

Marco Scott? Caleb thought. He looked at the man he knew as Walter Barnes and he could see the name Marco Scott was causing no confusion, nor was this intrusion much of a surprise. He looked like a man with a job to do and a new but minor obstacle thrown in his way.

"Scott, get the hell up on deck, now," the voice said, more emphatically this time.

Scott, nee Barnes shifted his Taser to his left hand, pulled Caleb's Beretta with his right, a move so smooth and quick it was done before Caleb was even aware of the opportunity it presented. Scott pointed the Beretta at Katie, then waved it toward the companionway, signaling her to get up on deck.

Katie hesitated, her eyes shifting from Scott to Caleb. Caleb wanted to shout, to tell her to stay put, but he was not sure that was the best move. Whoever was on deck was some enemy of Scott's, and that meant he was probably the closest thing to a friend he and Katie had on board.

Caleb met her eyes and gave his head a small nod and Katie stood and moved forward as best she could with her hands cuffed behind her. As she stepped toward the companionway, Scott stepped up behind her, her body shielding him from the deck above. He grabbed her under the arm, half lifted, half pushed her up the two short steps until her frame all but filled the small door. Then he jerked her to a stop, leaving her standing there, blocking the entrance.

In that instant Caleb realized that their time was up. Any plans that Scott had had for killing them in a more clandestine way were past, he had to finish them now and then get clear because someone had come for him.

As if confirming that conclusion, Scott, who had been looking past Katie to the deck above, turned toward Caleb, raising the Beretta as he did, and his eyes went wide as he realized his intended victim was already in motion.

Caleb, his leg cocked under him, launched himself off the coil of rope on which he had been dropped and flew across the small space separating him and Scott. The Beretta fired, the sound like a bomb going off in that small space. Caleb felt the bullet tear through the flesh of his left arm, but by the time Scott had squeezed the trigger Caleb was already too close for him to aim at body mass.

Caleb heard Katie scream. He slammed into Scott in nearly the same instant that the gun fired. Scott was driven back against the bulkhead and Caleb heard him grunt in pain as he drove his two hundred and forty-five pounds against the smaller man. He leaned hard to his left, pressing Scott's right arm against the bulkhead so he could not move it, could not bring the gun to bear. Scott jerked his hand back, trying to get it free, and Caleb heard the gun drop into the bilges at their feet.

"Son of a bitch," Scott said, the words coming out like a snarl. The Taser was in his left hand and he swung it around, cocked his arm back, trying to find a way to shoot it into Caleb's body.

Caleb leaned back, and just as Scott was bringing the Taser up, he slammed his forehead down on the bridge of Scott's nose. Scott staggered back, blood already running down his face. Caleb stepped up to hit him again, but Scott still had some fight in him, and he was clearly skilled in this sort of thing.

Scott cocked his leg and gave Caleb a powerful kick in the stomach that sent him flying back, smashing against the side of the cabin, struggling to keep on his feet with his hands held fast by the cuffs.

Caleb made a growling noise, ready to push off at Scott once again, when he saw Katie half turn and stumble down the companionway steps, landing in a heap on the deck of the cabin. Whoever was on deck had shoved her out of the way and now his body filled the companionway, a silhouette with the dull sunlight behind him, the unmistakable shape of a gun his hand.

The stranger on deck turned toward Scott, leading with his gun, as Scott turned toward him, left hand coming up. Caleb heard the pop of the Taser going off, heard the strangled scream of the man on deck as the pain hit him and his muscles clenched up with the amps running through them. The man fell back and Caleb could see only sky, but Scott had apparently had enough. He tossed the spent Taser aside, grabbed up his drawstring bag and leapt for the companionway, pulling the bag open as he did.

Caleb pushed himself off the side of the cabin. "Katie, are you okay?" he shouted.

"Yeah," Katie said, struggling to her feet.

"Come on," Caleb said, charging for the companionway. He was not sure what he might do on deck, but somehow it did not feel safe to remain below. He had to know what was going on topside.

He took three steps to the bottom of the companionway. He could hear the stranger screaming in pain through clenched teeth, heard the footfalls of Marco Scott running aft.

Caleb stumbled as he tried to move fast, his hands pinioned behind him. He found the step with his foot, then the next, bending over to get his tall frame through the short, narrow doorway. He stepped up on deck. Whoever had come aboard and been Tasered had fallen behind the lobster tank and bait table and Caleb could only see his feet kicking.

He looked aft. Scott had reached the transom and pulled a knife as he ran, flipping the blade open and slashing the painter of the Boston Whaler even as he vaulted over the back end of the *Lisa Marie* and onto the deck of his own boat. Scott's forward momentum drove the Whaler away from Caleb's boat, and by the time Scott gained his feet there was five feet of water between them.

Behind him, Caleb heard Katie stepping out on deck, but his eyes were on Scott and the Whaler, watching in impotent anger as the gap opened up. Then Scott tossed something—a ball or a rock, it looked like—onto the *Lisa Marie*'s deck.

The dark sphere hit the planks with a hard sound and rolled forward, toward where Caleb stood. Caleb's first thought was, *What the hell is that?*

His next thought was, *A grenade...*

It was an M67 fragmentation grenade. He had seen them before, even detonated one once.

"Shit!" he yelled. He stepped forward quick, lashed out with his foot, caught the grenade like playing kick-the-can and sent it hurdling aft. He had a half-formed hope that he might kick it clean overboard, but he saw it hit the transom of the boat and bounce back inboard. He spun around. Katie was standing behind him, blocking the companionway. He hurled himself at her, knocking her back down through the hatch, the two of them falling back into the cabin. Caleb twisted as he fell, trying to change the angle of his body so he would not come down right on top of her, a thing that might be as fatal as the grenade.

Katie hit the bottom of the boat with a thud that drove a grunting, wheezing sound from her gut. Caleb landed beside her, his shoulder slamming into the deck inches from her right side, his body jarring with the impact as the grenade detonated on deck.

The sound of the explosion was magnitudes louder than the Beretta had been, even with the bulkhead between them and the deck above. Caleb heard shrapnel tearing through the cabin, heard the windscreen blow apart, the twang as chunks of grenade ricocheted off the boat's metal gear. He shuffled over to Katie, trying to cover her body with his, though by the time he was in a position to shield her from the blast, it was over.

They lay silent for a second, not moving, marveling at the fact they were still alive.

"Oh my God…" Katie said, the words no more than a whisper. "Oh my God…."

Caleb rolled over and got his feet under him and struggled to stand. Katie rolled the other way and with a much more graceful and coordinated action gained her feet as well.

They had to get the damned cuffs off them, but first Caleb wanted to see what damage had been done to his boat. He stood at the bottom of the companionway stairs and looked out, his head a foot or so above the level of the deck. What he saw was not encouraging.

The grenade had exploded in the after end of the boat, which was probably good. It had blown the port quarter and half of the transom and a big section of the deck clean off. Caleb looked through the ragged, shattered planks to the open water beyond and he caught a glimpse of the Boston Whaler kicking up a tall rooster tail as Scott made good his escape.

He turned his attention back to his damaged boat. If there was any damage below the waterline it could not be too extensive or the *Lisa Marie* would have been listing harder than she was. The live tank and bait table, however, had taken a serious beating. The port side of the tank had been torn apart, the water gushing out and running over the deck as the pump continued to circulate the seawater. Half a dozen lobsters were thrashing and waving on the deck of the boat.

Caleb saw movement to his left and he remembered the stranger who had saved them and he wondered what condition he was in, if he had been ripped apart like the live tank. He was afraid to look, but he could see whoever it was was getting to his feet, so he could not have been too badly hurt. The tank, apparently, had taken all the shrapnel that might otherwise have cut him down.

"Hey!" Caleb called and the stranger straightened and Caleb could see him over the shattered edge of the tank. Billy Caine.

Chapter Twenty-Six

Billy had been in Caleb's thoughts, and not in a good way, though it had been a couple of weeks since he had seen the man. Billy's beard, which had been close-cropped when Caleb had seen him last, seemed shorter still. His round glasses were askew and he straightened them as he looked around. He was wearing a light canvas shirt and the same sort of cargo shorts he had been wearing when they first met. He held a nine millimeter pistol in his right hand, which he tucked into the back of his shorts.

"What the hell are you doing here?" Caleb asked, trying to swallow his surprise.

"Long story," Billy said. He looked down at the two metal probes from the Taser still stuck in his chest and belly. He scowled at them, grabbed the wires and jerked them out, displaying no reaction as he did.

"Look, we're in these friggin' cuffs, come cut us out," Caleb said. Billy looked over at him as if pulled from his thoughts. He stepped over, drew a folding knife from his pocket, and with a deft flick of his wrist snapped it open. Caleb stepped aside as Billy came down the companionway stairs, turned around and felt Billy's knife slice through the plastic restraints. He lifted his arms, relishing the feeling of release.

"Billy? What the hell are you doing here?" Katie asked as she turned to have her own cuffs cut free.

"Long story, as I told Caleb," Billy said. "And we have other issues. Like the fact that the boat is sinking."

As Billy spoke, Caleb heard the bilge pump he had recently installed kick on. He looked down at the bilge below him. The water was rising over the floorboards and already swirling around his black rubber sea boots. "Ah, shit," he said.

"Yeah, that's about it," Billy said. "Look, we're not too far from shore. We can swim. If you can't swim there are PFDs, right?"

"No way," Caleb said. "No way I'm letting the boat sink." He pushed past Billy and up onto the deck. He stepped over to the wheel and snatched the mic from the radio. He was bringing it to his mouth when Billy's hand clapped down over it.

"What are you doing?" Billy asked.

"Calling the Coast Guard," Caleb said. "I'm not letting the boat sink."

"We can't have jurisdictions overlap," Billy said, his tone calm but commanding. "No Coast Guard. We'll have to keep it floating ourselves."

Billy kept his hand firmly on the microphone, raising Caleb's level of anger exponentially as the seconds ticked by. Five seconds, ten seconds, the two men stared at one another, options running through Caleb's head: listen to him, ignore him, kick his ass?

He was willing to admit that if it had not been for Billy Caine he would now have two of his own nine millimeter slugs through his skull, so by way of thanks he decided not to argue. He moved the mic back toward its clip and Billy let go of his hand.

"We got to try and stop the leak," Caleb said. "Katie, under the port bunk there are some of those wax toilet bowl seals. Go get them." Katie nodded, dived below. Caleb grabbed his sweatshirt hanging in the cabin. It was well-worn and stained, with Hopefleet written across the front in block letters. He grabbed Katie's as well, much newer with the University of Iowa logo on the front. He ran aft, his boots splashing in the water that the pump in the live tank was still spewing out over the deck.

He stopped by the wreckage of the stern and dropped to his knees, leaning out through the shattered planks to assess the damage. The transom was blown apart as were many of the planks on the port side all the way aft, and there was a big, ragged hole in the deck. As the boat rocked in the swells the water lapped over the now-open section of the rail and into the gap between the deck and the bilges, filling the boat with every dip. But Caleb was certain there was more water than that coming in.

He reached his hand through the opening the grenade had left and felt down below the water. He could feel the splintered wood where the planking below the water had suffered in the concussion. He could feel the flow of water as it ran past his fingers and into the hull.

He took his sweatshirt and plunged it into the water and with his fingers he jammed the cloth into the cracks as best he could. "Okay," he said to whoever was behind him, "that should slow things down for now." He turned and looked up. Billy was watching him. He had the look of a guy who wanted to help, who was used to helping, but did not know what to do. Katie stepped up behind him, half a dozen boxes containing wax toilet bowl seals in her hands.

"Good," Caleb said. "You guys, soften the wax up by working it in your hands and let me have it."

Katie handed two boxes to Billy and tore two open herself. They threw the boxes on the deck and began to mash the wax rings together until they were shapeless lumps in their hands, growing softer as they worked them.

"Here," Billy said, handing his lump to Caleb. "Is that soft enough?"

Caleb took the proffered wax. He could feel the warmth from Billy's hand in the soft, sticky material. "Yeah, great. Do the last two." He lay down on the deck and inched his way through the ragged gap in the port quarter of the boat. Finally he was far enough outboard that he could look down at the rent planks just below the waterline. It was bad, but not disastrously bad. He took the lump of softened wax and reached down into the water and pressed it into the gaps opened by the blast.

"More," he said, holding his hand up and behind him, and he felt Katie pressing her ball of wax into his palm. He jammed that one into the cracks as well, working it with his fingers so it went as deep into the seams as it could go. "Is there any more?" he asked over his shoulder.

"Two more, that's it," Katie said. "Here they are." Caleb put up his hand and was once again rewarded with a ball of wax. He pushed that into the last of the holes he was able to see. He hoped that was the worst of it sealed.

"Okay," he said, pulling himself inboard and getting to his feet. "That's the best we can do." Billy was standing back, apparently unsure of what to do next, but Katie had switched off the pump that circulated sea water to the lobster tank, and had been circulating sea water all over the deck. Now she was retrieving the scattered lobsters, removing the bands from their claws and tossing them back into the ocean.

"Breaks my heart," she said.

"Me too," Caleb said. "But I'll be happy as long as we don't join them on the bottom."

He stepped around the shattered tank and up to the wheel, ran his eyes over the controls. The tank seemed to have shielded everything on the starboard side from the brunt of the blast, such as the engine controls and Billy Caine. There was no damage that he could see.

Here goes... he thought as he turned the key in the ignition and was greeted by the welcome sound of the diesel growling its way to life. He turned around. Katie was just throwing the last of the lobsters overboard.

"Katie, get forward and cut the anchor away, just cut the line, no time to screw with getting it up."

Katie nodded and went forward, jumping easily onto the rail and moving forward, pulling her folding knife as she did. She knelt by the anchor rode, began working the blade across the strands, and a few seconds later Caleb felt the bow swing as the rope was cut through and the *Lisa Marie* was free from the bottom.

Caleb shifted the boat into gear and eased the throttle forward, listening to the sound of the engine, trying to feel through his hands and his feet if there was something not right beyond the gaping hole in the stern. The boat felt sluggish, which was to be expected, since the pump had not freed the hull of all the water that had come in. As long as it could more or less keep up with the inflow, that would be enough.

He spun the wheel and eased the throttle forward a bit more and the *Lisa Marie* turned onto a more southerly heading, the shore of Hopefleet passing down the port side now.

Katie hopped back down to the deck and stood beside him. "Well, what do you think? We gonna make it?"

"Don't know," Caleb said truthfully. "It's a race now, between us and the water coming in. I'm going to try and make Kettle Cove. If we can get right onto the marine railway at Downeast Marina we should be all right."

"That's...what? Ten miles?"

"Gonna be close," Caleb said. "We'll radio ahead, have them get the railway ready for us. And I don't give a crap what Mr. Caine thinks about using the radio."

At the mention of Billy's name they both turned and looked aft. The man was standing by the starboard quarter. He had Caleb's binoculars and he was scanning the water and the islands to the west.

"He said we can't have jurisdictions overlap," Katie said, her voice dropping in a conspiratorial way. "What do you think he meant by that?"

"Don't know," Caleb said. "I intend to find out. But right now we have other things to worry about."

They continued to skirt the coastline south, but it was no more than five minutes later that Caleb knew there was a serious problem. "Katie," he said. "Take the wheel, will you?" He could feel the boat was slowing despite the increased turns on the propeller. He could feel the sluggish motion underfoot, sluggish even for a heavy wooden boat.

Katie stepped up and took the spokes of the small brass wheel, and Caleb moved to the port side and down the first step in the companionway to the cabin below. He looked around in the dim light.

"Oh, shit," he said.

The pump was not keeping up, not even close. The water was five inches over the floorboards, running side to side in small waves as the *Lisa Marie* rocked in the westerly swells. PFDs and spare buoys were floating in the bilge water.

Caleb turned and stepped back on deck.

"Well?" Katie asked.

"Not good," Caleb said. "I think the vibration of the engine and prop is opening everything up. We're not going to make Kettle Cove."

"So...call the Coasties? Despite him?" She jerked her head over her shoulder to indicate Billy Caine aft.

"No, too late. They can't get here in time to help. There's a small beach about a quarter mile from here. We'll run her up on that," Caleb said, then looked aft and called, "Billy!"

Billy lowered the binoculars and hurried forward. "No sign of Marco Scott, so that's good," he said.

"Not our biggest problem now," Caleb said. "We're not going to make it to Kettle Cove, so we're going to beach it at a place a little south of here." It was not a radical idea. For generations lobstermen had been running their boats onto the beach at high tide and letting the ebb leave them high and dry so they could clean or repair the bottom. At one time it had been the only practical way to get at the places below the waterline. Now it was the easiest way to avoid the cost of a haul-out.

Billy nodded. "What can I do?" he asked.

"Bail," Caleb said. "You and me, we're going to bail while Katie drives the boat."

"Bail? Really?" Billy asked.

"Really," Caleb said. "There's no better bilge pump anywhere than a frightened man with a bucket."

He led the way down into the cabin. The Beretta was just visible under the water where Scott had dropped it. Caleb snatched it up and turned to face Billy as he jammed the weapon back into the holster in the small of his back. He found two five-gallon buckets among the jetsam washing back and forth. He handed one to Billy and the two of them began scooping water and throwing it through the companionway onto the deck, where it ran out of the scuppers aft. Caleb could not tell if it was doing much good, but every bit of what the Coasties would call "dewatering" was for the better.

"Caleb!" Katie's voice came down the companionway. "I can see the beach!"

"Okay!" Caleb shouted. He turned to Billy. "You keep at it, I'm going to bring the boat in."

Billy nodded and Caleb went up on deck again, stepped over to the wheel. Katie pointed to the beach, two hundred yards to the south and right off the port bow, though Caleb's eyes had gone right to it as soon as he had come topside.

"Good," he said. "I'll take it from here."

"You want me to bail?" Katie asked.

"No, you get some lines to tie off to the trees once we're high and dry. Use some of that pot warp, the dock lines will be too short."

Katie bounded off to do that and Caleb eased the wheel a bit to port. High tide was about three hours past, which was not good. With the tide in that state they would not be able to get far up the beach, and they would only have a few hours between the time the falling tide left the boat aground and the rising tide lifted it again.

Caleb shifted his eyes between the beach and the depth sounder as he approached. He did not want to go aground until he was as far up the sand as he could get. He turned the wheel to port, bringing the *Lisa Marie* toward the shore at a steep angle, the depth beneath his keel dropping fast.

He looked behind him. Katie had fished two coils of spare rope for the lobster traps out of the cabin and was laying them out on deck.

"One on the Sampson post and one on the stern cleat, port side!" Caleb called and Katie looked up and nodded. He turned the wheel a bit more and the *Lisa Marie*'s bow was pointing directly at the shore. Billy stepped up out of the companionway, his legs soaked by the seawater, his shirt and hair soaked with sweat. He looked forward, through the broken windshield.

Caleb glanced at the depth sounder, which showed the water growing rapidly shallower. "Here we go," he said and he spun the wheel hard, turning to starboard, swinging the damaged port side toward the shore. The keel hit with an ugly, grinding sound, but Caleb was sure the bottom was sand and gravel, not ledge, and he knew the soft impact had not done much damage.

With a shudder *Lisa Marie* came to rest and Caleb switched off the engine. The quiet was startling, but Caleb did not pause to appreciate it. He jumped over the side. The cold ocean water flooded his Grundens and his sea boots and swirled up as high as his waist, but no higher. He pushed his way through the water, fifteen feet toward the shore, then turned back to the boat. He had never seen *Lisa Marie* from this angle, just off the beam and standing waist deep in the water, and he had to admit she looked good, nice lines, her bow high and proud-looking. Despite the fact that she was going down.

Katie was at the bow, the rope in hand, and she tossed it to Caleb. Billy had the stern line—Caleb guessed Katie had instructed him to take it—and he threw that as well. Caleb caught the coils and paid the rope out as he headed for shore. He came up onto the beach, water streaming from his oilskins, his boots still filled and heavy with the Atlantic Ocean. The gunshot wound in his left arm burned with pain, but he knew the bullet had only torn up a little flesh, no more.

He found two trees, solid enough and within reach of the lines, and made them fast, pulling as much slack out as he could. Satisfied, he waded back toward the *Lisa Marie*, pleased to see she was tilting a bit to starboard. She was in no danger of sinking now because her keel was already resting on the bottom.

Katie had kindly set a boarding ladder that they kept stowed in the cabin over the side and Caleb climbed it and hopped down to the deck. He looked around at the shattered rail and transom, the lobster tank, half blown apart with shrapnel still embedded in it, the shards of windshield jutting out from the frame.

He looked at Billy Caine. "Okay," he said, "I think there are some things that need explaining."

Chapter Twenty-Seven

Billy took off his round glasses, found a dry corner of his shirt and wiped them off. "Yeah, we do need to talk," he agreed.

Caleb sat on *Lisa Marie*'s starboard rail, pulled his sea boots off and dumped the water over the side. He stood and slipped the shoulder straps of his Grundens off and dropped the rubber coveralls to the deck and stepped out of them. The cool breeze ran over his sweat-and-salt-water-soaked clothing and felt delicious. Katie followed suit, pulling her boots off and shedding her orange oilskins.

"Okay," Caleb said. "Talk." He was very aware of the gun that Billy had in his waistband, was watching Billy's hands, ready to move on him if he went for his gun. But Billy did not seem much inclined to reach for his weapon. Instead he sat wearily down on the rail a few feet away from Caleb. Katie leaned on the undamaged side of the lobster tank.

"All right," Billy said. "You might have guessed that environmental testing is not all I do."

Katie snorted at that. Caleb smiled, as much as he could in those circumstances. "Yeah, we got that," he said. "Do you do any environmental testing at all?"

"Oh, yeah," Billy protested. "I really am an environmental scientist. But I'm also employed by…other people, let's say."

"Other people?" Caleb asked. "Like, industry people? Government people?"

"Let's just say I'm not at liberty to discuss that. Which is the way a government operative might put it."

"'Can't have jurisdictions overlap,'" Katie said. "That was what you said when Caleb wanted to call the Coasties."

"Yeah, jurisdictions," Billy said. "It's never good when you have agencies tripping all over each other. But that's all I'm going to say about that. Here's the thing. You get these big internationals like IGP and AGO and they start trying to get their hands on a community and it can get rough. That guy who tried to kill you, Marco Scott, he's about as rough as they come. And I'm pretty sure he's working for AGO, trying to do what he can to keep International Gas and Power from getting their hands on the fuel farm."

"He kept asking about Howard Cox," Caleb said. "Why I was screwing with Howard Cox."

"Are you screwing with Howard Cox?" Billy asked.

"No," Caleb said. "At least, I wasn't before. Not until Cox hired these guys to beat the crap out of me."

That made Billy sit up a little straighter. "Beat the crap out of you? Did you get hurt?"

"No," Caleb said. "It didn't work out so well for them. Anyway, I tried to find out why Cox was interested in me, and that kind of turned to crap, too."

Billy nodded. "It's like I said back in the Hopefleet Tavern when I found out you were the guy. Cox is a mean son of a bitch, his whole kindly grandfather thing notwithstanding. I think he's up to his ass in this. That's what I'm here looking into. I was trying to warn you that night. To the extent that I could, and not give too much away. But it's out of the bag now."

"I don't know if Cox is up to his ass in this, but I did find some things," Caleb said. "When I was…looking around his house."

"Oh? What did you find?"

"It was an e-mail," Caleb said. "From Cox to Dick Forrester."

"Really?" Billy said. He sounded very interested.

"Yeah," Caleb said. "It gets better. Cox was asking for AGO to pay this bill to a printer in Lewiston. It was more than seventy thousand dollars. And here's the biggie—the print job was for promotional material for Cox's gubernatorial race."

Billy Caine leaned back and whistled. "Wow," he said. "Okay, now this all makes sense. Cox is planning to run for governor and AGO is funding it. But of course Cox can't let anyone know that. And in exchange, Cox makes sure IGP doesn't get the lease in Hopefleet."

"Looks like," Caleb said.

"Was there anything more?" Billy asked.

"No," Caleb said. "Cox wrote something about using another e-mail address. I guess he's not dumb enough to conduct that business on his home computer. Must have another one somewhere else."

"Of course," Billy said. "Like I said, Cox is no amateur at this stuff. The connection to Dick Forrester, that must be why Cox thinks you're out to get him. I mean, Cox obviously didn't kill Forrester, he was working with him. So he must think you did."

"Which is why he got this Barnes guy, or Scott, or whatever his name is, to come after us," Katie said. "But how did you know he was on board? Trying to kill us? And how did you get aboard?"

"I had a kayak," Billy said. "Came out in a kayak and I let it drift away. Figured I was either coming back on this boat or I wasn't coming back at all."

"Okay," Caleb said. "But that doesn't tell us how you knew Scott was on board. Or where we were." He was going to make Billy answer, and he guessed he would not like what he heard.

"Ah…yeah…" Billy equivocated. "So, I was pretty sure you were tied up in all this somehow. Didn't know how, but I thought you were a player, so I…well, I put a tracking device on the boat, so I could see where you went. You wouldn't believe how nutty the pattern is, the way a lobsterboat cruises around every day. It's like you're staggering around drunk."

"But how did you know Scott was aboard?" Caleb pressed.

"Scott, I knew, was a bad guy. I've been following him since he got to town. I watched from the end of Hopefleet Neck with binos, saw him come aboard your boat. Then I used the tracker to see where you guys went. Had the kayak on my car, ready to go."

"Okay, that makes sense," Caleb said, and it did make sense, though Caleb was not entirely sure it was the truth. He recalled Scott sweeping the boat for RF transmissions, the look he had shot at Caleb, the acoustic blocking device. Billy, he guessed, had been listening as well as watching. Once his bug was disabled he must have been prompted to kayak out and see what was going on.

"So look," Billy said, leaning closer to Caleb and Katie. "Things are coming to a head here, as you can see. You guys are not safe. Scott's not going to stop. So I need you to work with me to put an end to this crap."

"Happy to," Caleb said. "But I have more pressing matters. Tide's going out, which means I have a window of maybe six hours to get this boat seaworthy enough to make it to Downeast Marina and get hauled out."

Billy nodded slowly, as if he was considering this, as if it was his decision which problem, his or Caleb's, would take priority. Caleb found that supremely annoying. He was about to make clear that the problems of two little gas companies didn't amount to a hill of beans in his world when Billy spoke.

"Okay, yeah, I see you gotta save your boat, first thing." He pulled out his phone, pushed a few buttons. He held it up for Caleb and Katie to see: the Google satellite image of the shoreline on which they were marooned. "Looks like if we can get through the woods ashore here we'll find Reid's Lane, and that will take us to 54 and then it's only about a mile to where I left my car. I can give you a ride to wherever you want to go.

"Good," Caleb said. "Let's go."

It was a scratchy business pushing through the woods and the undergrowth, worse for Billy who was wearing shorts, but it was no more than fifty yards and then they broke out onto the dirt road called Reid Lane. Twenty minutes later they were in Billy's Subaru Outback, the seats wonderfully soft, the air conditioning on full force.

"My truck's back at the co-op," Caleb said. "Can you take us there?"

"Sure," Billy said. He looked in his mirrors, then pulled off the shoulder and onto 54. They drove in silence for a minute, then Billy started in again.

"Here's the thing," he said, in a tone that suggested he was getting down to business. They had not talked about anything of any importance on the walk back to the car.

"The vote on the LNG terminal is in two days. Now, I...we...the folks I work for, we don't give a crap about how the selectmen of Hopefleet vote on this. Not our business. But it looks like Cox is being bribed by Atlantic Gas and Oil to vote against it to stop IGP, and that's a crime and *that* we do care about. We care that the vote is honest, and not driven by bribes or promises of campaign contributions or anything like that."

"Okay," Caleb said. "So how does that involve me?"

"I don't know," Billy said. "But for some reason Cox thinks it does. So you have to convince Cox that he can't get away with voting against the LNG terminal because he's been bribed. You need to

211

convince him you have evidence that's he's taking cash from AGO and you'd be willing to expose him."

Caleb frowned and looked straight ahead as the road passed under the car. He had an uneasy feeling about all of this. "Why do I have to convince him?" he asked. "Why don't you tell him you have the evidence?"

"Because, to be perfectly honest, I don't," Billy said. "Cox is a tricky son of a bitch. We've never been able to get anything on him. This e-mail you found is the only evidence I know of, and I can't hit Cox with it because it was obtained illegally. And in my...position...I can't just confront him and tell him I have evidence when I don't."

"But Caleb doesn't have a 'position,' is that what you're saying?" Kate spoke up from the back seat. "You can use him because he has no connection to whatever government agency or whatever you work for? Complete deniability for you?"

Billy was silent for a moment. "Well, yes, I guess it's fair to put it that way. Even if it does make the whole thing look more nefarious than it is."

"The whole thing stinks," Caleb said. "I don't want any part of it. I'm just a guy who catches lobsters. I have no interest in any of this crap."

Billy pulled the Subaru into the parking lot of Hopefleet Lobster Co-op and came to a stop just behind Caleb's truck. He turned to Caleb. "I told you when we first met, you weren't going to have much choice about taking sides. I still think I'm right. I think it's time to decide."

"I did decide," Caleb said. "Cox, IPG, AGO, whatever the hell their initials are, they can all bite my ass. I don't have a dog in this fight. Thanks for the ride."

"And for stopping Marco Scott from killing you both?" Billy prompted.

"Yeah, thanks for that, too."

"He won't stop, you know," Billy said. "He'll be back. And I might not be there."

"I'll take my chances," Caleb said. "Once they take the vote, the deed is done. Then Scott or Cox or anyone has no reason to kill me." He opened the door and stepped out and Katie did the same. He closed the door and bent over and looked back through the window. "I only have to live for two more days," he said.

"Good luck with that," Billy said. He put his wagon in reverse and backed out of the parking lot. Caleb and Katie watched him go.

"Huh," Katie said. "That's a twist."

"What?" Caleb said.

"Well, we were thinking maybe Billy was the guy behind all this. Turns out he's on our side. One of the good guys."

"You think he's a good guy?" Caleb asked.

"Well, he saved our lives, like he said. That makes him pretty good in my book."

Caleb nodded, but he was frowning as well. "Maybe," he said. "But honestly, I don't think there are any good guys in this massive steaming pile of manure."

They climbed into Caleb's truck and headed back to Caleb's house, and *en route* Caleb explained to Katie how he hoped to patch the boat up enough to get it back to Downeast Marina and the safety of the marine railway. Ten minutes later he pulled into the drive and hit the garage door opener. He and Katie climbed out and fought their way through the tangle of junk that filled the two car bays.

"How long have you owned this house?" Katie asked.

"A little less than a year," Caleb said, pushing a lawn mower out of the way.

"How in hell did you manage to accumulate all this stuff in less than a year?" she asked.

"It's a guy thing," Caleb said. "And a Maine thing. A girl from the Midwest wouldn't understand."

"You got that right," Katie said. "Let me know when you're ready to have a garage sale. I'll be happy to help."

Caleb cleared a path to the shelves at the back of the garage and found some cans of a two-part epoxy repair compound they could use to seal the rents in the hull.

"I've seen lobsterboats that were practically made of this stuff," he said as he handed the cans to Katie and grabbed up some rubber gloves and putty knives and other necessary implements. "Put those in the bed of the truck, okay? I have to get some things inside."

He unlocked the door and disabled the alarm and climbed the stairs to the master bedroom. He went into the closet and stuck the key in the gun safe lock, swung the heavy door open. The Beretta was already on the front seat of the truck, so Caleb pulled out the Windham Weaponry .308 rifle and the four magazines he had.

Caleb put the weapon in a fleece-lined bag and zipped it closed. He wished he had something that did not look so obviously like a gun bag to carry it in, but he didn't, and the soft case was at least better than the hard case, which made him look like an assassin heading off for a hit.

And he was not that. He was not a killer; he did not wish to be one. He wanted to be a guy who caught lobsters. He had left his old world behind, a world that existed at the junction of violence and glamor, great wealth and massive corruption. He had tried to turn his back on all that, and yet, for his sins, it had followed him, the intrigue, the violence, the ambiguity between good and bad. Here it was, polluting the new world he was trying to create.

Caleb Hayes might not be an assassin heading off for a hit, but what he was, where he was going, what he would do—those things he did not know. He closed the gun safe and turned the key.

Chapter Twenty-Eight

Katie Brennan put the cans of epoxy and the other things in the bed of the truck, then climbed into the passenger seat and leaned back against the soft upholstery. The truck was new, like Caleb's house, part of this new life he was apparently constructing. Like the house, it was comfortable, comfortable in the way of new pickup trucks. It had none of the battered, sparse, utilitarian quality of the trucks she remembered her father driving when she was little.

She sighed as she eased back and let the padding embrace her. She was tired, possibly more tired than she had ever been before. She was no stranger to physical exertion; it took a lot of labor to wear her down. She was no stranger to mental exertion either, after her undergraduate work, and now halfway to a master's. But this was something very different.

They had nearly died, which was out of the ordinary for her. They had been cuffed, beaten, dragged below, kidnapped, threatened at gunpoint. Nearly blown up, nearly sunk. Katie realized that this was the first moment she'd had to herself since all that had gone down, the first time she had not had something or other to distract her.

A strange, disconnected feeling came over her, a sort of swimming feeling, like being suddenly underwater, not knowing which way was up.

Is this PTSD? she wondered. *Can you get PTSD two hours after something happens?*

She realized her hands were trembling, just a bit. She swallowed hard. She looked over her shoulder, momentarily afraid that someone was coming up behind the truck. She was suddenly uncomfortable sitting alone in the cab. She thought about climbing out and going into the house and finding Caleb.

Then she saw the door open and Caleb step out and close it behind him and she breathed easier. *Don't be a wimp,* she told herself. *Don't be such a friggin' wimp.*

Caleb walked toward her, fishing his keys from his pants and smiling at her through the windshield. He opened the driver's side door and Katie noticed that he was carrying a long canvas bag that looked very much like a gun bag. He slid it in behind the seats and climbed in, shutting the door with a slam.

"What's that?" Katie asked.

"It's the .308. You remember, from when we went shooting?"

Katie glanced back. The gun bag was just visible between the seats. "You think we're gonna need that?" she asked.

"Don't know," Caleb said. "It's like any emergency gear. You gotta carry it and hope you don't need it." He looked over at her, a half smile on his face, and then she saw his expression change. He reached over and rested his big hand on her shoulder, a light touch. "Are you okay?" he asked.

Katie shook her head and said, "Yeah, I'm fine," and as she spoke she realized her words and body language were contradicting each other so she stopped shaking her head.

They were quiet for a moment, then Caleb said, "You know, the first time I got into a really ugly situation, when it was over, I puked my guts out."

Kate gave a weak smile. "You've been in situations like that before? Like what happened today?"

"No," Caleb said. "Not like that. I've been shot at a few times, and I've been in a lot of personal combat situations. But I've never been cuffed and nearly shot before. It's kind of weird."

"Kind of," Katie agreed.

"Look, I can take care of the boat myself," Caleb said, his voice soft and sincere. "Really. If you want to go home, shower...sleep, have a drink, whatever, I can take care of this."

"No," Katie said, and she felt herself rally, felt the strength coming back to her like a flood tide. "No, I'll help. I'd feel like a total shit if I bailed on you now."

"Okay, good," Caleb said, smiling, and Katie could see that he really meant it, that he was glad she would be with him. It occurred to her that maybe Caleb Hayes, unflappable, unafraid, might also be human enough to feel the need for company after so traumatic a morning.

He started the truck, backed up onto the lawn and turned around. He put the truck in gear and Katie remembered something else that had been clawing at the back of her mind since their near-death experience with Marco Scott.

"I'm going to check my e-mail if you don't mind," she said, pulling her phone from her back pocket. "My mom gets kind of wiggy if she doesn't hear from me."

"Of course," Caleb said. "If she's the kind who worries, you might want to gloss over some of what's been happening."

Katie pressed the stand-by button on her phone and the screen blinked on. She shuffled into the corner of the seat as if trying to get more comfortable, though in truth she was positioning her phone so that Caleb could not see the screen. She pressed the Google icon, and when the search engine appeared she typed *Jenny Carter*.

In less than the blink of an eye a list of hits appeared, newspaper articles and social media sites. There were a few pictures lined up, each showing a beautiful girl, about Katie's age, smiling at the camera. Some seemed to be selfies, some were taken by others, but they all showed a smiling girl with blond hair and straight white teeth. A girl of notable beauty.

Katie scrolled down. The articles were mostly a year or so old. *Woman, Last Seen at Celeb Party, Still Missing...Police Question Celebs about Missing Woman...Jenny Carter's Parents Plead with Middleton, Public for Help...* Katie frowned and squinted at the screen.

"Everything okay?" Caleb asked, and Katie jumped at the sound of his voice.

"Huh?"

"Everything okay? Your mom worried about you?" Caleb said.

"Oh, yeah, she's fine. Just some news about an old friend."

"Nothing bad I hope," Caleb said.

"We'll see," Katie said. She turned back to the phone, touched her finger to one of the headlines, an article from the *Los Angeles Times*.

> *Police in Los Angeles questioned film star Trevor Middleton today concerning the disappearance of Jenny Carter from Middleton's Malibu home three days earlier. Carter, twenty-one, was last seen attending a party at Middleton's*

beachfront home in the company of approximately one hundred others attendees, including some of Hollywood's most prominent names.

"No one seems to recall when she left, or with who," said police detective Robert Short. "We're still talking with witnesses, but everyone is cooperating with the investigation."

Carter had only arrived in Los Angeles from her home in Salina, Kansas, two months before her disappearance. According to her mother, Patricia Carter, who still resides in Salina, Jenny had moved to California with ambitions of becoming an actress or model. When Jenny failed to contact her mother for three days, Mrs. Carter called police, who discovered the young woman had not returned to the apartment, which she shared with two other women, since telling them she would be attending the party at Mr. Middleton's home. When Ms. Carter failed to answer calls to her cell phone or show up for work at the Santa Monica restaurant where she waits tables, police began a missing persons investigation.

Among those interviewed were Trevor Middleton, the owner of the property, and Caleb Hayes, Middleton's longtime friend and bodyguard, and now owner, with his wife, of the elite C&S Security. C&S Security is known for its ties to the entertainment industry and boasts numerous clients among the Hollywood elite. Neither man is considered a suspect or person of interest. Police asked that anyone who might have information on Jenny Carter's whereabouts to contact them, but declined to further discuss an ongoing investigation.

"Here we are," Caleb said and Katie felt the truck brake to a halt.

"Huh?" she said, looking up quickly from the phone. "Oh, we're here?" She was trying to sound casual, but to her ears her voice seemed strained, with a guilty quality.

"Yeah, we're here. Like I said," Caleb said. "Everything okay?"

"Oh, yeah," Katie said. "Just this text I got from an old friend back home. She's pretty screwed up and I think she's about to screw herself up even worse."

"Sorry to hear that," Caleb said. "You can still bail on getting the boat floating if you want."

"Oh, no, that's cool. Nothing I can do for her. But I can probably help you."

"If you can slop epoxy on a leaking boat, you can help me," Caleb said. He climbed out of the truck and Katie climbed out of the truck. Caleb pulled the .308 out from behind the seat and they grabbed up the gear they had stowed in the bed and headed down the hill to the dock.

That swimming sensation that Katie had felt earlier was worse now, her head spinning with this new information. She had seen Caleb's visceral reaction, like he had been punched in the gut, when Scott had spoken the name Jenny Carter. What the hell was that about?

Among those interviewed were Trevor Middleton, the owner of the property, and Caleb Hayes…

The *Los Angeles Times.*

Neither man is considered a suspect or person of interest.

But Caleb's reaction was not that of a man who had no knowledge of what had happened to the girl. It was not the response of someone with nothing to hide. And Scott must have known that, because he was using the girl's name to get a rise out of Caleb.

Katie followed Caleb down the dock, a can of epoxy in one hand, putty knife and rubber gloves in the other. Her mind was spinning, her eyes on the gun case in Caleb's right hand, and on the slight bulge in the small of his back where his shirttail hung over the Beretta thrust into his holster.

Who the fuck are you? she wondered.

They came down to the floating dock, the little shack with the scales and the lobster crates where Jimmy Moody ruled his kingdom.

"Hey, Jimmy," Caleb called cheerfully. "My skiff's out on my mooring. Could you give us a ride out there?"

Jimmy looked around, confused. "Where's your lobsterboat?" he asked. It didn't make sense that someone should show up on the dock with his lobsterboat gone and his skiff tied to the mooring. It was like some hole rent in the space/time continuum.

"Long story," Caleb said. "My boat's taking on water, I gotta go out and patch it up." He held up the can of epoxy as evidence.

"Okay," Jimmy said. He still sounded a bit skeptical, but he led them down the dock to his skiff and drove them out to Caleb's mooring.

Five minutes later Caleb and Katie were underway, moving as fast as Caleb's skiff and the fifteen horsepower engine driving it could go. Their long wake stretched like a beaten path back to Kettle Cove as they left it behind. Caleb was in the stern, hand on the outboard's throttle, and Katie was in the bow, looking forward, her hair streaming behind, Casco Bay opening up in front of her.

Katie felt a slight rhythmic jarring as the skiff bounced over the small choppy waves. Talking over the outboard was difficult, so they didn't. And that was fine with Katie. She was happy to have a bit more time to think, and to try to make sense of all this.

And despite the pounding of the boat and the wind and spray in her face and the noise of the outboard, she was able to sort through her thoughts, to start to make sense of the whole situation.

To the extent that she could.

I gotta talk to Caleb about this, she concluded. She had run through her various options: let it drop, do more digging around, wait and hope that Caleb would mention it himself. None of that would work, none of it was right.

She recalled what Caleb had said about krav maga, the style of fighting he used so effectively. You just go right in, no hesitation. Overwhelm your opponent. It was good advice, applicable to more than just hand-to-hand combat. She would ask.

Whatever Caleb's part is in this, it can't be too bad, she thought. And she hoped that she was right. She had slept with the guy. She could not believe, could not stand to contemplate the possibility that she had misjudged him that badly.

But then, something about his story had never sat quite right with her. She could understand his deciding to abandon the whole sleazy Hollywood thing in favor of fishing on the coast of Maine. She would have done the same thing. But to dump it all and run as quickly and completely as he had done? There had to be something more going on there.

They ran northeast along Hopefleet Neck, and the shoreline seemed to crawl by as the skiff made all the speed it could, which was maybe five knots, and Katie wondered if they even had enough gas for this. The skiff rarely made any trip longer than the two hundred feet between the dock and the *Lisa Marie*.

"There!" Caleb called. He was pointing to some place off the starboard bow. Katie could see it too, the *Lisa Marie* just coming into view around the point of land that defined the small cove in which they had beached her.

The tide had been half out when they put *Lisa Marie* on the beach. It was further out now, and the lobsterboat was high and dry, tilted over on its starboard side, the seaward side. Katie could not tell if the tide was still going out, or if it had reached its low point and was creeping back in again. Either way, they did not have much time to make their quick and dirty repairs before the flood tide lifted the boat once more.

There was ten feet of wet sand from the tide line to where the *Lisa Marie* lay on her side. Caleb ran the bow of the skiff up onto the sand and Katie jumped out and pulled the boat a foot or so farther up. She fished the small anchor out of the bottom of the boat, carried it up the beach and set it into the sand. That way the skiff would not drift away as the tide came in and their attention was on repairing the damage the *Lisa Marie* had suffered from the grenade.

Caleb stepped out as well, into a foot of water. Like Katie, he had left his sea boots on the *Lisa Marie* and opted for canvas and rubber sandals. He grabbed up the cans of epoxy and Katie walked back down to the water's edge and retrieved the rest of the things they had brought.

"This stuff dries pretty fast," Caleb said, holding up the can of epoxy. "If we get it on now we should be good to go by the time the tide comes in."

Katie nodded, but her mind was not on epoxy and damaged planks. She was thinking about Jenny Carter, the picture of the smiling girl seared in her mind. *Among those interviewed...Caleb Hayes...*

They walked side by side up the beach to where the *Lisa Marie* lay stranded and pathetic-looking, like she was some forlorn wreck. Caleb looked at Katie with a half-smile on his face. "It's like *Gilligan's Island*," he said.

Katie looked back at him, but she had no reaction because she did not get the allusion he was making.

"*Gilligan's Island*?" Caleb prompted, but saying it again did not clarify anything, so he said, "Never mind."

No screwing around, go right in, Katie thought. She was not very good at confrontation, at initiating any sort of serious discussion. It was more her style to ignore issues if issues could be ignored, and that had never done her much good in any relationship. This time she

221

was determined to take the initiative. This would not be allowed to fester.

They had an hour and a half, she guessed, before the boat was floating again. An hour and a half with nothing to do but watch the epoxy dry and get to the heart of what had happened in Los Angeles all those months before.

"All right," Caleb said. "Let's do it." He led the way along the *Lisa Marie*'s side, aft, toward the damaged stern. Their feet sunk a bit in the hard-packed sand as they walked, mussel shells crunching underfoot.

"Hey, Caleb..." Katie said.

"Yeah?" Caleb said.

"There's something we have to talk about...it's...we can't...I have to talk to you about this." She cursed herself for her bumbling approach.

"What is it?" Caleb said, and she could hear the genuine concern in his voice. They stepped around the boat's starboard quarter, and the tree line on shore, which had been hidden from view, now spread before them.

"It's about..." Katie said and that was as far as she got. The crack of a rifle sounded from somewhere among the trees, and in the same instant a fist-sized hole was blown in the *Lisa Marie*'s transom, a shower of splinters fanning out over the wet sand.

Chapter Twenty-Nine

Before Katie was even aware of what had happened, Caleb reacted. He spun around, still clutching the cans of epoxy, and leapt at her like a football player, wrapping his arms around her and pushing her back. She felt her feet come off the ground as she went airborne and then she and Caleb tumbled back behind the boat.

They were still falling when the second shot went off, the bang of the gunfire and the shattering sound of wood blown apart coming at the same instant. And then they hit the ground and Katie felt her body jar with the impact, felt her arms fling wide, the putty knives she was holding flying from her grip, and then everything came to a stop.

For a long moment they just lay there, Caleb's arm around her, both of them breathing hard as if they had just made love. Caleb's head was up, his ear cocked toward the shore. There was no sound, save for the lapping of the waves, the cry of a gull somewhere far off, and the distant ring of a bell buoy.

"Are you all right?" Caleb said at last. He spoke softly, almost a whisper.

"Yeah, I'm okay," Katie said. She pushed herself to a sitting position and Caleb moved his arm and sat up as well.

"Scott?" Katie asked.

"Don't know who else it could be," Caleb said. "But then, there seem to be all sorts of people I don't know who want us dead. Could be the friggin' Good Humor man, for all I know."

He stood and pulled the Beretta from his waistband and stepped closer to the side of the *Lisa Marie*. He inched his way forward, toward the bow, and Katie followed behind. Caleb stopped a few feet aft of the curved stem. He stood motionless, listening, and Katie listened as well. She heard nothing, and neither, apparently, did Caleb.

With a quick, darting motion, Caleb stepped forward, looked around the bow and then stepped back, the whole action taking a second at most. If the shooter had even seen him he had not had time enough to react. The silence remained unbroken.

"So now what?" Katie asked.

Caleb frowned and looked around, as if searching for an answer on the beach or among the islands scattered around Casco Bay. "Not sure," he said. "This son of a bitch kind of has us pinned down. I think we can get to the skiff. I think the *Lisa Marie*'s shielding us. But once the skiff is clear of the beach he could take us out easy if he's a decent shot. And I'm guessing he's a decent shot."

"Okay," Katie said. "We can't leave in the skiff now. But if we wait until it's dark we could get away then."

"Probably," Caleb said. "But by the time it's dark the tide will be in and my lobsterboat will have sunk."

"So, let the damned lobsterboat sink," Katie said. She could not imagine why he had even made so stupid a point. He looked at her and she looked back at him.

"Oh, my God," she said, "you still want to save your boat!"

"Well, yeah," Caleb said. "It's my boat."

Katie shook her head. *Incredible*, she thought. "Look, Billy's not here, let's just call the Coast Guard," she said.

"Radio's up there," Caleb said, nodding toward the cabin above them. Anyone standing there would be an easy shot for the sniper on shore.

"I'll call them," Katie said. She pulled her cell phone from her pocket and pressed the button to bring it to life. She looked at the wedge of bars at the top of the phone. Nothing. Not even a hint of signal. Which was often the case on the coast of Maine. "Unbelievable," she muttered.

"The *Lisa Marie*'s our best way out of here," Caleb said. "If Scott or whoever it is has a night scope, which he might—I would if I were him—he could still take us out even if it's dark. If we can get the *Lisa* floating we can drive it out of here, stay down below the rails, get clear of the shore."

"But we have to fix the leaks first," Katie said, "and they're on the other side of the boat. We won't even get the can of epoxy open before the guy shoots us dead."

"Yeah, I thought of that," Caleb said. He looked down the beach to the skiff, which was now floating free with the incoming tide and tugging gently at the anchor line. "So, here's what we do. We wait until the tide comes in and floats the lobsterboat. Then we cut the stern line and swing the boat around and patch up the leaks. This epoxy stuff, it'll work underwater, so it's not a problem if the boat's floating. We just have to work fast so it doesn't sink. Then we cut the bow line and we're gone."

"Easy peasy," Katie said. She did not try to disguise her sarcasm.

"You have a better idea?" Caleb snapped, the anger in his voice sharp and genuine. "Look, I didn't ask for any of this shit, okay? I told you you didn't have to come, but here you are, so if you can think of a better way to not get our asses blown off, I'm all ears. If not, then just do what I fucking tell you."

Katie pressed her lips together, Caleb's words stoking the anger that was already smoldering in her. "Fine," she said. "Whatever the hell you think." She turned and leaned against the side of the boat, folded her arms. She knew it made her look like a surly teenager and she did not care.

Caleb stepped off, moving quickly down the beach to the skiff, bending over at the waist as he moved. Katie scowled at him, wondering what he was doing, but she was too angry to ask. Caleb reached the skiff and no shots came and Katie guessed he had been right that the *Lisa Marie* was blocking the shooter's view of the smaller boat. Caleb grabbed up the rifle, still ensconced in its gun bag, and the oars, and trotted back to the side of the boat.

"Now what?" Katie asked.

"This gun wasn't doing us any good in the skiff," Caleb said, biting off the words, and he said no more. Instead he unzipped the bag and pulled out the long, black gun, the steel gleaming dull in the pale light of the day. He set the butt down in the sand, leaned the muzzle against the *Lisa Marie*'s side. Then he leaned against the boat as well, he and Katie five feet apart, looking out over the water of Casco Bay, waiting for the tide to raise their boat, their only means of escape.

They stood in silence for a few moments, then Caleb pushed himself off and stepped away. "This guy in the woods is probably going to guess we're armed, so he won't cross the open ground to come after us," he said. "But I have to make sure."

He moved toward the bow once again, but this time he dropped to his hands and knees and then onto his stomach in the wet sand. He crawled forward a foot on his elbows, then lay flat and looked out under the bow of the boat, where the curve of the stem made a narrow, wedge-shaped space between the hull and the sand. If anyone was watching from shore, even if he was looking through a high-powered scope, it would be very difficult to see Caleb's face.

Caleb stood and came back to where he had been standing before. His pants and shirt were soaked through and sand was clinging to him. "Okay, seems like he's staying put for now," Caleb said.

Katie made no reply. She was still seething with anger, and she knew half of the anger was the fallout from all the suspicions and fears and confusion she had been feeling since she had brought up the articles about Jenny Carter on her phone. She was exhausted, and for the second time that day, she was in clear and present danger of being shot and she had had enough.

"Look," she said, turning quickly toward Caleb, who looked a bit startled by her tone and her abrupt move. "There's something I have to know. I need honesty from you, okay? What's the story with Jenny Carter? What's that all about?"

Caleb's eyebrows came together and he tilted his head a bit and he looked just as he might have looked if Katie had slapped him with no warning. "Jenny Carter?" he said, as if trying the name out for the first time. "How do you know about Jenny Carter?"

"Marco Scott," Katie said, her anger not abating at all as she spoke. "He said something about her. I saw your reaction. I could see there was something there, that he'd hit a nerve, big time. So who is she?"

"Someone from the past," Caleb said.

"I know," Katie said. "I know some of it. I Googled her. In the truck. I know about her, how she disappeared from some party at Trevor Middleton's house."

Those words struck like more blows to the face, but harder. Katie could see the fury rising up in Caleb as he stood straighter, his scowl growing more pronounced, his eyebrows furrowing deeper. She was angry too, and suddenly frightened, but she stood her ground and met his gaze. She held her lips tight and waited for a response.

"If you Googled her, then you know everything I know. She came to Trevor's party. She was some girl from some shit-ass place in the Midwest hoping to be a star. That's what the papers said. There were a million like her, and if they were hot enough they could always get into an A-list party. So that's what she did. I saw here there. Trevor saw her there. And then she was gone. And I don't know where the hell she went."

They glared at one another, and for a moment neither moved or spoke.

"You," Katie said at last, "are so full of shit."

"Oh, yeah?" Caleb said. "What the hell do you know? Katie Brennan, Ace Detective." He leaned in closer to her, spoke each word slowly and distinctly. "You...don't...know...a...fucking...thing."

Katie's hands balled into fists. She wanted to hit Caleb Hayes more than she had ever wanted to hit anyone in her life, more than she had wanted to hit Mike Morin at his worst moment. But if she did, it would be a token gesture, no more. She could not hurt him and she knew it and that knowledge made her madder still.

Caleb snatched up one of the oars that was leaning against the hull and Katie had a sudden idea that he might hit her with it. She had no idea what he had done to Jenny Carter, what he might be capable of doing. She wondered if she should run around the far side of the boat, hope that Marco Scott was not interested in gunning her down.

"Take this," Caleb said, "and when I tell you, stick the blade out beyond the transom. Just a bit. Don't show yourself." He snapped the words as if he could just barely bring himself to speak to her, then he stepped toward the bow of the boat once again, and once again he lay down on his stomach and peered under the keel.

"Now!" he called in a half shout, half whisper. Katie stuck the blade of the oar past the transom, a little above shoulder height. She held it for a second, five seconds. Nothing happened, and she was about to ask if she should pull it back when she heard the crack of the rifle and felt the oar jerk out of her hand and spin away down the beach, the blade shattered.

"Shit!" she shouted and jumped back further behind the boat. She turned. Caleb was there, stepping back from the bow.

"Okay, I see where the shot came from," he said. He picked up the .308. "Come here," he said. He walked toward the bow once again and Katie followed behind, too angry to ask him what he planned. He lay down once again, but this time he put the muzzle of the rifle under the keel and twisted it around, sighting over the barrel. He stood, leaving the gun in place.

"Tide's coming in," he said, nodding toward the water's edge. The skiff was floating free and half the sand that had been exposed when they had first arrived was now under water. "I need to go aboard and cut the stern line free so the stern will swing around when the boat's lifted. I need you to distract the shooter. You know how to use the rifle. Just squeeze off some rounds when I tell you."

Katie looked at the rifle and then back at Caleb. "I'm not going to shoot anyone," she said. "I can't kill anyone."

Caleb looked at her for a long few seconds without replying and she wondered what hurtful things he was considering. Then he said, "You won't. The gun's just aimed in his general direction. You won't hit anything but trees. Just distract him, okay?"

Katie nodded. She did not know what to say. She knelt down by the stock of the gun and reached her hand for the grip.

"Don't expose yourself," Caleb said. "Don't try to aim, just pull the trigger a few times, then get the hell back behind the boat."

Katie nodded again, looking up at him over her shoulder. Caleb slid himself onto the *Lisa Marie*'s starboard wash rail. With the boat resting on its starboard side, and the port side high, Caleb was still hidden from the tree line. But he would have to get up to the port side and expose himself in order to cast the stern line off.

"Okay," he said, "on three, you fire off a few rounds."

Katie nodded.

"One, two…" She took her eyes from Caleb, reached out and put her finger on the trigger, the angle awkward and unnatural.

"Three." Katie pulled the trigger and the gun went off with a powerful blast, leaping up and back, but it was caught between the sand and the keel and it stayed more or less in place. She squeezed off another and another and then jumped back just as the rifle in the woods cracked and she heard the wicked buzz of a round passing within feet of where she stood.

She could see Caleb half walking, half crawling up to the port side, to the stern where the line was tied off. She wondered if Scott would figure that out, start firing at the side of the boat. She wondered if the planks were thick enough to withstand the rifle's bullets.

Caleb reached the stern cleat, port side. He remained crouched as low as he could, reached up and found the cleat and untied the figure eight wrapped around it. Katie tensed for the sound of rifle fire coming from the woods, but there was nothing. Then she heard a thump beside her and Caleb rolled over the wash rail and dropped to the sand four feet away. He looked at her. He was breathing hard.

"Okay," he said. "Stern line's free. You can get the gun. Be careful."

Katie nodded and took the few steps back toward the bow. She leaned over and gripped the top of the .308, the black steel still warm from the burst she had fired. She lifted it and carried it back to where they had been standing beside the boat. She did not put it down.

Caleb looked out toward the advancing tide line. "Once the boat is floating we can swing it around and patch the stern," he said. "We'll have to haul the skiff up here and put the epoxy and the other stuff in it."

Katie nodded. She knew what Caleb was doing, that he had timed that stunt to distract her from her line of questioning. In the past she might have let him get away with it. She had let other guys get away with similar crap. Because, she suddenly realized, she had never considered any of the others worth the effort. Whenever any relationship had hit some snag, she had always preferred to let the whole thing rot on the vine rather than go to the trouble of having a real conversation.

But she was not willing to let Caleb go that way. And she was still angry, very angry.

"We still have an hour before the boat's floating," she snapped at him, "and we still have things we need to talk about."

"We have nothing to talk about," Caleb said, his voice low, menacing. "I told you every damned thing I know, which is nothing. I don't know what happened, okay? Just drop it. It's none of your business."

Katie glared up at Caleb as Caleb stared off over the water, his face set in a grim look of fury. She wondered how far she could push him, what he was capable of doing. She knew she could not drop it, like he wanted her to. She adjusted her hold on the gun, a subtle move that she did not think Caleb had missed.

"It most certainly is my business," Katie said. "Unless you want me to walk away right now, unless we're done completely, you bet it's my business."

Caleb turned his head and met her eyes. She had given him an out, a way that he would not have to speak another word about the whole affair. He just had to let her go, let her make a complete exit from his life, and then he could continue to stew in silence.

He looked like he wanted to speak but did not know what to say.

"You didn't just give up your old life in LA," Katie said. "You ran away from it. Your business, your wife, everything. You ran, and no one runs like that unless they're running from something."

Caleb's scowl deepened and she saw his hands clench into fists and his muscles tense as if he could no longer contain this thing that he was holding inside. Katie's hand slipped down the side of the rifle until her finger was resting on the side of the trigger guard.

A growl built in Caleb's throat, the sound of anger escaping like steam, and the growl turned into words and he said, "It's none of your business." He raised his hand, and, moving so fast Katie could barely see it, he swung around and slammed the fist into the side of the boat, so hard Katie thought he must have broken knuckles or fingers or both.

He turned back and seemed to fall against the *Lisa Marie*'s hull. He closed his eyes and tilted his head back until it, too, was resting on the side of the boat.

Katie stared at him and he seemed to dissolve right before her eyes, like when the tide finally reaches the sandcastle you're building on the edge of the surf and that first good wave washes the structure right away, leaving only soft mounds of sand where hard edges once stood.

He opened his eyes and swung his head around and looked at her. She could see the tears standing out just above the edge of his beard.

"I buried her," he said, his voice low, strangled. "God help me...I let her die and then I buried her."

Chapter Thirty

The tide was lapping on the beach, the gulls crying off to the south. Somewhere in the woods a killer with a rifle was crouching and looking for a shot that would end their lives. But Katie Brennon was no longer aware of any of that.

Her eyes were on Caleb's face, the tears running down his cheeks. The anger was gone, the fury blown away like smoke, and in its place was something broken and pathetic. She did not speak. She was sure Caleb was not done.

"I was the one who got her into the party," he said at last, choking out the words, visibly fighting to maintain control. "Like the whole thing wasn't enough of a nightmare, I was the one who invited her there in the first place."

Katie nodded. She still did not speak, did not want the sound of her voice to fracture this moment.

"Trevor did a shoot that morning, down at Venice Beach," Caleb continued, and his voice sounded as if every word was causing him pain. "There's always people, you know, lots of people who crowd up by the tape to see what's going on. I was doing security, heading up the team. Trevor never trusted the studio goons. So I met her there, and she was beautiful. God, she was beautiful, and that's saying a lot in LA, you know? Trevor pretty much had a standing order that girls like that, they got invited to his parties, so I went over and talked to her and invited her. That night. Malibu. A real A-list affair, you know? And you better believe she was happy about it."

Caleb sighed deep, closed his eyes again and fell silent. Katie still did not speak, because she did not think Caleb was done, and she was right.

"I was doing security at the party, too. Working, not taking part.

231

I saw her show up, said a few things to her, just small talk. Then, a few hours later, I'm in the living room. Trevor's bedroom was in a loft, overlooking the rest of the house, kind of like my place but a hell of a lot nicer. Anyway, I look up and I see his bedroom door is half open. But Trevor's out by the pool, I can see him through the glass. So I know something's wrong, because no one else is supposed to be in the master bedroom. Way too much chance for trouble, everyone having a camera with them, or God knows what."

He paused again. Swallowed. Then went on. "So I go upstairs and there she is, in Trevor's bed. Still dressed, just lying there, kind of trying to look sexy. I tell her she has to go, but she says she wants to stay, give Trevor a surprise when he comes in.

"'No way,' I tell her. 'Out.' So she stands up and I realized she was pretty drunk, and next thing I know she's got her hand over her mouth and she's saying she's going to puke. Last thing I want is her puking all over Trevor's bedroom so I rush her into the bathroom and she makes it to the toilet and starts hurling. And while that's going on I hear some yelling downstairs, something falling and breaking. The girl, Jenny, she's still hunched over the pot, so I run downstairs. Party crasher, it turns out, but a big guy, drunk and belligerent. I throw his ass out. And I forget about her. Jenny. I forget I left her upstairs.

"I've been playing this whole thing out in my head for a year now. It's like a movie I've watched a hundred times. Later, after a lot of folks have left, Trevor calls me up to his room. He's panicked, absolutely panicked. And he takes me into his bathroom. He had a Jacuzzi, of course. Always kept it full when he had a party. In case he needed it at a moment's notice. And there she is. Her clothes are on the floor and I can see her under the water and she's friggin' dead."

Katie sucked in her breath. "Oh, God…" she said, her voice soft.

"Yeah," Caleb said. "She's dead. I mean, eyes open, completely submerged. I hauled her out of the water as fast as I could, but no breath, no pulse. If you've seen a dead body you know, there's a certain look. You can't mistake it. I was going to call 9-1-1 anyway, but Trevor…"

Caleb frowned and looked like he was gritting his teeth. He looked out over the water, taking control of himself.

"Trevor was crying…actually crying…and pleading with me not

to do it. He was in the middle of negotiations about a movie…a fucking movie! And he didn't want any scandal screwing it up. The cops, the tabloids, they'd be all over this. Sure, it was an accident, we knew it was, but maybe the cops would think something different. And he begged me…begged me…just to make it all go away."

He closed his eyes again and Katie took a step closer to him. She realized she was still holding the .308 as if she intended to use it, so she set it down with the butt on the ground and the muzzle against the lobsterboat's hull. The incoming tide was inches away from washing over their feet.

"He talked you out of calling the cops?" Katie asked.

"Yeah," Caleb said. "And it wasn't that hard to convince me, because I had fucked up, you know? I left her there, forgot about her, and I didn't want anyone to know that part. It would have been a huge shit storm, huge scandal. The papers, TV, TMZ, they would have been all over that like you can't believe."

Katie nodded. She could believe, could imagine the sensation, the wall-to-wall coverage. "So…" she said, soft as the lapping water.

"So…my job was protecting Trevor Middleton, right? That was my duty. Protect him. And not just from physical harm, but from any harm. It's what I did."

"You thought it was your duty? To stop any stories about this girl drowning in Trevor's Jacuzzi?"

Caleb smiled, a wry smile without a trace of humor in it. "Yeah," he said. "Only doing my duty. That's what I've been telling myself for a year, and it's such bullshit even I don't believe it anymore. I did it because I'm a chickenshit coward. I was terrified of losing it all. The money, the prestige. My wife. Terrified of going to jail. I kept thinking they would call it manslaughter. Or maybe say I drowned her. It seems stupid when I look back, but I was just a coward, that's all. So I put Jenny Carter in the trunk of my car and I drove many, many miles out into the desert and I buried her. And there she remains."

"Oh, my God…" Katie said, her voice still low, her head swimming. She had no idea what to think. It was all rushing in like the tide. Shock, revulsion, sorrow, pity. She looked up at Caleb. The tears were coming down his cheeks now, unimpeded and unchecked.

"I lied to the cops, I lied to the reporters. The only one who knew besides me and Trevor was Susanna, my wife. And she sure as hell was not going to say anything because she was more terrified of losing it all than I was. I watched Jenny Carter's parents on TV pleading for information on what happened to their daughter. I saw the agony in their eyes. And I said nothing."

Katie nodded. She could make sense of the words, but not how she was reacting to them. "So she's lost, forever?" she said at last. "Jenny Carter? No one will ever find her?"

Caleb's eyes were closed tight, but he shook his head side to side. "No," he said, his voice small-sounding. "I took the GPS coordinates. I have them. I know where she is. But because I am still such a coward I haven't said anything. Waiting until there's no chance of any evidence being left. Told myself I was protecting Trevor, like I've been doing all along. But really I did it because I was too afraid to lose what I had. And the irony is that, after what I'd done, I couldn't stand any of it any more. So I tossed it all away."

Now Katie closed her eyes and tilted her head back and leaned against the boat. They stood there for a long time, silent, motionless, sifting through all that had just been said. The sun was a pale disk sinking toward the west, the muted light falling on them and on the side of the *Lisa Marie*.

Katie felt something cold and wet on her feet. She opened her eyes and looked down. The incoming tide had risen above the edge of her sandals and was now flooding into them. It would not be long now. She wondered if Marco Scott, or whoever it was, was still in the woods, was looking for his shot.

Caleb pushed off the boat and splashed softly into the water, reaching down below the surface and retrieving the skiff's small anchor. He pulled the skiff, now floating free, toward him like a cooperative animal on a leash. Then he pulled the skiff up the beach until the bow grounded out again, this time only a few feet from the side of the boat.

Katie bent over and retrieved the cans of epoxy and the tools they had brought with them and set them in the boat. They stood again in silence. Ten minutes. Fifteen minutes. The water crept up over their feet and then over their ankles.

Finally Katie broke the silence. "Think he's still there?" she asked. Her voice came out like a croak and she coughed. The words sounded strange and intrusive.

"Let's see," Caleb said. He picked up the undamaged oar and

stepped to the transom and thrust the blade out into the clear. He dipped it up and down. Five seconds, ten seconds, fifteen. Nothing.

"Maybe he gave up," Caleb said. He came back amidships, took hold of the davit and stood quickly on the wash rail to look through the cabin windshield at the tree line, fifty feet away.

"I don't..." he managed to say, no more, before his words were cut short by the loud crack of a rifle. The frame and the Plexiglas on the port side of the windshield blew apart and Caleb was hurled back into the shallow water creeping up around the boat.

"Caleb! Shit!" Katie yelled, kneeling beside him. Caleb sat up, shook his head.

"I'm okay," Caleb said. "He missed. Barely. Son of a bitch has moved. Must be looking for a better angle."

He stood and once again they sheltered behind the boat, shifting a little further aft to keep the *Lisa Marie* between themselves and the shooter's new location. And they waited.

The water inched up their legs and the *Lisa Marie* began to sit more evenly, and by unspoken but mutual consent, Katie and Caleb set aside all that had happened over the past hour and focused on their most immediate concern, which was getting off the beach without getting shot.

"If Scott or whoever is moving south along the shore, that's going to help us," Caleb said, "because it makes his angle worse for the starboard quarter where we have to work."

Katie nodded. He was right. Scott seemed to be inadvertently moving away from the place where she and Caleb would have to get at the hull.

"There's about a forty-minute pot life to that epoxy," Caleb said next. "So once the boat's nearly floating we'll mix it up and get ready. We'll have to move fast."

"It'll only take forty minutes for this stuff to dry?" Katie asked. She lifted one of the cans and squinted at the label in the dim evening light.

"No," Caleb said. "Real drying takes longer. It just stops being workable after about forty minutes. And hopefully it'll stay put long enough for us to get to the boatyard."

Ten minutes later the *Lisa Marie* made a grinding noise and rolled a bit more to port as the tide lifted the low side. Caleb untied the rope on the skiff's anchor, then stepped toward the stern of the boat and hitched the line to the starboard stern cleat.

From the woods on shore the rifle barked loud and a spray of splinters exploded from the port side, as the bullet tore through the wash rail.

"Shit!" Caleb shouted, stumbling back and almost falling in the process. The bullet had passed near him, but it had a random, unaimed quality. Katie did not think the shooter had actually been able to see Caleb; he had just gone for a lucky shot. And nearly got one.

The *Lisa Marie* rolled a bit more. The water had risen enough that she now floated nearly level, her keel grinding a bit in the sand.

"Here goes," Caleb said. He heaved on the rope he had looped over the stern cleat and the boat began to swing, just a bit. "Almost free," Caleb said. "Mix up the epoxy, one to one."

Katie nodded. She found the screwdriver on the seat of the skiff and pried the can of epoxy and the can of hardener open. Some of these things worked at different ratios of epoxy to hardener, but this was one part to one part of each, which made things easier. Each can was about three quarters full, and she hoped that would be enough to repair all the damage the grenade had done. She pulled on the rubber gloves. *For protection*, she thought, and smiled grimly to herself. Then she dumped both cans into a bucket they had brought, stuck a stir stick in and worked the thick mixture around.

Behind her she heard Caleb give a strangled grunt. She turned. He was heaving on the line, trying to pull the lobsterboat around, its keel apparently still touching the sandy bottom. He jerked hard and the boat shifted, jerked again and the *Lisa Marie* moved another foot. Then one more time and the keel came free and the boat swung around, so first the starboard quarter and then the transom was facing them.

Two shots from the shore, one ripping through the side of the cabin, the other whining overhead. Caleb pushed his shoulder against the side of the boat to stop the swing and Katie leapt forward, bucket in hand, like an emergency room doctor with a patient who was crashing on the stretcher.

She had intended to use the putty knife to work the epoxy into the cracks, but now she saw that was too fussy by far. She reached into the bucket and pulled out a big handful of the goo, about the consistency of stiff oatmeal, and slapped it on the most obvious rent in the lobsterboat's side. Some of the wax Caleb had applied was still there, but most was gone, and Katie spread the epoxy thick, pressing it in between the planks and smearing it side to side.

Once again she reached into the bucket and pulled out a handful of the mixture and worked it into the cracks. The rifle fired again, the bullet ripping through the handgrip on the top of the trunk cabin, and Katie saw that the shooter had indeed done them an unexpected favor, changing his position as he had.

"There!" Caleb said, pointing to an open seam just below the waterline. Katie nodded and worked more epoxy into the damaged wood. Caleb stepped around her, pulling the Beretta from his holster as he did. With the boat still shielding him he stuck the gun around the edge, pointed it in the general direction of the shooter, and fired off four rounds in quick succession. He pulled his hand back as a rifle bullet struck the *Lisa Marie* somewhere near the bow.

Katie scraped the last of the epoxy off the bottom of the bucket and applied it to the planks.

"That going to be enough?" Caleb asked.

"Better be," Katie said. "That's all there is."

Caleb nodded. He looked around as if for something else that needed doing. The *Lisa Marie* was now perpendicular to the beach, the bow pointing toward the trees and the sniper hiding there, while Katie and Caleb hid behind the stern.

"Okay, here we go," Caleb said. He nodded to the transom overhead. "You go over first," he said. "The shooter won't be set up for the first one over."

"But he will for the second?" Katie asked.

Caleb shrugged. "Maybe, maybe not."

"Give me the pistol," she said, holding out her hand. "I'll cover you, like on the cop shows."

Caleb gave a half smile and handed the Beretta to Katie. "There's a tall pine just to the south of us. I think that's where the shooter moved to," Caleb said. "Just aim in that general direction. You won't hit him, so don't worry."

Katie nodded. Caleb bent over and interlaced his fingers. Kate set a foot in his cupped hands and a hand on his shoulder. "One, two, three," Caleb said and straightened and raised his arms and all but threw Katie over the back end of the boat. She rolled over the last few inches of the rail, fell in a heap onto the deck. The pistol flew from her hand but luckily did not discharge. A rifle shot screamed by overhead.

Katie shuffled across the deck on her belly and grabbed up the gun. She shuffled forward until she was under the cabin roof. "When I shoot, you go!" Katie called back, trying to yell as quietly as she could and still be heard.

"Ready," Caleb called. Katie turned the gun on its side to check that the safety was off. She breathed in and out a few times, deep breaths. Then in one smooth motion she came up on her knees, elbows on the boat's rail, and brought the gun up to a firing position. She found the tall pine, or what she hoped was the tall pine, and started squeezing off rounds, one, two, three, the gun bucking in her hands. She felt the deck jar as Caleb landed in the stern.

"I'm in!" he shouted and Katie dropped to the deck. She put her hands over her head and closed her eyes, waiting for the rifle shot, but none came. She opened her eyes, looked up. Caleb was crawling toward her, commando-style as she had done, holding the .308 in his hands.

"Okay, so far, so good," he said and he stopped a few feet away. He looked up and Katie looked up. The key was hanging from the ignition switch. Caleb got to his knees and turned it and the big diesel coughed to life, the sound growing smoother as the engine quickly warmed. "Oh, crap," he said.

"What?" Katie asked.

"One thing I forgot about," Caleb said. "Bow line's still tied off."

Katie nodded and frowned. She had forgotten that as well. The *Lisa Marie* was floating free, the water with any luck not rushing in through the damaged planks, but they were still tied to the shore, one end of the line tied to a young oak tree, the other made fast to the Sampson post on the boat's exposed foredeck.

"Here," Katie said, handing Caleb the Beretta. "You've spent enough time on the shooting range, you should be able to hit a five eighths line at ten feet."

Caleb took the gun and smiled. He popped the magazine out, pulled a fresh one from his pocket and snapped it in place. "You put the boat in reverse and give her some gas, put some tension on the line. Do it on your knees, don't stand. I'll try the Annie Oakley thing."

"Got it," Katie said. Caleb walked on his knees to the port rail. If the shooter was where they thought he was, then he was just off the starboard bow and would not see Caleb there. Keeping low, he climbed up onto the rail and shuffled forward along the side of the cabin.

Katie felt herself tensing. If the shooter was not where they thought, or if he had shifted his position again, he would shoot Caleb down like he was a turkey on a limb. Katie's mind was still a whirl of emotions, spiked with a big shot of fear, but she was at least certain she did not want that to happen.

"Ready," Caleb called. Katie could no longer see him behind the side of the cabin. No shots came, so she guessed the shooter could not see him either. She stood on her knees and clicked the gearshift into reverse and nudged the throttle forward.

The lobsterboat responded quickly, a living thing once again, backing away from the beach, her bow swinging slightly. Then the bowline tied to the oak came taught and Katie staggered a bit as the boat jerked to a stop. For a second everything seemed to come to a halt, the sound of the engine drowning out all other sounds, the boat held motionless between the thrust of the prop and the tension on the rope.

And then four things happened, with just a fraction of a second separating them. Caleb fired the Beretta, the sound nearly deafening, even over the roar of the straining engine. The bow line parted with a snap and the *Lisa Marie* jerked back, shoving Katie against the wheel in front of her. And on shore the rifleman fired, the bullet ripping though the cabin top overhead, leaving a long, oval gap where it tore through the wood.

Katie grabbed the wheel and looked astern, but the *Lisa Marie* was backing nicely away from the beach, moving perpendicular to the shore. From the corner of her eye she saw Caleb coming back over the rail, half rolling onto the deck and keeping low as he, too, looked astern.

"Okay, good," he said. He spoke loud to be heard over the engine, the first time in hours either of them had spoken much above a whisper, and Katie found it jarring. "Just keep down on the deck like this. You should be able to keep her more or less backing away from the beach. I'm going to go see how much water we're taking on."

Katie nodded and Caleb crawled off toward the companionway. She sat up a bit, her back against the cabin bulkhead, holding the bottom spoke of the wheel in her left hand and looking port and starboard to orient herself. She knew there was deep water there and nothing to hit and her only concern was getting as far from the shore, and as far out of rifle range, as quickly as she could.

A minute, two minutes, and the shoreline was lost to sight from her low angle and she could see nothing but sky in her limited field of view. She got up on her knees and raised her head, peering tentatively over the dashboard and through the shattered windshield. The beach and the trees were a good two hundred yards off, and no shots had come since they had gotten underway. She was about to call down to Caleb, tell him she was going to shift the boat to forward, when he leaned out of the companionway.

"Not bad," he said. "Water's still coming in, but I think the pump can keep up with it."

"Good to hear," Katie said. "I think I should shift gears here and head for home."

Caleb nodded. Katie reached over and throttled down, shifted into neutral and then into forward. She turned the wheel and pushed the throttle ahead and the *Lisa Marie* built speed as she headed south.

She heard Caleb breathe a big sigh. He was looking out toward the shoreline, and as the boat's bow began to lift he stepped up out of the cabin, standing at full height. Katie took that to mean he thought the danger had passed and she too stood, grateful to be off her knees.

"Better ease off that throttle a bit," Caleb said. "We're just limping now."

Katie nodded and pulled the throttle back. The noise of the engine dropped by half and the *Lisa Marie*'s bow settled down. At the same instant she and Caleb turned and looked back at the distant beach. The sun was setting fast now behind the overcast sky, coloring the water and the shore in grays and browns. They could see nothing but sea and sand and trees. No one moving, no telltale flash or puff of smoke.

"Looks like we're safe," Caleb said. Katie could hear the irony in his voice.

Chapter Thirty-One

Marco Scott was angry. Very angry.

That would not have been obvious to anyone watching him or speaking with him. Anger, joy, frustration, satisfaction, Scott's outward appearance did not alter in any appreciable way with any change in mood. He would not yell; he would not raise his voice. But the man on the other end of the phone call would appreciate his level of fury. They had worked together often enough. He would hear in the words and the questions how very angry Marco Scott was.

Everything had gone perfectly at first, and then it had not.

The plan was simple enough. Get onboard the bodyguard's boat, gain enough trust to buy himself the few seconds needed to draw the Taser. Not a great problem. A few seconds were bought cheap. Drop the big man with 5,500 volts, subdue the girl. Cuff them, anchor in some out of the way place. Find out what they knew, why they were harassing Howard Cox.

Or not. It was not crucial that Scott find the reason, only that he make the harassment stop, and stop for good.

He had a plan for that as well. Double tap to their heads and after dark drive the boat out into the deep water. On the coast of Maine you could find a couple hundred feet of water just a few miles off shore. Blow a big-ass hole in the bottom of the boat with the M67 grenade, drive the Whaler back to shore. Problem solved.

The plan had been simple because it had to be, because Scott had not been given anything like the time needed to put together something more elaborate. Those idiots with more money than brains, who thought themselves the great manipulators of men, had waited until it was nearly too late. As usual. And as a result, Scott had not been given the time to do the advance work that would assure success. And so the end result was failure.

These thoughts and others were stewing in his head as he tied the Whaler up in the slip he had rented at the marina in Brunswick. The sun was near setting, the late afternoon growing dark and lost in shadow. Anyone watching him approach would have seen little more than a dark shape and red and green running lights moving over the still water.

He had spent most of the day heading south toward Portland in an effort to expose and shake off any pursuit. He had no idea what forces might be set against him. In the end he decided there was no one, at least no one following him, so he had headed back to the marina and idled up beside the dock.

With the boat tied fore and aft, he sat in the seat behind the steering console and pulled his cell phone from his pocket. He punched in a number he knew by heart. It was time to talk to the man who was actually running this show, and that was not Howard Cox.

The phone was answered on the second ring, the voice young-sounding but at the same time displaying a tone of authority and command. "Yeah?" Ryan Miller, the lawyer Howard Cox had recruited to join him at his K Street firm, the man who had eased Cox out of the place so artfully the old man didn't even realize he'd done it.

"Ryan? It's Marco Scott."

Marco Scott was not worried about using his name. He knew to what lengths Miller had gone to make certain that line was secure.

"Marco," Ryan said. "You done up there? I heard that—"

"No, I'm not done," Scott said. The fact that he had cut Miller off in midsentence would tell the man all he needed to know about Scott's frame of mind.

There was a pause on the line. "What happened?" Miller asked.

"I was set up, that's what happened. All was fine, and then guess who showed up? Billy Caine."

"Billy...Caine?"

"Yes. I think you know who he is."

"Yes," Miller said. "Yes, I do."

"I was not informed that Billy Caine was involved in this."

"Neither was I," Miller said, interjecting the words. "And that has to mean Cox didn't know, either. He would not have failed to mention a thing like that."

"I was not informed about the bodyguard, either," Scott continued, "this Caleb Hayes. I was led to believe he was just some dumb piece of meat who made his living standing around looking tough. But he's not. He's had some training, knows what he's doing. If you had called me a week ago I would have been able to find all this out, and not walk into it like some idiot."

"Yeah, yeah, I know," Miller said and Scott hoped for Miller's sake that the frustration in his voice was not directed at him. "Look, I'm sorry about this. Howard's made a huge mess out of all of it. I can assure you these problems will be reflected in your compensation."

Good answer, Scott thought.

"So where are you at now?" Miller asked.

"Pretty much where I started. Except Caine knows I'm here and Hayes and the girl have seen me. So I guess, in truth, I'm three steps back from where I started. But if you still want me to take care of this, I can. Not Billy Caine—I'd need more time for that—but Hayes and the girl, I can still take care of them. I know that's what Cox wants."

"Yeah, well, Howard thinks he's still a kingmaker," Miller said. "But I'm getting calls from people a lot higher than him on this. There's some movement and I'm not sure how it's going to shake out."

"So you want me to forget about Hayes?"

"No," Miller said. "But right now, just stick by Cox. We have to keep him alive for another couple days, at least so he can vote against this LNG thing."

"Hayes and the girl know my face now. My voice."

"Yeah, don't worry. You'll get a chance to take care of them. Soon, I promise. But for now just stand by."

"Yeah," Scott said and pressed the button to disconnect. He frowned as he looked off at the pale disk of the sun behind the high clouds, sinking behind the skyline of jagged pines. Marco Scott did not like to stand by.

Caleb Hayes took the helm from Katie and Katie stepped aside and with a grateful sigh sat on the wash rail. Caleb looked back over the stern. The beach and its adjacent shoreline were now lost to view behind the point of land. Even an expert marksman had no shot now. He felt his body relax in a way he had thought he would never feel again.

He turned to Kate, opened his mouth to speak, then closed it and turned away. He didn't have the heart to ask her to stand again. He could give her a minute at least.

It was about a minute later when he turned back to her. "Katie, would you go down into the cabin and see how much water's coming in?"

"Yeah, sure," Katie said, weary but willing. She stood, climbed down the few steps to the cabin. A minute later she stuck her head out. "It's about at the floorboards, but not above," she reported. "Pump's running steady, but it seems to be keeping up."

"Good," Caleb said. "Good news."

"You want me to stay down here and watch it?" Katie asked.

"Naw, why don't you stay up here. As long as you check it once in a while, that'll be good."

Katie nodded and climbed up the steps and took her place on the rail. Caleb kept his eyes forward, but he was aware of her presence and glad for it. Not since the night at Trevor Middleton's house, with Jenny Carter lying dead on the bathroom floor, had Caleb experienced such a ride of anguish and terror as he had over the past few hours. How Katie felt about all that, he did not know, but he wanted to make it right with her because he wanted things to be as they had been.

He did not think they were done discussing it. He longed to get it all out, get it behind them. And he dreaded it as well.

Hopefleet Neck stretched out along their port side and Caleb fished his phone from his back pocket. He knew from experience that there was cell reception to be had on that part of Casco Bay. He hoped he had juice left in his phone, and was relieved to see the screen light up when he hit the button. He scrolled though his contacts, hit a dial button.

The phone rang three times before it was answered.

"Downeast Marina." Caleb recognized the voice of Buddy Johnson, the owner of the boat yard.

"Buddy! Caleb Hayes here," Caleb said.

"Caleb? What the hell? I was expecting you three hours ago."

"Yeah, sorry, had more problems than I thought. Anyway, I'm

on my way now and I think I might even make it. You good to haul me out?"

"Sure," Buddy said. "Just bring it right onto the railway and I'll be there to meet you."

"Thanks," Caleb said. "Be there in about twenty minutes." He disconnected the phone and asked Katie to take the wheel. He climbed down into the cabin and looked around. It was even more of a shambles than usual, but as Katie had reported, the water was down by the floorboards and not getting any higher. Caleb felt guardedly optimistic about their chances.

He rummaged around until he found a small blue tarp and carried it up on deck. He picked up the .308 from where he had leaned it against the cabin side, ejected the magazine, cleared the chamber, wrapped the weapon in the tarp and set it down again.

It took them another fifteen minutes of motoring, with Katie heading down into the cabin every few minutes to check the level of the incoming water, before they rounded the point and Kettle Cove opened up in front of them. This brought on another level of relief, a sense of troubles banished. They were home, and even if that sensation had no connection to reality, still, they both could feel it.

Caleb motored past Hopefleet Lobster and further up the cove to where Buddy Johnson's marine rail ran down into the water. He lined the bow up and drove the *Lisa Marie* slowly between the rails, and Buddy, who was indeed waiting, grabbed the bow and guided the boat onto the cradle, the wooden structure that would hold the boat upright as it was hauled ashore.

Ten minutes later the *Lisa Marie* was clear of the water, snug and dripping in the cradle, and Buddy set a stepladder against the side and climbed on board. He stepped down onto the deck and in the glare of the work lights mounted on the marine railway he looked slowly around. Caleb untucked his shirt so the tail would fall over the Beretta in the holster and said nothing. He knew Buddy would need a moment to process what he was seeing.

Finally Buddy spoke. "What...the hell...happened here?"

Caleb and Katie exchanged glances. "It's those friggin' lobsters," Caleb said. "Once they get to be hard-shells they get a wicked attitude. It's nearly impossible to control them."

"Yup," Buddy said, still looking around. "I guess so. Looks like they're even starting to arm themselves, 'cause those sure as hell look like bullet holes. And I can't even imagine what happened to your lobster tank."

"It wasn't pretty," Katie offered.

"I guess not," Buddy said.

"Look," Caleb said. "If you and your guys could just fix this up and keep it to yourselves I would be very grateful." He leaned over and casually picked up the .308, wrapped in the blue tarp, and cradled it under his arm, trying to hold it as unlike a gun as he could manage.

Buddy looked at the bundle and then up at Caleb and it was clear he knew perfectly well what was wrapped up in the tarp. Then he nodded his head. "Okay," he said. "We can do that. But if you're in some kind of trouble, need some help, you just let me know. Got all sorts of ways to help a fellah."

"Thanks, Buddy, I appreciate that," Caleb said. "But I just want to get back on the water quick as I can."

He let Katie climb down the ladder first, then followed, the .308 still under his arm. He exchanged a few more words with Buddy; then he and Katie headed off down the road for the short walk to Hopefleet Lobster and the parking lot where they had left Caleb's truck.

Caleb unlocked the doors and set the guns behind the seats and he and Kate climbed in. He let himself sink into the soft cushion and once again felt the fine sensation of relief wash over him. He looked over at Katie and their eyes met and they gave one another half smiles and shook their heads in mutual disbelief. Caleb had no idea what Katie might be thinking at that moment. He was not so sure how he felt himself.

He started up the engine, backed up and turned. It was dark enough now to call for headlights, so he switched them on. They rode for a while in silence, then Katie spoke.

"It looks like Billy was right," she said. "Scott's not going to stop. I don't want to get all dramatic, like this is a movie or something, but we saw his face, you know? We can identify him. Don't you think he'll keep trying to kill us? If for no other reason than that?"

Caleb was quiet for a moment. He had been wrestling with that same thought, but had not reached any conclusion. "I don't know," he said. "He might. But then, I have a fair amount of expertise in making sure guys like him don't kill me or the people I'm protecting."

"Yeah, but you had, like, a staff then," Katie said. "Now it's just you. And even if you can keep yourself safe, you can't protect me all the time. And I imagine this Scott asshole now wants me dead as much as you."

Caleb nodded. "Yeah, you have a point," he said.

"We should call Billy. See what he has to say. See if he can help," Katie said. "You saw what he can do."

"I saw him get tased," Caleb said. "I saw him nearly get blown to bits before I kicked the grenade away."

"You know what I mean," Katie said. "He works for some kind of government agency. They must have resources. People. Stuff that can help."

"All right," Caleb said. "We'll call Billy." He did not see a way out of this. And besides, Katie had a point. He'd have to ride this train to see where it stopped.

But in the end they didn't have to go to Billy Caine, because Billy Caine came to them.

Caleb turned his truck off Route 54 onto Ash Point and rumbled down toward Hopefleet Sound. He turned again into his driveway, his headlights sweeping across the front of his gray-shingled house and Billy Caine's Subaru wagon parked in the gravel drive. The hatchback was open and Billy was sitting in the back, one leg draped over the bumper, one propped up on the bed, and leaning against the side. The picture of patient ease.

"Well, look who's here," Caleb said as he pulled up beside the Subaru and shifted into park. He switched off the headlights and he and Katie tumbled out of the truck.

Billy had climbed out of his car and was standing, waiting, as Caleb shut the door to the cab. "There you are!" Billy said. "Where have you been? I've been waiting for...like, two hours. I didn't think it would take so long to get the boat to the marina."

"Took longer to patch up than we thought it would," Caleb said quickly, getting his explanation in before Katie could give the full story. He hoped Katie would take the hint, keep quiet about Scott and the ambush. He wasn't sure why. Just his natural inclination, he guessed, to always keep the cards close to his chest.

"I guess it did," Billy said.

Katie came around the back of the truck, gave Billy a weary

smile. "Billy! Good to see you again. And in better circumstances. We were just talking about you."

"You were?" Billy said.

Caleb gave Katie a sideways glance, wondered if she had said that just to keep him from backing out of his promise to talk to Billy. If so, it had worked. He had to say something now.

"Yeah, we were," Caleb said. "We were talking, and we think you're right. This Scott guy isn't going to stop until we're both dead. Particularly since we can identify him now. So we figure the best way for us to get out of this is to work with you."

Billy nodded. "I agree," he said. "And I'm glad you've come to that conclusion as well. We don't have a lot of time. The vote on the LNG terminal is coming up. That's the big one for them. They're going to put the pressure on. Like I said before, we don't care which way Cox votes, as long as his vote isn't being bought by AGO or anyone else."

"Right," Caleb said. "And tell me again, who are 'we'? Who exactly do you work for?"

Billy smiled. "Tell you again? I don't think I told you in the first place. And, honestly, there's not a lot I can say. Let's just say it's a very, very big organization. Funded by your tax dollars."

Caleb nodded. "Okay, that narrows it down. So, how are we going to play this?"

Billy pointed with his thumb to the house. "Should we go inside and talk about it?" he asked.

Caleb thought about the deadly accurate rifle fire that he and Katie had just survived. He thought about the ring of dark woods that surrounded his house, perfect cover for a shooter. "Yeah, sounds good," he said.

He opened the door of the truck, pulled out the .308 and shut the door. He took two steps toward the house, then stopped and put the gun down on the hood of Billy's Subaru. "Excuse me a second," he said. He put his hands down on the hood and stretched his back, arching like a cat, groaning with the pleasure of it. He stood and grabbed each elbow in turn and stretched his upper arms.

"Been a long day," he said, "and I'm feeling my age."

He unlocked the door to his house, disarmed the alarm and led the way into the kitchen. He distributed cold beers and gestured for Billy and Katie to sit in the living room, which they did, then he took his place in the big armchair. He turned to Billy.

"Okay, this is your territory. What do we do?"

"We stop Cox and Scott before they kill you," Billy said. "And Katie becomes collateral damage."

"'Collateral damage,'" Katie said. "Oh, that's flattering."

"We could publicly expose Cox's corruption with the e-mail you found," Billy continued, "but that causes all sorts of problems, like the small matter of your breaking and entering. I think the way to go is to confront Cox, one on one. Let him know that you didn't kill Forrester, that you don't care about any of this crap, but that you can and will expose him unless he calls Scott off and drops this quid pro quo with Atlantic Gas and Oil."

Caleb considered that. "It sounds very reasonable," he said at last. "You think Cox is in a mood to be reasonable?"

"I don't think he'll have a choice," Billy said.

Caleb turned to Katie. "What do you think?"

"Like you said, it sounds reasonable. To be honest, I'm not so sure Cox is going to see reason, but it's worth a try."

"You want me to set it up?" Billy asked.

"Sure," Caleb said.

"Good," Billy said. "I'll make it happen." He stood, took one last pull from his beer, and Caleb and Katie stood as well. "I'll be in touch once I have something worked out. We'll figure out the details then."

Caleb and Katie nodded, muttered their agreement. Billy let himself out and then it was only the two of them and an uncomfortable silence.

"I'm…I'm not sure where I'm at right now," Katie said, haltingly. "About us."

Caleb nodded. So much to process. He might be the most loathsome of creatures in her eyes now. Or maybe he was a hero after getting them off the beach. He had no idea how she felt, or how she should feel.

"I understand," he said. "But I also don't think you should go home. Not with Scott still out there. Why don't you take the bed upstairs and I'll crash on the couch? Honestly, with everything that's going on I think I'd rather cuddle with the .308 anyway."

Katie gave him a look that suggested that she would not have appreciated the joke in the best of times. She bid him goodnight, headed up the stairs to the master bedroom. He set the alarm and padded off to the downstairs bathroom with its promise of a hot, soothing shower.

He stripped off his shirt and started to unbuckle his pants when he realized his cell phone was still in his back pocket. He pulled it out and set it on the counter by the sink. He remembered that moment of surprise when he had turned his phone on and found Billy Caine's kids grinning at him. Wrong phone.

And then another thought organized itself in his head, like something solid forming out of the ether.

Billy at the Hopefleet Tavern, accidentally walking off with Caleb's phone.

Marco Scott, holding him at gunpoint, demanding answers. *Two weeks ago you sent a text to Howard Cox.*

Caleb stood up straight, looked down at his phone, and suddenly he felt everything falling into place.

Chapter Thirty-Two

The text Caleb had been waiting for came in around 1:20 a.m., Eastern Standard Time, 10:20 in California where it had originated. The buzzing of the phone on the coffee table woke him, but it took him a moment to remember where he was, so deeply had he been sleeping.

Couch... he recalled. He picked up the phone and swiped the screen. Read the text. Nodded. But there was nothing he could do about it at that hour so he put the phone down again, and, certain he would not be able to fall back to sleep, was thoroughly unconscious five minutes later.

The living room windows were east facing, and though Caleb had closed the curtains the evening before, he had done so imperfectly. As the rising sun reached the top of the spruce on the far side of Hopefleet Sound, a thin vertical shaft of light managed to work its way through the narrow part in the curtain and hit Caleb square in the face.

He blinked and then shut his eyes against the onslaught and then with a groan pushed himself to a sitting position. He was dressed in a tee shirt and cotton shorts. His muscles felt sore and tight, but his head was now clear of the beam of light so he opened his eyes. The Windham Weaponry .308 was lying on the coffee table and his cell phone beside it. He looked around. All was well, no immediate threat to life or property.

We'll see how long that lasts, he thought, and with another groan pushed himself to his feet.

The coffee was half brewed and bacon popping and sizzling in the pan when Katie finally came down the stairs to join him. She was wearing one of his flannel shirts and carrying her filthy, salt-water-soaked, mud-and-sweat-stained clothing in a bundle under her arm.

"Morning!" she said, but before she joined him she crossed to the small laundry room by the side door and threw the clothes in the washing machine. She filled the rest of the space with clothes from Caleb's hamper and twisted the knob. Caleb had a mug of coffee on the granite counter of the island by the time she arrived.

"Ah, coffee!" she said with sincere appreciation. "Thanks."

"Thanks for throwing my clothes in the wash," Caleb said.

"Least I could do," Katie said. "After all, it's your machine. And your soap and water and electricity."

"True," Caleb said. He took a deep and welcome mouthful of coffee.

"You sleep okay?" Katie asked. "How was it with your .308?"

"Not as good as I'd hoped," Caleb said. "How about you?"

"Yeah, I slept well. I was pretty out of it," Katie said. She took a tentative sip, looked up at Caleb. "I missed you."

He looked back at her, into her eyes, blue like the blue of the ocean far off shore. "I missed you, too," he said.

They were silent for a moment, not an awkward silence exactly, but the silence of two people who were not sure where to go from there. Then Caleb said, "Bacon's on."

"I know," Katie said. "It's the only reason I got out of bed."

"Two eggs over easy, sourdough toast?"

"You got it."

Caleb turned toward the refrigerator, then turned back. "Hey, I got a text last night. Read this." He slid the phone over to Katie.

Katie picked it up and read. "Who's this?" she asked.

"My buddy in LA," Caleb said. "The guy who can track down the phone numbers."

"'Dude,'" Katie read off the screen, "'you know I like a good challenge, but that was a seriously hard nut to crack. Lots of layers, but the phone number in the end belongs to a company called International Gas and Power, headquartered in New York City. That's all I could find. JK about not knowing what to do with lobsters. I've got the water boiling so send the lobsters soon.'"

Katie put the phone down and looked up. "So...?" she said.

"So, you remember I texted him to ask about Billy's number?"

"No," Katie said. "Honestly, with all the crap that's happened this week I can't remember jack."

"We tried calling the number on Billy's card, remember? And it seemed like his company, whatever it was called, was legit. But I asked my buddy to see if maybe the phone number belonged to some other company. Turns out it belongs to IGP."

"So…?" Katie said again.

"Have some more coffee," Caleb said. He refilled her mug. "So, the company that Billy says he works for is some division of International Gas and Power. The guys who want to build the LNG terminal in Hopefleet."

"The company that Cox is voting against," Katie said.

"Exactly. Now the caffeine's reaching your brain," Caleb said.

"But didn't Billy tell us he worked for the government?" Katie asked.

"Actually, he didn't," Caleb said. "He just implied it. I don't know why he didn't just outright lie. Maybe he was afraid we'd catch him in it. Anyway, I'm going to make a phone call, see if I can find out more." He looked over at the clock on the wall in the dining area. "Once places start opening."

He made breakfast and they ate at the island in the kitchen. Caleb wanted very much to have it on the deck: a high pressure system had moved in overnight, blowing out the clouds and humidity and promising ideal weather. But after their experience under sniper fire the day before, he opted for them to stay inside. His cameras and motion sensors had not picked anything up, but extra caution was warranted, he felt.

"Good day for lobstering," Katie observed. "Too bad we don't have a boat."

"Yeah, looks like we're tourists today," Caleb said.

"And I guess I'm out of a job."

"Not necessarily," Caleb said. He had been thinking about this very thing. It had surprised him how very much he did not want Katie Brennan to go off and find other work. "I really want to get the boat fixed up as fast as I can. I was going to work on it with the guys at Downeast. I'd be happy to pay you if you want to help. Might be good experience. Even fisheries yahoos should know how to fix boats."

Katie nodded. "Do you really need my help?" she asked. "Or are you just doing this for me?"

Caleb leaned back and looked at her. "I don't *need* your help," he said. "I want your help."

Katie nodded again, and Caleb hoped that she understood that he was being as honest as he could be.

They finished breakfast and Katie moved the clothes from the washer to the dryer. They cleaned up the breakfast dishes and had another cup of coffee.

Soon the dryer buzzed and Katie emptied it, then changed from Caleb's flannel shirt back into her own clothes.

It was five minutes past nine when Katie emerged from the downstairs bathroom. Caleb had his laptop on the granite island and he stared at the screen as it booted up. "I'm going to call International Gas and Power's headquarters, see if they have a Billy Caine in their employ," he said, even before Katie could ask.

"Wouldn't he be using an alias?" Katie asked. "If he's really involved in all this intrigue, you think he's using his real name?"

"I don't know," Caleb said. The home page appeared and Caleb typed *International Gas and Power* into the browser. "That time in the tavern, when he bought a round, I saw his driver's license and a credit card and they had his name. You can fake all that stuff, but it's difficult and expensive. They might not go to the trouble if they don't think it's worth it."

"You noticed all that when he opened his wallet?" Katie asked. "Nosey, much?"

"Training," Caleb said. "You gotta keep your eyes open." He clicked on the most promising search result, scrolled around the website until he found what he was looking for. He picked up his phone and dialed the number, a 212 area code. New York City.

The phone was answered on the second ring, a female voice, cheerful, thoroughly professional. "International Gas and Power. How may I direct your call?"

"Yes, hello," Caleb said, trying to match her good cheer and professionalism. "I understand there's a division of your company called New England Environmental Testing and Analytics? Could I be connected to them, please?"

There was a pause at the other end, just long enough to signal confusion. "I'm sorry," the woman said. "I don't believe there's any division of this company by that name."

"Huh," Caleb said. "Well, I'm looking for a fellow named Billy Caine, or William Caine. I thought he was with New England

Environmental, but maybe I was wrong. Do you have a company directory? Can you tell me if you have a William Caine?"

"One second, please, sir," the woman said. Caleb could hear the telltale clacking of computer keys. "Yes, sir, there is a William Caine in our directory, but he's part of IGP's security division. Would you like me to transfer you?"

Caleb had been expecting something like that, but the confirmation still made him feel as if he had been punched in the gut, and shocked him into silence.

"Sir?" the woman asked.

"Oh, ah, no, that's good," Caleb said. "I'll try another number I have for him. Thanks." The woman was still going through her courteous sign-off when Caleb punched the disconnect button.

"Security division?" Katie asked. She had been leaning in, listening.

"Security division," Caleb said.

"But we don't know what that means," Katie said. "Remember, he did save our butts when that Scott guy was going to blow our brains out. Security could mean he's trying to stop the other guys from killing us. Or anyone else."

"It could," Caleb agreed.

"But you don't think so," Katie said.

"I don't know. Innocent until proven guilty and all that. But I did have an idea. Might tell us more about the game Billy's playing."

He went upstairs to his bedroom and changed into jeans and another tee shirt, then came down again. He picked up the .308 from the coffee table. "Okay, let's head out," he said to Katie.

"Are you taking that?" she asked, nodding toward the rifle.

"Yeah. Like the Boy Scouts say, 'Be Prepared.'"

"I don't think that's the sort of thing the Boy Scouts had in mind," Katie said.

They left the house and Caleb set the alarm. "Mind if we take your car?" he asked.

"Sure," Katie said. "Why?"

"I'm thinking it might be less loaded down with tracking devices than my truck is," Caleb said. He opened the passenger side door and laid the rifle on the back seat, amid a strew of Starbucks cups and running shoes and empty bags of chips from Trader Joe's and various articles of clothing. He picked up a green bikini top, which was made of precious little fabric and held it up, looking askance at Katie.

"Give me that," she said, reaching through the driver's side door, snatching it from his hand and tossing it on the floor behind the seat.

Caleb covered the rifle with the tarp he had taken from the boat the day before and struggled to climb into the passenger seat. "You should clean this thing once in a while," he said.

"Yeah, yeah," Katie said, climbing into the driver's seat and settling her sunglasses on the bridge of her nose. "Where to?"

"You know Middle Bay Canoe and Kayak?" Katie nodded. "There," Caleb said. Katie started the car and backed up in a big half circle. Five minutes later they were swaying along Route 54 heading toward Brunswick.

"I had another thought," Caleb said.

"Uh oh," Katie said.

"You remember yesterday? The guy in the woods, shooting at us?"

"Bullets flying? Nearly killed us? Yeah, I remember that."

"Well, here's the thing," Caleb said. "I think we mostly kept down, hidden, but sometimes we were exposed. And when the shooter tried for us, he missed. But you remember when you held out that oar? He nailed it. Shot it right out of your hands."

"What are you getting at?" Katie asked.

"The guy was a hell of a shot," Caleb said. "But he kept missing us. It makes me think maybe he wasn't really trying to kill us at all."

"Well, we know Scott wanted to kill us," Katie said. "I think he was pretty clear about that."

"Exactly," Caleb said. "So maybe the shooter wasn't Scott."

"Then who else could it have...wait...do you think it was Billy shooting at us?" Katie asked.

"The possibility occurred to me."

"Why would he do that?" Katie asked.

"He wants me to convince Cox not to vote against the LNG terminal. Now we know why. He works for International Gas and Power. Part of his argument was that this guy Scott was going to keep coming after us unless we made this thing go away. So maybe he wanted to drive that message home a bit. He knew where the boat was beached. Besides, when we showed up at my place last night he said he'd been waiting for hours, but when I put my hands on the hood of his car it was hot, like he'd just been driving."

"Wow! Who's Sherlock Holmes now?" Katie asked.

"No, not Sherlock Holmes," Caleb said. "Encyclopedia Brown. I lifted that technique right out of one of those books."

Katie turned her PT Cruiser onto Middle Bay Road and then onto Mere Point. Five miles later she turned into a big gravel parking lot. A small wooden building with doors and windows flung open sat at the far end, and ringing the lot were metal racks half filled with bright-colored plastic kayaks. The sign on the building read Middle Bay Canoe and Kayak. Beyond that, the upper part of Middle Bay glinted in the morning sun. Katie braked to a squeaky stop.

"Okay, now you're going to see some real Sherlock Holmes action," Caleb said.

"Oh, yeah?" Katie asked.

"Yeah," Caleb said. "Maybe. We'll see." They climbed out of the car and approached the building, but they had only gone a few steps before someone stepped out from the dark interior to greet them. He was a young guy, mid-twenties, with dark hair, a few days' growth of beard on his face. He was wearing shorts and a tee shirt and had the lean body and deep tan of someone seriously committed to outdoor sports.

"Morning," he said, friendly and casual. "I'm Jason. Can I rent you folks some boats?"

"No, thanks," Caleb said. "I have a boat. But, do you mind if I ask you a question?"

"Shoot," Jason said.

Caleb pulled out his phone and pressed it on. The screen filled with a picture of Dick Forrester, smiling at the camera. It was the kind of picture taken for corporate PR purposes, and Caleb had found it online earlier, along with Forrester's obituary.

"That guy that drowned a few weeks back, the guy from Connecticut? Did you rent him the kayak?"

"Yeah..." Jason said, his voice wary now. "Why? I'm guessing you're not a cop, and I already told the cops all about this."

"I'm not anything," Caleb said. "Well, yeah, I am something. I'm the lobsterman who pulled him up on his trap."

"Oh, dude!" Jason said, relieved and smiling. "That must have been one sucky surprise!"

"Yeah, it was that," Caleb agreed. "But tell me, is this the guy you rented the kayak to?" He held his phone up and Jason took it, squinted at it, then turned so his body cast a shadow over the screen. He held it up close and was silent as he studied it. He turned back to Caleb.

"No, I don't think so," Jason said. "I'm pretty good with faces, you know? And I don't think that was the guy."

"Okay," Caleb said. He turned to Katie. "Can you bring up that picture of Billy you had on your phone?"

"Sure," Katie said. She pulled her phone from her back pocket and poked at buttons until she had what she wanted. She handed the phone to Jason who once again turned so the screen was shaded from the sun.

He took less time with the second photo. "Yeah, dude, that's him!" Jason said, turning back to them. "That's the guy I rented to the boat to. Poor bastard. I told him to wear a PFD."

"Yeah," Caleb said. "Sometimes people do dumb things and you don't know why they do it. And sometimes they end up dead."

Chapter Thirty-Three

Billy Caine was not a musician. He knew nothing about orchestral music and did not particularly like it. But he had an idea of how it felt to be a conductor, and he liked that very much.

His home for the past month had been a suite in the Best Western in Brunswick. Excellent accommodations. Not terribly cheap, but International Gas and Power was picking up the tab, so that part was of no concern. Nor would it have been in any event. IGP was paying him enough that he could have afforded much better than the BeWe without feeling a dent in any of his bank accounts, domestic or offshore.

He didn't think of his suite as a room, or a home, or anything of that nature. He called it, in his own mind, Master Control. He had turned the hotel's flat screen TV into a monitor which, with the press of a button, would show the display from any of several electronic devices he was currently employing. He had tracking devices and hidden video cameras and RF listening devices. He had various cell phones and laptops, each running some different application. He had all the principals in this current operation under his watchful eye, and he was playing them all like puppets.

Like a conductor, he thought. *The Leonard Bernstein of surveillance and manipulation.* He liked that even more than the clockmaker simile.

The suite was getting a bit stale now, and he knew there was an

259

unpleasant odor. He could smell it when he entered, was aware of it until his nose acclimated once again. The array of equipment meant that he could not have housekeeping do their work. He could not afford to have nosey maids yapping about what they had seen. Once, two weeks earlier, he had packed it all away and let them give the place a cleaning. But since then he had kept the Do Not Disturb sign hanging from the doorknob. He had distributed tips liberally. No questions were asked.

He stood and stretched and went into the bathroom. There was one lone towel left on the rack. Every few days he would call to the desk and ask for fresh towels and meet the housekeeper at the door and exchange his old ones for new. He considered doing it now but dismissed the idea. No need. He had no more than a day or two before he was gone from this place, his job done, and done well.

Caine used the bathroom and then returned to the desk on which his various blinking screens were arrayed. He looked at the read-out from the tracking device on Caleb Hayes's truck. It hadn't moved all morning. Hayes and the girl, Katie, must have been sufficiently freaked out by their brush with death on the beach that they did not care to venture out of the house. Billy had an image of Hayes sitting on the edge of his couch, wide-eyed, clutching the .308.

Tough guy, Billy thought. *Tough bodyguard. Your ass is mine.*

He picked up his cell phone and punched in a number. The line at the other end rang and Billy heard Caleb's voice. "Hey! Billy?"

"Yeah, it's me," Billy said, putting the brightness into his voice. His helpful tone, a touch of concern as well. "You okay?"

"Yeah, yeah, all's fine," Caleb said. No change in his voice that Billy could hear, save perhaps for a touch more anxiety. That was good. Hayes had been stewing all night over his predicament.

"Okay, look," Billy said. "I've got this set up. I've been in touch with Cox. He doesn't know who I am, but he knows I'm someone he had better pay attention to. He's set to meet you. Tonight. Midnight at the fuel farm. He'll come alone."

"The fuel farm?" Caleb said. "That's a nice touch. Sounds like a great opportunity for Scott to kill me with a sniper rifle. You sure this is a good idea?"

"Look, this isn't the amateur hour, okay?" Billy said. "Scott shooting you? Won't happen. Cox knows what you have on him, and he knows it all goes public if anything happens to you. I made sure he knows it. You show up, you give him a print-out of what's on that flash drive, you tell him as long as he doesn't do AGO's bidding no one will know any of it. Hell, there's nothing stopping him from still running for governor. Just not with AGO's backing."

There was a pause on the line as Caleb seemed to consider this. Of course he would be hesitant. There was no guarantee things would play out as they hoped. But Billy guessed that the fear of Marco Scott would be enough to push Hayes over the edge.

He smiled to himself. *Cox, you stupid bastard*, he thought. *You called Scott into this to save your ass, and now Hayes is so scared of him he'll do what I want.* Billy Caine enjoyed irony.

"Okay," Caleb said. "Midnight at the fuel farm. I'm alone, Cox is alone."

"That's right," Billy said. "I'm going to stay clear until it's over. I don't want my presence to screw this up. We'll meet up after and you can tell me how it went down."

"You got it," Caleb said and disconnected.

Billy sat there for a long moment, staring at the sundry screens but paying them no attention. *Good...* he thought. *Good.*

It was falling into place. He was standing above them all, waving his wand, and the various players were doing as he directed.

Cox had been harder than Hayes to conduct, and that was no surprise. Cox was a crafty old bastard, no stranger to this sort of thing. But he was ready to crack. One day left before the vote. Cox votes against the LNG terminal and Caleb Hayes exposes his connection to AGO. International Gas and Power's hands remain clean, because Hayes has no connection whatsoever to IGP.

Beautiful.

Billy picked up one of the disposable phones. He connected the recording device to the earphone jack and hit record on the tiny unit. He had recorded it all, all the conversations with Finch. Insurance that would last a lifetime.

Satisfied that all was working, Billy punched in a number. He waited as the phone on the other end rang half a dozen times, enough for Billy to start growing annoyed, before it was answered.

"Yes?" Daniel Finch was there. Billy could just picture the little puke in his Forty-Ninth Street office. Probably standing in front of the plate glass windows, looking down on Central Park like he was God overseeing His creation.

"It's me," Billy said. He used his low, expressionless voice, more like a growl, because he knew it unnerved Finch and gave him, Billy, a huge psychological advantage. "Looks like we're set. Cox is meeting tonight with the lobsterman, and he'll be told in no uncertain terms that his vote must change. Cox is on edge now. He'll crack."

The silence at the other end of the line lasted longer than Billy liked. Then Finch spoke. "The vote's in two days," he said. "What makes you think Cox will crack now?"

"Because I have pushed him as far as he can stand. The lobsterman knows about his connection to AGO, and he's willing to spill it if Cox doesn't play."

More silence. "You said Cox brought in muscle?" Finch said at last.

"Yeah, and it blew up in his face. Makes the lobsterman even more eager to help me."

"The lobsterman can connect you to IGP," Finch said. A statement, not a question.

Caine could feel his irritation climbing like mercury on a hot day. "No, he can't," he said. "Hayes thinks I work for the government. He is unaware of my connection to IGP. He has no way of knowing."

More silence. Finch was not displaying the sort of fearful uncertainty that Caine had come to expect from him. In their earlier discussions, Finch had seemed like a man out of his depth, a man grateful for the fact that he, Caine, knew how to handle the situation. That was how Caine wanted him. But he was not acting that way now.

"Look," Caine said. "Cox and Hayes are meeting tonight, and one of two things is going to happen. Either Hayes scares Cox into cooperating with us, or Cox's muscle kills Hayes, in which case I can implicate Cox in murder because I will be videotaping the whole thing. Either way the old man is ours."

"Yeah," Finch said at last, "but here's the situation. We have some things moving at this end, some things still in play. We may have to take another tack here. Hold off on Cox. Don't approach him with this stuff until I tell you. I'll be in touch."

And then Finch disconnected.

For a long moment Billy sat there with the phone still pressed to his ear. He was still staring at the screens on the desk and still not seeing them.

Hold off on Cox...? He had spent the past month carefully manipulating Cox and Hayes and all of these bumpkins in Hopefleet, and now the little prick in New York was telling him to hold off? He had written a masterpiece here, his *Magnum opus,* and this Finch asshole wanted him to stop before the music had reached its climax?

"I don't think so," Billy Caine said out loud. He would kill them all before he let that happen.

When Caleb finished talking with Billy Caine he hit the disconnect button on his phone and the screen showing Billy's number vanished. For a long time he just stared at his background—a picture of the bell buoy, red number 18, between Littlejohn and Great Chebeague Islands—and the smattering of application icons that half obscured it.

He was sitting in the big white upholstered armchair in his living room, Katie on the edge of the couch, four feet away.

"Well?" Katie said at last.

"You know," Caleb said, looking up at her at last. "I actually half believed Billy *was* a government guy. And now I'm embarrassed as hell to admit it."

"Huh," Katie said. "Well, you figured it out long before I did. Actually, I didn't figure it out at all. So I guess that makes me even more pathetic."

"No, you're not pathetic," Caleb said. "This is just more in my sphere of experience. I'm sure if we were talking about, say, the mating habits of marine gastropods you'd be way ahead of me."

"That's too titillating for me," Katie said. "So, what'd he say?"

"We have a meeting. Tonight. Me and Cox. At the fuel farm, of course. I give him a print-out of the thumb drive to show him I have it, tell him not to do AGO's bidding, which apparently is another way of saying do what IGP wants, and then we're good. He leaves me alone."

"Right," Katie said. "You're not going, of course."

"Of course I'm going. Billy went to a lot of trouble, here. It would be wicked rude of me to just blow him off."

Katie sat more upright and looked at Caleb as if she could not tell whether or not he was kidding. Which she probably couldn't. "Are you serious? You're really planning to go?"

"Of course," Caleb said. "If I don't go, then this thing just drags on and on. Time to put an end to it."

"Even with what you know about Billy? That he probably killed that Forrester guy? That he was probably the one shooting at us from the woods?"

"Yeah, even knowing that," Caleb said. "Especially knowing that. I'm not walking in blind and stupid now. Before, I didn't have a clue who the players were or what they wanted. Now I know. So now, when I go in, I can be ready. To end all this crap."

Katie leaned back in the couch. "You're not...you're not...planning on, like, killing anyone, are you?"

Caleb did not respond immediately. He held her eyes, tried to gauge what was behind the question. Was she afraid he would go to jail? Was she wondering whether or not he was some sort of psychotic killer? Was she afraid *for* him, or *of* him?

"I'm not intending to kill anyone," Caleb said. "I've never killed anyone, and I don't want to start now. But neither do I intend to be killed over something that was none of my doing. So if there is killing that takes place, it won't be me doing it. Unless I have no choice."

The silence hung like smoke between them. And then Katie said, "Fair enough."

They spent the rest of the day talking, planning, assembling what they would need. They drove Katie's PT Cruiser down to the fuel farm and once they were sure they were alone they scouted the place out. They drove into Brunswick so Katie could get some things from her small apartment on Federal Street. They went back to Caleb's house. They barbecued. They talked. They enjoyed one another's company. And then, when the sun set and the hour approached eleven, they loaded gear in the truck and then they drove off so Caleb could get to his meeting with Howard Cox, so long in coming.

A mile from the gate to the old naval facility, Caleb pulled into an overgrown dirt road, switched off the headlights and killed the engine. A streetlamp on Route 54 cast a fractured light through the trees, enough that he could just make out Katie's face.

"You good?" he asked.

"Yeah," she said, soft and not sounding entirely certain. "You?"

"Yeah," Caleb said.

They were quiet for a moment, then Kate spoke again. "I've been thinking," she said. "A lot, to tell you the truth."

Silence. "Yes?" Caleb asked.

"You gotta make this thing right, this thing with Jenny Carter. I mean, I know you can't...you have to..."

"I know," Caleb said. There was no anger in his voice, because for once the thought of Jenny Carter didn't fill him with anger and despair, and he took that as a good sign. "I told you before. I was a coward. I *am* a coward. But I'm going to make it as right as I can."

In the dark Katie nodded. "You're not a coward," she said. "You can be afraid and still not be a coward. God knows I am."

"Thank you," Caleb said. "I don't know if I can let myself off that easy, but thank you."

"I'm being selfish," Katie said. "Because I want to be with you, and I want you to be with me, and I don't think you can really be with anyone until you deal with this. In a way that brings you some peace."

"You're right," Caleb said. "I've known that. For a while now. Maybe since I met you."

In the muted light Caleb could see the white of Katie's smile. She leaned over and she kissed him and it was not a perfunctory gesture. "See you on the other side," she said. She shuffled away, opened the door and hopped out. Caleb watched her in the mirror as she got what she needed from the bed of the truck and then disappeared into the trees.

After she was gone, Caleb remained where he was, sitting in the cab of the truck, running through what he hoped would happen over the course of the next hour, working out contingency plans if it did not.

He thought about the strange and winding path that had brought him to this place and the odd situation in which he found himself now. He shook his head. Then he started the engine and backed up, switched on the headlights, and pulled his truck onto Route 54, heading off to where Howard Cox and God knew who else would be coming for him.

Chapter Thirty-Four

Caleb turned off Route 54 and onto the narrow road that led into the fuel farm. There were a smattering of private homes near the entrance to the facility, but beyond that it was only fields and a few abandoned buildings slowly returning to nature. Since the navy had given up the facility, the gate in the chain link fence was never closed, and Caleb drove right through, past the small brick building that once had housed the men and women who guarded the place, and into the sprawling, hundred-acre grounds.

Where once there had been storage tanks for aviation fuel, there were now only fields overgrown with tall grass and milkweed and a smattering of empty red brick buildings. The roads that ran off in either direction were broken now, with weeds poking through the cracks. It looked like what Caleb imagined the whole world would look like a few months after some deadly virus had wiped out mankind.

He continued further onto the grounds. He couldn't see beyond the sweep of his headlights, but he knew the road ran gently downhill for about half a mile until it terminated at the shoreline and the massive dock where the fuel ships used to tie up. If the sun had been up he knew he would have had a lovely view of Middle Bay and some of the waters where he set his traps. If the sky had been really clear he would have been able to see Mount Washington in New Hampshire, ninety miles away.

But he could see none of that now. He could see only the tall weeds reaching up from the ground as his headlights swept over them, the gray hardtop of the road under his wheels. He rolled his window down, hoping to catch some sound, some hint of an enemy in wait. He could hear crickets and smell the cool evening air and the tang of the ocean all around, but he detected nothing else.

The meeting place had been set by Billy Caine. The western end of the fuel farm, down by the water. In front of the brick building that stood by itself at the bottom of the long slope. It was a fairly specific location, but Caleb needed to get there first. He wanted to pick the exact point that he would park his truck, where Howard Cox would stop his car and the two of them would talk at last.

He had spoken to Billy Caine that evening, finalizing the plans. "You know what to do," Billy said. "Give Cox the print-outs. Tell him there are others who are onto him. If anything happens to you or Katie, if he does AGO's bidding, voting against the lease for the LNG terminal, it all goes public."

"Okay," Caleb said.

"But look, you're on your own," Billy said. "I can't be part of this, so I won't be there; I won't be anywhere near the place."

Bullshit, Caleb thought.

"Okay," he said.

Caleb had no doubt that Caine would be there, somewhere. He expected the man would be watching, maybe shooting video of the meeting, but he would not join in. He did not think Billy Caine would risk being shot when he had Caleb Hayes to take the risk for him.

With his foot off the gas, Caleb let his truck roll slowly down the sloping road to the water at the far end of the open space. He considered turning off his headlights. There was a half-moon and Caleb could see it was casting a tolerable amount of bluish light on the landscape. But he did not think it would be enough for him to keep on the road, and anyone watching would have seen him already, so he kept the lights on.

The single-story, flat-roof, brick building was visible now in the light of the high beams, and beyond that Caleb could see a grassy lawn that seemed to end abruptly, but he knew it dropped away about ten feet to the beach below. Beyond that he could see the dock and glinting water of Middle Bay. He drove around to the front of the building and stopped. He shut off the lights and the engine, and the dark and the quiet enveloped him.

He sat for a moment and listened and breathed, letting his senses tune into the night. Crickets, breeze in the tall grass, the lap of water. Somewhere far out in the night the buzz of a boat's engine. He could make out the tiny spot of green light, and a white light above it, moving fast over the water, the starboard side of a small vessel underway in the dark.

It was a beautiful summer night, but Caleb was only aware of that on an intellectual level, a theoretical level. His mind was too roiled with consideration, his senses too sharp, his thoughts coming too fast to really appreciate the aesthetic qualities of the place. He reached up and turned off the dome light of his truck, then picked up the manila envelope beside him, opened the door and stepped out. He wanted to get his night vision as sharp as he could.

He leaned against the truck and listened, pulling apart every sound, but he could hear nothing out of the ordinary. If Cox was already here, or Scott or Caine were already here, he could not tell. But he didn't think so.

He was wearing one of his flannel shirts, untucked, and jeans, and he realized he was dressed a bit more warmly than was quite appropriate, but there was nothing he could do for it now. Despite the clothes, he had a vaguely naked feeling, an underdressed feeling, and he realized it was the absence of the weight of the Beretta on his belt or shoulder holster that he was sensing. He had been instructed not to bring the gun, and he had complied. If Cox or Scott had even suspected he was carrying it, the whole thing would go south fast.

The clock on his dashboard had read 11:34 when he shut the engine off, so he guessed he had twenty minutes or so before anyone arrived. He remained motionless, playing out in his mind how things would go down if they went down the way he hoped. Which, he knew, was very unlikely, but if it was even close he thought that would be good enough.

He heard something move off to his right, a rustling sound, and he tensed, took a tentative step away from the truck. Something moving through the undergrowth; it sounded big, big like a bear or a moose, but Caleb knew that even a porcupine could sound massive rustling through the bracken on a still night. He listened as the sound seemed to grow closer, then began to recede again. Too much noise to be a person trying to move stealthily. Whatever it was didn't care how much noise it made. Caleb stepped back toward the truck, let his muscles relax.

And then he heard the car. It was some ways off, probably just coming through the gate in the chain link fence and moving down the hill. He looked over the hood of his truck and could see the headlights sweeping over the tall grass. He turned away, not wanting the lights to ruin his night vision.

He could see the beams sweeping along the edge of the water as the car came closer. It was coming along the far side of the fuel farm, making a big loop around the property, but Caleb knew the road it was on would join up with the one on which he was parked. They would meet by the water, as planned.

In his peripheral vision he watched as the car came down the hill, then swept around the bend toward the shoreline and the brick building in front of which he had parked. Caleb walked around behind his truck, putting it between himself and the oncoming vehicle, turned his back on the car and shut his eyes. He listened as the car came close, stopping about twenty feet away, he guessed. The engine stopped and even through his eyelids Caleb could tell that the headlights had been doused. He opened his eyes, turned, and stepped around the truck.

The door of the car swung open and the dome light snapped on and Caleb shut his eyes again, but not before he caught a glimpse of Howard Cox climbing out of the driver's seat. He had never actually seen the man before, save as a shadowy figure he was disarming and tossing onto his couch, but he recognized him from the research he had done, the pictures online or in newspapers. In the pictures, Cox looked happier than he seemed in the brief glimpse Caleb had just had.

"Hayes?" Cox's voice was raspy, the anger barely contained. "Hayes, is that you?"

"Shut your car door," Hayes said. He did not want his night vision interrupted, and he did not want to be illuminated in any way that might help a shooter hiding in the grass. He heard the slam of the car door and opened his eyes.

The moonlight was falling on Cox's nearly bald head and his slight frame. He was not a big man, but even in the dark there was an energy, a presence about him. He had spoken less than half a dozen words, but his tone was forceful, without a hint of fear.

"Yeah, Cox, it's me. Hayes." Caleb took a step away from his truck, a step toward Cox, and Cox did likewise. Ten feet away, Cox stopped.

"Okay, Hayes, I'm here," Cox said. "Are you the one who called me, set this up?"

"No," Caleb said. "That was someone else. Someone who's very interested in what you're up to."

"And you're not, you son of a bitch?" Cox spit. "You've been harassing me for a month now. You killed Forrester, didn't you? Drowned him on your lobster trap. Fucking brilliant, I have to say. The last person the cops would guess did it is the guy who discovered the body and called it in. And it sends me a hell of a message."

"Brilliant. You're right," Caleb said. "Makes me wish I'd thought of it. But look, I have this file. It's a print-out of what was on your computer. You know what it is. I'm just giving you this to show you I really do have it." He stepped forward, held the envelope out with his extended hand. He clenched his teeth, ready for what he was sure was coming, surprised it had not come yet. Hoping it would come the way he had guessed it would, the way he had assured Katie it would.

And then the bushes thirty feet away seemed to explode in light and sound, and in the same instant Caleb felt the hammer punch of the bullet hitting his chest. He staggered and another round struck him and sent him reeling back, spinning as he fell.

He hit the blacktop and lay motionless, his face pressed to the asphalt, which still held some of the warmth of the day. His ears were ringing a bit from the blast of gunfire and he felt the ache in his chest where the rounds had struck.

He tried to discern what was going on from the sounds he could make out through his dulled hearing. He heard Cox's feet shuffling, thought he heard the rustle of brush, and then the quiet was torn apart again by a blast of gunfire, the sound different, louder, with the authority of a larger weapon. The shots came from the brick building in front of which they were parked. Came from the roof.

Caleb heard Howard Cox shout in surprise and for the first time heard fear in the old man's voice. He heard the sound of feet running, soft soles, but they had a distinct sound as the runner made no attempt to move with stealth. The gunfire kept up, *bang, bang, bang*. Caleb could hear the sound of bullets screaming through the air. He heard the soft-soled footfalls come closer, heard Marco Scott's voice, a voice he would not soon forget, shouting, "Get in the car! On the passenger side!"

Caleb reached up under the tail of his shirt. His hand snagged on the edge of the Kevlar vest, but he brushed past it and reached higher. His fingers wrapped around the hard plastic handgrip, secured at exactly the right angle for this grab. He jerked the weapon free, rolled over, extended his arm, lifted his head.

Marco Scott was ten feet away, stepping quickly toward him, his pistol held low but ready. Coming in for the *coup de grace*. Caleb could see the surprise on Scott's face as the man he thought he had already killed rolled over, raising a weapon. Scott's gun started to come up as Caleb pulled the trigger. In the moonlight Caleb could see the glint of the two thin strands of wire playing out at supersonic speed. He could see Scott stop dead in his tracks, his body clench up and double over as the voltage hit him.

"You're not the only one with a Taser, bitch," Caleb said.

Katie Brennan watched the whole thing play out from her perch on top of the brick building, hunkered down behind the two-foot section of wall that encircled the roof.

She had made her way to the building down a path beaten through the woods, one that she and Caleb had found earlier in the day. She made the climb up to the roof by way of a route she had earlier scouted out and practiced; up on the edge of an abandoned Dumpster, a big step up to the sill of a window, then a foot on the window frame to boost her up to where she could get a handhold on the edge of the roof.

She had been a gymnast in high school, and while she no longer felt the same sort of agility and limberness now as she had then, she had not lost it entirely. Of course, climbing the side of a building was something quite different from the parallel bars. And she had never done a gymnastic routine with an assault rifle slung across her back.

The climb had not been easy, but it had not been as hard as convincing Caleb to accept her help in the first place. She did not need to put her life on the line, he insisted, for the crap that had been visited on him. He could not tolerate the thought of what might happen to her—physically, psychologically, legally—if things went wrong.

She had countered that he could not do this job alone, that Scott would want her dead, too, and thus she already had skin in the game. That she had proved herself already.

"There is one thing," she had told him. "I'm not going to kill anyone. Understand that; I'm not going to kill anyone." He did understand it, and he most emphatically did not want her to kill anyone. Her job was to sow confusion, create fear and panic. The .308, they agreed, would serve that purpose well.

They had gone over and over what would happen if things went right, what might happen if they did not, what Katie should do in any of those scenarios.

It had been thrilling at first, the whole thing, like an amped up version of playing soldiers. The black clothing, the black face paint which Caleb had insisted upon, though it seemed excessive and histrionic to her, the night vision goggles. Moving through the trees and the tall grass, senses alert, pausing every fifty feet or so to listen, to look around.

She had been alone in that big, open field, as far as she could tell. She had climbed up onto the roof with little difficulty, though the effort left her breathing harder than she felt she should have been. She tumbled over the edge of the roof, hit the warm, rough, tarred surface and crouched low just as Caleb's headlights appeared a quarter mile away at the top of the slope, coming through the chain link fence.

At least I hope that's Caleb, she thought. They were expecting at least one other car, and Caleb had wanted to get there first.

She hunkered down behind the short wall and took off the night vision goggles and suddenly the whole thing did not seem as illicitly thrilling as it had been. Not as much fun. She was no longer alone, which meant this was no longer play-acting. Someone was here. Caleb or Howard Cox or Marco Scott or Billy Caine. Someone. Someone intent on violence and she was an integral part of it, even if no one but Caleb knew that.

The lights grew closer as the vehicle swept down the hill, and from their height above the road Katie was pretty sure it was a pickup truck, and as it came closer she was certain it was Caleb's. She moved along the edge of the roof, only the top of her head and the upper part of her black-painted face showing above the low wall as she did, following Caleb's truck as it swung around the building and came to a stop.

The headlights and the engine switched off and Katie put the night vision goggles on once more. Caleb opened the door and Katie watched him, or what seemed to be a greenish-black ghost of him, step out of the truck and lean against it. He had the manila envelope in his hand.

For a long time they waited, an excruciatingly long time, it seemed to Katie. Again and again she scanned the brush and the trees that surrounded the periphery of the open space where Caleb had parked, but she could see nothing beyond vegetation. Once she heard something moving in the brush and the sound made her jump, made her heart pound so hard she could feel it in her chest. She lifted the rifle part way to the firing position and peered out in the direction of the noise. Half a minute later a fat porcupine came waddling out of the undergrowth and ambled off toward the trees. Katie sucked in a breath, noiselessly, and then slowly let it out.

As she did she heard another noise, another vehicle somewhere in the distance behind her. She started to turn when she saw the headlights on the edge of her vision. She pulled the night vision goggles off and looked up the hill, still kneeling, still concealed by the low wall. This was a car, she was fairly certain, not a truck, the headlights lower than Caleb's had been.

She felt her pulse rate nudge up, like pushing a boat's throttle ahead. She licked her lips, which were getting dry, and crouched down a bit lower, so her head was below the level of the short wall, in case some hump in the road caused the oncoming headlights to bounce up and reveal her crouching there. She pulled the night vision goggles back on and listened.

She could hear the car coming around the far side of the fuel farm, coming from the opposite direction that Caleb had come. She felt her stomach tighten; she felt vaguely nauseous. Katie Brennon prided herself on never being afraid, or at least rarely being afraid, but she was afraid now. When Caleb had laid out how this would all happen, it had seemed perfectly reasonable, but now his plans seemed like a ridiculous jumble of nonsense, this mission of theirs a perfect opportunity for Marco Scott to finish what he had started aboard the *Lisa Marie*.

The car stopped, a door opened. Katie heard a voice—it had to be Cox's voice——say, "Hayes? Hayes, is that you?"

She was on her knees, hunched over behind the wall. Now she rose slowly, lifting the rifle as she did, easing it over the wall and resting it on the bricks as she watched the two men below her, not one hundred feet away. They were talking lower now, and Katie could not hear what they were saying. If Caleb had guessed right, then Scott was out there somewhere, waiting for his chance. If Caleb was right, Scott would be armed with a handgun, and when he fired he would not go for a head shot, he would go for body mass, and after Caleb was down he would finish him off.

If Caleb was wrong about that part, he would be a dead man inside a minute.

She watched Caleb, rendered in the weird green and black of the night vision goggles. He stepped toward Cox, extending the manila envelope as he did. Cox reached out his hand and the bushes at the edge of the lawn seemed to explode with light, blinding in the goggles, and the sound of the gunshots ripped through the air.

"Shit!" Katie shouted, despite herself. She squeezed her eyes closed, opened them again. Caleb was staggering back. She could see the torn fabric of his shirt and she knew the rounds had stuck him square in the chest and she knew that he was wearing a Kevlar vest, but she did not know if it had actually stopped the bullets or not.

"Shit!" she said again as Caleb hit the side of the truck and went down, falling from her sight. She was breathing hard and her mind was reeling from the shock and the light and the noise.

And then she remembered. She had a job to do. Create chaos, flush Scott out. Caleb had assured her that if Scott was there to protect Cox then he would not remain in hiding if the bullets started to fly.

She put the butt of the .308 to her shoulder, sighted down the barrel, swiveled the gun around until it was pointing in roughly the direction that the shots had come from, but high enough that she was not going to hit anyone. She squeezed the trigger, felt the gun slam back against her shoulder. She wasn't wearing hearing protection this time, and the sound of the gun was deafening, disorientingly loud, but she squeezed off another round and another.

To the right of where she was aiming she saw a figure come out of the brush, moving fast, and though he was a couple hundred feet off and distorted by the night vision goggles, Katie had no doubt that it was Marco Scott. A calm had come over her now, despite the noise and the wild muzzle flash and her not knowing whether Caleb was alive or dead.

She swiveled the gun down at Marco's feet, tracked his legs with the sight, and once he stepped out of the line of fire she squeezed off another round. She could see the asphalt explode behind him, as if urging him on. She had the feel of the gun now; she was acclimated to the recoil and the noise.

Katie turned to her left, swinging the gun around until the barrel was pointed at Cox's car. She pulled the trigger, watched with satisfaction as the bullet tore a section from the roof. She fired again, saw the rear driver's side window blow apart.

Then Marco Scott was there, shouting something, his pistol held low at his side. He had been running, but now he slowed and Katie could see he was moving toward Caleb, who was still out of sight from where she was crouching behind the wall. Without thinking, she centered the barrel on Scott's chest and tracked him as he moved toward Caleb's truck.

And then she realized what she was doing, realized that once Scott lifted his gun to fire at Caleb she would have to make a decision whether to shoot him or not, and she would have a fraction of a second in which to decide. And the result of that decision would be permanent and irreversible and it would alter the course of her life from then on.

She felt her stomach knot up, felt panic rising in her throat. Still looking over the barrel, she saw Scott stop suddenly, saw the gun start to come up from his side. She put a fraction more pressure on the trigger and then she heard the dull pop of the Taser, saw the silver wires glinting as they flew, and saw Scott seize up as the steel bolts hit him and sent the current coursing through his body.

Katie realized she had been holding her breath. She let it out, eased her finger off the trigger. "Perfect," she said to herself.

This whole thing had played out just as Caleb had planned. She saw Caleb struggling to his feet, his shirt torn in the front, but otherwise unhurt. He looked up in her direction and waved. She smiled and felt herself relax, just a bit.

Now Caleb would put plastic cuffs on Scott, cuffs of Cox, leave them there lying on the ground amidst their guns and the envelope of damning evidence. She and Caleb would hightail it away from the scene, and if no one else called the police in response to all the gunfire, if they didn't hear the sound of sirens coming in twenty minutes, they would make an anonymous call themselves.

Caleb knew for a fact that Alex Henderson, publisher of the *Hopefleet Buoy*, monitored the police scanner. If the police were dispatched he would hear it and would certainly head for the scene.

The sheriff's deputies would no doubt call the ambulance from Hopefleet Fire and Rescue with their staff of volunteers, who would likewise witness this very bizarre and incriminating scene. Whatever story Cox made up to explain this situation, he would never shake the cloud of suspicion. Nor would he dare drag Caleb or Katie into this. He would not want them telling anyone what they knew.

If they really hit the jackpot, the police would discover that Marco Scott was wanted for something or other. Actually, that did not seem so unlikely. They would arrest him, and Cox's troubles would only grow deeper from his association with a wanted felon.

As for Billy Caine, his work in Hopefleet would be done. There was nothing more for him to do than just crawl back to wherever he had come from.

Howard Cox had been moving around the front of his car, heading for the passenger side door, when Caleb downed Scott with the Taser. Now he stood frozen like a jack lighted deer, and Caleb grabbed his arm, spun him around and pushed him down on the hood. With a practiced ease Caleb drew Cox's arms behind him and slipped the plastic cuffs on his wrists, then bent down and whipped another set around his feet, leaving him bent over the hood.

Katie shifted her gaze to Marco Scott, sprawled on the blacktop. He was starting to move, the effects of the Taser starting to pass, but he had dropped his gun and Caleb was advancing fast, pulling another cuff from his pocket.

Almost done, Katie thought. And no sooner had she thought it than gunfire blazed in the dark, the muzzle flash illuminating the scrubby brush a couple hundred feet in the direction opposite of where Scott had been hidden. Three shots in rapid succession and Katie saw Caleb pitch forward, arms flung out as he went down on the blacktop ten feet from where Scott was struggling to sit up.

She jerked her head to the left. Another figure was coming out of the tangle of bushes and even if she had not recognized Billy Caine she would have known it was him. Who else could it be?

"This wasn't supposed to happen, Caleb!" she said out loud as she swiveled the .308 around. So far Caleb had guessed right about how this would play out. But he had also guessed that Billy would not interfere with their taking down Marco Scott and Howard Cox. And this time he was wrong.

Katie tracked Caine with the gun. He was running toward

Caleb's truck. Katie understood that Caleb had been shot, maybe for real this time, maybe a head shot, but her mind was moving too fast for that to mean anything. She aimed at the ground just in front of Caine and squeezed the trigger and squeezed it again. Puffs of smoke came off the asphalt by Billy's feet. He stopped short, turned and raised his gun in her direction. Katie ducked her head and heard the bullets slamming into the brick wall. She felt the vibration of their impact and tiny shards of brick stinging her face.

"Son of a bitch!" she said. She popped her head up again. Caine was once again running for Caleb's truck. She looked over at the scene just below her. Caleb was still sprawled out on the ground. Marco Scott was pushing himself up into a sitting position. Howard Cox had rolled onto his back and was trying to stand.

Katie turned and leveled the rifle at Billy, who was no more than fifty feet from where Caleb lay. Billy, who had just shot Caleb, and if he hadn't killed him yet he would in the next few seconds. She wasn't thinking about consequences now, not thinking at all. She drew a bead on Billy's chest and tracked him with the gun as he ran. She pressed down on the trigger, applying more and more pressure, keeping the gun aimed true at the center of her target.

She squeezed the trigger. It didn't budge. The magazine was empty.

Chapter Thirty-Four

Perfect, Caleb thought as he pulled the plastic cuffs tight around Cox's ankles, stood and shoved him unceremoniously down onto the hood of his car.

This was a moment that had concerned him, one of many. He had to get Cox secured so he couldn't run off, but do it before Scott had recovered enough from the shock of the Taser to grab his gun or put up a fight.

But the timing was going to work, he could see that. Cox was bound tight and Scott was only now flailing to stand. One kick to the side of the head, not even a particularly hard one, and Scott would go down again and be lucky if he could move at all.

Caleb left Cox where he was, took two steps toward Scott, still sprawled on the ground, and suddenly his world seemed to come part around him. From behind, the blast of gunfire and three bullets slammed into his back with enough force to blow him off his feet, to knock the breath clean out of him. The noise and the shock and the pain stunned him and he went down and hit the asphalt hard, sprawled flat on his chest, mouth open, gasping.

Caine...he thought, the only word that would form in his mind. It had to be Billy Caine, the wild card. He had guessed Caine would not interfere and it seemed he had guessed wrong and now he might well die because of it.

More gunfire. Caleb was barely aware of it as he struggled to breathe, but there it was. He thought it must be Caine, shooting as he ran, and he wondered why he didn't save his bullets, just step up behind him and put a bullet in his skull. There was nothing Caleb could do just then to stop him.

And then Caleb managed to suck air into his lungs and as he did he realized the gunfire was coming from above and to his right. Katie. It had to be Katie from her sniper's perch.

Don't kill him, don't kill him... Caleb thought. He knew Katie did not intend to kill anyone and he didn't want her to. If there was killing that had to be done, he would do it, but he feared she might do something rash now that the bullets were flying.

More gunfire, not the .308 but a smaller weapon. Caleb had air enough in his lungs now to push himself up off the ground. He could feel agony in his side and back and was sure some ribs had been broken by the impact of the bullets. But the Kevlar vest, yet another leftover from his former life, had done its job.

Billy Caine was twenty feet away, gun trained on the rooftop as he squeezed off rounds, and Caleb saw his chance. He pushed off with his arms and his feet, flung himself toward the bumper of his truck. There was no chance he could get to Billy before Billy put a bullet through his head, but he could at least get the truck between the two of them, and that was something.

He hit the ground and rolled. The agony was all but unbearable, but he kept rolling and came up onto his feet, crouched behind the grill of his truck. It was quiet, no gunfire either from Billy's pistol or from Katie on the rooftop. Caleb could hear the soft footfalls as Billy Caine made his cautious approach.

Caleb saw movement to his right and looked up in time to see Marco Scott diving behind Cox's car. Scott, like Caleb, was looking to put a vehicle between himself and Caine. Scott's gun was still lying on the blacktop where he had dropped it when the Taser had locked his muscles up, but it was beyond Caleb's reach. He could never get to it before Billy gunned him down. A head shot would be easy enough at this distance.

So, Billy, you son of a bitch, who are you going to shoot? Caleb wondered. He had no idea what was driving Billy Caine now, what his motive was. Who he most wanted dead. He knew only that Billy had put three rounds into the back of his Kevlar vest and that likely meant he, Caleb, was high on that list.

Caleb inched back and around the far side of the truck as he heard Billy's careful approach. He paused. Quiet. He looked up at the roof of the brick building but could see nothing of Katie.

This would be a good time for you to start shooting, he thought.

From the other side of the truck, not ten feet away, Caleb heard

James L. Nelson

the distinctive sound of a magazine ejected from a handgun and a new one snapped into place. Caine reloading. *Any time, Katie...* Caleb thought.

More steps now, as Billy worked his way around the front of the truck and Caleb backed away. *We can't keep this up for long*, Caleb thought. The cops might well be *en route*. Random gunfire was not unusual in the countryside in Maine, and the nearest houses were at least half a mile away, but this much gunfire might be enough to attract someone's notice.

Still, Caleb was pretty sure Billy would shoot him before that. Soon he would have only the truck's bed for protection, and the bullets in Billy's gun would punch right through that sheet metal as if it wasn't there.

He heard Billy take two quick steps and with no conscious thought Caleb dropped and rolled under the truck, then rolled again to reach the far side. He lay on his stomach and saw Billy's feet moving fast down the truck's length and stop near the tailgate. He saw Billy swivel around, take a step, pause.

He knows where I am, Caleb thought and he braced himself to roll out the far side, when he heard the deep-throated report of the .308 from the roof, heard a bullet come screaming past. He saw Billy's feet stop, turn, heard three shots fired back at the roof.

Son of a bitch! Caleb thought. He had a sudden vision of Katie taking a round right in the forehead, of her being tossed back onto the roof, dead before her body even stopped moving. But then the .308 barked out again and a bullet tore through the bottom of the truck and hit the pavement five inches from Caleb's head.

"Son of a bitch!" he shouted and his eyes shut by reflex and bits of asphalt bit into his skin. He rolled out from under the truck as another round ripped through the bottom of the bed. He got to his knees just as Billy came around the front, aiming his pistol at the rooftop, squeezing off rounds as he put the truck between himself and Katie firing down on him.

Caleb stood, took two quick steps forward, clapped his hand down on Billy's hand and twisted the gun free. It was a practiced move, one Caleb's hands could do with no conscious thought. Take the gun, turn it around, aim the business end at the assailant.

It was an easy grab against someone with no training, but Billy Caine was not an amateur. Even as Caleb wrenched the gun free Billy

280

swiveled around, leading with his left hand, aiming a blow at Caleb's throat. Caleb saw it coming, ducked his head, took the blow on the temple, painful and disorienting. He tried to switch the gun around in his hand, to get the grip in his palm, his finger on the trigger, but Billy followed up with a right to the side of his head.

Caleb twisted aside and the fist grazed his cheek as it passed. He felt the gun fly from his uncertain grip, heard it clatter on the ground. Billy took a step toward him and drove a powerful fist into Caleb's solar plexus, a blow that would have put him down for good if Billy had not forgotten in the heat of the fight that Caleb was wearing a Kevlar vest.

As it was, Billy's fist made a dull thumping noise and the impact was enough to send a shudder of pain through Caleb's chest, but not enough to drop him or even give him pause. Caleb stepped up, swinging his right elbow, and caught Billy on the side of the head. The blow made Billy stagger and Caleb stepped in again and grabbed the back of Billy's neck.

But Billy Caine was not done. He swung his left arm in a wide arc, grabbing the arm Caleb had on his neck, knocking it free and locking it in a powerful hold, bending it in a way that would snap it like a stick.

Caleb howled in pain and instinctively brought his foot up hard between Billy's legs. The kick might have ended the thing if it had landed as Caleb hoped, but it didn't. It was, however, enough to break Billy's grasp. Caleb pulled his arm free, took a step back.

Behind Billy, Howard Cox's car turned over, the engine roaring as the driver pressed the gas. Caleb spared a glance, just a fraction of a second, but it was enough to catch a glimpse of Marco Scott in the driver's seat. While he and Billy had been going at it, Scott must have shoved Cox into the back and leapt in behind the wheel. Caleb's eyes darted down to the blacktop. The gun that Scott had dropped was gone.

Billy Caine could not look; turning his head would have been the end of him, and he knew it. Instead he lunged, moving in fast at Caleb, hoping no doubt to finish him in time to at least get a shot at Marco Scott. Left, right, his fists came in at Caleb's head, but Caleb was ready this time because he knew it was Billy's only play. He couldn't go for a body blow, not while Caleb was wearing the vest.

Caleb had his hands up and as Billy's fist came at him he swatted it aside, sending Billy off balance. He saw Cox's car leap ahead as Scott slammed it in gear and hit the gas. He saw Scott's arm reaching out through the open window.

Billy's arm sailed past Caleb's head and Caleb grabbed it and pushed, turning Billy full around. He thrust his arms up under Billy's arms, pressed the man against his chest. Billy had half a dozen ways to get out of that hold, but he never had a chance to try one of them. Cox's car, still accelerating, came up with them and Marco Scott aimed his gun and fired round after round as he screamed past. Caleb felt the impact of the bullets as they hit Billy Caine and tore on through, he felt the lead hitting his Kevlar vest, but their power was spent passing through Caine's body and they felt like the weak punches of a dying man.

The shriek of squealing tires filled the night and then it was gone and the roar of the engine in Cox's car receded. Caleb dropped his arms and Billy Caine's body slipped to the ground at his feet. He stepped back. Four neat holes in his chest, they looked like black spots against the fabric of Billy's shirt.

*Nice grouping...*Caleb thought.

Billy's eyes were open and unblinking. The man was dead, probably had been before Caleb laid him on the ground.

Caleb took another step back and looked around. The night was silent, the scene of violence and death suddenly still. "Katie?" Caleb called, as loud as he dared. His hearing had been dulled by the gunfire, his voice sounding odd and far away. "Katie?"

He had expected her to call back from the top of the roof, and when she didn't he felt another wave of fear, but then she appeared out of the shadows by the side of the building, her clothes and face black, the .308 in her hands. She came up to him at a jog, stopped five feet from where Billy lay. Her eyes were wide and focused on the dead man.

"Oh, shit..." she said. She was quiet for a moment, then said, "I didn't...?"

"No," Caleb said. "It was Marco Scott, his parting gift."

Katie looked up the road in the direction Scott had driven off. She looked back at Caleb. "Well, it almost worked as planned," she said. "Now what? Do we call an ambulance?"

"No," Caleb said. "He's way beyond that. Let's leave him for some early morning dog walker to find."

"Really?" Katie said. "That's kind of…grim."

"Yeah, but it'll buy us some time, which we might need. Because we didn't manage to resolve one damned thing tonight." Caleb reached out a hand for the rifle and Katie passed it to him. "Would you mind picking up the file?" he asked, nodding toward the manila envelope lying on the road. "That won't do us any good now."

Katie went to retrieve the papers and Caleb stepped over to his truck. He put the rifle in behind the seats and picked up the Taser and put that in as well. He pulled out a flashlight and a pair of cloth gloves, the sort that lobstermen wear when handling gear. He slipped the gloves on and picked up Billy's gun in his right hand, wiped the surfaces clean with his left. He slipped the magazine out of the grip and extracted the unspent rounds, then put them in his pocket.

"Don't need whoever finds him accidentally shooting himself," Caleb explained. "Or anyone else." He clicked the magazine into place and set the gun back on the ground.

Next he handed the flashlight to Katie, who clicked it on. In the muted light of the moon it seemed very bright and it gave Caleb a vulnerable, exposed feeling, so he moved fast. He pressed his hands against Billy's front pockets, but he could feel only car keys in one, nothing in the other.

He half rolled him over and pulled his wallet from his back pocket. He thought of Richard Forrester's wallet, his own inability to suppress his curiosity. *This is how all this crap started in the first place,* he thought as he flipped Caine's wallet open. He saw what he expected to see: driver's license, credit cards, a few hundred dollars in cash. And a hotel key card in a paper sleeve.

Caleb pulled the key card free. The sleeve said Best Western, and handwritten on the line provided was the room number, 104. Caleb looked at the card tucked into the sleeve. Not one card but two. He pulled one out, stuck it in his pocket. He put the sleeve with the second card back in Caine's wallet, put the wallet back into Caine's back pocket. He was careful not to step in the pool of blood that was spreading out from Billy Caine's lifeless body.

"All right, let's get the hell out of here," he said.

"Sounds good to me," Katie said. She sounded calm, like she was coping well enough. The shock of the thing would come later, he knew. He hoped she would stay with him, let him help her get through it.

They climbed into his truck and shut the doors. Caleb started the engine and drove slowly out of the fuel farm, headlights off. They reached the top of the drive and passed through the chain link fence to where the road met up with Route 54. Caleb glanced at the clock on the dashboard. 12:48. If they met any other vehicle on the road at that time of night, there was a good chance it would be a cop. Caleb switched the headlights on and turned onto Route 54.

"Where are we going?" Katie asked.

"Back to my place," Caleb said. "To clean up. Then to the Best Western to see what there is to see."

At first, and for the duration of the drive home, Marco Scott intended to leave the old man cuffed and writhing in the back seat of his Lexus. Furious as he was at the night's events, it would have given him quite a bit of pleasure. But after driving for a mile or so, it occurred to him that there was a better than even chance of encountering a cop at that time of night, and an explanation would be difficult to produce.

He pulled over to the side of the road and fished his folding knife from his pocket. He said nothing as he opened the door to the back seat, leaned in and slit the plastic cuffs. Cox sat up, cursing and rubbing his wrists. Scott reached down and picked up the cuffs and stuck them in his pocket. If it came to that, he didn't want to have to explain those either.

Cox climbed into the passenger seat and Scott climbed behind the wheel and pulled the car back onto Route 54, bound for Cox's house a few miles away. Cox was raving about what had just transpired, barely forming coherent sentences, but Scott didn't care because he wasn't listening. He was far too involved with his own thoughts to worry about anyone else's, least of all the half-crazed old man beside him.

Stupid, stupid, stupid... Scott chastised himself. He knew better than to step into any situation that he himself had not organized, but still, against his better judgment, he had allowed Cox to set this thing up. He had hoped he might turn it to his advantage, find some way to get the upper hand.

He recalled the look on Billy Caine's face the instant before he pulled the trigger, and that made him feel a bit better about the whole thing. He remembered how Caine's body had jolted with the impact of each shot. He would have liked to kill that Hayes guy as well, but he had to be satisfied with what he had. Billy Caine had fucked with him more than once over the years. This last time, aboard the lobsterboat, he had really gotten the upper hand.

Well, no more, Scott thought, and he smiled to himself.

At last Cox stopped talking, to Marco Scott's relief, and they drove the rest of the way to Cox's house in silence. Scott stopped the car in the driveway and shut off the engine. Cox turned to him.

"You're planning on staying, right?" he said. "That asshole Hayes is still out there and God knows what he's planning. If he comes by I would be grateful if you would kill him this time and not screw the whole thing up again."

"I'll stay," Scott said. "As long as I need to."

They climbed out of the car and Scott waited and listened for anything unusual as Cox disarmed his alarm and unlocked the door to his house. Scott considered the change of plans that had been relayed to him earlier that evening. Another reason he had not wanted to agree to the rendezvous with Hayes. It was now pointless.

At least Caine's dead, Scott reminded himself.

They stepped into the house and Cox turned on the lights and locked and dead bolted the door. He poured himself a generous glass of scotch. He did not offer Scott a drink.

"You have a gun, don't you?" Scott asked.

"Yes, I do," Cox said.

"Why don't you get it?" Scott said. "If there's trouble, two guns are better than one."

Cox frowned as if he thought this was a stupid idea, but he did not protest. He crossed the living room, pulled open a drawer in his desk. He pulled out a semi-automatic handgun and shut the drawer again. Scott pulled out a pair of tight leather gloves from his back pocket and slipped them on as Cox crossed back to him.

"I just bought it," Cox said, holding the gun up. "After that bastard Hayes stole my last one." Somehow he managed to make it sound as if that, too, was Scott's fault.

Scott reached out and Cox handed him the gun. He slid the magazine out, checked that it was fully loaded. He clicked the magazine back in place and set the gun down on the narrow table behind the couch. He nodded toward the armchair positioned at a right angle to the sofa.

"Sit," he said.

Cox frowned again, but he sat. And no sooner was he down than he was talking again. "Okay, so you killed the guy that Hayes was fighting with, but Hayes is still alive and he's going to pull out all the stops now. The vote's the day after tomorrow…"

"How do you know I killed the guy Hayes was fighting with?" Scott asked. He had thought Cox was flat out in the back seat, unable to see.

"I told you, I sat up as you were driving away," Cox said. "Weren't you listening? So how do we deal with Hayes?"

Scott picked up one of the small throw pillows that were strewn around the couch. The design was a nautical signal flag. *Nice*, he thought. He casually squeezed it in his hands.

"Actually," Scott said, "it turns out there's been a change of plans. Way up the ladder. We're not worried about Hayes anymore. Or IGP getting the lease on the fuel farm. Doesn't matter. That's done."

"Done?" Cox spluttered. "Bullshit. Either way, I'm the controlling vote. If they want the lease or they don't want the lease, I'm the one they have to make happy. I have the vote. And what's more, I have the dirt on them. I know all the dirty little machinations they've been up to."

"You're right," Scott said. "You are the controlling vote. And you are a serious threat to all of them. As long as you're alive."

He took two quick steps across the room, reached the armchair just as the implications of what he had said registered on Cox's face. Cox opened his mouth and Scott pushed the pillow down over his face, pressing his head back against the chair, using two hands to be certain all the airways were cut off.

Cox's arms and legs thrashed as he punched and clawed at Scott's hands and arms, but they had no effect on Scott, made no impression on him whatsoever. Scott turned his face away to prevent a stray nail from lacerating his cheek, which would leave skin, DNA evidence, signs of a struggle, under Cox's fingernail. He heard Cox screaming a muffled scream through the pillow.

The pounding grew weaker as Cox fought for air but found none. The kicking dropped off until it was no more than a feeble twitching of the legs. Cox's arms dropped to his sides and Scott lifted the pillow from his face.

Howard Cox was not dead. His mouth was open and he was still making faint gasping noises. His eyes blinked and blinked again as air found its way into his lungs. Scott stepped over to the sofa, picked up Cox's pistol. He pulled the slide and chambered a round, then stepped back to where Cox sat, still all but motionless, on the chair.

Scott lifted Cox's right hand and put the butt of the pistol into his palm and fitted his index finger over the trigger. Cox, just barely conscious, made some sound in his throat, made some effort to resist, but the effort was so weak as to be hardly noticeable. Scott bent Cox's arm around. With his left hand he forced Cox's jaw open and with his right he thrust the gun into Cox's mouth. Cox's eyes went wide and he seemed to give his head a barely perceptible shake. Scott slipped his own finger over Cox's and together they pulled the trigger.

Chapter Thirty-Six

Caleb drove his pickup back to his house on Ash Point Road. He and Katie did not speak, each lost in their thoughts. He pulled into the drive, turned off the engine. He turned to her.

"You okay?" he asked.

She did not answer right away. "Yeah," she said.

"This isn't like when we broke into Cox's house," Caleb said.

"No," Katie said. This time they had left a dead guy behind. Duplicitous bastard he may have been, he was still a human being, and now he was dead.

"You saved my life, you know," Caleb said. "Literally. You saved my life."

"You're welcome," Katie said.

They climbed out of the truck and walked around to the side of the house and Caleb unlocked the door. "You should wash that black stuff off your face," he said.

"Do you have any cold cream?" Katie asked, and then, seeing Caleb's expression, added, "Dumb question?"

"Yeah," Caleb said. "But under the sink in the downstairs bathroom there's some of that hand cleaner with pumice. That should take it off."

"And that's what leading dermatologists recommend," Katie said.

Caleb went upstairs to change his shredded shirt. He unbuttoned the three remaining buttons and slipped it off. Three slugs were still embedded in his Kevlar vest and they could connect him to the crime scene, so he made a note to get rid of them when he was not so tired. He undid the Velcro straps and removed the vest. He stepped into the bathroom and looked at himself in the mirror. Big, ugly black and purple bruises had already formed where the bullets had struck. He took a deep breath and felt the stab of pain in his chest.

Yeah...a couple of broken ribs, for sure, he thought. He knew the sensation well.

He stepped into his closet and found a shirt pretty much identical to the one that had just been ruined by gunfire. He pulled it carefully on and headed down the stairs. Katie was leaning on the back of the couch, waiting for him. Her face was mostly free of the black makeup, but it glowed red from the scrubbing with abrasive cleanser.

They went back out the side door, out into the cool night air, the quiet sound of frogs and crickets. The adrenaline that had been pumping though Caleb's veins was starting to dissipate. He felt a weariness such as he had not felt in a long time, but he knew he had to keep going. They had a few hours' window, no more.

They drove up Route 54, and they had the road to themselves at that time of night. Their conversation was intermittent and brief, as if they were trying to conserve energy. Caleb caught Katie starting to doze a few times, then jerking awake.

Slowly the country dark of Hopefleet yielded to the lights of Brunswick, which, if not a city, at least constituted a town large enough to have amenities such as hotels. Caleb pulled into the parking lot of the sprawling and well-lit Best Western. He avoided the big, welcoming overhang that led to the lobby and instead drove along the north wing of the building, pulling into a parking space near one of the side doors. He shut the truck off and he and Katie climbed out and shut the doors as softly as they could.

The hotel's side door was locked at that time of night, but Billy Caine's key card opened it with a swipe. They stepped into the cool, air-conditioned entrance and followed it down to a long hall lined with identical doors. Caleb read 132, 136, 138...

"This way," he said softly and nodded to his left. They walked side by side, trying to look as much like they belonged there as they could, but they encountered not one other person before reaching 104, the number on Caine's card sleeve. A Do Not Disturb sign was hanging from the handle.

They paused, and before Caleb used the key card he glanced up and down the hall and then thought, *Could I look more guilty?* But no one was there so he swiped the card through the reader and was rewarded with a green light on the lock mechanism. He twisted the handle and opened the door for Katie, then followed her in.

"God, it stinks," Katie said in a soft voice. She was right. There was a distinct odor of unwashed clothes and old sheets and stale food. Caleb ran his hand over the wall by the door and found the light switch. The lights revealed a living room and kitchen and Caleb realized this was not just a room, it was a suite. There were clothes tossed around and on the counter in the kitchen various stacks of pizza boxes and cartons of Chinese take-out.

"Can't say I'm real impressed with the housekeeping staff," Katie said.

"I suspect that Do Not Disturb sign's been there for a couple of weeks. Whatever Caine was up to here, I don't think he wanted anyone to know about it, including the maids."

The light from the single overhead fixture cast a glow further into the living room and Caleb and Katie stepped tentatively forward. There seemed to be a desk of some sort at the far end of the room. It was still lost in the dark, but Caleb could see an array of green and red lights like some odd, colorful constellation indicating electronic equipment. He stepped to his left and found another light switch and flipped it up.

A single floor lamp in the far corner came on and threw off light enough to see the entire room. Katie gave a low whistle. "Wow, look at that," she said.

The table, actually two mismatched tables shoved together, was covered with screens and laptop computers and cell phones and various other surveillance gear that Caleb recognized from the old days, the days he had tried to leave behind. He stepped over toward the tables, running his eyes over each bit of gear in turn.

"What is this stuff?" Katie asked, stepping up beside him.

"Surveillance equipment," Caleb said. "GPS trackers. RF receivers for God knows what." He pulled a pair of rubber gloves from his back pocket and snapped them on. He stepped up to the closest laptop and pressed one of the keys. The screen came to life. The image was grainy, taken with a camera in night vision mode, but it was unmistakably the office in Howard Cox's house.

Caleb minimized the screen, looked at the icons for various applications spread over the desktop. He nodded. "Yeah, he had some good stuff," Caleb said. "Real industrial grade stuff. Not cheap, and very effective. He could see whatever the hell he wanted to see.

Listen to whatever he wanted to hear."

He stepped back and looked at some of the other things spread out on the table. The simplest looking of all the devices was a silver box not much bigger than a cigarette packet, wires running in and out. Caleb picked it up and looked at it closer.

"What's that?" Katie asked.

"Looks like a recorder. Just a simple recorder, hooked to the cell phones. I'm guessing Caine was a cover-your-ass kind of guy. Probably had records of everything, in case his superiors decided to turn on him."

Caleb pressed a rewind button on the side of the box. He stopped it, hit play. Billy's voice came from the speaker, as if he were there and talking to them.

"It's me," they heard Billy say. "Looks like we're set. Cox is meeting tonight with the lobsterman, and he'll be told in no uncertain terms that his vote must change. Cox is on edge now. He'll crack."

A brief silence, then another voice, whoever was on the other end of the line. "The vote's in two days. What makes you think Cox will crack now?"

"Because I have pushed him as far as he can stand. The lobsterman knows about his connection to AGO, and he's willing to spill it if Cox doesn't play."

Another pause, then the second voice. "You said Cox brought in muscle?"

"Yeah, and it blew up in his face. Makes the lobsterman even more eager to help me."

"The lobsterman can connect you to IGP," the second voice said.

Caleb turned off the recorder and looked at Katie. Katie shook her head. "Unbelievable," she said.

"Yeah," Caleb said. "But I should have seen it."

"Why?" Katie asked. "Are you some kind of mind reader? Give yourself a break. How could you have figured any of this out? Actually, you did figure it out."

"Took me long enough," Caleb said. He rewound the tape, listened to a few more selections. Various conversations between Caine and this unknown guy. Caine's superior, apparently. Caleb heard no conversations between himself and Caine, though that did not mean they weren't there.

"So now what?" Katie asked. "We have to figure out who the guy is that Caine was talking to."

"No we don't," Caleb said. "The cops will do that, easy enough. And they'll be here about twenty minutes after someone finds Caine's body."

Katie nodded. "Right," she said.

"Let's go," Caleb said. "Let's go sleep. I don't know about you, but I'm more wicked exhausted than I have ever been in my whole damned life."

It was two days after the deaths of Howard Cox and William Caine that Daniel Finch finally saw an article in the *Portland Press Herald*. He was sitting at his big desk in his office on Forty-Ninth Street, the curtains drawn across the floor-to-ceiling windows as defense against the morning sun. Steam from his latte was twisting and curling off the surface of the liquid as he read the online version of the Maine paper.

Hopefleet Rocked by Two More Deaths

Hopefleet – The quiet fishing town of Hopefleet was stunned by the death of two men, one a prominent citizen, the other a visiting scientist, which occurred sometime Wednesday night. Howard Cox, 72, a longtime summer visitor who had recently moved to Hopefleet and had been elected to the board of selectmen, was found dead in his home, the apparent victim of suicide. Cox's body was discovered Friday morning by a neighbor who grew concerned when Cox failed to answer his doorbell despite his car being in the driveway.

The second fatality was that of William Caine, an environmental field scientist for New England Environmental Testing and Analytics. According to police, Mr. Caine was the victim of an apparent homicide, having suffered multiple gunshot wounds to the chest. His body was discovered at the former navy fuel farm in Hopefleet on Thursday morning by a woman walking her dog. New England Environmental Testing and Analytics, for whom Mr. Caine worked, had been hired by the state to measure environmental hazards in the ground surrounding the area where Caine was found dead.

*That site is now being considered for the construction of a liquid
natural gas terminal.*

*Like Mr. Caine, Selectman Cox was intimately involved
with the debate concerning the construction of the liquid natural
gas terminal in Hopefleet. As the only member of the board of
selectmen to oppose the terminal, Cox was poised to cast the
deciding vote that would have ended attempts by International
Gas and Power to build the facility. Asked if there was any
link between the two men, or if the proposed terminal played a
role in their deaths, Cumberland County Sheriff's Department
Detective Mike Berry said, "We can't comment on an ongoing
investigation."*

*A month prior to Wednesday's fatalities, the body of
Richard Forrester, an executive with Atlantic Gas and Oil, a
chief rival of IGP, was found tangled in the traps of a local
Hopefleet lobsterman, Caleb Hayes. Police at that time said
there was no connection between Forrester's death and the
negotiations over the former navy facility. Forrester had
apparently been visiting Hopefleet on vacation at the time, and
his death was ruled an accidental drowning.*

Finch scanned the rest of the article. A brief bio of Cox and one
of Caine, which happily made no mention of IGP, meaning that the
reporter had been satisfied with the cover and had not tried to dig
deeper into the truth of New England Environmental Testing and
Analytics.

*William Caine...*Finch thought. All this time, and he had never
known who this man was, the one he called the Enforcer. And now
he was dead and he, Finch, knew he had been right all along. Caine
was not as tough or smart as he'd thought he was.

Asked if there was any link between the two men... Finch read the
words again and smiled. It should be obvious even to the inbred
locals in Maine that there was a link. The death of a guy like
Forrester, a man intimately involved with the LNG industry, was
beyond coincidence; two more would blow the probabilities out of
the water. But they could not prove anything, that was the important
part. They could suspect all they wanted. Howard Cox was the only
one who knew anything for certain, and he wasn't talking.

Okay, time to collect on this debt, Finch thought. He picked up his phone, flipped open his address book, punched in the number written there. The phone rang three times and then a woman answered.

"William Davis's office. How may I help you?"

Finch frowned. This was supposed to be a direct number to Davis, the man who held the position equivalent to Finch's at Atlantic Gas and Oil. Howard Cox's handler. For obvious reasons Finch did not care to go through AGO's switchboard, did not care to have caller IDs flashing his name or that of International Gas and Power. The discussion he was planning on having with Davis was, among other things, an egregious violation of the Sherman Act.

"Yes, I'd like to speak with Mr. Davis, please," Finch said. He considered just hanging up but decided to wait and see if Davis came on the line. He did not want to call back.

"I'm afraid Mr. Davis is not available right now," the woman said, but her tone was not that of a secretary giving a routine answer. There was something different about it. More edgy, defensive.

Finch pulled the phone away from his ear and looked at it as if the problem might be in the receiver. Not only was the woman's tone odd, she was not supposed to have answered this line in the first place. No one but Davis had ever picked the line up before.

An uncomfortable feeling began to brew in Finch's gut. This had all been carefully planned. He had agreed that IGO would back out of the Hopefleet thing, let AGO have the terminal they were hoping to build in Searsport, further up the Maine coast, in exchange for not contesting a tar sands deal IGP was eyeing in Canada. What had, a week before, been an ugly struggle for a foothold in Maine had become a win-win for both companies through careful negotiations and a healthy dose of felony collusion.

Davis had taken care of his Howard Cox problem and, it seemed, William Caine had taken care of himself, which made Finch's job all that much easier. It had all fallen neatly into place. But now Finch was not so sure.

"When do you expect Mr. Davis back?" Finch snapped, his voice sounding more irritable than he wished it to, but he was having a hard time containing himself.

"I..." the woman stammered for a second, then continued. "I'm afraid I can't say when Mr. Davis..."

Before she could finish, the intercom on Finch's desk buzzed, a soft and unobtrusive sound, but it made him jump nonetheless.

"Son of a bitch!" Finch said.

"Sir?" the woman on the phone said, but Finch ignored her. He punched the intercom button.

"Julie, damn it, I told you not to fucking interrupt me!" Finch barked.

"I'm sorry, sir," his secretary's voice come over the speaker. "There are some men here to see you..."

"Not...now..." Finch said, giving free rein to his anger and irritation. "I told you—"

"Sir, they're from the FBI," Julie said. "And...ah...they're very insistent that they see you, sir."

Finch stared at the intercom. He heard the voice of the woman on the phone, the woman who had answered William Davis's line. She was asking something, but Finch could not make out the words. Slowly he set the phone back in the cradle. Whatever happened from that moment on, he knew that his life would be altered in some profound way. He understood that he was, just then, experiencing the moment when everything in his life changed, when it all spun off on an entirely new trajectory, and that trajectory would not be a good one. Not good at all.

"Sir?" Julie's voice came over the intercom. "Sir, are you there?"

Epilogue

A week after the death of Howard Cox and William Caine, three days after Cox was laid to rest in a funeral service attended by a sizable percentage of Hopefleet's citizens, Caleb Hayes left town. He did not intend for the trip to be a long one, but he did hope that the result would be profound, both on his life and the lives of a few others.

After having slipped unseen from Billy's room at the Best Western, he and Katie drove back down Route 54 with the sun just cresting the eastern horizon. They spoke little. They both felt stunned, like they had been hit hard on the side of their heads, by what they had seen in the hotel suite and all that had gone down over the past week.

They arrived at Caleb's house as the rising sun was washing over Hopefleet Sound and bathing the gray shingles and white trim in a warm orange light. They went inside and Caleb did not bother to set the alarm. They climbed the stairs and fell onto the big king-size bed and slept.

They slept through the morning and into the evening. They awoke to find the light streaming in from the opposite side of the house from where it had been when they first drifted off. They showered, and again, being concerned with environmental stewardship, they showered together. Then they got back into bed and made love. Then they slept some more, then they made love again. Then they barbecued steaks.

"Will the cops come to talk to you?" Katie asked. She was seated across from him at the round glass table on the deck, the shadow of the house falling over them, the remnants of her meal littering her plate, condensation running down the sides of her cold beer bottle and forming a pool on the tabletop.

"Oh, yeah," Caleb said. "Soon, I imagine. I'm not sure how

they'll fit me into this. Or you, for that matter. So I don't know if they'll show up to talk or to execute a search warrant. Which means we have some things to do."

He and Katie finished their beers and then turned to doing the things he had in mind. Caleb pulled out his gun cleaning kit and had Katie give the .308 and the Beretta a good going over until it was impossible to tell when they had last been fired. While she worked on the granite countertop on the island, Caleb retrieved his Kevlar vest and extracted the misshapen rounds still stuck in the fabric. He walked down to the water's edge and threw the spent bullets in, then found a decent-sized rock, wrapped the vest around it, bound it with seine twine and threw that in as well. Last into the Sound was the external hard drive with the file taken from Howard Cox's computer. The print-out had gone up in flames on the barbecue hours earlier.

It was around 9:30 p.m. when they finally heard the knock on the door. Caleb opened it, recognized the man standing on his stoop. "Detective Berry, right?" Caleb said.

They wanted to talk to Caleb and asked if they could come in. Caleb opened the door wide and gestured for them to enter. He was glad to do this in his home for several reasons. The offices for the Cumberland County Sheriff's Department were in Portland, an hour away, and Caleb did not much feel like spending two hours, round trip, in the back of a police car. But more to the point, if they weren't going to stick him in an interrogation room, it probably meant they did not suspect him of much.

He invited them to sit on the couch. He introduced them to Katie, reminded them that they had met her that afternoon on the dock after Caleb had pulled up the body of Richard Forrester.

The questioning lasted nearly two hours.

"Did you know Howard Cox?"

"No. I know who he was, I don't think I ever met him."

"Did you know he suspected you were trying to intimidate him in some way?"

"I had an idea. He sent some goons around to kick my ass. At least, they said he had sent them."

Berry nodded and his partner nodded. The detectives knew Mainers well enough, and lobstermen well enough, not to ask why Caleb had handled the issue himself and had not called the police.

Caleb had the upper hand, but Berry did not know that. Berry had listened to the tapes that Billy had made, Caleb could tell by the questioning, but the detective assumed that Caleb had no idea they existed. But not only did Caleb know about the tapes, he had a pretty good idea of what was on them. The thing he did not know, the crucial thing, was whether or not his name was mentioned, or whether there were recordings of any of the brief conversations he himself had had with Billy on the phone.

Guess I'll find out soon, Caleb thought. He remained calm, waited for Berry to pull that trigger.

"Did you know William Caine, the man who was found dead at the fuel farm?"

"Yeah, a bit. Katie and I took him up to do samples by the fuel farm...what? A month ago?"

"Yeah, about a month ago," Katie said.

"Did you know he worked for International Gas and Power?" That was Berry's partner, going for the change-up.

Caleb shook his head. "No, he didn't. He worked for some environmental testing company. He gave me his card. Want to see it?"

They did want to see it. They asked to take it as evidence and Caleb let them. Caleb was the soul of cooperation.

"Caine was apparently working with some lobsterman," Berry said. "Some of the evidence we found referred to a lobsterman."

"You're a lobsterman, right?" Berry's partner interjected. Caleb almost smiled at the clumsy attempt to trip him up.

"Yeah, I am," Caleb said. He did not bother to mention the fact that many other people in Hopefleet and thereabouts were lobstermen as well.

"But you're not the lobsterman Caine was referring to?" Berry asked.

Caleb shrugged. "I don't know what Caine was telling anyone. Maybe he meant me. I wasn't working with him, except that one time we took him to the fuel farm, but maybe he was telling people I was. Sounds like the guy was into some pretty serious shit. Who knows what he said or why?"

When it was over the two detectives thanked Caleb and Katie and left. Twice more, Berry called with follow-up questions and Caleb was just as helpful as he had been the first time. He and Katie read reports in the *Portland Press Herald* about what the ongoing investigation was revealing. It was all compete bullshit, but whether that was because the detectives could not uncover the truth, or were feeding the press disinformation, they could not tell.

He wondered if they had found the .308 slugs embedded in the asphalt, or the spent brass Katie had left on the rooftop. If so, he never heard about it. But he was satisfied that they could never charge him or Katie with killing anyone because they hadn't killed anyone.

The next day Katie went home, and Caleb was fairly confident that she was safe in doing so. Marco Scott had disappeared. He was a dangerous man, a killer, but he was a professional killer and revenge was probably his last concern. Staying clear of Hopefleet would likely be a higher priority now.

That same day had been slated for the selectmen's vote, the big one, the one that would determine whether or not an LNG terminal would be built on the grounds of the old fuel farm. It was the vote that had been so long anticipated, which was why the selectmen's ultimate decision was so very anticlimactic.

There was considerable discussion, of course, but after all had been said it was decided to put the issue to the vote of the town. With the apparent suicide of a third of the board of selectmen, the other two did not feel it was right to move ahead on their own. Let the democratic process play out. Pass the buck to the people and let them continue to argue the point for another two months.

The following Monday, at the civilized hour of 9:00 a.m., Caleb and Katie met at Downeast Marine and set to work on getting the *Lisa Marie* back in shape for fishing. "The law says we can leave our traps unattended for thirty days," Caleb said as they surveyed the damage. "But I hope we'll be back on the water way before that."

They left the work of removing the damaged planks on the stern to Buddy Johnson's crew and set about repairing the havoc done to the cabin. They cut away the shattered wood left in the wake of the rifle bullets, made wooden plugs to fill the holes, epoxied them in place and smoothed it all over with more epoxy and filler. For three days they worked side by side, repairing the nightmare that had been visited on their boat, and then Caleb announced he had to go.

Katie was there on the morning he left. "I can't make this right, you know," he said. "Maybe I can make it better, but I can't make it right."

"It can't be made right," Katie said. "You're doing all that can be done."

"I'm still doing it in the most cowardly way imaginable," Caleb said. "I still don't have the guts to face it."

Katie nodded. "You're just a guy," she said. "You're a long way from applying for sainthood. So you're no better or worse than any of us."

He got in his truck, having removed the various tracking devices hidden on the underbody, and drove. He drove as far as he could drive in a single day, which brought him to a place called Robinson Township, just north of Pittsburg, Pennsylvania. He checked into a Day's Inn Motel, had a drink, had another, then went to sleep.

The next morning he found a big-box office supply store and bought some innocuous-looking stationary with paper and envelopes. He used the GPS on his phone to find a Goodwill store, and there he was able to locate a manual typewriter with enough ink left on the ribbon for his needs. He drove twenty miles west, across the Ohio River to Steubenville and found a post office and purchased a sheet of stamps.

He parked his truck in a Wal-Mart parking lot, far from the store and any other vehicles. He pulled out a pair of rubber gloves and worked his hands into them, then set the typewriter up on the armrest between the front seats. He opened the box of stationary, pulled out a sheet of paper and rolled it into the carriage.

He stared at the blank sheet for a long time. It was not as if he was trying to figure out what to write; he had envisioned this moment for ten months or more. He knew exactly what he would say. He had written the words in his head over and over again. Had flagellated himself with them. He had been looking at the seemingly random numbers scrawled on the file folder for even longer than that. He all but had them memorized, but he had brought the file with him, just to be sure.

Now he was having a hard time making his fingers work.

Finally he gritted his teeth and started pounding the keys.

Your daughter Jenny's body is buried at 34° 42' 26.8164" N 117° 44' 13.0524" W

I am very sorry.

That was it.

He rolled the sheet of paper out of the typewriter, replaced it with an envelope. He typed out the address of Jenny Carter's parents, double-checking it against what he had written in the file, though that, like the coordinates, was something he had read a thousand times and knew by heart. No return address. He would keep an eye on the *Los Angeles Times*. He would know if the Carters had received his letter.

Gloves still on, Caleb peeled a stamp from the sheet and affixed it to the letter. He set the letter, the paper, and the typewriter on the passenger seat and covered it all with a blanket. He thought about eating but knew he would not be able to swallow anything. Except a drink. He really wanted a drink but took a pass on that as well.

Instead he drove south to Wheeling, West Virginia, and once it was dark he found a mailbox and deposited the letter. It gave him an odd feeling to do so after having so long thought about it. A jumble of feelings, really: fear, relief, guilt. An unappetizing mix. He left Wheeling and drove east on US Route 70. In the town of Claysville he found a Dumpster at a construction site. He wiped down the typewriter and tossed it in the big green box. He stopped again at a town called Speers and dropped the stationary and the stamps and the rubber gloves into a trash can on the sidewalk of a strip mall.

Then he climbed back into his truck. He looked around at the dark storefronts, their black windows reflecting the light from the lampposts that illuminated the parking lot. His was the only vehicle there, save for an old Ford Mustang that looked as if it had been abandoned. He put his truck in gear and rolled out of the parking lot and onto the street that fronted it, accelerating slightly as he drove off, north east. He was ready at last to go home.

If you would like a heads-up about new books by James L. Nelson, along with other good stuff cheap (actually, free) please visit our web site at:

www. JamesLNelson.com

And sign up for our (occasional) e-mail newsletter.

ACKNOWLEDGEMENTS

This book has been kicking around in my head for more than fifteen years. I am delighted to finally bring it to fruition, and grateful to the many people who have helped me in that process. My deepest thanks to Brian Tarbox, lobsterman, educator, my friend and chief lobstering advisor, for all his help with this book and so many things over the years. Thanks as well to Bud Moody and Roy Knight for all they taught me about the business of catching lobsters. Thanks as ever to Steve Cromwell, both for his great work on the cover and his editorial work as well. Thanks to Jonathan Nelson, my son and official photographer, for the cover photo. And thanks as well to my son-in-law Patrick Lockard for the insights into krav maga. Alicia Street at iProofread and More gets thanks and credit for her herculean efforts to correct my many typos and misspellings. And thanks as ever to Stephanie Nelson for her input and support and for always picking up the bar tab.

And of course, to Lisa, for everything

Glossary

anchor rode – the rope by which a boat is tied to its anchor, or tied to the chain attached to the anchor.

band – to place the thick rubber bands on a lobster's claws. Also, the rubber bands used in this process.

beam – the widest part of a boat, generally the center of the boat from bow to stern

bilge – the lowest part of a boat, where any incoming water first accumulates.

bow – the front, or pointey end of a boat.

bowline – a secure knot that forms a loop in the end of a rope.

buoy rope – a rope attached on one end to a lobsterman's buoy and at the other to the first lobster trap in a **trawl**.

companionway – the door and stairs leading from the deck to a space down below.

freeboard – the outside of a boat's hull from the waterline to the top of the rail.

gunnel – the upper edge of the side of a boat.

hauler – a hydraulic winch that drives a round wheel grooved to hold a rope and used for hauling up lobster traps.

head – a marine toilet.

Homarus americanus – scientific name for the Maine Lobster.

keeper – a lobster within the legal limits for catching.

painter – rope attached to the bow of a small boat.

PFD – personal flotation device, a lifejacket.

pogie – a small fish commonly used for lobster bait.

pot warp – the type of rope used to connect lobster traps in a **trawl**.

quarter – the rear-most corners of a boat's hull.

Sampson post – a stout vertical post near the bow to which the anchor or mooring line is made fast.

scuppers – openings through the **freeboard** at the level of the deck to drain water.

shedder – a lobster that has recently shed its shell. When these lobsters leave their burrows the fishing generally improves.

short – a lobster that is too small to be legally caught.

snatch block – a type of pulley with one side open so a rope can be looped over it. The **buoy line** is looped through the snatch block and run to the **hauler**.

stern – the back end of a boat.

thwart – the seats in a boat where rowers or passengers sit.

trawl – a number of traps attached to one another with a rope called a ground line. A trawl generally consists of two to eight traps, the number dictated by local customs and regulations. Sometimes referred to as a stringer.

trunk cabin – the low structure built over a boat's cabin to give more headroom below.